I'LL BE HOME...

HEATHER LONG

TATE JAMES

Not all heroes wear plaid.

Also, for Stephanie, she's wanted us to write together forever. Happy now?

For Rasputin, the cat, even if all he did was distract one of the authors.

For Stitch, the dog, cause she thinks she's a cat. She also distracted one of the authors.

Ava was the goodest girl ever.

FOREWORD

Dear Reader,

Surprise! We wrote a holiday book, technically we wrote a dark reverse harem with a holiday twist set in winter in the lead-up to Christmas. That said, we wrote a holiday book.

Why?

Well, there are any number of reasons but the simplest one is we wanted to write one because it was both a carrot and a stick to finish previous projects. At this time, we should probably freely admit we one hundred percent wrote this for us.

The biggest takeaway is that we had a blast writing this and after more than seven years of working together, we pretty much know how the other one thinks. We also know just what to do to twist the knife a little with each other.

I'd like to say we're sorry in advance (but we are so not sorry) for the ride ahead. Curl up in a cozy spot, grab yourself the beverage of your choice (hydration is important) and get ready to read. Fair warning this is not your typical holiday tale and it is so not one of the holiday movies that we love to consume this time of year.

Or is it?

Eh, we'll let you be the judges. Now, for those of you who require trigger warnings, I've placed them at the very end of this foreword (and hopefully on the next page for those of you in the ebook). For those that don't, pop on off with you to read and we'll see you at the end.

Thanks for checking out I'll Be Home..., we can't wait for you to get to know them all!

Happy reading.

xoxo

Heather & Tate

P.S. The dog does not die.

TWs: SA on the page in a flashback. If you want to skip it, it's Chapter 20. Kidnapping. Threats of violence. Actual violence. Discussion of trafficking. Smuggling. Be kind to yourself, this is a dark romance.

CHAPTER
ONE

Thank fuck today was my last day until the New Year. I'd saved up every bit of my leave so I could escape for the bulk of the "holiday" season. Every year, as soon as the school supplies left the shelves, they rolled out Halloween and always at least *one* aisle of Christmas. These days it seemed to start sooner and sooner.

Garland and fake snow festooned the shop windows, lights gleamed, and the music blasted out of the speakers. From the shops to the restaurants to the elevator at the building playing host to the offices of *The Arigin*, I couldn't escape the jingle-jangle of holiday cheer determined to suffocate me to death.

Foot tapping, I turned up the music in my earbuds. Queen could drown out anything. As soon as the elevator reached the floor of the magazine's editorial office, I stepped out, coffee in hand and strode down the corridor. I literally had to sign two pieces of paper and review my copy and I was done. Out.

The offices reeked of pine, cinnamon, cranberries and other "Christmassy" spices. As if visual and auditory torture weren't enough, I had to drown in the sensory overload of too many

1

damn candles, potpourri, and more. Aleta at reception beamed a happy smile at me that just seemed to make my scowl deepen.

When her smile faltered, I grimaced then shook my head even as I gave in and turned off the music to my earbuds. Unfortunately, that meant letting the Christmas station torture resume. "Sorry," I said. "Bit of a headache."

"Oh," she said, a picture of sympathy. "You should probably go take something before you go see Connie."

My excuse of a headache was about to become a real one.

"I don't have an appointment with Connie." The editor and I got along fine with several miles of Internet between us. Mostly because I was stubborn and he was pushy. That said, he was the best damn boss I'd ever had, and he never got weird about me preferring to work at home or out of the "office." Nor did he choke off a story if I had an idea.

He trusted my instincts, and I'd learned to trust his experience.

"He said to send you to him as soon as you came in," Aleta told me with a sympathetic wince. "Maybe he wants to give you a holiday bonus?"

"You already told him I was here, didn't you?"

Aleta lifted her shoulders. "Jerry at the desk told me you were on your way up..."

Fuck my life.

"Right, fine. Let's get this over with. Then I'm off for the rest of the month."

"Lucky!" Aleta called.

It wasn't luck if you planned. I weaved my way through the cubicles, lifting my chin to some of my coworkers and waving to others. A lot of us worked remote. Some worked in the office. *The Arigin* thrived on the jagged, uneven precipice between gossip and investigative journalism.

That finite difference was like porn. We knew it when we saw it.

At Connie's door, I knocked twice before pushing it open.

"Firecracker!" My editor-in-chief called out his nickname for me, ending his call and tossing the phone onto his desk. "Aleta said you were coming up, but I thought you might try sneaking off before talking with me."

I forced a smile and gave a small shrug. "You know me too well, Connie. What's up?"

"Come in and close the door, Firecracker. We need to chat." He gestured for me to come inside fully, and I groaned internally.

It wasn't that I didn't like my editor; we respected each other just fine. But he had a way of throwing me curve balls when I least expected it, and the grim look on his face hinted at bad news. On my last day before a month of personal leave? That didn't bode well.

"Oh, uh, I was just here to sign off on my timesheets and expenses for the year, then I need to head off. I've got an early flight to St. Barts tomorrow, and still need to pack." I gripped his office door, not coming any further inside and silently praying he'd just let me leave.

His glower darkened. "Sit down, Firecracker." It was a command, not a request. Damn it.

Gritting my teeth, I closed the door and did as I was told. Perched on the edge of the chair, I crossed my ankles and folded my hands in my lap.

"Thank you," Connie muttered, taking off his glasses and placing them down on his desk. "Now, I know you always take December off because you're allergic to Christmas cheer—"

"I'm not *allergic*," I grumbled. "I just *dislike* it. Strongly. And I hate the cold."

3

Connie gave me a deadpan glare in return. "As I was saying. I fully appreciate you had plans for your time off, but—"

"Wait," I interrupted again, no doubt getting his blood pressure up. "What do you mean, *had*? I *have* plans. Present tense. *Have*."

Connie didn't smile. He wasn't playing. "Had, Firecracker. I've got a lead on a story, and you're the only one I trust to do it justice."

My mouth fell open, and a whine of disbelief escaped. "Connie... *no*. I have leave. For a month. You approved it yourself, eight months ago. I booked flights and a hotel and—"

"And the company will compensate your loss for canceling, but this story is not one we can miss the opportunity on. Or are you not the same woman who told me she wanted to win a Pulitzer?"

Christ. I really did want one. "Can't it wait until January?" I pleaded. "I really don't want to stay in the city through December." Because bloody everywhere in North America seemed *obsessed* with Christmas, and it was utterly inescapable. That was why I spent every December on a beach somewhere *far* away from the snow and cheer.

"That's fine," Connie told me in a gruff voice, picking up his glasses once more. "Because you're not staying in the city for this story. It's an out of town assignment."

Confusion rippled through me. "Oh." I frowned. "Well... what's the story?"

Connie grinned. He knew he had me, and he was right. I was intrigued about *what* story was so important it couldn't wait, and was potentially worthy of a Pulitzer if I could pull it off.

"Kids," he told me, putting his glasses on and sorting through the file folders on his desk. "Missing kids."

My brows shot up and my spine straightened. He was

right, this *was* a story with teeth. A million times better than the current rash of *Ten Ways To Wear A Skort This Christmas* and *How to Not Hate Your Family When They Come to Stay* type articles our online site had been running. My last investigation piece had been about a doggy daycare running a fight ring.

"I'm listening," I murmured when he paused for dramatic effect. "Please elaborate."

Connie barked a sharp laugh, finding the file he'd been looking for. "Ah, here we go." Instead of handing it over, he held onto it. Building suspense, the old goat. "So, these kids have been just up and disappearing, but local authorities aren't doing anything to try and find them. Just writing up reports and filing them in the *no one cares* box."

A bad feeling curled through my gut. "Why? What are their parents doing about it?"

"No parents," he replied, sparking a fire of dread in me. "The kids are disappearing from a group home situation. An orphanage, like in bloody old-time England. Did you know they still existed? I thought they were all just group homes now."

My mouth went bone dry. "Um, yes. I knew that. So... who is reporting them missing? The grandm— um, the matron? Or whoever is running the home?"

Connie shook his head. "Nah, for all accounts she's denying these kids ever existed. It was some concerned towns-folk who raised the alarm. First to local authorities, then when that led nowhere one of them reached out to my nephew Jimmy because she knew he knew reporters. So they reckon if the press gets wind of the story, maybe something will get done to find the kids, you feel me?"

I nodded slowly, my mind whirling. Connie had no idea that I was an orphan myself. I'd entirely fabricated my family and backstory when I'd applied for my job at *The Arigin*—as well as changing my name. He couldn't be pushing this story on me for personal reasons, right? It was just a coincidence.

"Um, that's great that the people in town care enough to make noise about it," I murmured, mentally detaching from the content. Orphanages were rare these days, but they existed. It was just a coincidence. "You want me to poke around and write an exposé? Push the lazy local sheriff into actually investigating where these kids are disappearing to?"

Connie shot me with finger guns. "Got it in one, Firecracker. Bring this story back to me by the twenty-third and I'll give you the front page the day after Christmas."

I blew out a long breath, sagging back into the chair as I thought it over. St. Barts was calling to me with its white sandy beaches, cocktail service, lush well-oiled men... and yet. The chance to sink my teeth into an investigation that cops were willfully ignoring? Even if these kids were just running away, the lack of professionalism from law enforcement would make a juicy story.

"It's probably nothing sinister, you know?" I warned my editor, seeing as he was grinning with the glee of a big story on the horizon. "Chances are, these kids are being mistreated in their home, and they've just had enough. So they take off and disappear. Change their names, move to the other side of the country, never look back. It's easy to disappear when no one is looking for you."

I should know.

Connie shrugged. "Maybe so. But then the story is on the mistreatment of children in these group homes, the fraudulent use of government funding at the cost of children's well-being, and the local sheriff's collusion with the organization. Either way, there's a story there, and *you* are the one who can crack it open like a nut. You're my nutcracker."

I glowered. "Don't you dare make Christmas analogies around me, Connie. I swear to fuck, I will quit."

He scoffed. "No you won't. So, do I have you on board?"

I groaned, running a hand through my mid-blonde hair. I'd just touched up my highlights in anticipation of a month at the beach, goddamn it. "I have to see whether my flights can be canceled, and then the hotel might not offer credit and—"

"And we will reimburse you," he reiterated. "And you can take an additional week of paid leave once you turn this story in."

Oh, damn. He was a sweet talker, old Conrad Aitken. Still... I never took the first offer.

"Two weeks additional paid leave, a Christmas bonus *and* the four I already had scheduled." I countered, hating that I even said the words *Christmas bonus* out loud. But I knew better than to leave even a nugget of wiggle room.

Connie shrugged. "Deal." He shook my hand, making it official, then pulled an envelope from the folder he was holding and tossed it across the desk to me. "You were getting a bonus anyway."

I sulked, opening the envelope to look at the check inside. It was a good bonus, I had to admit grudgingly, written out to *cash* like I always requested. It wouldn't be much good having checks written out to Rachel when that wasn't my real name. I had the papers that said I was Rachel Dean, and I had an account, but I liked distance. I liked cash. "Fine. You got me. Are you going to hand over that folder, or what?"

Connie passed it across, and I noted my chosen name— Rachel Dean—scrawled on a post-it stuck to the front. "Better pack a coat, Firecracker," he told me with a smirk. "It's cold where you're heading. Flight leaves at nine tomorrow; tickets are in the folder. Rental car will be booked for you on the other end, and accommodation is all arranged. Have fun." He pushed back from his desk and grabbed his keys, phone, and briefcase. "I need to run. Charlene has her parents visiting, so I'm going to catch a quick eighteen holes before I need to go home."

I frowned, anticipation and dread returning twofold. "Wait, hold up. Flight? Cold? Where are you sending me?" I scrambled out of my chair as Connie headed for the door.

"Oh, crap. I didn't say *where*? I thought I did." He quirked a bushy brow at me, and I shook my head. "Huh. Old age setting in. You're heading to Northland, Rachel. Most picturesque Christmas town in Minnesota. Enjoy!"

On that bombshell, he hightailed it out of the office. Running away like a goddamn coward, and for good reason. I was *furious* and outraged, but not for the reason he thought I'd be pissed.

Sending the Christmas hating Grinch to *Vogue Magazine's Prettiest Place for Christmas* was one thing. But this was a hundred times worse for me, because there was only one orphanage in Northland... and it was the one I'd grown up in.

Fuck that. No way in hell I'll be going home for Christmas. Not this year, not any year.

CHAPTER TWO

Online research got me absolutely nowhere. Despite the urge to puke just typing the name *Northland* into the search engine, I made it work for me. If I could find anything that meant I could do the story from a distance, I'd totally do it. Apparently, Northland was still locked away in its 1950s-era love affair. Not even the local paper was online.

What. A. Joke.

Then again, who went to picturesque Northland to surf the web? Irritation left every one of my nerves scraped raw. My flight was booked for the following day, and since I didn't even have a cat to worry about, it wasn't like I had to change my plans beyond repacking my suitcase.

The Arigin would compensate me since I had to pay penalties on the hotel and the flight. I fired those off to accounting so they could just add it to my next reimbursement check. I downed an entire bottle of wine while repacking, and it was the only thing that let me sleep. Unfortunately, nightmares showed up like the cracked little elves they were to torture me, so I couldn't really say I'd gotten any rest.

More than twelve years had passed since I escaped. I wasn't that kid anymore. I sure as shit wasn't helpless. I'd become the person I wanted to be, and I made a goddamn difference. It wasn't fair, not that life had *ever* been fair. Still, here I was. One mention of the town that time should have forgotten and fucking buried, and I was a wreck all over again.

Maybe I should look into therapy one more time. It hadn't worked the last time around. Maybe it would now.

The lack of sleep and wine headache made for a pleasant morning on the way to the airport. At least they booked me in first class, which meant I could get a gallon of coffee in the lounge before boarding. The folder sat in my carry-on bag like a brick with my laptop, digital tablet, and change of clothes. I was aware of it every single minute.

I'd read through it from front to back. Three times.

I didn't think it would reveal anything new on the flight. So I turned up the first audiobook I'd chosen for the beach and tried to lose myself in the story of the rock star at a prep school. Wealthy, infamous, and celebrity being pursued by three assholes. I could actually relate to one of those.

Still, the story helped throughout the flight and through the delay when the next flight was held up by a damn storm. Instead of early afternoon, it was after dark when I finally landed. As tempting as it was to grab the rental car and go to a local hotel, I stowed my bags and got on the road.

The sooner I got there, the sooner I got the hell out of there. The very last thing I wanted to do was be in Northland. Every mile ticking by as I left the city and headed further west and north, the more the sour sensation hit my stomach.

It was still snowing. It was dry, thankfully, and not coming sideways. Didn't make for the best driving conditions, but didn't make for the worst either. My phone buzzed, and the sound interrupted the book. I'd synced my phone with the rental first thing. Though it hit me I'd missed the last however many chapters of the book.

I was gonna have to start over. That was fine. I'd started a second after finishing the first. I couldn't even remember if it was the second in that series or not. Whatever. I hit the button on the steering wheel.

"Do I have any new messages?"

"You have one new message from Connie the Dick Editor."

A snicker broke through my black mood. He really deserved that title today.

"Firecracker, check in when you get there. Weather says there's a series of snow storms heading that way. And yes, I know you could be on the beach. Winkie face, purple heart, balloon."

I hated him so much right now. Even if the phone's auto-speech didn't stand a chance of mimicking his real voice.

"Would you like to reply?"

"No," I said automatically. I wasn't there yet, so I'd check in later. As it was, the distraction helped. The last time I'd been on this road, it had been aboard a Greyhound bus. I'd been traveling on the cheap using every carefully hoarded dime to the best effect. I lived on a diet of super cheap, terrible fast food and bus travel. Six months to find a new place, a new name, a new job, and I went to a local community college.

Hard work and me were close acquaintances. One year into community college and I scored a scholarship to the local university. It wasn't enough to cover living and food expenses, but it took care of classes and books. I made do.

I started selling online articles a year out from my degree and never looked back. By the time I graduated, I'd *become* Rachel Dean. It had taken me years to get comfortable in that skin, as that person, with her idealized family, and socially awkward brother, not to mention the almost but not quite alcoholic father.

The stories I'd told had become my own. I was Rachel Dean. So why was it that every mile I got closer to Northland seemed to strip another layer of her away? Agonizing inch by inch, the drive flayed her from my skin. Ten miles out, I stopped for gas that I didn't need and coffee that I did, even if both sucked. The guy behind the gas station counter grinned at me; his fuzzy beard practically screamed Santa.

It was like hell had thrown open the doors to welcome me back. "Merry Christmas, young lady," the man called as I headed for the doors again. I raised my cup and gave him what I hoped was an actual smile and not the Grinch-green sickly one it felt like. The air was cold and smelled of snow with hints of woodsmoke and pine.

I barely made it to the trash can on the other side of the car before I threw up. My stomach rolled at the stench of it. I really hated this time of year. I rinsed out my mouth with some water, and tablet chew for cleaning my teeth. Then sipped the godawful coffee, replacing one terrible flavor with another.

The snow continued to be steady as I followed the GPS directions, not that I needed them. The closer I got to arriving, the slower I went. Passing the No-Tell Motel that sat back from the highway nearest the Northland exit added to the curdling feeling in my stomach.

Not even the bedbugs liked to stay there.

The rear of the car slipped a little as I followed the circular exit. In the distance, the flicker of lights told me I was almost there. I slowed at the sign that said Welcome to Northland. The sensory assault was all in my head. It didn't matter that I was in the car or grown. It didn't matter that I wasn't a scared teen on foot, trying to get back to the...

A flash of a red light jolted me out of the memory along with the car's shrieking proximity alarm and sudden braking, but it was too late. I hit something. No—not something

Oh shit.

"No, no, no, no!" I chanted, cold sweat breaking out all over and my stomach bottoming out. Had I seriously just hit a *person* with my car? Surely not. That was the whole point of that stupid proximity alarm thing, wasn't it?

My hands shook so badly I needed to try three times before my seatbelt unbuckled, then I popped my door open and nearly slipped ass over tit on a patch of ice. Fuck this stupid cold town and all its bad energy.

"Oh, come on!" I groaned, seeing the unmistakable bulk of a human on the ground halfway under the hood of my car. Guilt and fear swirled through my head so hard I nearly fainted while bending down to check if I was about to be charged with manslaughter. Holy hell, I couldn't go to jail.

My trembling hand hovered over the person's black coat a moment while I tried to work up some courage.

Pull it together, Rayne!

The unexpected internal use of my real name jolted me so much that I smacked my victim's shoulder, then gasped. Was he dead? It was a man, that much I could see now. How fast had I been driving?

"Hey, uh, I'm so sorry... sir? Are you... uh... okay?" As soon as I said it, I winced. Of course he wasn't fucking *okay* I'd just run him over.

Swallowing hard, I moved my fingers to his throat to check for a pulse. His skin was hot, and to my intense relief, his pulse was strong.

"Oh, thank fuck," I exclaimed, giving a slightly unhinged laugh. "Okay. You're not dead. That's good. Not dead is good.

Uh… Sir, I'm going to call an ambulance, okay? Just… wait here."

"Seriously?" A gruff voice moaned from halfway under my car, making me damn near pee my pants. "Wait here? You hit me with your car and your advice is *wait here*? Call the fucking cops, you appalling driver."

My jaw dropped and outrage bubbled within my chest. "What? No, I didn't— I mean, yeah I guess I did, but you just *appeared* out of nowhere!"

The guy shifted, then gave a hiss of pain and panic flared up inside me once more.

"Fuck, shit, just stay still. Please? You could have something broken. Let me just call the ambulance and—"

"There are no ambulances in Northland," the man snapped, irritation clear in his voice as he slowly wiggled out from under my front bumper with little groans of pain. "And probably no cell service, with those storm clouds rolling in."

My mouth opened and closed pathetically, and I shook my head. He was being dramatic, I was sure. With an exasperated noise, I circled back to my open door and leaned inside to find my phone. Of course with the abrupt braking it'd ended up in the passenger seat footwell and I leaned in to get it, pointing my ass straight in the air.

"Listen, uh, maybe I was too harsh, Miss…" the man said from behind me, and I glanced up to find he was on his feet. On his feet and probably getting an eyeful of my rear end.

"Not at all!" I called back, my fingers finally snagging on the pesky runaway phone. "It's entirely my fault, let me call someone and—"

I retreated from my awkward position, sweeping my long hair off my face as I straightened up. Then I damn near fainted, again.

"Ho-ly fuck," the man murmured, his eyes wide as he stared back at me.

My heart skipped a beat. Literally just fucking skipped. An intense rush of fire flooded my belly and my face heated. His short hair was a shock of pure white—not blond or gray—but the dusting of stubble on his strong jaw was dark. He was tall. Very tall. And broad, like he could just pick me up and throw me across the bedroom if he wanted to.

"Frost?" I squeaked, shock making me dizzy.

He shook his head slowly as if in disbelief. "Rayne," he finally muttered, then sighed. "What the fuck are you doing back here?"

All that warm fuzziness drained out of me like the plug had just been pulled. The affection of our old friendship fled as fast as it'd come, and in its wake I was reminded of how heart-broken this man had left me all those years ago.

I sniffed, wrapping my arms around myself as I straight-ened my shoulders. "Work," I snapped. "What are *you* doing here? Last thing you said to me was that you'd never come back. I guess that makes you a liar, huh?"

My former friend gave a shrug, then winced with pain. "Yeah well... it's far from the worst I've been called. Go home, Rayne, wherever the fuck that is. You don't belong in Northland."

He grasped his arm, then cast a derisive look at me from head to toe before turning to walk away. Just like that. Just *you don't belong* and that was it.

Fuck that. Frost Jackson didn't get off that easy after all these years. So I did the only thing I could think of. I scooped up two handfuls of snow and hurled it at his back as hard as I could.

Smack. Bullseye.

THREE

"What the fuck..." Frost growled as he turned back toward me. There was a faint grimace of pain on his face, one I could see clearly now that he was illuminated by my headlights.

I'd already scooped up another handful of crunchy snow and packed it into a ball. It was flying toward him before the thoughts fully formed. I'd always been a southpaw, a left-handed pitcher. I wrote with my right, but I did just about everything else with my left.

"What the fuck are you doing, Rayne?" Frost demanded, all harsh lines and snarling voice. What the fuck was I doing?

Therapy.

Another handful of snow flew at him, he stalked back toward me as I pelted him. He managed to block a couple, but the next caught him square in the face and he jerked his head. One minute he was up, the next he was on the ground on his ass.

There was a peculiar kind of satisfaction that crawled through me at the whump of air he released when he hit the ground. I scooped up another handful, packing it as I took two steps forward. He lay there on the ground, scowling upward, and then those ice blue eyes locked on me.

"Don't tell me where I belong," I told him. "You don't get to do that. You sure as shit don't get to tell me what to do. I haven't seen you in more than a decade and you dismiss me?" The earlier heat in my belly blew up into a fiery inferno, chasing the cold out of my veins.

The combination of shadows and light dancing over his visage couldn't disguise the high cheekbones and angled jaw that used to make me tease him that he would be the perfect fae. Oddly, what had seemed almost delicate back then had turned so intensely masculine it was impossible to ignore. The ferocity in his eyes reflected a severe dislike that I actually found myself craving.

So much better than the stunned wonder.

"You hit me with your car."

"Did I?" I cocked my head as he pushed himself up, his expression tightening again. "Felt like you jumped out of nowhere onto it." Then again, beyond the shock of his damn near white blond hair, the rest of him—"You do know when you're out at night you should wear something reflective, right?"

He was almost head to toe in black clothes, from his boots to his coat. If he'd had on a knit cap or something, I probably wouldn't have seen him at all. The clothes seem painted on, particularly since against the snow and the road, he looked huge.

Idiot.

"You planning to hit me with that?" The dry remark pulled my attention away from the considerable breadth of his shoulders. When I frowned, he nodded toward my hands, and I glanced at the snowball I was still gripping.

Flicking a look back at him, I twisted and flung it away toward the side of the road. Ahead of us the lights of the town were still there, but we were all alone out here on this stretch. The fact I was right there in Northland hit me all over again.

"I'll take that as a no," he said as he rose to his feet. The glimmer of pain in his voice raked some guilt through me. Without another word, he began to walk away—again.

This time there was no mistaking the limping.

Get in the car, I told myself. *Get in the car.* It was bad enough to be back here. That was enough memories. I didn't need him or this… But the echo of the internal command didn't really register and I didn't move. He kept moving, slow and steady, but every step seemed more pained than the last.

Goddammit.

"Frost," I called, but he didn't stop.

Climbing back into the car, I started after him. He moved all the way over to the other lane like he wanted to get out of my lane but he was hardly going to outrun my car.

I rolled the window down as I pulled up next to him. "Frost."

"Go away, Rayne."

"No," I retorted. "Get your stubborn ass in the car. There's got to be an urgent care somewhere. I'll take you there—or drive you back to wherever you're staying."

"No." The parrot of my own response was not endearing. He kept shuffling forward, the grimace on his face permanently etched.

I pulled a little past him. At the rate he was going, it would take him forever to get back. Particularly that in the twenty some odd minutes since we ran into each other—yeah too soon—I hadn't seen a single other vehicle pass us.

"I said get in the car," I ordered as I slammed it into park and then climbed out to confront him. Frost, unlike most men, actually towered over me. But I'd liked it when they'd all hit that growth spurt. I'd always been tall, and I used to tower over the other guys. So it didn't faze me a bit when he tried to loom over me.

"I said no." Mutiny should not look so damn hot. Nor should his nearness send the heat rising through me like it was shimmering off desert pavement.

I pulled up a clinic on my phone—holy shit I had a signal—there was one not even ten minutes away. I showed it to him.

"Get in my car, I'm driving you here and I'll leave you. I don't care. But I'm not driving away and then finding out tomorrow you died from stupidity."

The corner of his mouth kicked up a little higher on one side. "Considering you hit me with your car, not thinking getting in it would afford me a high intelligence score."

I rolled my eyes. "Car. Now."

"You're really not letting this go, are you?"

"Nope."

He glared off past me, past the car, and just stared into the distance. Dislike radiated off of him. No problem, I wasn't doing this for the hugs or the kisses. In fact, I'd have been happier if we'd continued to never see each other again.

"Fine," he said as if reaching a decision changed everything. He jerked his gaze back to me so fast it landed like a visceral blow. "You drop me off then you go the fuck away, deal?"

"Deal." If by *go the fuck away* he meant *go to the hotel my company had booked* then sure. I'd come this far, I'd faced my fear of returning to Northland; no way in hell was I leaving without my story.

He glared at me for a moment, then huffed a sigh and opened the door of my rental. The back door. Then he slid inside with a muffled groan and slammed it shut behind him.

"Seriously?" I growled, throwing my hands up as I got back into the driver's seat. "For the record, Frost Jackson, you're an even bigger prick now than you were as a teenager. And that's saying a lot."

He didn't reply, and since he was sitting in the backseat like I was some kind of fucking Uber driver, I couldn't read his face. Infuriating fuck.

Neither one of us spoke for the drive to the urgent care clinic, but the closer we got into the middle of Northland, the more nauseated I grew. By the time I pulled up in front of the medical center with its twinkling Christmas lights and massive tree in the front window, I was ready to throw up.

Without a word, Frost opened his door and got out. Then slammed it behind himself.

"What the fuck?" I growled, getting out myself and hurrying after him as he pushed through the front door. "Your manners haven't improved, I see. How about *thank you, Rayne*? If I'd left you, you'd still be limping here by dawn, and why are you holding your arm like that?"

He whirled around to glare at me, his handsome face fierce. "Thank you, Rayne, for running me over like roadkill then bullying me into your car with your incessant whining. We had a deal, remember? You need to leave. Now."

I folded my arms defiantly. "The finer details of the deal weren't specified. I am staying until you get seen by a doctor and I know for sure you won't be suing me for injuries."

His eye twitched. "I swear to fuck, Rayne—"

"Rayne?" someone asked, interrupting us. I glanced past Frost and flinched when I recognized the woman behind the reception desk. "Rayne Dear? Is that you, sweetheart?"

The nausea intensified. It was nothing against the woman herself, but more the memories seeing her conjured up. "I go by Rachel now, Mrs. Kane."

Frost scoffed a derisive sound and stalked away from me, heading over to the receptionist who was still staring in shock. "Candice, is the doctor available at all?"

Mrs. Kane blinked with confusion refocusing on Frost. "He's with a patient right now. What happened, hon?"

Frost shot an icy glare in my direction, then sighed. "I believe I have a dislocated shoulder."

The receptionist gasped, pressing her hands to her mouth. "Oh my goodness, Frost! How did that happen? Did you slip on the ice? Gosh it's so dangerous out there. You really should be more careful. Let me go and tell him you're here. It won't be long." She started to hurry away, then paused and turned back to face me. "Don't you go disappearing, Rayne. I'll be right back."

"It's Rachel," I called after her, but she was already gone through the swing door to the consultation rooms.

"You can leave now, *Rachel*," Frost sneered. "I won't go reporting your dangerous driving to the cops."

I glared daggers back at him. "Why are you being such an asshole, Frost? We haven't seen each other since the day you turned eighteen and left me for dead. If either one of us has a good reason to hold a grudge, it's me."

"Why am *I* being an asshole?" he repeated, outraged. "You hit me with your car, Rayne!"

"Uh..." a new voice interrupted and my gaze jerked to the swing door. It *wasn't* Mrs. Kane who'd just stepped into our argument, but goddamn I wished it had been. "Frost... you got run over by... Rayne?" The doctor's lips twitched with amusement. "You got run over by a Rayne Dear?"

"Hilarious," I snapped, seething anger replacing my shock at seeing yet another ghost from my past. "It's Rachel, now. Rachel Dean."

Frost scoffed again, but the doctor just offered a lopsided

smile. "I see. Well... whatever your name is, I'm surprised and confused to see you here. In Northland. Candice said it was you but I had to see with my own eyes..." He trailed off, his gaze tracking over me from head to toe. Slowly. Way too slowly. Fucking hell, time had been *good* to him.

Clearing my throat, I pointed to Frost. Redirect that intense stare away from me. "Frost has a dislocated shoulder and he was limping. So, you know... can you please fix him, *Doctor Buddie?*"

Frost's childhood bestie grinned wide, not taking his eyes off me for even a moment. "He'll live. I'm more interested in knowing why *you* are here, Rayne."

"Rachel," I growled.

"Rayne," he replied, still grinning. "Actually, I could do with an extra set of hands to get Frost's shoulder back into the joint. Can you help?"

I shook my head. "Nope. I just wanted to make sure he wasn't going to die, and now I can go."

"Finally," Frost muttered, sour as a fucking warhead.

The doctor ignored him, still focusing on me. "You sure? It's painful. For him, I mean. You might get to see him cry."

Against my better judgment, I snickered a laugh. "Fine, I'll help."

Inflict pain on Frost? How could I say no to an offer like that? Especially when it was an offer made by the insanely sexy grown-up version of my first crush. Alfred Buddie, a fucking *doctor*. As if he needed to be more of a good person.

CHAPTER FOUR

"C'mon," the *doctor* invited me with a wider grin. "It's so damn good to see you."

"Hey Alf," Frost said, cutting between us with a scowl. "Hello? Remember me? The patient?"

"Like that's the first time you've had a dislocated arm, please." Alfie practically scoffed as he gave him a gentle shove on his good shoulder. "Room five. You know the way." While he spoke to Frost, he didn't take those sexy, dark eyes off me.

Fuck, the man had no right to be this good looking. Like Frost, he was tall, and like Frost, he'd built out. Alfie had always been beautiful. Alfie in scrubs was kind of superhero-like. Alfie in dark blue scrubs with tatted up arms, a dark beard that looked soft and silky, and bedroom eyes definitely achieved the divine.

When he held out a hand to me, I almost reached out to clasp it. The reaction was automatic and the desire intense. Alfie had always been the easiest of us, the one who showered me with affection. He would throw an arm around me and cuddle me when I needed it.

It was like I could practically feel the weight of that arm curling around me. That was crazy. What was really jacked was the intense longing to *lean into* the contact. Like seriously, what the fuck? Gorgeous or not, Alfie had cut bait and left town just like Frost and the others. Left and never looked back.

Well... I suppose the fact they were here *now* meant they'd looked back at some point. Still, not a mood or past we needed to unearth or fucking repeat. I wasn't a kid anymore. So I dug my fingers into my palms and strode past him like I knew where I was going.

Which I did—he'd said room five.

Frost practically glowered at me as I turned into the room. The scorching blaze of dislike rolling off of him threatened to push me out of the room. Too late, though, 'cause Alfie was right behind me, and the man was practically a damn furnace. The weight of his hands landing on my hips was unsettling on so many levels.

Before I could really process that he was touching me, he lifted me and moved me right into the room before closing the door behind us.

"You mind if we get some privacy here, *Alf?*" Frost practically vibrated with all the unspoken vitriol blazing out of his eyes.

"Have a seat and let's get you out of the coat. I need to check the shoulder," Alfie told him, his ease and cheer not remotely dissuaded by Frost's scowl. "It's really good to see you, Rayne. You—you haven't changed at all."

I wasn't alone when I snorted, 'cause Frost's echoed mine almost perfectly. This time when our gazes clashed, he just shook his head and then went to work trying to get his coat off without moving his arm too much. Alfie wasn't paying any attention to him at all; his focus hadn't left me.

"Right, I'd say the same except none of it is true, and you're definitely nothing like I remember." No, they were both better —grown men now, rather than the boys I'd known—and I needed to check out of this conversation before my hormones shook off the shock-therapy of being back in Northland to get onboard an entirely different kind of Pole-r Express.

Did I really just go there? Groaning internally at the terrible joke, I went to help Frost because he really seemed to be struggling.

"I have it," he snapped at me as I freed the cuff of his jacket from his watch. Or whatever the hell that satellite on his wrist was supposed to be. It flashed an alert that I didn't even get a glimpse at because I got the jacket pulled over it and then off of his arm.

"Yeah, you totally looked like you had it." I backed off as his jacket hit the floor. It landed with more of a clank than fabric should have, but whatever. "So why are you here?" I asked abruptly, focusing on Alfie. "Both of you are here? This is not exactly the hopping spot for medicine."

Or whatever it was Frost was doing with his life. Was scowling lumberjack in the wilderness a career path? At least he wasn't wearing flannel.

"Did some time with Doctors Without Borders," Alfie said as he examined Frost's shoulder. He tested his range while Frost continued to scowl. It couldn't be comfortable. "It's definitely out."

"You know, people leave Northland," I pointed out. "I shouldn't have to tell you that."

"Yet, you can't seem to help yourself," Frost said through gritted teeth. "Will you just pop the fucking thing back in, Alf? This dog and pony show has gone on long enough."

"You know how I feel about Alf," Alfie said with the first display of his "fuck around and find out" smirk since I'd walked into the clinic. If his bedroom eyes and gorgeous looks weren't enough, that bad boy smirk that gave his shining too damn good to be true guy veneer the perfect varnish.

"Fuck my life," Frost said.

"You seem to have done that. C'mere, Rayne." Alfie curled his fingers in a beckoning motion and I raised my eyebrows.

"You really want me to help you pop his arm back in."

"Yep," Alfie said, his grin growing. "C'mon, you know you want to. Get over here."

"I will gut you," Frost said to Alfie, but Alfie just chuckled.

"Not with your arm dangling like that you won't. Stop being a whiny little bitch and man up. Show Rayne you can handle it."

All at once the venomous glare Frost had been shooting me found a new target. Alfie looked pretty fucking pleased with himself. "Dick."

"Jerk," Alfie retorted, then he had me gripping Frost's arm from the front as he moved behind him. Even through the thick long sleeves of his shirt, the heat seemed to sear my fingers. What would it be like to touch his skin—

"What are we doing?" I asked, ready to get the hell out of here. We were crammed into this little exam room, and I was completely surrounded by them. While they weren't quite between me and the door, it wasn't as wide open as I would prefer.

"Just hold his hand and brace," Alfie said as he gripped his shoulders. "On three, pull."

"Who? Me or—"

"Three," Alfie said and Frost's hand flexed around mine like he could crush it. I tugged. I'd probably have more success moving a truck with a rope pulley than I did moving Frost, but there was still a sickening *thwok,* and I winced as Frost swore a string of syllables.

Then he jerked his hand off mine and moved away from us as he stretched his arm.

"Easy," Alfie told him, the dry teasing all gone. "You need to go easy on that for the next couple of days. I'll get you a sling."

"I don't need a fucking sling," Frost said, snagging his jacket before he cut a look at me. "You can get lost now, Rayne. All fixed, and I said I wouldn't sue. Now you have the Boy Scout as a witness." With that, he slammed out of the room.

"Good to see you too," I muttered before slanting a look at Alfie. "I guess you know, good to see you too, by the way. I'm going to get going." I came to Northland to write a story about missing kids, not missing assholes from my past.

I didn't even make a step before Alfie caught my arm and hauled me backward. He spun me around and I didn't have a second to utter a single syllable before his mouth slammed down on mine.

A shocked gasp was all I got out before my body reacted against my will. My lips moved with his, my body curving into his hold as our tongues danced. Alfie had always been an amazing kisser, and things had only gotten better with age.

His huge hand cupped my ass, pulling me closer as I grasped onto his neck. Then all of a sudden I *remembered*.

Shoving him away with a pained groan, I stumbled backwards.

"What the fuck was that?" I spluttered, pressing the back of my hand to my lips. I could still taste him, like fucking Earl Grey tea, and my head swirled.

Alfie just grinned, his own lips shiny from our less than chaste kiss. "God, it's good to see you, Rayne. I lied before. You have changed *a lot*." The way his heated gaze ran over me this time felt downright intrusive... and erotic.

My mouth gaped and no words came out. He'd rendered

me speechless. Then my face flamed hot once more with embarrassment, thinking how natural it'd been to melt for him.

"Yes, Alfie, I have. I'm not that pathetic little girl who used to crush on you, and I sure as fuck have more self-respect than to let you pretend we're even remotely *okay* after all these years." I tensed my thighs, trying to convince myself that it was *not* okay to take things just a little further. "I'm here for work, and that's it. You stay out of my way, I'll stay out of yours. Clear?"

Alfie shook his head. "You're still so hot when you're angry, Rayne-drop. And in denial."

My eyes widened. "I am *not* in denial."

He smirked, moving closer until he was right in my personal space once more. "Yeah, you are. Because you kissed me back." With that, he smacked a quick peck on my mouth and moved to leave the room. "I've got to see some more patients, but I'll find you later. Count on it."

I stared at the open door to the room that he'd vacated as the smell of the urgent care invaded my senses. It was—clean, medicinal, and ordinary. Those were so at odds with the last thirty—well forty-five—okay fine more like one hundred thirty seconds of intense lip action where my tongue tripped into his mouth that I swore dissociated for a second.

"Rayne dear?" Mrs. Kane said, and it had me blinking back to reality to find her glancing in the room with that kind, almost too sweet smile. "You alright?"

What the fuck was I doing, standing here swooning over a kiss? The rest of my brain kicked into gear, and the holiday music filled in the vacuum of sound around me, and I didn't want to rock around a damn tree any time of year.

"I'm fine," I said with a shake of my head decrying my words. "I just need to get moving, and I was making a list."

"Checking it twice?" The tease killed my vague attempt at humor.

"Probably going to have to check it a few more times than that." I motioned toward the door. "I need to head out, and I go by Rachel now." Not that it sounded all that confident to me.

"Well don't be a stranger, Rayne. It is so good to see you doing well. I worried." With that and another quick wink, she headed back to the front leaving me to gape after her. *She worried? What the fuck?*

Nope. Not going to deal with this right now. I had reservations calling my name and Christmas capital or not, once I was in my room, I could shut it all out. Or at least pretend too.

I used to be really good at pretending.

Thankfully, I made it out of the clinic without running into Frost the grump or Alfie the god—

Not. A. God. Rayne.

Great, now *I* was calling myself Rayne. I hadn't even been here an hour and the walls between me and my past, erected with blood and mortar, were falling down. I had to do better. The cold air was a slap in the face, but so were the scents of cinnamon, gingerbread, and chocolate on the air.

It was all nausea-inducing. There was a note stuck to the windshield wiper, and I jerked it off. If I got a ticket after all that, it would be just fucking perfect. No, it was a note advertising Santa's village at the center of town: come sit in his lap, tell him your tale, and get a cheerful ho ho ho and a cup of hot cocoa. There was even a candy cane sealed to the flyer.

I shredded the whole damn thing and walked it over to a trashcan rather than let it in the damn car with me. The ten or so steps gave me time to soak in the red and white flashing lights, the dancing snowmen, the festooned windows. Everywhere you looked, Christmas blasted back with an inescapable in-your-face attitude.

Back in the rental, I followed the directions to one of the newer hotels in Northland. Since making their appearance in *Vogue*, it looked like Northland had truly trended upscale. The palatial Northland Lodge blazed with warmth and Christmas cheer. I pulled into the valet and handed over the keys then gave them my name before going to check-in.

Thirty minutes and a brand-new headache later, I retrieved the car and my removed luggage. Apparently, they were overbooked.

Everywhere was overbooked.

There was no room at the inn or the lodge or any other of the new establishments because *everyone* was here to see the *Prettiest Place for Christmas.*

The cosmic joke of it all just dug the knives in a little deeper. Eyes closed, I leaned my head back against the seat as I debated my next steps. A knock on the window jolted me out of the momentary peace. The young valet stared at me with some concern, so I rolled the window down.

"You okay, Miss?"

"No," I told him. "Not in the slightest. But I'll figure it out. I just need to find a hotel…"

He winced then dug a hand into his pocket to come up with his little ticket book and a pen. He wrote something on the back of the claim ticket I'd given him and handed it back to me. "They usually have space. It's not as fancy, but it's also close."

How close was close?

"Thank you," I said after eyeing the name. The Ginger Bridge Boarding House. I wasn't planning to stay that long but then…

"Have a good night," he said, then patted the top of my car before he jogged away to meet another guest who'd pulled up. Despite my canceled reservation, there were still more people and families pouring into the glittering monument to Christmas excess.

It wasn't until I shut the window and closed out the obnoxious music that it hit me. The kid hadn't said Merry Christmas or some version of Happy Holidays.

"Congratulations," I told him via my rearview mirror. "You might have just become my favorite person in Northland."

I put the name of the boarding house into the GPS. Fingers crossed, they'd have room cause if I left this damn town, I might not come back.

And I still had a job to do.

CHAPTER
FIVE

The Ginger Bridge Boarding House was some kind of cosmic joke. It had to be, there was no other explanation for how obscenely comical the cottage was. The whole damn thing looked like a gingerbread house, right down to the oversized "candy" adorning the exterior and the candy cane door bell.

Sitting there in my car, staring at the garish decorating, I seriously considered backing down and leaving town. Going back to the city and telling Connie to get fucked. I could get a new job somewhere else.

But... kids were going missing from the orphanage I'd grown up in, and my gut told me something awful was happening. If no one else was investigating, then I owed it to my own childhood to do my best.

Ruffling my fingers through my hair, I pulled up my metaphorical big-girl panties and climbed out of the car. It was likely that this place had no vacancy either, so I didn't bother unloading my luggage before heading up the colorful pebbled path.

Wrinkling my nose, I tugged on the faux candy cane and groaned as the doorbell rang *Jingle Bells* inside. This assignment just kept getting worse. Right as I thought no one was home, the door opened to reveal a plump old woman in a frilly apron.

"Good evening, poppet," she greeted me with the kind of smile that made her cheeks all round and rosy. Had to be fake. "Are you looking for a room?"

I hesitated, on the verge of saying *no*. Then sighed. "Yes, I am... my company made a reservation over at The Northland Lodge but apparently they overbooked and I got bumped. So the valet suggested I try here, but I totally understand if you're fully booked too."

"Not at all!" she exclaimed. "I have one room left, and I think it was kept just for you." She nodded like fate had somehow played a hand in this encounter. Fucking Christmas people did my head in.

"Oh. Cool." I jerked a thumb over my shoulder. "I'll just grab my luggage then?"

She nodded again, flapping the tea towel in her hands. "Yes, of course! I was just pulling some cookies out of the oven. Grab your things while I rescue my baking, and then I'll show you the room."

Cookies. Of course she was baking cookies. I gave a tight smile and retreated down the pebbled path to where I'd left my car. I popped the trunk open, then closed my eyes and took a few deep breaths, trying to convince myself to push my Christmas aversion aside for the sake of the story. I could do this.

Sucking in a deep breath, I grabbed my bags out and headed back inside. Sure enough, the woman—Ginger, perhaps—was humming along to Michael Buble's Christmas album while transferring fresh baked cookies onto a cooling rack.

"Do you like gingerbread, poppet?" the woman asked with a grin. "Oh jolly gosh, I haven't even introduced myself. I'm Ginger." She dusted off her hands then offered me one to shake.

I returned the gesture with a small wince. "I'm Rachel."

"What brings you to Northland this Christmas, Rachel?" Ginger seemed politely interested as she finished transferring her cookies and rinsed off the baking sheets. "You don't strike me as the typical Christmas tourist."

For the first time since returning to my hometown I smiled genuinely. "You're perceptive, Ginger. I'm here for work, actually. It's safe to say I'm definitely not the Christmas tourist type." I sniffed, the sweet, spiced aroma filling my nose. "But that doesn't mean I don't appreciate homemade cookies..."

Ginger laughed, tossing her cloth onto the counter. "Good, because I love to bake. I'll show you your room then come back and ice them once they've cooled a bit. When they're ready, I'll be sure to deliver some to your room." She winked, then led the way to the ornately decorated staircase just past the foyer.

She puffed a bit as she climbed the stairs slowly, but I was in no hurry while dragging my heavy suitcase with me. It was a far cry from the valet and bellboy service at the Northland Lodge, but it was somewhere to sleep, so I couldn't complain. In the morning I'd call the office and make them sort it out.

"Here we are," she announced, breathless, as we reached a closed door at the end of the landing. Instead of a room number, the name plate read *Blitzen*. She must have noticed me staring because she tapped it with a red glittery fingernail. "All my rooms are named after reindeer. Just fitted the vibe of Northland, you know?"

Oh. I knew.

She didn't wait for my reply before unlocking the door and handing me the old fashioned key on a snowflake keychain. "All yours, poppet. I'll be back with cookies shortly and to check if you need anything."

Not hanging around to make awkward small talk, she bustled back down the stairs and left me to drag my suitcase into the room named *Blitzen*.

To my intense relief, the interior of the room was *significantly* less decorated than the rest of the house. Not to say there was nothing Christmassy—the red plaid bedspread and fairy lights around the window frame ensured it was in keeping with the theme—but if I squinted I could pretend it was just a room.

The room itself was huge, with a king size bed and a reading chair by the window, but to my dismay I discovered no attached bathroom. Where was the bathroom? And how many people would I have to share with? I was accustomed to staying in five star properties while on assignment so definitely hadn't packed shower sandals.

Of course, the moment I started thinking about the bathroom, I needed to pee. So I dropped my suitcase and stepped back out into the corridor. Surely there was one close by, or Ginger would have mentioned it. Right?

Then again, she didn't even ask for a credit card or ID before she handed me a key and shuffled off.

I went left first but only found two more rooms labeled *Prancer* and *Dasher*, so I tried the other direction. The door directly beside my room had no name plate so I shrugged and tried the handle.

In hindsight, yes I could have knocked first... but I was tired and anxious and hungry and just not really thinking straight. So when the handle turned without any resistance from the lock, I opened it without hesitation.

"Oh *fuck!*" I yelped, locking eyes with a man's naked asshole. I'd clearly just walked into someone's room—*not* the bathroom—and that someone was currently engaged in some vigorous activity with a long legged woman who was bound and gagged beneath the man. That explained why I hadn't heard any moaning to tip me off, I supposed.

"Get out!" the man barked, not even pausing for a moment as he pounded the woman's cunt so hard it *had* to hurt. Maybe in a good way.

I should have left. I *absolutely* needed to leave. And yet I stood there fucking *frozen* and watching like some kind of deer in headlights. Porn headlights. There was just something... strangely familiar about the man's ass. Was that weird? Yes, definitely.

So I stood there. Watching. Like a goddamn creep. Then again, the man wasn't stopping so maybe he didn't mind an audience? I couldn't speak for the woman because her mouth was securely gagged with... was that a Santa hat stuffed between her scarlet lips? Oh come on.

The man glanced over his shoulder ever so quickly, like he was checking if I was still there, then reached down to wrap his hands around the woman's throat. I gasped in horror, thinking he was about to murder her right in front of my eyes, but nope... she was into breath play. That much was evident in how her body quaked and spasmed beneath him, her eyes rolling back into her head with her orgasm.

He didn't release her throat, though, even though she'd come already. He just gripped her tighter as he pounded her pussy harder, chasing his own release and eventually coming with a deep grunt and delicious moan.

Fuck. Why were my panties soaked?

The man released his partner's throat and slowly withdrew from inside her, giving me an eye full of his huge, condom clad dick as he shifted to get off the woman. She... *fuck* she wasn't moving at all. She was totally unconscious. Dead?

"You killed her!" I gasped aloud, despite the fact I was *still* trespassing on an intimate moment that I had no business trespassing on. Why was I still in this guy's fucking room? Shit maybe it wasn't his room at all, maybe it was hers and she was actually in distress and needed help. What if—

"She's fine," the guy drawled as he stood to peel off the condom and toss it in the waste bin. He was positioned in a strip of shadow, obscuring his face to the point of anonymity but that body... that *dick*... there was no obscuring that. Holy sweet baby Christmas. "She'll wake up in a moment and beg for more." He leaned over to tug the Santa hat roughly from the woman's slack mouth and tossed it aside. Then he went to work untying her wrists from the wooden headboard.

I swallowed hard. "Oh, I see. I was, um, I was looking for the bathroom. My room doesn't have one attached and I looked further down the hallway but it wasn't there and your door didn't have a nameplate so I figured—"

"You figured you'd enter without knocking then hang around for the free show?" His deep voice was like a caress over my skin. It relaxed me and gave me an intense feeling of security. Part of that was probably his physical size—what was with the men in Northland today?!

My breath caught. Why was my pulse racing so fucking hard? "Um, I'm sorry that was... uh, I was just..." Just *what* Rayne? Just so turned on I'd frozen like a statue, unable to look away from the up close and personal porn show? Fucking hell, I was glad I'd packed my vibrator because it was going to get a work out tonight.

The woman on the bed suddenly regained consciousness with a spluttering gasp, sitting up with a hand to her throat.

She blinked big doe-eyes, *her* face illuminated by the light of twinkling fairy lights around the headboard.

"What—?" she started to say, then frowned in my direction. "Oh, I thought I hallucinated her. Weird. Are you... joining in?"

My brows shot up so hard I was surprised they remained attached to my face. "N-no! No, I'm so sorry, I was just—"

"Looking for the bathroom," the man finished for me in that low, amused voice just *dripping* with sex. "So you said. And yet... you're still here."

"Well, if you're not joining us, I'm going to take a shower." The woman hopped up off the bed, naked as the day she was born with tits bouncing like a fucking adult Disney princess. She leaned in to kiss the man who still stood beside the bed in shadow. "You gonna join me, baby?"

He kissed her back, giving a small moan of approval while grasping two handfuls of her ass. "In a minute. Will you be quiet this time or shall I bring the hat?"

She giggled. "Bring the hat." Not bothering to grab any clothing or even a robe, she crossed over to where I stood there like an *idiot*. "If you change your mind, I eat pussy like it's my job." She winked, then sashayed past me, entirely unconcerned by her nudity as she opened the door *across* from this room. The one I cringed to see was labeled *bathroom*.

"Spoiler alert, it is her job," the man rumbled, making me nearly jump out of my skin at how close he sounded. I'd been so focused watching the naked woman, I hadn't noticed he'd approached.

Now my head whipped back around to find all six-foot *fuck-knew-how-tall* of him standing right there in front of me. Still naked. Still swinging an enormous cock like a badge of honor. But that wasn't what made my eyes widen to the size of saucers and my mouth go suddenly dry.

43

I should have seen it coming. Frost was here, as was Alfie. Of course they hadn't come back to town without *him*. The leader of their little band of misfits, Nicholas Klores.

"Nick?" I squeaked in utter disbelief. Now I knew why that firm backside had seemed so familiar.

He stared back at me, his pine green gaze confused and showing not a single trace of recognition. "I'm sorry, have we met?"

Rage flooded through me. *Have we met?* The audacity of this man to ask *have we met* when the last time we'd seen one another, he'd been promising me forever. Swearing he'd come back for me, and asking me to *wait for him*.

Have we fucking *met*?

My mouth opened to spew obscenities at the gorgeous man, but then my vision went all spotty and my axis tilted. This time I really was going to faint, except when it came to Nick... *Saint Nick*... I was fainting from overwhelming *anger*.

Lying bastard.

CHAPTER
SIX

The sound of a heated argument nearby was what woke me and I lay still to listen. There was no sense in announcing I was awake when they were clearly arguing about *me*... unless there was a different Rayne in Northland right now.

"...fairly fucking obvious she didn't know it was me until I was standing right there in front of her," Nick was growling, his deep voice still doing sinful things to my insides.

"Naked," Alfie added, terse as fuck.

"That's usually how I like to fuck, Alf, yes. Naked," Nick snapped back.

"And then when she saw it was *you*..."

"I pretended I didn't recognize her," he muttered.

"Because..."

Nick made a frustrated sound. "I panicked! Rayne was the last fucking person I expected to walk in on me balls deep in Donna, so she caught me off guard. If you two knew she was in town, why'd no one tell me?"

"And miss this amazing reaction? Not for the world," Frost

scoffed, speaking for the first time since I'd woken up. So they were all there, then.

Alfie made a long-suffering sound and I could picture him scrubbing his hands over his face. "In fairness, we didn't think she'd be staying here."

"I followed her to the Northland Lodge," Frost commented quietly. "I assumed that's where she'd booked her room."

"She probably did, but they habitually overbook their capacity, remember?" Alfie murmured thoughtfully.

"Fuck," Nick swore. "This is the last thing we need."

"No shit," Frost answered him. "'Course, you can stop playing fainting damsel there, Rayne. I saw the eyelids move."

Flicking my eyes open, I was greeted to the sight of all three of them basically hovering around my bed. Frost was still all in black, Alfie was in his dark blue scrubs, and Nick—well, at least he had pants on.

"Knew it." Frost sounded positively smug about it as he patted my cheek. I slapped his hand away and then sat up abruptly. Thankfully, I was still on the bed, so when the room swam in a circle around me, I didn't fall over.

"Easy." Alfie all but shoved Frost to the side and put a hand on my shoulder. "You passed out and were out for a good—fifteen minutes." He checked his watch then with the guys.

Well, that wasn't embarrassing.

"I'm fine," I informed him and shook off his touch. I was just *fine*. My panties were wet, my pulse was dashing, and I swore it felt like I'd done one too many shots of whiskey and now I had a hangover from hell—a hangover in Christmas hell with my own personal elves.

"Great," Frost said. "I'll grab your stuff and put it in the car and you can get out of here."

"She can't leave," Nick said in the same breath Alfie uttered, "She doesn't need to be driving."

"Neither of you get an opinion." Frost sounded downright testy as he turned those ice-cold eyes in my direction. "You need to go. In fact, we had a deal."

I swore, these assholes were just making my headache worse. Then my body reminded me of what started all of this in the first place. I needed to pee. I pushed off the bed. The feeling of the rug under my feet hit me—where were my shoes?

They were gone. Along with my jacket. I did a quick mental inventory. Where was my phone? Alfie had a hand under my elbow and despite the swimming head, the sick feeling in my stomach, and my violent desire to urinate, I found myself wanting to lean into the contact.

Which meant, hell, fucking, no. I jerked my arm out of his grasp. "You have a touchy feeling problem there, Alfie. Stop. Touching. Me."

I could barely think with all of them around me. The uneven sensation fought a valiant effort against my embarrassment, but the fact I really needed that bathroom before I pissed myself won out over all of it.

Abandoning Alfie, I cut to the side to go around Frost without touching him and went wide of Nick. The feeling of all three of them staring at me followed me out of *my* room and down the hall. A low sound of half-choked laughter hit me and I glared at Nick who'd actually followed me out into the hallway.

"I forgot," he admitted with a nod toward the bathroom. It was almost an apology. If apologies included smirks and not sounding remotely sorry. Ignoring him, I let myself inside the room with all its porcelain fixtures and a—kill me—Merry Christmas bedecked shower curtain. Thankfully, it was empty of any nude blondes. I half-wondered where she'd disappeared to, but only half.

"Don't lock it," Alfie said from the other side, startling me as I shut the door before I even made it one step. Did he fucking teleport down the hallway? "If you pass out again, we need to be able to get to you."

I wasn't passing out again. But I didn't argue with him or even acknowledge him. I just turned, pressed in the little button on the door handle to lock it. Flimsy lock. I doubted it could keep me out, much less the three bears out there.

Fuck, I needed to pee. I ignored my pale, haggard, coffee-deprived image reflecting in the mirror, yanked down my jeans, and did my best to ignore all the crocheted doilies, decorations, and other elfin delights of Christmas staring at me as I peed.

The relief was a slightly less intense orgasm. Nick could do so much better—as evidenced by the ripple of muscle in his powerful ass as he'd rocked Donna's world. Lucky bitch. I almost inhaled my spit when I recognized what I was doing and I shook my head.

Just no.

I didn't care about Nick's glorious glutes or Alfie's agonizing kisses or Frost's glacial eyes.

I didn't give a damn about any of them. I was here to investigate missing kids, not rediscover the past with three assholes. *Remember the headline, Rayne. Remember the story.*

Bladder finally relieved, I cleaned up and washed my hands. The hints of steam and shampoo remained in the room. Oh, I wonder if I interrupted Nick getting to join Donna in the shower.

Pity.

Anyway...I looked like shit. But it had been a *long* day, and it wasn't getting any shorter. As much as I'd like to hope that the silence outside meant they'd all fucked off to whatever holes they'd climbed out of, I didn't have that luxury. I wasn't a little girl, and I wasn't afraid of anything, certainly not them.

When I opened the door, all three of them jerked to a halt in the middle of what looked like a very intense, *silent* argument. I'd seen a couple of hand signs I recognized, but they all three focused on me again and I huffed out a breath. "This town really needs a few other things to do if you're all still lurking."

Then I turned heel and headed back to my room. I needed to call Connie tonight. Or another hotel. Maybe I could stay somewhere one town over and drive in. Even as I tried to weigh the mental plans, the fact those three paced me back to my room seemed to swallow all of my attention.

At the still open door, I paused and turned, barring them from entering. "I can't say it was good to see all of you, because it wasn't. But I'm tired and I'm not in the mood to chat, so goodbye, good night, whatever."

Then I stepped back, but the door didn't close because Frost had a hand on it, keeping it where it was. "That's nice, Rayne," Frost told me. "We don't care if you're tired. We have questions."

"Actually," Alfie said, shooting Frost a dark look. "We do care." Then he snapped those dark eyes to me. "I care. Especially since you passed out. We need to talk about any medical conditions you have, special considerations. People don't just faint for no reason."

"You're not my doctor, and I'm fine. I've just had an extremely busy day, and I was supposed to be enjoying some peace, quiet, and room service right about now, but here I am. So nothing for you to see or do. Good night."

I tried to close the door again, but Nick sighed. "Rayne, we're not going anywhere until we talk. I have no problem having this conversation right here."

I rolled my eyes. "Of course you don't. You don't even lock

the door to your room when you're railing a girl. You always were a bit of an exhibitionist."

A smile flashed across his face like he was proud of himself, but it faded nearly as soon as it appeared. "No one told you to open the door."

No, they hadn't. "Clearly. Now would you guys please fuck off."

"No," Frost said, folding his arms as he all but invaded my spot in the open door. I had two choices, back up or stand breast to chest with him.

I retreated, and the smirk on his face said he knew it. "What," I said, cobbling together the armor that had served me on numerous stories over the years. They were not the first unfriendly subjects I'd had to interview in order to get to the heart of a story. So fine, if they wanted to ask questions.

So would I.

"What do you want?" I asked and it was Alfie who sighed.

"Look, sit down at least? Put your feet up?"

"No," I snapped at him in the same tone that Frost used, and then I grimaced. I didn't want to agree with Frost on anything, and his equally annoyed expression when we locked gazes said we agreed—again.

"What are you doing in Northland?" Nick asked.

"What are *you* doing here?"

"We live here," Frost retorted.

"Here?" I motioned to the gingerbread house around us. "I know it says boarding house but..."

"Not here, here," Alfie said with a sigh.

"No, we have a bigger place. Just getting renovated, so we stay here." The explanation from Nick offered up some information... not a lot, but some. They had a *bigger* place? So they lived in Northland? But for how long? And why did they have to leave their house to renovate? Who renovated in December anyway? "Your turn."

"I'm here to do a story on Northland, America's prettiest city for Christmas." I lied with a straight face and a smile in my heart. "They made *Vogue,* and there are lots of people hungry for every bit of Christmas cheer they can consume, so where better to find it than in Northland itself?"

Their three faces were varying levels of disbelief. "You came to Northland to do a story about Christmas?" Alfie seemed to struggle with the idea.

I had no idea why. Christmas had never been a bright spot before they left, but back then I didn't actively *hate* it like I did now. "Sure." My story was as plausible as theirs.

"Rayne," Nick said as he straightened and took a step forward.

"Actually," I said, "it's Rachel. I changed my name a long time ago. You can call me Miss Dean. Or you can say nothing at all. I'd be fine with that. But I answered your questions. You know why I'm here. You know why you're here. Now, I'm closing the door and you're fucking right the hell off."

All three of them stared at me, and it was Nick who finally let out a harsh sigh, raked a hand through his hair, and dropped back a step. "Fine. We're going. I'm next door, so just yell if you pass out or something. Alf is down the hall if you need him to play doctor."

"It's not Alf," Alfie grunted. "Dick." Yet he followed Nick, the only one who didn't move was Frost. He glared at me and I glared right back.

"I'll be watching you," he said finally and it provoked a memory of what he'd said before. He'd followed me to the Northland Lodge. He'd stormed out of the clinic and got a vehicle from somewhere and then followed me?

"I'll be sure to put a little pep in my step just for you," I said as he finally stepped back and let me shut the door in his face. I locked it then leaned back against the closed door so I could sag in relief.

My hands were shaking with the dump of adrenaline, and I closed my eyes as I got my breathing under control. Of all the gin joints in all the world, why the fuck were those three back here? And why *now*?

After more than a decade of silence? How did that end up happening? Rubbing a hand over my face, I looked at the room. It hadn't changed since the first time I walked in here, so why did it seem so different? As much as I wanted a shower, no way I was going back to that *shared* bathroom.

Not right now.

So I found my phone—it was still in my coat pocket. The coat had been hung up. My suitcase was set on a stand, and my shoes were lined up neatly inside it. I dug out some comfortable pajamas, changed into them, and bundled my feet into socks. It was chilly in here. My stomach protested. I had a bottle of water inside my backpack, so I pulled it out to take my evening meds.

A knock at the door stopped me cold.

"Just me," Ginger called, "leaving you some hot tea and cookies. There's sandwiches in the fridge if you get hungry. We usually only serve breakfast, but it's late and I thought you might be hungry."

Then she was gone. Hot tea sounded divine, and I crept over to the door, violently aware of every creak in the wooden floors. I jerked to a halt when I realized what I was doing. What did I care if they heard me moving around?

At the door though, I opened it quietly and glanced down at the tray with the covered plate, the actual teapot, cup, and tea bags with sugar and milk as well as honey and lemon. She'd thought of everything.

Thankfully, the hall was silent and I made it back into my room with the tray and set it on the desk. After brewing the tea and getting it ready, I popped open the cover, braced for what kind of cookies she'd left me. If I weren't hungry, I could just ignore them but I needed something.

A choked sob stuck in my throat and my eyes misted over. The cookies were shaped like trees, but they weren't decorated for Christmas. There was icing done in the shape of flowers. There was a little note next to it that read: *For the not-Christmas tourist.*

I sniffled. They were the prettiest cookies ever.

I ate all four of them.

CHAPTER
SEVEN

Morning arrived with a kind of abrupt record screech that took me from a sexy scorching dream to ice cold reality. I sat up with a jerk, chest heaving as I sucked in the chilly air. Well, more than chilly since my breath was practically vapor. I swung my wild gaze around the room, my empty cunt clenching tight and sweat decorating my lip.

Twisting, I looked at the headboard to my bed then around the room again. I'd just been tied to a bed and had a gag in my mouth while Nick powered into me with so much force the bed itself fucking broke. The fact I was right there on the edge of an orgasm made me want to scream as I flopped back against the bed.

The cold in the room had me burrowing under the blankets. It was fucking freezing in here. A bit of snow fell in to land on the floor with an icy plop and I grimaced. The swish of a tail didn't—

Tail?

I sat up again. A cat sat on the windowsill, tail lashing as it eyed me. I'd cracked open the window the night before—more to air out the smell of sex from Nick, which apparently hadn't worked, and the other warm, masculine scents that lingered after I'd kicked them out.

But I'd only cracked it.

Apparently, the wind had other ideas. The cat kept staring at me and I stared back. Did Ginger have a cat? She hadn't mentioned it, and it was cold. Could hardly blame it for sneaking in here with the dipshit—that would be me—who left the window open.

"Okay, cat," I said. "I need to get up and close that window before I freeze. So if you're staying, get in here or get out. I'm pretty easy."

Teeth chattering, I shoved the blankets back and hurried over to the window. The cat didn't move until I was right there, then she hissed at me like she was seriously offended before she darted upward and over to another window.

Right, good. I pulled the window closed and shuddered as I danced in place. Hot shower sounded really good. Hot shower and clean clothes. The heater in the room was no match for the chill, so I grabbed one of the knit blankets to wrap around myself.

My nipples were peaked and hard and it had nothing to do with sexy times dreams about Nick. Me clenching my thighs was to keep from freezing to death as I turned to my suitcase, which was open where I'd left it to get clothes out the night before.

The smell hit me as soon as I was next to it.

No.

It didn't.

Cat urine was the absolute worst smell on the planet and it was all I could smell. Dammit. Head back, I stared up at the ceiling and considered screaming. Just—one good, oxygen-filled shriek. Getting a grip, I took the time to check.

Every single item.

I didn't know how the cat managed it, but the feline even managed to get my underthings. The room was cold. My clothes were soaked in cat piss. I was staying in what felt like a literal gingerbread house in the Christmas town from hell

Oh, and apparently, the three wise-ass jerks were also staying here. An image of Nick's very toned, very fit ass flitted through my mind. It was like burned there, forever imprinted. Trying to get a grip took several more deep breaths—through my mouth and not my nose 'cause the smell was killing me—then I dragged the knit blanket around me more firmly since I didn't have anything to put on over my tank top and shorts.

Damn cat.

Then I sucked up my pride and went in search of Ginger. She had to have something I could borrow, and hopefully a washer and dryer I could borrow. All the way down the hall and then down the stairs, I kept my eyes away from the other doors.

The sound of Christmas music led me to the kitchen where Ginger was sipping coffee and humming as she worked a crossword puzzle? Oh, so much better than cookies even if the ones she'd brought me the night before were amazing.

"Rachel," she said when she looked up, her smile wide and welcoming though her expression quickly turned to concern. The kindness rolling off her positively visceral, like a long-distance hug I couldn't avoid. "What happened?" She stood up. "You're positively blue."

"Would you believe I cracked open my window last night and a cat let themselves in and peed all over my clothes?" Even saying it aloud sounded insane especially with how plaintive my voice was. The last thing I wanted was for *anyone* to see me like this, but I really needed to fix it before the guys did.

Ginger blinked at me and I swore, for a second her lips twitched. "Rudolph is a bad kitty sometimes, but I can't—actually, I can and I'm so sorry. I'd offer to throw them in our washer and dryer but they aren't working. There's a small Laundromat just up the street, for locals only but I have a key. Let me find you something to wear, and I'll make you up a hot coffee, and then we'll get you all sorted shall we?"

All sorted turned out to be a pair of jeans that actually fit me, which with my long legs was fantastic, but the only tops she had that weren't tents turned out to be the ugliest Christmas sweaters ever. They were warm, they were clean, and they didn't smell like pee.

Fifteen minutes later with a huge tumbler of hot coffee that tasted divine, a breakfast sandwich that was even better, and all my clothing sacked up for washing, I headed out past my rental car and followed the block. At least my shoes and the socks I'd worn the previous day had avoided a similar fate. As promised, the little laundromat was just down the street.

It was a quiet little building with windows facing away from the street. I let myself in and juggled the bag over to the machines where I came face to face with the absolute *last* person I wanted to see.

"Morning Rayne," Nick said from where he was sitting atop one of the washers like the naughtiest elf on the shelf come to life.

Yep.

I was in hell.

"You look positively festive this morning," he commented when I stood there speechless. "It's nice to see your Christmas cheer in full swing."

"Fuck you, prick," I grumbled, snapping out of my daze and

making a beeline for the furthest machine from where he sat. As quickly as possible, I dumped my entire bag of laundry into the machine, then tossed in the bag itself. Glancing around, I realized the machine for detergent was displaying a large *Out Of Order* sign.

"Give me a break," I groaned under my breath, hanging my head with frustration then wincing as the tang of cat piss burned my nostrils.

"Phew, that is... pungent," Nick commented, having snuck up right behind me. "You let Rudolph into your room last night, huh?"

I rolled my eyes, stubbornly refusing to turn and look at him. "Yeah, thanks for the heads up on that. Asshole."

"Now, now, none of that. I was going to offer you some of my soap, but if you're going to be mean about it..." He waggled a big bottle of laundry detergent in front of my face and I bit my lip to resist the urge to smack it out of his hand.

Instead I gritted my teeth and silently prayed for patience. "Please, may I use your detergent, Saint Nick?"

I could practically *feel* his smug smile. "That's more like it, Rainbow," he purred, making my insides go all fucking fluttery, "Of course you can."

Rather than hand it over, he reached around me and opened the bottle. He measured out the capful and poured it in, all while keeping me bracketed between his arms. Then he added an extra splash, which I quietly agreed was necessary given the stench, before closing the lid.

"Thanks," I muttered, inserting my coins and starting the cycle running.

"It's the least I could do," he murmured, so quietly I thought I'd imagined it for a moment.

When I spun around to confront him, he had his back to me, returning his bottle of detergent to his own laundry basket beside the machine he'd been sitting on when I arrived. Like that simple act of sharing soap wasn't crazy sexually charged.

"What are you doing, Nick?" I asked in a harsh exhale, folding my arms over my stupid Christmas sweater.

He turned back around to face me, slouching way too sexily against his washer. "Laundry. What are you doing, Rainbow?"

I flinched. "Don't call me that."

"Why not? Alf called you Rayne-drop yesterday, and Frost called you—" He broke off with a grin. "Never mind."

I glowered, imagining whatever Frost called me was probably unkind. He was such a moody asshole and always had been. Alfie had always been sweet with me, Nick was always hot and flirty, but Frost and I were constantly at each other's throats, forever on the verge of clawing each other's eyes out. Except for that one night...

I shook off the memory, refusing to let my mind go there. To that night when Frost had been genuine and soft with me.

"I don't know how many times I have to say it, but once again, my name is Rachel. Not Rayne, not Rayne-drop, not Rainbow, not... bitch tits or whatever awesome nickname Frost thought up this time. It's Rachel. Got it?"

Nick licked his lips, slowly, like he knew what kind of dirty dreams I'd been having about him all damn night long. "Hmmm I see. I hear what you're saying, Rainbow, but I don't believe I can acquiesce to this request."

It took everything in me not to react like he so clearly wanted me to. He was baiting me, trying to make me angry and irrational. It wasn't going to work.

"You seem like a negotiating sort of man, Nick," I observed, and noted the way his brow twitched with interest. "What is it going to take for you to *acquiesce* on the subject of my chosen name?"

He shrugged. "Is it really such a big deal? You can use

Rachel all you like, but you'll always be my Rainbow deep down."

I shivered, trying so damn hard to ignore the girly butterflies his voice was causing inside my belly. "It's a big deal to me, Nick," I admitted, my voice cracking with more vulnerability than I'd have liked him to see.

He stared at me for a long moment, then pursed his lips thoughtfully. "Okay. I'll make you a deal."

My breath gusted out. "Thank you. What do you want? Because I'm already planning to call around the hotels today and find a new room somewhere else."

"Leave town," he replied.

My heart ripped in half and all the butterflies turned to ash.

"I can't do that," I snapped back. "I'm here for work. It's nothing to do with you, and believe it or not, this town *is* big enough to avoid one another."

He gave a small nod, seeming annoyed. Tough shit.

"Fine. Then I have a different request."

My mouth was so damn dry, and I shifted my feet uncomfortably. Everything about the way he stared at me was making me jittery and nervous. "Go on then."

He prowled back across to me, invading my personal space and leaving me trapped against the humming washing machine. "Let me re-do last night."

My brows rose with surprise. "You mean when I walked in on you plowing the snow in some tied up chick's vagina?"

His lips twitched. "I mean, when I pretended not to know you. That was wrong of me, and I want to try again. Will you let me?"

I was so damn confused.

"You want a reunion do-over where you're less of a lying

prick?" I still wasn't seeing the catch. There was always a catch with Nick.

He nodded, bracing his hands on the washer either side of me and leaning down to my height. "Yes."

Suspicion filled my chest and my eyes narrowed. "And that's all?"

"That's all," he agreed. "You go all wide-eyed with shock and ask *Nick?* And I react the way I should have, if my brain was even halfway functioning. Deal?"

A bit dazed and intrigued, I found myself nodding slowly. "Okay. Deal."

Nick flashed a grin, releasing the washing machine to straighten up and take a step back. "Good. Okay turn around, you were facing away from me, remember?"

Still sure he was up to something—but with no idea what —I did as he directed, turning around to face the washers and sighed. "Nick, this is—"

"Hang on, lemme get into the right mindset," he cut me off.

I rolled my eyes to the ceiling, praying once again for patience. He was messing with me, and I was too tired to see the punchline, which was undoubtedly right around the corner. "Can we just—"

"Okay, ready," he announced. "So just, pretend like you were watching Donna head to the bathroom then turn back around and recognize it's me."

I sighed again, rubbing the bridge of my nose. There wasn't enough coffee in the whole of Northland for this shit. Still, if it stopped him calling me Rainbow...

"Fine," I muttered, turning back around and then gasping so hard I nearly choked. My eyes widened so much they could have popped out and my jaw hit the floor. "Nick?" It came out as a shocked squeak because he was just standing there stark-naked, wearing nothing but a grin.

"Rainbow?" he replied with a fake surprise that nearly made me laugh. "Holy shit, it's really you."

Without giving me even a moment to recover from shock, he reached out and gripped the hair at the base of my skull, tilting my head back and crushing his lips to mine in a searing hot kiss.

Not even the strongest of grudges could withstand the power of Saint Nick on a mission, and right now... he had a point to make. Fuck, I was done for.

EIGHT

Kissing Nick had never been a passive sport. It hadn't been the first time he kissed me. The second... the third... and it sure as fuck wasn't now. Even as my brain sparked on every reason we *shouldn't* be doing this. His lips pressed more firmly, and I was groaning.

The feel of his tongue stroking against mine was like being lost on a liquid chocolate high dipped in the sweetest of strawberries. There was a bite and a silkiness, a demand and coax. I could fight one, but not the other. It was like he knew exactly how to dart in and around the barbed wire wrapped around my soul.

Flattening my hands against the solid wall of muscle, ink, and sex, I caught fire. Touching him was a mistake. Whatever chill had remained after the night went up in a violent conflagration. The hand on my nape drifted down my back, and then he clapped both palms to my ass and lifted me.

I landed against the machine, but not once did he let up on the kiss. He had my lips in his possession, and he wasn't giving them back. Saint Nick was the devil incarnate, pure magnetism, and I was absolutely trapped in his orbit. The distant part of my mind shrieking about what a terrible idea this was got gagged and shoved into a closet.

His mouth left mine as he kissed a path along my throat. My cunt was soaked, and I didn't have a single doubt who it was. Everything about him said, *flee, run, and get the hell out of here.* But I wasn't going anywhere. The fire spread against my abdomen as he shoved his hands under the ugly as fuck sweater.

"This is a terrible idea," I panted, the words slipping out from the closet I shoved them into.

"The worst," he agreed in the sexiest masculine purr, as though his voice dropped another octave, and I swore everything inside of me went hot, tight, and more than a little desperate. "Absolutely the worst, Rainbow..." The tickle of his tongue over my pulse was a tease, then he scraped his teeth against my skin before he sucked a hickey into place that went all the way down to my cunt.

The pulse was electric.

"We can't do this." The fact I can still string words together was a good sign right? I hadn't completely lost my mind.

Those hot hands under the sweater pushed it up and took my tank top with it. The air in the laundromat was so much cooler than his skin, and my nipples went hard as a rock.

"We can," Nick assured me, pulling that sinful mouth away from me as he dragged the sweater and shirt up and over. I had to lower my hands to help him, but he didn't strip it off; he just bound my arms behind my back, tangling shirt and sweater together. "Oh we definitely can—look at these beautiful breasts... I have missed you."

Me?

No, he wasn't talking to me. He was dipping his head to my chest. Heat bloomed before his mouth fastened over one nipple, and I bit my lip to keep from crying out. The power of his lips as he sucked hard then teased my nipple against his teeth left me almost whimpering.

It was just heavy petting.

"Nick," I panted.

"Hmm," was his only answer, and then he was stripping off my boots, and then the jeans were unfastened. Fuck...

"Nick, we can't..."

"We can," he whispered against the damp nipple, his hot breath feathering over it and sending out another wave of sensation. "Flatten your hands against the top," he ordered and I frowned. My hands were behind me. It wasn't exactly uncomfortable, but at the same time it took a little concentration to balance myself, and since he held all of my focus, I forgot to argue.

As soon as I had it, he peeled my jeans and panties down, and then I was as naked as he was and his gaze swept over me with a kind of raw hunger that threatened to choke me. The image of his ass in motion from the night before overlaid the dream that had held me hostage before that ugly wake-up call, and the present—it superimposed over all of them.

Dropping my jeans behind him, Nick gripped my thighs and pulled me forward. With me on the washer and him leaning into me, gaze fastened on mine, and we were nose to nose.

"Say it again, Rainbow..."

My neurons scrambled around looking for whatever the fuck he was asking about and coming up empty. "Say what?"

Those hot as hell fingers slid through my folds, and a slow grin turned up the corners of his mouth. "You're soaking for me, Rainbow—so just say it for me."

What the fuck? I wanted his hands on me, and he was

teasing two fingers around my clit like he was playing some game. The tension inside of me ratcheted higher.

"Say it," he whispered against my ear before he bit it.

"Say what?" I almost yelled.

"Saint Nick," he murmured before grazing my clit with the lightest possible pressure.

"Saint Nick?"

He chuckled, but it was dark and wicked and not remotely humorous. "Like you mean it, Rainbow. Beg Saint Nick like you mean it."

I groaned in both pleasure and pain. I called him that in my head just fine, but saying it out loud seemed *submissive,* and I was anything but. Then again, he'd earned the nickname of *Saint* because of the decidedly unsaintly things he'd done as a teen, so if I thought about it sarcastically then... maybe...

"Fuck." I gasped as he butted the tip of his cock against my core. "Damn it... this is *still* a bad idea."

"But..." he teased, knowing full fucking well I was gagging for his dick.

"But I need you to *finally* fuck me, Saint Nick," I confessed. "I need to know what it feels like to take all that saintly cock inside my—*oof!*" Words totally failed me as he pinned my thighs wide and thrust inside.

We'd fooled around plenty as kids, but we'd never gone this far. I'd thought about it *plenty* of times, though, and it was safe to say that the real deal was way, way better than imagination.

"Holy fuck, Rainbow, you feel so good. So ready for me. You've got no idea how long I've wanted to do this..." Nick groaned the words against my throat as he rocked his hips, thrusting deeper and making me whimper as I wrenched my hands free of the damn sweater. Clawing at his back, I fought to pull him closer, and the moment his hands released my thighs I had my legs wrapped around him and my ankles hooked together like a bow on a present.

"Yes," I gasped out as he started to pump in and out of me, setting a quick rhythm that told me he was just as worked up as I was. This hadn't been planned out in advance, and it had none of Nick's usual carefully measured control. Nope, this was pure instinct and emotion and nostalgia. Hot, sweaty, orgasmic nostalgia.

The washer beneath my ass bumped and shifted into spin cycle, and I yelped. It was vibrating and bouncing, but Nick didn't miss a stroke as his fingers toyed with my hard nipple and his mouth explored my throat like I was made of candy canes. Nick always did love peppermint candy.

"Are you gonna come for me, Rainbow?" he asked in a breathless, husky voice while pumping his hips faster. He gripped my hips, lifting me up a little to meet his strokes.

So soon? I mean, yes I was absolutely already there. But holy hell, that had to be a personal best. Usually I had to work for my orgasms in an awkward dance of getting my partner to push my buttons just right, but Nick had just valet delivered me right onto the precipice without even trying.

I moaned, my thighs clenching around his hips as he slammed deeper and his broad head rubbed deliciously over my g-spot. "Oh god, yes, right there, don't stop..."

"Not god, Rainbow," he grunted, repeating the motion again and again. "Say *my* name when you come. My name. I wanna hear you moan it, just like you did the first time I ate your cunt."

Shit. That was not fair play, but my orgasm didn't care for the rules. It crashed over me in soul shuddering waves, making me whimper and gasp, my body convulsing and my pussy gripping onto Nick's cock like it was a life preserver.

"Say it," he growled, and I nearly died.

"*Nick...*" I moaned. "*Saint Nick,* please don't stop. Don't stop. I can come again. Just fuck me harder."

Shock and delight flashed over his face as he shifted to meet my heavy-lidded gaze, then he did what I asked and thrust faster. His hips slammed into my pelvis, and the washing machine went nuts under my ass, like a fucking paid actor. The vibrations chattering through my ass did the trick as Nick stuffed me like a knitted stocking on Christmas Eve, bending me all out of shape and stretching me to fit all of him no matter how hard he had to stuff.

"Fuck, yes!" I exclaimed, feeling the heat of a second climax build in my pussy. "Oh my g—*Saint*. I'm going to come again. S-so g-g-good." My whole body was bouncing with the motion of the washer, the motion of the enormous ripped *saint* between my thighs, and with the waves of pure ecstasy coiling out from my cunt.

Why did I think this was a bad idea again? This was a fantastic idea. We should do this again.

"Shit, Rainbow, I'm coming too," Nick confessed, then crashed his mouth back against mine. His tongue plunged inside, absolutely dominating me and controlling my breath as he slammed his hard length into me with deep, jerky thrusts. I was still riding the tail wind of my second orgasm, and my inner muscles clamped tight, holding him deep as he released his hot load.

He kept kissing me long after he finished coming, just in no hurry to let me go. His tongue and lips seemed to be doing everything possible to memorize every millimeter of my mouth, or reacquainting himself as it may be. Reminding me how good we used to be together, and how long we'd spent learning how each other liked to be kissed. As if that could ever be forgotten.

A girl never forgot her first love, and in my case, I had three. That shit stuck on the mind and soul for eternity.

"Nick…" I whispered after kissing him for what seemed like an eternity. The washing machine just beeped to inform us the load was done, so that said a lot about how much time we'd taken.

"Hmm?" he rumbled, twitching cock still buried deep within me as he kissed my lips again.

I smiled, blissed out on endorphins. "Nick…"

He ignored me this time, diving back in for another tongue wrestle. I moaned but kissed him back until my belly started to curl with excitement again.

"Saint Nick…" I tried this time, and he paused. Then sighed and shifted his face back only far enough to meet my eyes.

"Yes, Rainbow?"

I narrowed my eyes. "We had a deal. You're supposed to stop calling me that."

His lush lips curled in a sly grin. "Did we? I don't recall any specifics laid out for that deal. Devil's in the details, Rainbow my love."

I frowned, then cast my mind over our conversation word for word. "Son of a bitch!" I hissed, giving him a shove. He stumbled back a step, dislodging from our intimate embrace and leaving me with my legs spread wide on the washing machine lid.

He stared with undeniable hunger for a moment, then paled as his eyes widened. "Oh shit," he whispered. "I didn't— *fuck*. Rayne! I didn't use a condom!"

It took a full second for his words to sink into my fizzy brain, then I glanced down to see the evidence of his point dripping down my splayed cunt. "Ah."

"Are you—"

"On birth control? Yes, I'm not an idiot. But considering I

literally walked in on you balls deep in a woman who is some kind of escort *yesterday*? I'm less concerned about pregnancy and more about STDs." I cringed and slid down off the washer. At least I'd seen him toss that condom yesterday. Good sign, right? "Pass me my clothes please?"

The guilty look on his face as he handed over my jeans still tangled with panties said it all. He was *also* concerned he could have given me something. Great. So great.

"I'll get tested today," he suggested with a grimace, running a hand over his sweaty face then pulling on his own pants. "Sorry, Rainbow."

I flinched, putting up a hand to say *shut the fuck up, Nick*. Gritting my teeth, I tugged my ugly sweater back on and looked around for my boots.

"Rainbow, I'm *sorry*," he repeated as I stuffed my feet into the boots. When I struggled, he boosted me back up onto the washer where we'd just fucked, and tied my laces for me. "I wasn't thinking."

I nodded quickly. "Oh, no, I know. That makes two of us. Nick... this was a *bad fucking idea*. I'm not in Northland for a trip down memory lane, I'm here for work. That's it. This—" I gestured between us "—was nice. But it can't happen again. Please, Nick, *please* don't tell Alfie."

His expression darkened like a storm cloud. "Why not? He told me you kissed him at the clinic."

My jaw dropped with outrage. "He *what*? Oh my fucking— nope, I'm not doing this. We are ancient history, Nick. *All of us* are ancient history. Don't go digging up graves now." I jumped back down off the washer and pushed him out of my way, making a quick beeline out of the laundromat.

The frosty air slapped me in the face like the wakeup call I so desperately needed, and I took slow, calming breaths as I stomped through the snow back to Ginger Bridge's Boarding

House. Each step I took, each wet slide of Nick's cum between my legs, solidified my resolve. I wasn't here for love or even lust.

I was here to do my fucking job. Kids were disappearing, and I was going to find them no matter what it took.

CHAPTER
NINE

It wasn't until I was all the way back into my room at Ginger's and freshly showered to wash Nick off my skin, that I realized I'd left all my laundry in the washing machine. Fucking hell.

Not wanting to put those jeans back on, I dressed in just the sweater and the pair of red and white striped wool leggings Ginger offered me earlier. I looked like a fucking mall elf but it was better than running around bare legged in the snow.

First priority had to be retrieving my belongings from the laundromat, but I was so reluctant to run into Nick again that I found myself turning the other direction and heading to the nearest coffee shop instead.

"Merry Christmas and welcome to Manger Coffee!" the festive-aproned barista called out with a cheery wave. "What can I get for you?"

"Uh, just black coffee, thanks. Biggest one you've got."

"Black?" The barista repeated, seemingly confused. "No festive flavor? Our specialty is a peppermint spicy mocha with vanilla whip, or I can make you a lovely pumpkin spice latte with heavy cream and a dash of butterscotch?"

I tried not to show my disgust too visibly, but those options sounded just goddamn awful. The only flavors I wanted in my coffee came in booze-form. "Just black. No festive flavors. Thank you."

The young woman looked puzzled like I'd just asked her to serve me a ketchup latte, but she nodded weakly and charged me nonetheless. Thankfully, she moved her smile packed with Christmas cheer on to the next person in line. Folding my arms, I paced away from the people hovering around the pick-up spot for their coffees and studied the town outside the window.

Business in the coffee shop was hopping. The door opened and closed with enough regularity that the jingling bells that kept playing blended almost perfectly with the constant drone of Christmas classics drifting out of the speakers. It was just loud enough to be impossible to escape, and yet the rise and fall of conversation, whistling milk foamers, and coffee grinders seemed to help drown out.

Torture.

Everything about this place from the scents of cinnamon, cardamom, nutmeg, apples, and eggnog to the music to the host of tourists and locals decked out head to toe like they were living in a Whoville Christmas Miracle just added multiple layers to the torture.

Insane.

It was all just *insane*.

"Rachel!" The call yanked my unseeing gaze off the legitimate collection of *elves* making their way up the street back to Manger Coffee. Desperate for the strongest of strong brews—black with no additional flavors, sugar, or cream—I weaved my way through the crowd.

The barista holding out the cheerful-looking cup flashed me a grin. "Merry Christmas, Rachel."

"Thanks—" She wasn't wearing a name-tag. "—very happy coffee goddess."

Her laughter startled me. Or maybe it was the surprise on her face. I wrapped my fingers around the cup, eager for both the warmth and the caffeine infusion. I had some investigating to do, and since I'd already made it to a coffee shop, maybe I could take a little wander down Main Street.

I sipped the coffee, ready for the bitter and the burn, which left me wholly unprepared for the wild taste of cinnamon infused coffee with a hint of brandy and super sweet whipped cream. I swore it was like a Christmas flavor bomb went off in my mouth. The fact I could taste coffee at *all* kept me from choking, but it didn't stop the spark of tears from burning in my eyes.

Torture.

Pure. Unmitigated. Torture.

A part of me wanted to stomp back up to the counter and demand to know what this was, and the rest of me said don't make a scene and get the fuck out of there. I grasped the latter impulse and followed an older guy out the door, even managing to nod to him as he held it open for me.

The rush of cold air didn't do much more than clear some of the peppermint madness from my nostrils. I attempted another sip of the coffee and grimaced. What the hell kind of *black* coffee was this?

I moved closer to the stores to avoid the heavier foot traffic as I made my way down a street I could hardly have forgotten, for all that Northland had truly grown the past decade plus— Main Street was as classic as it had always been, right down to the festive little storefronts that had truly been transformed into a Bavarian village classic. Not all the shops were familiar, but there were new restaurants, gift shops, and clothing stores all kitted out for the holidays.

Even as I studied the layout of the street, the festooned lamp posts, and the presence of actual *carolers,* it hit me how incredibly decked out the town was. Before, Christmas had been a big deal.

Now—it was big business.

Even the snow looked like it had been carefully curated and placed artistically. In the morning light, I could almost see the "magic" of it all. You know, if I canted my head and squinted.

I took another sip of the coffee and grimaced. I needed real coffee. There was a cheerful scrawl in green ink on the side of the cup. *Christmas Cup of Joe.*

Christmas.

I rolled my eyes. I really hated this time of year.

Three more steps and I tossed the cup into a trashcan and slid my hands into the pockets of the sweater. At least it had them. My phone was in one pocket and my room key in the other. More than one person tried to catch my eye and smile. I managed to keep my expression neutral and not lock gazes.

After encountering three ghosts of my past in the last twenty-four hours—the ache in my cunt reminded me of just how impacting one of those encounters had been—I wasn't in a great hurry to meet up with anyone else. The sheriff's office was right where I remembered it, located where four other streets intersected with Main to create the town star, rather than the town square.

They were so very proud of themselves. As I passed more storefronts opening for business, I started tracking how many teenagers and kids I could see. The high school wasn't that far from the town center. A lot of teens took free periods in the mornings and afternoons to work.

Locals as well as kids from the orphanage. It was a way to

earn some "pocket" money. I picked out a dozen easily, mostly guys, working on sweeping sidewalks or clearing them. Others were either bringing stock in or loading other stock onto trucks. That made sense: the guys were often in high demand for physical labor. Girls got the cleaning jobs.

Damn shame I'd lost my reservation at the Northland Lodge. I would like to have gotten a look at the cleaning staff. I checked my watch before heading across the road. I cast a glance at myself in a window as I passed it. My hair was pulled back into a messy ponytail that had gone more than a little frizzy. The Christmas sweater and striped leggings attracted more than a few open smiles and laughter. They were all enjoying themselves.

But I didn't look like me.

Relying on that, I made a point of checking the board out in front of the sheriff's office. Just like old times, all the town events were posted for the next several days. The tree lighting was done. There was plenty more to do including sleigh rides, snowmobile runs, cross country skiing, snow shoeing, toy making—that made me snort aloud.

Build your own toys with Northland's very own elves and add some brightness to their days.

Right.

I tracked the people coming and going while I took a picture of the "events" board with my phone. Good to know what people were doing. Where the crowds would be. Town events were fantastic for redirecting attention. While the notes Connie provided me had a lot of data, they didn't include *who* sent the tip in about the missing kids.

I had a list of kids that had gone missing. But of the ones on that list, only one of them had a family in town. Her name stuck out to me, so I wanted to take a look at what their crime blotter said.

Yes, funnily enough, even the prettiest place to spend Christmas had its very own blotter, probably bedecked in tinsel or some shit.

When a couple went inside the sheriff's office, I slipped in after them. While there were decorations everywhere in here and the poor schmuck at the desk wore a Santa hat, he was also in a uniform. Young.

Younger than me. Maybe twenty-five. Too young to remember much of when I'd been in town, so that was some luck, finally. I let them go first as I made a show of being attracted to the tree in the corner. There were little angel-like paper figures, toy soldier ones, and some snowman shapes that decorated it.

Each sheet included a name, an age, and some interests for local children and teens in need of some Christmas cheer. My stomach bottomed out as I skimmed the different ones. There was a sign that said if one caught your eye, to take the paper decoration off and affix it to the gift you wanted to leave.

Sounded so—reasonable. Just make some orphan or poor kid's day, right? Where else were they going to get presents?

"Sheriff Vynachts! There you are..." A woman called out an all too familiar name, and I took a picture of one of the "wish lists" before I snagged a selfie so I could look over my shoulder.

No fucking way.

The pot-bellied asshole striding inside with his well-trimmed white beard and damn near bald pate was sickeningly familiar.

He hadn't been *sheriff* then.

"What is it, Cherry? I'm supposed to be meeting the mayor over at the Christmas Cafe."

"Mrs. Mechante is on the phone. She said it would just be a minute."

A shudder passed through me as the sheriff grunted.

"Right, I'm coming. Yo, Brick, head over to the cafe and let the mayor know I'll be there in a few minutes."

"You want me to run over?" the guy at the desk said, and I tuned out the rest of his comments as I diverted to the door. I'd come back when the sheriff wasn't here. I timed it mostly right, hitting the door at the same time as Brick.

"I got it," he said to me with a dopey smile. "Have a merry Christmas ma'am..."

"Deputy," I managed before he got out a couple of steps, and he turned to me shuffling a hand up to his Santa hat that he tugged off, doffing it like he would his standard hat if he were wearing it. Which he wasn't.

"Yes ma'am?" He grinned so openly and easily.

His badge actually read Elf Brick, not—Deputy. "Are you a deputy or an elf?"

The quick laugh was so open, I almost felt guilty. Almost. "I'm definitely a deputy, ma'am. But this time of year, we're all elves. Sheriff Vynachts is our town Santa, you know."

Oh. I knew. "No," I said, dopeying up my own smile. "That's so fascinating. I'm pretty new here but—I heard him say you were going to a cafe?"

"Sure am, best Christmas cafe in this part of the state. Would you like me to escort you?"

I'd rather walk into hell and get toasted over a barbecue. "That would be fantastic, I'm still getting a feel for it here. Everything has a Christmas name..."

"Yes ma'am," he said in that aww shucks voice of his. "I'll be happy to show you around and tell you all about the town."

"That would be wonderful." I held out my hand to him. "Rachel."

"I'm Brick."

Yeah, I got that. "Well, I'm all yours, Brick." A little bit of a flirt and a hint of a smile and he offered me his arm.

He might not be the brightest brick in the box, but he knew everyone in town, and by the time we made it to the cafe, I was starting to put together a sketch of who was still here and who wasn't.

I had a lot more questions than answers.

And a new lead.

A real one.

CHAPTER
TEN

I had to *walk* back to the boarding house, and I didn't want to hurry or draw attention to myself until it hit me that I had never made it back to the laundromat.

Damn you, Saint Nick. It was still before three; if I moved my ass, I could get my shit dry, change, and grab the rental car then head out to sleigh rides on the other side of town. There was supposed to be hot apple cider, blankets, story telling, a bonfire, and a cranky old man named Tinker.

Tinker was my lead.

He was one of the few adults I knew from back then that I thought I might be able to trust. The more I thought about it, the more I had to wonder if one of the people reporting the missing kids wasn't him. He was a Northland fixture, but he didn't *work* for anyone. He just managed his life, his little store, and he repaired broken and unwanted toys.

Kind of like he was there for the broken and unwanted kids.

I double-checked my watch before I used the key that Ginger had given me to let myself back into the laundromat. It

87

was empty. The machines were quiet. The air had a hint of lemon and something far muskier. Sucking it up, I tried to ignore the fact I was about to touch the lid of the machine that Nick had totally blown my mind atop and just flipped it open.

The machine was empty.

Shit.

I spun around the little laundromat. All the dryers were empty too. I checked the other washers just to be sure.

My clothes were gone.

What were the chances that Nick took them back to the boarding house and dumped my wet things in my room? After the way I stormed out, that would be a reasonable payback right?

Something right out of our teen years?

I grimaced.

Yeah, I didn't have time for this, and I sure as shit didn't want to head out to the sleigh ride area in my elf-wannabe outfit. Okay, new plan, back to the boarding house to check and worst case scenario, I would go buy some new clothes so I could head out there. With one last glance at the washing machine, I gave myself a mental shake and hurried back out.

To my utter shock, however, when I got back to the boarding house and my room, not only did I find all of my clothes—but Nick had washed them, dried them, folded them neatly, and left them in perfect stacks on my freshly made bed. Atop it all was a red rose and a note.

I scowled at the rose and considered trashing the note.

But to be perfectly honest, I was just a little on the grateful side that I had pee-free clothes to wear that didn't look like Christmas threw up on me. Unsealing the envelope, I read the note.

It was short and to the point.

Roses are red. My Rainbow was too.

I definitely enjoyed fucking you.

Nick

P.S. You forgot something, but I wanted to make sure you had them before you left town.

The first two lines made me laugh, but that P.S.

Bite me, Nick.

Not that I planned on saying that aloud 'cause my thighs were already clenching 'cause yes, I'd enjoyed fucking him too. Hopefully any future notes would include his STD-free status.

The rose actually smelled fantastic, and the petals were soft. Shaking my head, I put it to the side with the note and ditched the clothes I had on. It was time to armor up in my own things. Five minutes later, I went from swooning over Saint Nick to wanting to throttle him again.

There wasn't a single pair of panties in my laundry. I had two bras and I felt like that was just dumb luck on my part, 'cause those were in my backpack with my laptop.

Asshole.

Commando it was. Like that was going to stop me from getting out there. The only luck that stayed on my side was avoiding any encounters on my way back out of the boarding house. Even Ginger wasn't there. That was good, right?

So, why was I actually a little disappointed when I got to my car without a single irritant in sight? 'Cause I was stuck in Christmas hell, that was why. I'd already dealt with the ghosts of Christmas past. It was time to nail the story for the ones of Christmas present.

Forty-five minutes later, I was drifting with the crowds as sleighs jingled away. It was like a pop-up village come to life right down to the miniaturized version of Northland that had visitors oohing and aahing. I cradled a cup of hot mulled cider, pretending to drink it while I followed the crowds.

There were booths, crafts of all kinds, hand-made wreaths,

and more. It was a tourist's Christmas dream come to life. Tinker was supposed to have a booth out here—he would be working on repairing broken toys—but I didn't see him. When a casual stroll didn't locate him for me, I made a point of checking each booth, then behind them. There was always something going on behind the stalls.

This field belonged to a local someone; they'd cleared paths to set up everything for the sleigh rides, which kept arriving and departing. I spotted a barn further out, so I angled toward it and managed to find Tinker's booth, but it was empty. It didn't look *closed,* in fact, the sign indicated he'd just stepped away. If they wanted to give the town elves and Christmas folk a place to break, this barn would be perfect, right?

After dumping the mulled cider, I slid up next to the barn and peeked inside. Just in time to see the back of Tinker's head explode away in a shower of blood and gore.

Holy shit.

I blinked twice, convinced I'd just imagined Tinker getting shot between the eyes, execution style, but to my dismay the scene before me didn't disappear. Nope, Tinker was dead. Big time dead. Chunks of skull and brain matter stuck to the window kind of dead.

Horrified, I gave a strangled scream before I clapped a hand over my own mouth. What kind of fucking idiot announced that they'd just witnessed a murder? The man with the gun heard me, too, because he instantly spun around to look in my direction, and I ducked out of sight in a panicked daze.

It was the sheriff. The fucking *sheriff* just murdered Tinker... and did it while dressed as Santa. What kind of sick fuck blows a mans brains out while dressed as the jolly fat man? My stomach clenched painfully, and I knew I needed to get the *fuck* out of there before I got caught. Before I joined Tinker all over the barn floor.

Sucking a breath, I crouched low and ran for my fucking life.

As soon as I reached the crowd once more, I slowed and straightened, hoping to blend into the crush of festive tourists and townsfolk. For a few moments as I forced myself to walk casually, I thought I was in the clear. Then I made the mistake of glancing over my shoulder and locking eyes with the red-faced Santa storming out of the barn. Where he'd hidden his gun, I had no clue, but when our eyes locked, his lips curled with recognition.

Very deliberately, he pointed a fat finger in my direction and called out an order to the muscular elf who'd followed him out. The elf looked in my direction, too, and nodded.

Fuck.

He couldn't just kill me in plain view of all these people, though, so if I stayed in public... I'd be safe. Right? That was the best I could think of as I turned away and drifted across to a local honey stall. Try as I might to look interested in the informative speech the stallholder was giving about antimicrobials and cross-pollination, I was strung tighter than a cello as I waited for the shoe to drop.

"Little Rayne Dear..." an uncomfortably familiar voice said behind me. "Of all the Christmas gifts, what did I do to get you back in Northland?"

Swallowing the urge to scream, I tightened my jaw and turned around. "You must be mistaken," I told the Santa-suit wearing sheriff. "My name is Rachel Dean."

His smile was pure malice. "Sure it is." His slimy gaze trailed down my body, and he gave a grunt. "You're all grown up. What a shame."

Bile rose up in my throat.

"Can I help you with something, Sheriff?" I snapped the question before catching myself. He was not in uniform, so I'd just admitted I knew who he was. Not that he noticed, too busy peering down my low-V neckline. Creep.

"I think you might have been snooping around where you shouldn't have been snooping, Miss Dear. Maybe we need to have a chat about what you saw, back at the station." He hoisted his belt as he said that, and the memory of him doing that same gesture in our last meeting hit me harder than a freight train. Cold sweat broke out over my skin and my pulse raced.

I shook my head. "No, thank you. I'm here on business, Sheriff, as an investigative journalist. It's in my job description to *snoop around,* but last I checked, *I've* broken no laws." I spoke loudly and clearly, ensuring the stallholder and several others nearby could hear every word. Witnesses.

I wasn't stupid enough to go screaming that the sheriff was a murderer. Unfortunately, I'd experienced first hand how allegations against Northland authority got handled, and I wasn't naive enough to think that'd changed. If anything, it would be ten times worse now that Vynachts was in charge. Slimy bastard.

He glanced around, noticing the attention we'd drawn, then gave me a narrow-eyed glare. "Maybe not today," he murmured, "but I'd suggest you find another town to spend Christmas in. You're not welcome in Northland, Miss Dear."

To my own surprise, I barked a laugh. "No shit," I scoffed.

His expression darkened, and he leaned in, grabbing my arm with his sweaty hand. "You tell anyone what you saw, and I'll do the same to you. Understood? You can't run from me. I own this town now."

Pure terror trickled down my spine at his words and his nearness, but I kept it in check as I nodded tersely and jerked out of his grip.

Shoulders stiff, I moved away from the lecherous sheriff.

He'd proven my theory that he didn't want to draw attention, so if I wasn't alone, he couldn't *silence* me. Just the idea of that made me gulp, but I knew all too well what the power players of Northland were capable of. A little casual murder was not so shocking in context.

For the next thirty minutes, I browsed stalls and even bought a few dumb ornaments to sell the idea that I was just an innocent tourist. All the while, I kept the sheriff in the corner of my eye, watching him watching me.

When he took his seat atop Santa's sleigh and his thickly muscled elves started organizing the line of kids to sit on his lap—which made me nauseous all over again—I took my opportunity to slip away. He was distracted, so I raced back to the parking lot and into my car.

My engine rumbled to life, and I breathed a short sigh of relief, locking my doors. I didn't know whether Sheriff Vynachts would actually kill me with no evidence I'd seen anything... but I wasn't hanging around to find out.

As I drove out of the parking lot, I glanced in my rearview mirror and startled when I recognized the body-builder elf standing at the edge of the tree line. Staring after me.

"I fucking *hate* this town," I said out loud, as if it was new information to myself. Fucking Northland needed a meteor dropped on it. Just burn it all to the ground and start afresh. Or don't. Scorched earth, forever to remain uninhabited.

Still, the more distance I put between myself and murder-Santa, the calmer I became. Something was seriously fucked up in Northland, and now more than ever I feared for what might have happened to the kids gone missing. I wouldn't be even a little surprised if their bodies were all buried in Vynachts' backyard.

Heading back toward Ginger's place, I kept my focus on the road since the snow was falling again. My incident with Frost played in my mind, so I shifted my foot to the brake pedal to slow down a little. But nothing happened.

Panic flared and I pressed the brake harder, expecting to feel the car tires lock up and the car to skid, but nothing happened. *Nothing.*

"Shit," I squeaked, my breathing so sharp I was starting to see spots. I was having a panic attack at literally the worst possible time.

"Calm down, Rayne!" I shouted at myself, desperate to control the panic. If I just kept my head, stayed on the road, and didn't accelerate, then eventually the car would slow itself.

That was great, in theory, but a blacked out F-350 loomed behind me a moment later, and I knew I wasn't making it back to Ginger's in one piece. I barely had time to brace myself before the truck rammed my back bumper and my car skidded across the slick road like a spinning top.

Around and around my car spun, then with the help of another ram from the truck, my rental flipped.

I screamed, clenching my eyes shut as airbags deployed and my equilibrium went to the shitter. My body rag dolled, held in place by only my seatbelt, but somewhere along the way my head smacked the window and I blacked out.

CHAPTER
ELEVEN

Consciousness swam back to me slowly, triggered by the crunch of boots on snow. For a moment, I thought it was Frost coming to save me. Why the fuck that was my first thought, I had no clue. But it was quickly rectified with the smashing of glass right by my dazed, bleeding head.

I cried out, jerking out of reach when the steroid-elf reached in to grab my hair. Fighting against the airbag and my own panic, I frantically released my seatbelt and scrambled across the car, away from the terminator trying to unlock the driver's side door. Fuck that for a joke, I wasn't sticking around to get dragged back to Santa's lair.

Flicking the lock on the passenger door, I shoved it open and tumbled out into the snow with a moan. Everything swirled and tilted, but I pushed to my feet and took off running nonetheless. I had to hope that Arnold Swartz-Elf was slow on his feet due to his size, or that he would take a minute to get past where his truck connected with my car... just *some* small mercy to give me a head start.

Aching all over and shivering violently, I raced into the woods with the hope of losing the elf in the trees. He'd be following my footsteps, but there wasn't much I could do about it. Not while running for my life, through snow, with a head injury.

Fuck this assignment, I *hated* Northland.

Luck wasn't on my side. About a hundred yards into the trees and I got hit by what felt like a grizzly bear. I went down hard, my teeth snapping together on my tongue and blood filling my mouth.

"Bitch!" the elf spat, grabbing a fistful of my hair and jerking my head back. He planted a knee either side of me in the snow, but he was likely used to wrestling much bigger opponents. In wriggling free, I sacrificed a good chunk of hair, but it was worth it. On all fours I scurried like an overgrown spider out of his reach and grabbed for any weapon I could find. It was pointless to run, and I sure as fuck wasn't going to lie down and wait for him to murder me, so when my fingers closed around a branch as thick as my forearm my chest surged with hope.

In one swift motion, I hefted the branch, swinging as I turned to get full momentum behind it as I smacked it into the side of my attacker's head. The force I put behind it should have cracked his skull open, *surely*, but the big lug just flinched then grabbed the branch in his meaty grip. He yanked, tearing it from my hands like taking a lollipop from a baby, then tossed it aside.

"Shit," I yelped as he grabbed me by the throat in one huge paw and lifted me clean off the ground.

Instantly, my air supply cut off and I clawed pathetically at his hand, my feet thrashing and kicking with my desperation about as high as it had ever been. There were several times in my life where I'd wished for death, but only one where I genuinely thought my time was up. This incident now made two.

The elf remained stoic as he held me aloft, barely even breaking a sweat as I damn near twisted myself in half trying to get free of his grip—*to get air*—but it was all for nothing. He was too big, too strong, and I was just a pathetic little girl that no one ever loved enough to stick around for.

The orphanage matron's voice echoed in my head as my lungs burned and my already throbbing head pounded so hard it felt like it was about to explode. All her little digs and manipulations when I tried to report what she was doing, convincing me that no one would ever believe an orphan. Why would they? My parents hadn't wanted me for a reason, after all.

She'd been right too. Not only had I not been believed, it'd made the situation worse. So, so much worse. And for the first time since Nick, Alfie, and Frost walked out of my life I had realized how truly alone I was.

Right as my vision went dark, the elf dropped me.

I crumpled to the snowy ground, coughing and choking as I sucked greedy mouthfuls of air, my hands circling my own throat protectively like I could stop it from happening again. He'd dropped me? Why? Fuck, who cared why, all that mattered was that I could breathe again and my would-be murderer was—

"Holy shit!" I exclaimed, realizing why the elf had dropped me.

He screamed the most blood curdling noise as an enormous white dog savaged his arm, ripping literal ribbons of flesh and flicking them across the snow in harsh slashes of color.

"Rayne!" a familiar voice shouted. From the trees, a black-clad figure appeared and I'd never been so relieved to see

Frost's infuriating face in my life. "Rayne, are you—" He broke off, staring at me in horror.

The growls and screams coming from the dog and elf respectively must have snapped him out of his momentary daze, and he frowned in their direction. "Jolly, *halt.*"

The dog immediately stopped trying to eat my attacker and sat back on his haunches, licking his lips.

"Fr-frost?" I whimpered, hugging my arms around myself. I was shivering nearly uncontrollably, and in the depths of my mind I knew it was equal parts shock to cold.

He ignored the agonized screams of the burly elf and crossed to where I lay in the snow, sinking to his knees beside me. "Rayne, you're bleeding." He cupped a hand to my cheek, turning my face ever so gently to the side. "*Fuck.*" The curse was a whisper that held so much emotion I nearly choked on it.

In an instant, Frost's soft expression darkened to something glacial and terrifying. "Jolly, *attack. Kill.*"

The huge dog licked his blood-stained lips again and launched himself at the screaming elf, this time latching onto the man's throat.

My mouth fell open and I stared in abject horror as the dog began tossing its head, savaging the man's throat. Frost was talking to me, but I couldn't understand a single thing he was saying. All I could focus on was the dog mauling a man *to death* just a handful of feet away.

"Rayne!" Frost barked, for what likely wasn't the first time.

I had no words, just shook my head. Numb. I was growing numb. At least then maybe I would stop shivering.

Frost gave an exasperated sound and shucked his coat, wrapping it around me in a flourish. Instinctively I huddled into it, savoring his body heat and rich smell. It was the instant flood of my senses that calmed me faster than a shot of valium, and my eyes drifted closed.

The sharp, deafening crack of a gunshot jarred me right back out of that sensation, though. My eyes popped open just in time to see Frost putting a gun away in the holster strapped to his rib cage.

What the *fuck*? Frost was armed? Why?

Then I put two and two together to shift my gaze to the savaged elf. The snow all around was stained bright red, and the man himself was little more than flesh ribbons and tattered green clothes. Frost had shot him. His dog had ripped him to pieces and then he'd shot him to... what? Finish the job?

"Fr-frost," I chattered into the sudden almost deafening silence. "I th-think w-we n-n-need t-to talk."

He just arched a brow, as if to say *no shit, idiot*. Then he sighed and ran a hand over his pure white hair. "Rayne... why couldn't you have just left town when you ran me over?"

Hurt and rejection struck me right in the chest, just like it had plenty of times with him. I thought I was over it, though. I thought I'd moved on from the stain Frost, Nick, and Alfie had left on my soul. But here I was, lower lip trembling at the idea that Frost *didn't want me around*.

I gave myself a mental slap. This wasn't the playground at school. He wasn't rejecting me from playing dodgeball with them. This was *murder*. I shouldn't *want* to be included in this.

And yet...

"Can you stand up?" The question jerked me back to the present. The ache in my chest echoed the one in my soul. My head hurt and my throat was killing me. Still wrapped in his jacket though, I gathered it a little tighter before I pushed myself up.

Hot breath hit my cheek, and I turned to see the dog staring at me with his red-stained muzzle. Even in the low light there was no mistaking that for anything else. Instead of some ferocious demon dog, the big beast just gave me an open, toothy grin. The copper scent on his breath rolled my stomach, so I made myself concentrate on standing.

"Rayne?"

I blinked and looked up at Frost again as he squatted slowly. Concern etched into his expression and turned his scowl into a deeper frown.

"What?" I demanded. "I'm trying to stand up. That's what you wanted, right?"

"I—" he started but cut off when I shoved my hand into the cold snow and pushed my knees under me. My jeans were soaked and cold. The denim stiffening and unpleasant. Oh maybe that was what was wrong with my legs, they were cold. Right, I shoved upward and stood on my own, then looked at Frost.

"See, I'm perfectly capable of standing."

Three things happened at once though. My vision tunneled, something hot rolled down my cheek, and the world turned upside down.

Fuck me, I was not fainting again...was I?

"Shit," Frost swore, and that was the last thing I heard as the ground rushed up to hit me.

When awareness clawed its way back through me, I wasn't on the cold ground anymore. I also wasn't in the woods.

"Tell me you took care of that son of a bitch," Alfie said in a voice so devoid of warmth, I barely recognized it.

"Oh, he's dead." Frost's earlier annoyance seemed absent. "Jolly made it hurt too."

"How is she?" Nick's voice held equally chilly notes.

"I'm worried about a concussion," Alfie said even as a gentle hand smoothed over my hair. There was a sensation of pressure, but no pain near my forehead. "She's got a deep laceration, here, but I got it closed. It also looks like the fucker ripped out her hair." Alfie was mad.

Really mad.

He didn't curse that often. But there was nothing friendly in his tone. But he was also not done. "You said she was talking earlier?"

"Yeah," Frost said with a harsh exhale. "She sounded bad, raw…"

"Good, I don't think he crushed her larynx, but this looks bad."

Something slammed and I jerked my eyes open as the crash echoed against the wall. No sooner did I open them than I winced at the light flooding my eyes and squeezed them shut. The throb of my heartbeat echoed inside my skull, and my stomach swam. Could you get dizzy lying down?

"Easy, Rayne-drop." All the ice melted out of Alfie's tone, and I had to fight the urge to roll over and burrow into him. "Dim the lights." The shine against my eyelids decreased, and I tried to open them again, carefully. The stabbing pain brought on by the brightness earlier dulled some. "There she is. Hey, beautiful."

"Where—?" Oh, I was croaking, and even pushing that one word out was painful. I managed to focus on Alfie; he was standing to my right, his expression encouraging—only his eyes were grim.

It was a *hot* look on him. I dragged my gaze to the left and stared up at Nick, who stood like a silent sentry. The ferocious look on his face promised all kinds of violence, and I swore my pussy rippled. The discomfort wiggling through me had nothing to do with my injuries and everything to do with the two of them.

Needing a break, I searched for Frost and found him standing in all his frozen glory at the foot of the bed. His eyes were hard and his lips compressed. The echo of that gunshot played over in my head.

So did his order to Jolly, the dog, to *kill*.

"Don't pass out again," Frost ordered, and I almost laughed. There was something deeply sexy and compelling about his hardass attitude, but in the unrelieved black outfit, his white-blond hair seemed to glow, and that helped distract me from my hormones.

Maybe.

"I'll work on that," I managed to push out. Still, it was hard to keep my eyes open.

"Good girl," Alfie soothed, and some distant, should-have-been-buried part of me preened under the croon in his voice. "Did he hurt you anywhere else?" The warmth of his fingers stroking down my arm lulled my racing pulse. Then the fact that my arm was bare registered and I frowned down at myself.

There was a sheet over my legs. My bare legs.

"Rainbow," Nick said, turning that damn nickname into a command, and I glanced up at him again. "You still with us?"

"Is this the concussion?" Frost demanded.

"Maybe," Alfie said. "Take it easy, both of you. She passed out, she was choked, you said her car was wrecked."

Nick's expression darkened. "It's trashed. We got it out of there, but I don't think the rental company is giving her the deposit back."

Right. Deposit. I should care.

At the moment, I didn't.

"Slow down," I said, trying to follow their words, but it was so hard to focus. "Someone pushed me off the road."

"We know," Frost said. "He won't bother you again."

"But he told him to do it..."

Sheriff Vynachts told him.

After he shot Tinker.

Hotness burned in my eyes and there was a warm palm on my cheek. "Don't cry," Alfie urged. "You're safe. I promise. No one is going to hurt you again."

Yeah, they couldn't make promises like that. "I need to get out of here..."

"Pretty sure that's what we've been trying to tell you," Frost snarked, and I wanted to flip him off, but I just shoved myself up. I was tired of being on my back with all of them over me.

The broken bits of the day were all falling back into place from cat pee to sex with Saint Nick to Tinker losing the back of his head.

Santa Claus sent an elf to kill me, and whatever was going on in this town, it was even worse than I remembered.

"Whoa," Alfie said, gripping my arms when I managed to sit up because I almost slid right off the table. The staccato rhythm beating out in my head intensified.

I was going to pass out again.

"Fuck."

The world went black.

TWELVE

The next time I woke up, the room was dark and I was wrapped up in a warm cocoon. The awareness trickling back in burst the dam. While I wanted to sit up, I arrested the urge. Both because I had zero interest in playing damsel in distress *again* and because there was an arm locked over my middle.

An arm attached to a very warm chest, which was pressed up against my back. A chest that clearly belonged to one of the three men who'd managed to plow their way back into my life and turn it upside down, because a very hot, stiff dick pressed against my ass.

"It's okay, Rayne-drop," Alfie said, his voice a caress that slipped out of the darkness to wrap around me like his arm was. He tightened his grip and pulled me back. That was when I realized I was also lying on his other arm as he curled it across my chest and then pressed a kiss behind my ear. "Sleep."

It was almost plaintive the way he said that, but I wiggled a little to try and roll onto my back. A mistake because it ground my ass against that very nice cock, and I closed my eyes at the surge of feeling as he tightened his grip.

"And as lovely as that offer is," he said in a sleep-drenched husky tone. "You need to recover first, sweetheart."

"Alfie," I finally managed to push his name out, and if it was possible, I sounded worse than I had earlier. My throat protested the vibration of sound.

"Hang on, baby," Alfie soothed before he kissed my ear again, then he shifted both of us, and helped me sit up but kept his arm looped around me as he leaned me against his broad—very bare—chest. I couldn't see anything in the dark room, but the bed might be mine at the boarding house.

I was going to go with that, because otherwise I was in another bed somewhere with Alfie, and while his presence did help, I still seemed to be lacking panties. The only thing I was wearing was an oversized shirt, and I wasn't sure if the rest of him was as bare as his chest.

He wrapped my hands around a bottle and then murmured, "It's just water. See if you can sip that."

I took the first sip slow and tentative. It was icy cold and felt like manna from heaven on my throat. I took another drink, then another. I guzzled down about half of it greedily before I let out a little sigh of relief.

"Better?" he asked.

"Yes," I answered, and while it still hurt to talk, it didn't hurt to talk as much as it had. "Where are we?"

"My room," he told me before he took a drink, then he shifted, and I realized he was putting the bottle back where he'd found it. "I didn't want you to stay at the clinic all night, and we wanted to clean you up. So we brought you back here."

"Oh."

With care, he gently manhandled me around until he was lying against the pillows and I was curled up against him.

"That's it, just oh?" Was he teasing me?

"I'm sorry, my head still hurts." Which wasn't a lie, I had a headache, and I was more than a little muddled.

He pressed his lips to my forehead. "I know, baby. You took some hard hits. But your skull is solid."

"Is that your way of telling me I have a hard head?" It came out way more of a complaint than I meant it to.

Alfie chuckled. "Maybe a little, but it's a good thing this time, Rayne-drop. You took some nasty hits. Lot of soft tissue damage to your throat. The concussion worries me more than anything, but you've been waking up and talking; these are both good signs."

"Is that why you're in bed with me?"

"You're awake now, aren't you?" He was answering a question with a question. "How bad is your head hurting?"

Gentle fingers probed along my scalp; their gentle stroke felt way too good, and my eyes drifted half-closed. "The roots of my hair feel bruised—I guess some of them are. He ripped hair out."

"I know he did," Alfie said, and there was steel running through the soft velvet of his voice. "It's not too bad, but what about the rest of you?" With each word, he kept petting my scalp, massaging away the bruised feeling.

"My throat is still sore, but the world isn't swimming—at least I don't think it is." It was kind of hard to tell considering how dark it was. The constant caressing of my hair though had my eyes drifting downward, and I tucked my cheek against his shoulder. "Alfie..."

"You can go back to sleep," he murmured and shifted us a little so I was tucked right up against him. I slid a leg up onto his thigh. His cock was right there, heavy, hot, and very engorged. His little groan penetrated the blanket of sleep, and I flicked my eyes open.

"You're naked."

"Better to keep you warm." He deadpanned the words like they were the most reasonable things in the world.

The corner of my mouth twitched. This wasn't funny. Or at least, it wasn't supposed to be funny. "I don't have any panties on."

"Mmmm, that's definitely keeping me warm too."

Nope. I shouldn't laugh. Yet—the giggle escaped. A second followed the first,and then Alfie let out a soft huff of laughter. I trailed my fingers up to his face; the feel of his short beard against my fingers was soft. Raising my head, I fought the giggles shaking me, but his laughter didn't help.

Then he swooped in, and his lips closed over mine, swallowing every single laugh. All of my humor evaporated as the five-alarm fire warning sirens went off in my head, but the stroke of his tongue against mine shut them down.

I was in bed with a very naked, very hot Alfie, and he devoured every sound coming out of my mouth as his hot fingers traced down my body. One by one, he flicked aside what objections my tired, sore brain could come up with. He skated the fingers out of my hair and then down my back.

The stroke of them over my ass shook another groan out of me, and Alfie rolled me over onto my back even as he nudged my legs apart. Before I could form a single protest, he slid a finger along the seam of my cunt then began to circle my clit.

A shudder erupted through me at the intimate contact. It felt almost too good, especially when he added his thumb to his forefinger and pinched my clit. The bolt of electricity that shocked through me made me almost cry out, but he kissed me again, smothering the sound before it went anywhere.

He kept his thumb in motion as he slid a finger inside of me, and I arched my hips. I forgot about the bruises and the headache. My world narrowed down to the sensual mouth he assaulted mine with, nibbling, licking, and sucking the sounds out of mine. The only other sensations getting through were his fingers as he worked one into me and then another.

The slick sounds of my pussy slicking his hand seemed almost abnormally loud, but he didn't slow the pressure. If anything, he increased it, adding a third finger to my channel. When he curled them against my g-spot, I bucked.

"That's it, baby," Alfie whispered against my lips. "Come on my hand."

This time, he didn't kiss away my whimper; instead he nuzzled along my jaw and then feathered kisses against my abused throat. I was the one muffling my sounds.

"Good girl," he coaxed as he added another finger and the combination of stretch burned but added even more unbearable pressure where he kept stroking me inside. I moved my hips with his hand, chasing the teasing caress of his thumb. Each time it grazed my clit, more sparks seemed to erupt. "Fuck my fingers, Rayne-drop—give me every bit of it, and then if you're a good girl and want more, I'll give you my cock."

For all the command lacing his words, his tone never shifted from that buttery soft croon that was urging me to keep going, to ride his hand, and I thrust up. I opened my mouth as he drove deeper, spreading his fingers even as he curled them. There was no control over the rhythm; he pushed me harder and faster.

Another whimper escaped, and his lips were at my ear. "You want this, Rayne?"

"Yes," I managed, and it came out almost as a wail. His chuckle was a sensual caress to my hearing before he bit down on my earlobe. The pain added to the pleasure, and he went still.

"Move," he told me. "Fuck my fingers, Rayne-drop. Take everything you want."

Shock almost knocked me out of that haze. But I wanted this; I wanted to feel good. I wanted to get rid of all the nightmarish images and the pain. He was leaning over me, half blanketing me, and I wrapped my arms around his neck.

"Good girl," he soothed and encouraged, and I rocked my hips, rolling them against the stiffness of his hand. He kept it right there. No matter how I moved, he didn't pull away or push in; he let me control it. The tension unfurling inside of me accompanied the familiar wave of an orgasm.

Vibrators were good at getting right to the point, but his fingers were so much better. My thighs trembled as I pushed my feet against the bed, straining up to chase the pleasure that was right there. His thumb moved, and I almost screamed in frustration, but he twisted his hand and his palm flattened against my clit as he kept his fingers curved.

The harder I drove him into me, the more firmly I ground against his palm. The hot pads of his fingers and the calluses on his hand added another layer of sensation. "Come for me, baby," he growled. "You're going to come now."

I couldn't do it on command—that was a fucking myth— but I dug my fingers into his shoulders as I kept thrusting upward and *then* it was right there. "Alfie," I screamed even as he clamped his mouth on mine to swallow my cries. The orgasm crashing through me shattered the bruises and the aches. I held onto him as I bucked, and he was right there, pushing me through that orgasm and right into another one.

The rush of release had me soaking his hand, and my inner walls fluttered and rippled as I fought to hold onto him. Heart racing, I clung to him as the tide ebbed. His hand still inside me, and his breath feathering my face, I'd never been more aware of a person than I was right now.

My panting sounded so loud, but not as much as it did when he began to ease his hand from between my thighs. I wanted to weep with the loss. Then he licked his fingers, the slurp unmistakable.

"You still with me?" Alfie asked, and I swore my pussy clenched in anticipation at the desire in his voice.

"Yes."

He shifted away, the blankets falling back to let the cooler air in to rub against my damp thighs. My nipples went tight under my shirt, and the smell of arousal was heavy in the air. There was a rip of foil, and I shuddered again.

Alfie had condoms. That teased something in the back of my pleasure-drunk brain, but I shoved it away. If I started thinking right now—I'd end up stopping and I didn't want to stop.

"Alfie?"

He went still. "I'm here."

"Fuck me… please."

"Oh," he said slowly and anticipation began to curl through me. He gripped my hips and manhandled me until my legs were wider and I was flat against the bed. "I plan on it." Then he lined himself up and thrust into me, hard and fast.

Fuck. Yes.

"Alfie!" I damn near screamed his name as he pushed my knees up to nearly touching my armpits, holding me tight, spread wide as he dicked me down.

"That's it," he purred, hips pumping with ferocity. "Fuck, Rayne, you feel so damn good. So much better than I imagined."

It was an echo of what Nick had said, but both statements rang true. I'd fantasized about fucking both of them, too, so it was encouraging to hear they'd thought the same way.

"Alfie, fuck…" I moaned his name loud, not giving a fuck who might hear.

Okay, that wasn't true. I knew exactly who I wanted to

hear, because I wanted payback for the lack of underwear in my clean laundry. As if summoned, the door burst open and a flood of light from the corridor silhouetted Nick's broad frame.

"Rainbow, what—"

"Fuck off!" Alfie barked, fully seated within my cunt and panting slightly.

"Keep going," I urged, cupping my own breasts and wetting my lips. "Don't stop, Alfie. I'm so close... again."

He only hesitated a moment before shrugging Nick off his mind and went back to fucking me as if we were totally alone.

"Very fucking funny, Rainbow," Nick growled, leaning his shoulder against the doorframe. "Payback, is it? Well, joke's on you because Alf quite likes an audience."

A surprised squeak escaped my throat as Alfie thrust deeper. He said nothing, which seemed to imply Nick was telling the truth.

Still, it was hard to hold a conversation when my world was being rocked by a man I'd once loved so hard it'd shattered my heart when he left. One of my three *first loves* and one of my three biggest regrets.

"You know what he likes more than having an audience?" Nick purred, stepping into the room and kicking the door shut behind him. Suddenly we were plunged into darkness once more, and I lost all sense of where he was. Not that it mattered when Alfie was doubling his efforts to fuck me senseless and doing a damn good job of it, too.

Then again... curiosity had been sparked. "What's that, Saint Nick?" I teased, breathless as Alfie pushed me closer and closer to climax.

All of a sudden, there were extra hands on my body. A rough, calloused palm cupped my breast and fingers tugged at my nipple, while Alfie still gripped my thighs.

"Team sports," Nick replied in a low rumble, his face so

close I felt his breath against my lips. Then he was kissing me, devouring me, and I exploded like Fourth of July fireworks.

Team sports? Holy fuck. My payback definitely backfired, and I wasn't even mad about it.

Maybe Northland wasn't the *worst* place to spend Christmas after all.

CHAPTER

THIRTEEN

The infuriating chime of my phone ringing was what woke me the next morning, or, that was my best guess of time. Alfie's room was still dark, but nowhere near as pitch black as it'd been in the night while he fucked me to the point of collapse.

Nick had slept with us the rest of the night. I actually slept, because I was way too exhausted for anything else, and that was something we'd need to address sometime after coffee. Now, though, I was alone in the big bed and cursing the sound of my phone.

It stopped briefly and then started again, making me groan. Had Frost retrieved it from my wrecked car? He could have fucking left it there.

With a sigh, I rolled over and snatched the device from the nightstand and peered at the screen. It was covered in spiderweb cracks—no shock there—and the caller ID displayed Connie's details. Fucking hell.

"Hello," I said on accepting the call. My voice was *rough,* but that was to be expected.

"Firecracker," he barked, "you sound awful."

I grimaced. "Yeah, I know." Sitting up, I reached for the fresh bottle of water sitting beside the bed and took a sip. "What's up?"

A short pause filled the phone line, then Connie huffed. "What's up? Rachel, I told you to check in when you got to town, and no one has heard from you since you left. I'm just hearing now that you didn't check in to the Lodge we booked so... where the hell are you?"

My head pounded, but it wasn't debilitating. A couple of aspirin should calm it down, combined with a huge coffee. Maybe a greasy breakfast? Oh, I'd kill for bacon.

"Rachel?" Connie barked again, making me realize I hadn't answered him.

"Sorry, Connie," I mumbled. "I'm just a bit... under the weather. The lodge had overbooked and was at capacity when I went to check in. So were *all* the other hotels in town, so I ended up at a little bed and breakfast thing on the edge of town. Don't worry, I didn't blow you off to sip mai tais on the beach." Though, I wished I had.

"Oh. Yes, that was what I thought. You're in Northland, though?"

"Unfortunately, yes." I yawned then winced at how much it hurt my throat. Fucking muscle-elf had really done a number, but at least I was alive. It was more than I could say for him.

Connie chuckled, clearly assuming I was just salty at all the Christmas cheer. "Aw come on, Firecracker, you might find some magic this Christmas. It's the prettiest place in America, remember?"

I rolled my eyes and climbed out of bed. My thighs hurt and my pussy ached, but those were the kinds of injuries I was more than okay sporting. Memories of the night flooded back into my head, and I needed to hold my breath to get a grip.

Team sports indeed.

"Oh. I remember just fine." I didn't mean it to sound so bitter, but now that I pulled the curtains open, I realized Christmas had exploded all over Alfie's room. He had his own *tree* for fuck's sake, all meticulously decorated with glass baubles and glittering decorations. Had he done this all himself? Or was he a victim of Ginger's enthusiastic theming?

"So, how's the story looking? Found anything juicy yet?" Connie sounded like he was practically salivating for some drama. Things must be boring as *fuck* in the office today.

I smiled, despite the gnawing anxiety in my gut. The sheriff would have a target on my back, now. If I wanted any chance of solving the mystery of missing kids, I would need to do it quick. And never let myself get caught alone again. Which probably meant asking for help...

"Maybe. It's early days yet. I'm not sure how much you already know, but this town has something of a history for mistreating the orphans."

Connie grunted. "Doesn't shock me. Not much does, these days. How'd you uncover that? Found an informant or chatty local already?"

I sighed, running a tentative hand over the back of my head where I'd lost more than a few strands of hair. "Something like that. I'll email through a story outline when I know what direction it's all going, okay?"

"Yeah alright. Maybe get some rest or something, kid. You truly sound like shit." Connie didn't sugar coat it for me. He ended the call before I could call him a dick, and I tossed my phone back onto the bed.

I'd lost the t-shirt somewhere in the tryst with Alfie and hadn't put anything back on before sleep, so now I was totally naked and left debating a nude dash back to my room. Considering I didn't know *where* Alfie's room was in relation to my own, I dismissed that idea pretty quickly.

After helping myself to a pair of his comfy boxer-briefs and a football t-shirt, I grabbed my phone then crept out into the hall and went in search of my *Blitzen* name plate. To my relief it wasn't a long search, and the door wasn't locked. Right, I had no idea where my keys were. Fine. Problem for later. Within fifteen minutes I was freshly showered and dressed in my own clothes once more.

Okay, *mostly* my own clothes. I kept Alfie's underwear because Nick had magically disappeared all of mine, and they were comfy.

Heading downstairs, I followed the mouthwatering scent of something to die for. Sweet and salty, maybe bacon—I didn't know what it was, but I needed it. The sizzle and pop grew louder, and the smell of coffee joined in the siren call to my soul. I pushed open the swinging doors to the dining room.

I barely made it a step inside when I locked eyes on Frost and he stared back at me, a large snowman-shaped bowl mug in his hand. Crashed on the floor at his feet was a huge dog that snored obnoxiously. White as Frost's hair and—the darkened stain around its muzzle wasn't quite red anymore.

It had been red, right?

The sound of a brute-elf's screams and the rending of flesh as the dog savaged him echoed in my mind. *Jolly, attack. Kill.*

Frost had issued that command, and that big boy had done it. I pursed my lips as I dragged my gaze up from the dog to meet Frost's icy gaze. He wasn't focused on my eyes, though, but on my throat. I adjusted the shirt a little, but I didn't get a chance to say anything before Ginger noticed me.

"Rachel!" The shock in her voice pulled my attention from Frost and the dog. "Oh my goodness, the boys said you'd been hurt." She pulled a pan off the burner and set it to the side before she hustled out of the kitchen. "Sit down; you shouldn't be running around. Your throat is a mess—did the seatbelt do that?"

"It was an accident," Frost said, the cold crispness of his tone turned buttery soft and soothing. "Seatbelt tried to strangle her when she slid into the ditch."

I cut a look at him, but he gave me a swift hard shake of his head. Ginger didn't know. Of course she didn't know.

"Yeah," I said, summoning up a smile as Ginger nudged me into a chair. "Just bad luck. I'll have to call the rental company later." I was going to need another car.

"We'll get you all taken care of. Coffee?"

"I'd kill for coffee," I admitted. "I'd kill twice if it's black with no sweetener or special flavoring."

Ginger laughed. "You went to Manger Coffee, didn't you?"

"So, everyone knows they can't make a decent cup of black coffee?" It seemed eons ago, but it was only the morning before. Fuck. In the last twenty-four hours, I'd been fucked twice, three times if I counted Alfie's fingers before his cock. Then there was the trip to town, the investigation, the Christmas hell sleigh ride, watching a man get murdered—twice I supposed counting the brute-elf—and had a hard face to face with the uglier bits of my past.

"Well, some people do like it," Ginger told me with a lot of kindness and a soft laugh. "But I remembered you don't like the Christmas stuff so—I made sure to brew a pot for you."

"Ginger, I officially love you," I told her as she left me to return to the kitchen and pour coffee.

"Are you hungry dear? I've got scrambled eggs with cheese, brown sugar and honey sausage, some fresh biscuits, and it wouldn't take any time at all to whip up some gravy."

If I was going to die, this was the way I wanted to go out. "Yes please," I said, almost drooling. A huff of sound came from across the table, and I just flipped Frost off. His laughter deepened. The sound was so open and utterly at odds with his behavior since I'd returned that I actually glanced at him.

The warmth in his smile and in his eyes was enough to make me forget a lot of things. Before I could comment on that though, Ginger returned with my coffee. "As promised, strong, black coffee."

"Dark like your soul," Frost said as he took a sip of his own. "Tasty."

He didn't deserve my snappy comebacks so I just extended my middle finger once again as I sipped the black, bitter drink. Pure unsweetened heaven. I moaned, closing my eyes and taking a bigger sip.

"God that's good," I sighed, licking my lips.

The dog snuffled, and I opened my eyes to find both Jolly and his owner staring at me with hungry expressions. Jolly, I didn't blame because Ginger had just carried out a plate of food for me, and even I was salivating at the scent. Frost... was a different story. Why the fuck was *he* staring at me like a starving man finding a thick loaf of bread?

"Did you get your eyes for Christmas?" I snarked, using a phrase we'd used a lot as kids.

Frost understood, his lips curving into a grin. "Yeah, I did. Do you like them?"

I rolled my own. *Smartass.* "I do, actually. They're pretty. Probably shouldn't wear them out with all that staring, though."

He scoffed a laugh. "Pretty?" he repeated. "I swear to fuck, Rayne Dear, you're the only person who has ever called me *pretty...*" The way he trailed off implied more to that statement. Like he meant to add *and lived to talk about it.*

I bit my lip, remembering the cold, businesslike way he shot the elf. I wanted to ask questions like *why* he was wearing a firearm, *what* he does for a living, and *how* he could kill seemingly without guilt or second guessing. But none of those questions managed to make it out of my mouth.

"Jolly is your dog?" I asked instead, sounding hoarse as my gaze shifted to the enormous canine. He'd lain back down on the ground but seemed to have shuffled closer to me as he watched my breakfast plate with huge eyes. A puddle of drool seemed to be collecting under his jowls, too.

"I'm his human, yes," Frost replied with a bemused expression, sipping his coffee. "Is that really what you wanted to ask me?"

Not even close. "What breed is he?"

"Dogo Argentino," he replied. "Abnormally large for his already large breed, though."

I nodded. "Yeah. I see that." I stared at the beast, and he stared back at me. Drooling. "Jolly, huh?"

Frost shrugged. "He usually is. Especially if you give him some bacon."

I looked to my plate, then back to the dog who shuffled closer to me on his belly with ears pricked up. If I hadn't witnessed him literally rip shreds of flesh from a man, I'd have given him scratches. As it was, though, I wouldn't be putting my hands anywhere near that mouth. Not for all the tea in China.

"He won't hurt you, Rayne," Frost said softly, like he could read my thoughts. "He's just a big puppy, really."

I bit my lip again, watching the enormous creature shuffle closer yet as though we couldn't see him moving. My spine straight, I tried not to shift my chair away. If Frost said he wouldn't hurt me... but try telling that to my subconscious.

"I think I'll keep my bacon all the same. Sorry, Jolly, maybe your master can help you out." I arched a brow at Frost then took a bite of the crispy bacon. It was so damn good. Salty, well-cooked, crunchy... delicious.

Jolly whined.

"No," I muttered, frowning at the polar bear on the carpet. "My bacon."

"Meanie," Frost accused. "How can you say no to that face?"

As if he understood, Jolly tilted his head to the side, really turning up the heat on his puppy dog eyes. Fucking hell, that wasn't playing fair.

Still, I was starving and the food was good so... tough luck. Shifting my chair to angle away from Frost and Jolly, I proceeded to eat almost my entire plate and drink my coffee as though they weren't even in the room with me. When I got down to my last sausage link and rasher of bacon, Jolly whined pathetically and my resolve cracked.

"Fine," I grumbled. "But I'm not putting my hand near those teeth." Instead, I tossed the sausage in the air and Jolly moved with shocking speed to catch it in his massive mouth. He barely even chewed before swallowing, so I quickly tossed him the rasher of bacon, too.

"Hey!" Ginger exclaimed, walking back in right as Jolly snapped up the bacon. "Did you just feed that beast in my dining hall? I thought we'd been over this, Frost Jackson: *no feeding the horse indoors.*"

"Wasn't me, Ginger," Frost replied with pure innocence all over his angelic face. "I tried to tell Rayne not to, but you know how Jolly gets when he spots a soft target."

I shuddered, remembering the *soft target* of muscle-elf's throat.

Ginger knelt down and gave Jolly a vigorous belly scratch, the huge dog rolling onto his back for it like some kind of overgrown pup. "You're too cute, Jolly-dog, aren't you?" she cooed, lavishing affection on the creature. "Big cuddle beast, you are. Naughty bacon stealing cuddle beast. Yes you are. Yes *you*."

She pushed back to her feet and fetched my empty plate and mug. "I'll get you another, Rachel. You look like you could use it today."

I glared daggers at Frost as she left us alone once more, and he just smiled back at me.

"What?" I asked when he said nothing.

His lips parted, then he sighed and shook his head. "Nothing. Never mind. I need to take Jolly for a walk, but when I get back I can drive you to the airport."

I frowned. "Uh... what for?"

Frost squinted back at me. "You're leaving Northland, aren't you?"

I should. The sheriff was a murderer and tried to have me killed. My childhood crush was some kind of cold blooded killer, and his best friends both fucked me better than I'd ever been fucked. I should be running for the hills and booking a therapy session with my long time psychologist Jannie.

"I'm not leaving," I said instead, giving Frost a stubborn glare. "Not until I finish the job I came here to do."

I expected him to dig in his heels and insist, but instead he just tipped his head to the side with interest. "And what is that, Rayne? What job are you here to do?"

"None of your business, Frost."

Again, he didn't argue. He just nodded thoughtfully and stood up. "*Come,* Jolly. Walkies."

The furry white rhino on the carpet jumped up to follow his master, and I blinked in surprise. That was *way* too easy, and now I was all kinds of suspicious of what Frost and Jolly were getting up to.

CHAPTER
FOURTEEN

Ginger returned with a fresh coffee for me a moment later, and I found myself torn between wanting to follow Frost, wanting to drink my coffee, and being utterly terrified of stepping out of the boarding house alone. My confidence fluctuated as I asked Ginger for a keep-cup so I could take my coffee with me, but then I froze just one step from the end of the front path.

"Going somewhere?" Nick's deep drawl shocked me out of my paralysis and my face flooded with warmth at the idea he'd caught me trying to follow Frost.

"Um, I... yes. Maybe. No. I mean, yes, I *need* to go somewhere but I..." Embarrassment flooded through me so hard it brought tears to my eyes, and I gulped back the sob in my aching throat. Nick didn't shush me or dismiss my emotional moment, he waited patiently and pretended nothing was amiss. Thank fuck. "I need to sort out a new rental car, and I want to follow up on what happened with Tinker."

No sooner did I mention that than another chill went through me. My head ached, my throat hurt, and I'd nearly been killed the night before. In the meantime, I had seen two men die. One of them deserved it; the other...

Nick quirked a brow, folding his thick arms over his chest. It was then that I realized he was dressed sharply in suit pants, thick leather belt, and crisp white dress shirt with sleeves rolled up to his elbow. On his wrist he sported that same enormous watch he'd been wearing at the laundromat yesterday. Fuck, was it only yesterday? Had I really slept with him and Alfie both in just one day?

"Tinker? What do you need to know about him?" The narrowing of Nick's eyes said he knew *something*. Or maybe my paranoia was just on high alert for no fucking reason.

I blinked slowly, recalling the fact that no one knew what I'd seen at the sleigh rides. No one knew that I'd witnessed Sheriff Vynachts shoot Tinker in the head. "He's dead." I told Nick. "I want to know what is being done about that."

Nick shook his head slowly, working that luscious lower lip of his with a scrape of his teeth. "He did die, but how do *you* know about that?"

"Because I *saw* it happen," I snapped. "I saw the sheriff *shoot* Tinker in the head at the sleigh rides. That's why he sent muscle-elf to kill me, too. He knew I'd seen and—"

"Tinker committed suicide, Rainbow. Or... that's the official story."

My jaw hit the snow. "Suicide? Get absolutely fucked."

"I think we know why you almost got killed yesterday," he murmured, brow furrowed. "Come back inside. We need to talk."

I huffed, stomping back up the freshly shoveled path with my coffee still firmly clutched in my cold fingers. I wasn't dressed warmly enough to be outside anyway. And Frost would have spotted me a mile away.

"Come up to my room," Nick ordered, and I stopped dead in my tracks.

"Not a chance," I replied, shaking my head. "We can talk in Ginger's sitting room." I gestured to my left where a cozy seating area was set up and completely dripping with decorations.

Nick shot me a sly grin. "Scared of what you might do with me if we're alone, Rainbow?"

"Yes." I shrugged and headed into the sitting room, choosing the single armchair so Nick couldn't go clouding my head with his strong manly scent and rippling forearms. All three of them fucking compromised me—that much was clear. I didn't need a concussion to tell myself that.

He followed, because I hadn't left him much of a choice in the matter, and sat down on the sofa so close our knees still touched. Fucking hell. After sleeping naked between him and Alfie and then waking up alone... there was more than a small measure of tension in the air.

"So, you witnessed Sheriff Vynachts kill Tinker yesterday?" he started, launching straight into the non-sexual stuff, and I breathed a small sigh of relief. Relief and maybe a bit of disappointment. Fair enough, though, this was probably a more urgent subject to discuss.

I jerked a nod, seeing the murder in full color detail within my mind. The icy shivers racing under my skin had me locking my ankles together—one over the other. Fisting the tumbler Ginger gave me, I wished it also had a couple of shots of alcohol in it or maybe that it was all alcohol.

"Rayne," Nick said in a voice that demanded I pay attention. It was the same voice he'd used to talk me down at the bus station when I was fifteen and wanted to run away. The same voice that quieted the nightmares that hit when I was sixteen and he snuck into my room. If the matron had busted him, it would have been huge trouble. The guys all slept in one wing of the school, and I was in the other.

"I missed you guys so damn much when you left," I told him, and that admission seemed to land like a slap across his face. It didn't feel any better for it to rip out of me like tearing open a wound that I thought had long since closed.

"Oh, there you are," Ginger said, her face flushed but her smile warm. "Nick, would you be a darling and tell Frost that I made a fresh batch of Jolly's favorite treats, and they are cooling in the kitchen? He can help himself when he's back."

"Of course," Nick said smoothly, rising to his feet. He shifted his stance, and it took me a moment to realize that he was putting himself between me and Ginger. Protecting me.

It was ridiculous. I hardly needed saving from her, despite the fact she lived in what might charitably be referred to as a Christmas snow globe. I took a sip of my coffee and tried to put my composure back together.

"Thank you. Rachel, I've left you lunch in the warmer on the counter. Meat pies, all freshly baked. So please just help yourself and if you two will forgive me, I'm off."

"You need any assistance?" The question was sober and serious, and I quirked a brow at Nick, not that he could see my face. But Ginger's smile didn't waver once, no matter what Nick's attitude suggested.

"No, stay with Rachel. She probably shouldn't be on her own today with that head injury. I'll be with friends down at the center. We're sorting out gifts."

"Thank you, Ginger." I mustered a smile, and Nick shifted to glance at me before she waved at both of us, and then she slipped out. The door jingled as it closed, and I stared after her a moment as Nick turned and reclaimed his seat. The bump of his knee against mine jerked my attention back to him.

"Tell me about Tinker," he said in a steady voice.

"I was at the sleigh ride... there's a lot of locals there along with the tourists. I was trying to find Tinker, to talk to him. But he wasn't at his booth. It looked like he'd just stepped away." It all replayed out in my head as I spoke. I took a sip of my coffee when my mouth went dry.

I walked Nick through it from when I headed to the barn to seeing the sheriff, all dressed up like Santa, put a gun to Tinker's head and then shoot him. Once I started talking about it, I couldn't stop. I fixed my gaze on my coffee cup and did my best to ignore every single Christmas light and decoration present.

My failed attempt to escape in the crowd. The sheriff confronting me.

"Wait—" Frost said abruptly, jerking me out of the space and yanking me into the present. "He *recognized* you?"

I didn't even know when Frost came back in, or that Nick's knee against mine was like a lodestone keeping me here and not there. The fact my knuckles were white and my hands were shaking kind of struck all at once. I put the coffee mug down before I dropped it.

"Yeah," I said. "He did."

"How?" Frost folded his arms, his feet planted like he was prepared for a fight.

I frowned. "How what?"

"How'd he *recognize* you? He was only a deputy when we were growing up here, and you never did anything to get in trouble with the law. Ever. No matter how hard we tried to corrupt you. So how and why do you know Vynachts?"

My stomach dropped and flashes of a younger *deputy* Vynachts filled my head. Of his mocking sneer when I reported the crimes committed against me, or the way he adjusted his belt while gaslighting me into believing I was powerless.

"That's irrelevant," I replied in a weak voice, unable to meet Frost's far-too-intuitive gaze. "Where's Jolly?"

"Don't change the subject, Rayne. What—"

"Let it go," Nick growled. "She clearly doesn't want to talk about it yet."

Oh? What gave that away? Maybe the fact that since realizing my slip up, I'd huddled in on myself, my arms wrapped around my body in some pathetic form of protection.

Frost glared daggers at his friend but kept his mouth shut and didn't push the issue any further. I wasn't dumb enough to think that'd be the end of it, though, since Nick had added *yet* on his observation. As though he was confident I would want to talk about it at some stage.

He was dreaming. I'd never tell them what I'd gone through after they left. Not in a million years.

"Carry on, Rayne," Nick coaxed. "The sheriff tried to get you to come into his office?"

I jerked a small nod. "I declined, because I'm not an idiot, and he seemed to leave it at that. And then..."

"And then Buddy the Elf tried to throttle you to death after cutting your brake line and running you off the road," Frost finished for me. "I'm up to date on that part."

"Someone in here talking about me?" Alfie asked, entering the room with a grin. "I heard my name."

Frost rolled his eyes. "I said Buddy the Elf, not Alfred Buddie. Narcissist. Rayne was about to tell us why she knows—"

"She was doing nothing of the sort," Nick corrected. "We were just discussing *why* Rayne was nearly killed last night, and it sounds like Vynachts has a target on her back. So that means it's not safe for her to remain in town." That last part was delivered with a hard edge aimed at Alfie.

My sexy doctor scowled, stuffing his hands into the pockets of his scrubs. "But she can't leave."

Nick flicked a quick glance my way, then scrubbed his hand over his face. "I know."

"Yes, she fucking *can*," Frost countered. "You just don't *want* her to, which is an entirely separate conversation."

"*She* is sitting right here," I spoke up, growing increasingly frustrated. "And *she* still has a job to do in Northland and won't be leaving until it's done. This shit with Vynachts only makes me more convinced I have to see it through."

Frost swung his obstinate glare back my way. "See *what* through? What job are you here to do, Rayne?"

I glared back at him. "I could ask the same of you, Frost. What *are* you all doing here? And why are you carrying a concealed weapon and strolling around with a dog trained to *kill* on command, hmm?"

"She's got a great point," Alfie muttered, giving Frost a sidelong glance. Then he checked his phone and gave a snap of his fingers. "Shit, is that the time? I have a patient in ten minutes. I better... you know... be anywhere but here." He shot me an impish smile then disappeared as quickly as he'd appeared in the first place.

Nick gave a quiet chuckle and patted my knee. "I actually need a word with Alfie before he runs back to the clinic. I'll be right back, Rainbow."

That just left me and Frost once more.

"Well?" I prompted. "I'm waiting for those answers, Mr. Jackson."

He cast a dark scowl at Nick's retreating back. "Chicken shits," he muttered, then refocused on me. "Fine. Tit for tat, Miss Dear. You tell me why you're in town, and I'll tell you why my dog likes the taste of Santa's not so little helper."

I smiled. "Nice try. If I tell you why I'm in Northland, you tell me why *you're* in Northland. That's what tit for tat means in this context."

Frost shrugged, moving to take Nick's vacated seat. "Fine. Ladies first."

Was he messing with me? If I opened up... would he? Frost wasn't one to lie... but he definitely danced around the truth sometimes.

He'd saved my life the day before, though. That had to earn him some level of trust. Despite the decade-old grudge I held against him... I *needed* their help right now. Otherwise I really wouldn't make it out of Northland alive.

FIFTEEN

"Where's Jolly?" Granted, I might be deflecting a little, but it was a fair question, and he hadn't answered the first time I'd asked.

"He's in the back, having his breakfast," Frost answered. "Now, back to why you're in Northland."

"You're like a dog with a bone," I pointed out and then looked at my coffee tumbler. 'Course it wasn't much use as another delaying tactic. It was empty. I didn't even remember drinking all of it.

"Ha ha," Frost deadpanned, and my lips twitched as I caught him staring at me. "Tick tock, Bad Weather."

I made a face. There was a nickname I could live without. Still, there was familiarity in it. "I'm an investigative journalist, and I'm here in Northland for a story, which I told you." I finally let go of the lifeline of the coffee tumbler by setting it aside and then shifting in the seat. The longer I sat here, the stiffer I seemed to get.

Look at me, now I was trying to distract myself. *Enough*, I told myself. *Enough.* Focusing on Frost, I raised my brows, and he nodded once.

"Well, the story is about missing kids." The fact it felt like I was pushing a boulder uphill to even admit that part was unsettling enough. "Not just kids from the Northland Home for Misfit Children." That wasn't the actual name, but for some reason, calling it that when we were kids helped. Probably some psychological bullshit...

"Kids ran away all the time," Frost said like it was totally reasonable, and I rolled my eyes.

"No shit, Sherlock. Thanks for the insight. If it were one or two kids, that would be one thing, but the numbers are a lot higher than that, and they are *climbing.* According to the reports we got, we're looking at more than fifty in the last eight weeks alone." Anger surged through me. "While I have a damn good idea of *why* those kids might want to bail, we're not talking just teenagers or kids close to aging out. These are kids as young as six or seven, others pre-teens. They're just—gone. Then they vanish from the system."

A muscle ticked in Frost's jaw. "If they aren't in the system —how do you know they're gone?"

"Ah," I said, with a shake of my head. "Your turn. Why are you in Northland?"

"Told you the first day: our house is being renovated."

"Your house?"

"Yep," he said, and I shook my head.

"And you three live together?"

"Go back to the system, Bad Weather. How do you know they're missing if they aren't in the system?"

"I could nut punch you and feel good about it." Probably not the nicest thing to say, but Frost actually smiled. The slow grin turned my insides upside down. It was really not fair.

"We'll get to my nuts later," Frost said, easily. "Stop

deflecting. You're not a coward."

I scowled at him. "Dick."

"Whatever." He gave me a pointed look.

"Whoever keeps erasing them isn't as good as they think they are," I said. "I've got confirmation of a dozen kids who existed on one date and then disappeared on another. Including reports that detail financial provisions from the state."

If I hadn't been staring at him, I might have missed it, but my answer definitely surprised him. Enough that he opened his mouth as if to ask, but my pointed look had his jaw snapping closed with a little click.

"Why are you three living together?"

"Why is that so hard to believe?" He said with a sigh. "Because Alf is a do-gooder and Nick wants to fix everything?" That told me a lot about all three of them, but I fought to keep the hunger for knowing everything about them from showing. Sure, I wanted answers. Who wouldn't? Thirteen-ish years was a long time. We weren't those stupid kids with even stupider dreams anymore.

But I really did want to know. "Living together," I prompted because I wanted more than a yes or no answer.

Finally, Frost shook his head. "We live together cause that was always the plan." The huff of exasperation he let out as he kept staring at me was kind of insulting.

"What?" 'Cause clearly he wanted something from me.

"Nothing," he said after a minute, his lips compressing. "Look, we got a place, and it needed renovations."

Right, he was playing coy. "If the purpose of this is to get me to trust you, you suck at it," I pointed out. "You want me to spill my guts, but you're holding back."

"So are you," Frost snapped. "You have been since you hit me with your car."

"Should have hit you harder," I muttered, and Frost snorted.

"Probably should have been paying attention. Then you could have." The verbal volley held just a hint of amusement.

"There's always tomorrow." At his mock scowl, I stuck my tongue out at him. It was childish, and I'd never known anyone who could push my buttons the way these assholes could and at the same time.

"You need a new car for that," Frost retaliated.

"Well, I guess you're safe."

"For now," he finished it like I hadn't left it off just for him. I swore we were both glaring but there was a glimmer of something akin to heat gleaming in his eyes. Amusement? Exasperation?

Honestly, I was right there. I didn't know whether to punch him or kiss him. The second one conjured all kinds of tension that had my cunt clenching. I was not a sex addict, but there was something to be said for melting all that tension in Frost.

Melting Frost.

The corners of my lips twitched. He raised his eyebrows, but his nostrils flared. Then an inappropriate giggle escaped me. I had to lift my shoulders as I admitted, "There's always tomorrow."

For a moment, I wasn't sure he followed. He was safe—for now. Tomorrow was another day, right?

It was what we used to say.

His smile startled me so much I swallowed my next chuckle. Standing, he held out a hand to me and I clasped it without thinking. "Let's go, Bad Weather."

We were halfway across the living room when it occurred to me to ask, "Where are we going?"

"Not the airport, which is where I should be taking you." The exasperation was back. "But I thought I'd introduce you to

Jolly—officially. Since I want him staying in your room if you're not in one of ours."

I was still processing that as he walked me through the dining room and then out through a door on the far side of the kitchen that went out to an enclosed porch where Jolly glanced up from the dog bed he lounged on. It was red with white trim, and looked like a Santa hat.

There was a tree out here and fairy lights. It wasn't quite dripping the Christmas that the indoors was, but it was warm and cozy. "Ginger made Jolly his own room?"

That was—so nice of her.

"Something like that," Frost said. "Jolly, come."

The dog bounded up. He really was huge. His soulful eyes struck me as he gazed up at Frost then at me.

"Freundin," Frost said as he held my hand toward Jolly. The strength in Frost's grip steadied me. Steadied my nerves as Jolly wuffled at my hand. "Rayne is a friend."

Jolly gave one bark. The sound was a deep bass that seemed to rumble from his soul. Then he licked my hand and I laughed. "Hello there," I said, trying to keep my voice calm. Jolly focused on me. "You're a pretty boy. Especially when you're not tearing someone to pieces."

"He was protecting you," Frost said, stroking his thumb along the side of my hand. "He wasn't trying to hurt you."

"I know," I said, glancing up at him. "I just—I've never seen a dog do that."

"Jolly's trained. Well trained. Once he knows you're a friend, a part of his pack, he'll protect you."

"He's your dog—what will Ginger say if he's upstairs?" That was my excuse? Yeah that didn't really work for me either.

"Rayne," Frost said, and it pulled my attention up to him again. While he still held my hand, he moved his free hand up to my throat. The stroke of his fingers there was slow and very gentle. The reminder of those bruises skittered through me, and I shivered. "Jolly will make sure this doesn't happen again. So will I. Clearly, Nick and Alf plan to stake out your bed or drag you to theirs."

Dislike kissed those last few words, and I tilted my head as I studied him. What did he want me to say? That I didn't plan to be in their beds? That I didn't want to be there? "I didn't even know you guys were going to be here." It wasn't an apology, and I didn't intend to make one. "I had no idea I would ever see you again."

"Yeah," Frost said slowly, still stroking my throat. "I'm getting that impression."

"What do you want me to say?"

"That you'll leave." Those words stung and robbed me of breath. "I want you to fucking say you'll choose to be safe and get the hell out of here." A muscle ticked in his jaw. "But you're too damn stubborn."

"You used to like that about me."

That earned me a flat look. "I *never* liked your stubbornness, Bad Weather. It was always a terrible sign that you were going to do the hardest, damndest things, and if we weren't really careful, we wouldn't be there to keep you safe."

The barely repressed anger in his voice didn't help his case. Especially *after* they left. They hadn't been there and what happened... "It's not your call about what I do. Or where I go. I'm not a kid anymore. None of us are. I have a job to do, and I'm going to do it."

I didn't care how fucking scared it made me. If anything, that just pissed me off.

"No shit," he said, damn near echoing my tone from earlier. "You keep telling yourself that. But you being here, now? If you want to stay, you're going to do this our way."

"Frost—"

"No," he snapped, and this time he closed the distance between us, pulling me to him. Frost was anything but cold.

Heat rolled off him and threatened to consume me. The hand he wrapped around my throat had no force; he didn't squeeze, but I was intimately aware of his chilled fingers where they burned into my skin. It was like he could erase the bruises, and for the first time since I woke up, I didn't feel the brutal elf's grip, only Frost's.

"You want to stay. You want to do this job. I don't like it, I don't have to like it. But you *will* do it our way. You *will* let us look after you. And *you* will do as you're told."

"Or what?" Fuck me, if I was going to play with Frost, I was definitely getting burned.

"I'll lock this gorgeous ass up, and make sure you stay out of trouble." The thing was, he was dead serious. "I'm tempted to do it right now. Alf and Nick are too damn far down memory lane to realize what you need."

"Excuse you?" I tried to pull back, but he had an iron band in the form of his arm around me and the other was his hand on my throat. It trapped me more effectively than a pair of shackles. I flattened my hands against his chest. At this angle, I still had to tilt my head back to look up at him and it kept my throat open to his grip.

"No, I don't need any excuses, Bad Weather. I need reasons, and you keep—being you." The last exploded out of him, and I frowned.

"Me?"

"Yes," he said with a glare. "You. You're so damn you…"

Then he slammed his mouth down on mine, and all I could do was squeak. Not because I didn't want it but because I met him halfway. Kissing Frost Jackson had been a goal of mine once upon a time, and he was right.

I had no problems rushing right into the damn storm.

CHAPTER

SIXTEEN

No sooner had I lost myself in the euphoria of kissing Frost—after all these years of wondering—then he was shoving away, holding me at arm's length with anguish etched across his handsome face.

"No!" he growled, that anguish shifting into anger. "This is a bad idea. *You* are a bad idea, Rayne, always have been, always will be." With that cryptic and downright gutting statement, he brushed past me and stormed out with Jolly hot on his heels.

Stunned, I turned to follow then pulled up short when I found Nick standing just behind me. Had he seen Frost kiss me? Or me kiss him back? He must have. Was that why Frost pulled away so abruptly?

Confusion swirled through my head, and I rubbed my bruised throat. "Um..."

"He doesn't mean that," Nick told me, just in case I needed confirmation he'd just heard Frost rip my heart out and stomp on it. "He's... holding onto an old grudge where you're concerned. We all are, to be fair."

My jaw dropped in outrage. "*You're* holding a grudge? Over *fucking what*, Nicholas Klores? What the hell do the three of you have to hold a grudge over when *you all left me?* Not the other way around. You. Left. Me. You all swore you'd protect me no matter what, and the second you could, you disappeared. Took off out of Northland and never looked back. Every single one of you. You. Left. Me. If anyone gets to *hold a grudge* here? It's me."

His eyes widened. "Is that what you think?"

A laugh as caustic as acid rolled out of me. "It's what I *know*, Nick. So whatever bullshit hurt Frost is imagining, he can shove it right where the sun doesn't shine. I don't need this shit."

Sick to my stomach with rage, I shoved past him, jerking out of his reach when he tried to grab my arm. I was way past the point of being placated with his sexy low rumble. The speed I took the stairs up to my room was just shy of a run, and thankfully I'd left my door unlocked. I really needed to find my key, but for now I could lock it on the inside.

Furious and bewildered, I paced the carpet of my room back and forth, replaying every second of that scene with Frost in my mind. Then tentatively recalling our *last* moments together... way back when Frost turned eighteen. He was the youngest of the three boys—only by a few weeks—but that meant he was the last to leave me. He was the one who *truly* left me alone.

Right as my mind spiraled back to that night, a movement in the corner of my eye caused panic to flare up. My breath hitched then released when I spotted the cause: a piece of paper slipped under my door.

Wetting my lips, I crossed the room to pick it up. It was folded in half, and when I flipped it open I recognized the Northland Medical logo at the top. Patient name: Nicholas Klores.

On it, there were a lot of details but the most important part had been circled with a red marker pen. *Negative.*

I snorted as I stared at it, then crumpled it into a ball. That was nice. At least STDs weren't on the list for this year's holiday fiasco.

Holding a grudge against *me*. They had a grudge against me. I swallowed the urge to scream incoherently, then went in search of my laptop. I needed to get a new rental car delivered, not to mention report the other one damaged—

I hadn't even popped open the laptop when it hit me I would need a police report and insurance claim. Right, I could just rent one myself; the other had been rented via the magazine. Then deal with it *after* I had the story and turned this insane town over to the state troopers or the FBI or someone.

The headache pulsing behind my eye redoubled like a drummer boy on crack. The hammering seemed to vibrate through me and echo off the walls. The fear and fury clawing through me threatened to choke me out worse than Brute-Elf, but I forced myself to suck in one deep breath after another.

Then the pounding echoed again. The noise was—not just in my head.

"Sheriff's Department," the shout carried up from below, and I went ice-cold. Hurtling over to the window, I peeked through the lacy curtains. There were two sheriff cars parked outside.

My stomach dropped at the pounding on the door carried up along with their shouts.

Shit.

Shit.

Shit.

I lurched to the door to my room. Ginger was gone. So were Frost and Jolly. Alfie was at the clinic. Was Nick—

"Stand aside," a booming voice ordered from downstairs,

and I shrank back against the wall as adrenaline hammered through me with the race of my pulse.

"I'm thinking no," Nick said with such utter calm, I wanted to scream. I couldn't see who was down there, and the voice didn't sound like Vynachts, but that didn't mean he wasn't there. "Can I help you gentlemen?"

"Son, this doesn't concern you. I have a search warrant…"

"Let's see it," Nick said, and when I crept over to the stairs, I managed to squat down and get a look via the mirror. The angle was terrible, but Nick had the door barred and he braced one foot against it.

"Excuse me?" the deputy said.

"I said, let me see the warrant. I'm an attorney, Nicholas Klores of Dewey, Skrewem, and Howe."

"This isn't your property," the deputy argued.

"Doesn't matter; currently, occupancy is determined by the signature in the ledger. Mine is in there and I'm present. So let's see that warrant. Since I am not the actual owner of the property, I have no right to just allow you admission without verifying your credentials."

Dead silence greeted him.

"You need to check with your boss or a judge. I'll just close this back up and let you do it."

They slammed a hand against the door when Nick would have closed it, and I forgot how to breathe. These people were capable of killing. Nick needed to not piss them off.

"We're here to find Rayne Dear."

"I'm sorry, what?"

"Rayne Dear," the deputy repeated, and Nick, of all the responses he could have had, chuckled.

"You might want to try over near Kringle's Field. They have reindeer there."

I had to clap a hand over my mouth at Nick's perfectly deadpan delivery.

The deputy, however, was *not* amused. "You want to keep interfering in an investigation, Mr. Klores, we can take you downtown for questioning."

"You could try, but then you'd be abridging my rights. I'm not interfering at all. I've been very cooperative. You can show me the warrant for the reindeer, or you can go. Totally up to you. But I think it's Judge Dickens this week. I have his number..."

"Here," the deputy said after an aggrieved silence where all I could imagine was they were glaring at each other. The mirror distorted my view, and I couldn't make out more than a blur or two.

I glanced down the hall. Should I lock myself back in my room? Was there another way out from up here?

"I'm sorry, gentlemen," Nick said. "I'm afraid the warrant isn't going to get you inside."

"That's it, we're going to arrest—"

"As I was saying," Nick stated, his tone cooling to something far more frigid. "Your warrant indicates you're looking for a Rayne Dear. Only if you look at this guest book right here by the door—I said look, Deputy Wilkins is it? You're capable of reading it from there. No one named Rayne Dear has checked in."

"There's a woman staying here." Suddenly the deputy didn't sound so sure about that.

"Well, now, that's a little personal, I mean there was a woman here. Besides the owner that is. But she left yesterday."

"Where did she go?"

I didn't move a muscle. If they caught Nick lying, they could arrest him, right? Also—attorney? He was an attorney? That fit my smooth talking saint to a tee.

"Back to her place," Nick said. "Far as I know, she's got an apartment over in the new village."

"The woman staying here was a local?" Now the deputy sounded really confused.

"Didn't say she was staying here, she just spent a few hours and then went on her way." Nick sounded deeply satisfied, and I wanted to punch him all over again. Yes, there had been a woman here—the lovely Donna.

Fuck me.

I scrubbed a hand over my face, and then Nick pushed out onto the porch with the deputies and closed the door firmly behind him. It cut off the conversation and left me in the dark, but he knew I was here.

He just wasn't going to let them in.

I eased back into my room, moving as quietly as I could. Time to pack. Staying here was potentially a threat to Ginger. The guys could clearly take care of themselves, but since Vynachts already knew where I was, it was time to relocate.

Bag packed, I charged up my phone while I searched for a car rental online—would they be able to get ahold of car rental records? Then I smirked: let them. I had identification as Rachel Dean, and I hadn't signed that guest book as either name.

They could keep looking for Rayne Dear. Rachel Dean had work to do. I finished the order for the car and booked it with the magazine's credit card. Connie and I could deal with that later. There was a rental place about a mile and a half away.

Not ideal, but I could store my luggage in the laundromat, then walk. I could hide my hair and use a neoprene mask; it was cold.

The minute I opened my bedroom door, however, Nick pushed away from the wall opposite my room and prowled forward.

All the moisture in my mouth fled at the sight of the dark look in his eyes.

More—at the gun he wore in a holster on his hip. "You already booked a new place, Rainbow?"

Yanking my gaze up to meet his, I debated my answer.

"Don't lie," Nick said. "Those deputies will be back soon and I want you safely out of here so they can search, but you need to be secure somewhere *while* they look."

"I'm going to get a rental car. I was going to stick my stuff in the laundromat, go get it, and come back."

"Bad idea. If he's already searching for you and knows you were staying here, then you've already been spotted. We're going to do this a different way…"

"Nick—"

"Argue with me later. While I have no problems with the debate and poking holes in your argument, I don't want them trying to arrest you. Then I would have to shoot them, and that's a lot more paperwork than I feel like dealing with right now."

Confusion swam through me as he held me hostage with his far-too-sober stare.

"You'd shoot them?" First Frost, now Nick.

"To keep you safe, Rainbow? I'd do a lot worse. Now, will you trust me long enough to get you out of here?"

My knee-jerk reaction went in two different directions. Part of me wanted to say fuck no, especially after that grudge comment and everything else. They'd wanted me gone from the moment they saw me.

Now, Alfie and Nick didn't want me to leave. "Dick doesn't fix anything between us," I told him, and I wasn't sure if it was more for him or for me.

"I know," he said, not sounding remotely happy about it. "But we can settle that later, too."

"You sure you want to—considering your *grudge?*"

Nick wrapped a hand around my nape and dragged me forward as he pressed his forehead to mine. "Do I have your attention?"

He didn't shout; if anything, his voice got softer. A shiver rippled up my spine. His grip was firm but not remotely painful.

"Yes," I told him. "Don't make me regret it."

"Definitely not my plan, Rainbow. Trust me long enough to get you secure—then we'll talk."

"I still have a job to do." I wouldn't be dissuaded.

"We'll talk about *that* too."

"Nick—" I was such an idiot sometimes. "Can I trust you?"

"I fucking hope so," he admitted, and then he pressed a kiss to my lips. This wasn't drenched in passion or need but in the firmness of an oath and a promise.

"Me too," I whispered under my breath when he let me go. Finally, I surrendered the suitcase, and he gave me a small, but encouraging smile.

"That's my girl. Let's go."

I followed him down the stairs. I wasn't his girl.

"We'll see about that," Nick said, tossing me a look over his shoulder before he ushered me to the backdoor. Shit, had I said it aloud?

I clamped my jaw shut. No more traitorous mouth. Or gasps. I was already in enough trouble.

Didn't need to borrow more.

Ten minutes later, huddled in the back of his car under a blanket, I repeated that as a mantra as we skidded on ice and gunshots rang out.

CHAPTER
SEVENTEEN

"Stay down!" Nick roared as he spun his truck to a sliding halt on the snow. The decision shocked me speechless for a moment, then I quickly accepted the fact that Nick was not the kind of man to be chased at high speed through perilous icy roads while being shot at. Nope, that was victim behavior, and that was something Nick had never been.

I thought he was stopping the car to get out or... something? But instead he pointed the hood toward the nondescript silver car that'd been chasing us, with the passenger shooting out the window. He—whoever he was—was a terrible shot, thank fuck, but Nick had shoved me into the footwell for safety nonetheless.

The engine revved and I barely got a terrified scream out before Nick let off the brake and rocketed toward the silver car.

"Brace!" he barked, just moments before we collided.

My head bobbled, but my protected position meant the worst I copped was the padded leather of the car seats rather than anything to exacerbate my concussion further.

"Stay there, don't move," Nick ordered, jerking the handbrake up once more and unbuckling his seatbelt. "No matter what you hear, Rainbow, you don't fucking move."

Not waiting for my agreement, he was out of the truck and slamming the door behind him. Fear and shock held me immobile until the distinctive cracks of gunshots rang out through the air, and I flinched violently. The memory of Frost shooting the mauled elf was still so fresh in my mind that I started trembling.

Nick told me not to move. Not for anything. So I stayed right where I was, arms wrapped around my knees until the front driver's side door opened once more.

"Rainbow?" Nick's voice set an overwhelming blanket of calm over my shaking shoulders. "You okay?"

"Yep," I squeaked. "You?"

His low chuckle should not be turning me on under such an intense situation, but I didn't control my own hormones, that much was clear. "Always, sweetheart. You're fine to climb back through here."

He slid into his own seat and waited while I clambered most ungracefully through to the front and fumbled my seat belt. After missing the buckle for the third time, he gently took it from my hand and locked me in,

"Hey, Rainbow," he said gently, cupping one huge hand to my cheek. "We're okay. I'll keep you safe, always."

I believed him, I did. But he'd told me that once before and then left me... and the things that happened when I had no one protecting me... I shivered. "I know," I whispered, tears pricking at the backs of my eyes. This whole cursed assignment was the worst kind of trauma therapy imaginable.

Nick's thumb stroked over my cheek, then he gave a heavy sigh before releasing me. "I need to get this mess cleaned up before it raises any red flags," he informed me with an apologetic smile. "Or any *more*, I should say. Sheriff Vynachts really wants you dead, Rayne. It feels more desperate than simply witness silencing."

The question was implied, and I knew I couldn't hold onto my secrets forever. This one, though... I couldn't say it out loud. The trust between us was still too fragile, and I was doing everything in my power to hold my shit together as it was.

"It is," I said. "I know he's connected to these missing kids, and he knows I know." That was the truth without delving too deep into my past.

Nick's head whipped around to stare at me a moment, bewildered. "He is?"

I pursed my lips, not ready or willing to say more. Nick understood and turned his focus to his phone. When he pressed *dial*, the ring tone sounded through his truck's speakers and he shifted into reverse while waiting for an answer.

"Not fucking now, dickhead," Frost growled on accepting the call. "I'm not in the mood for—"

"I need a scene clean up," Nick announced, cutting off whatever Frost wanted to complain about. "On the corner of Partridge Lane and Pear Street."

"I'm on my way," Frost replied, all business. "What happened?"

Nick's lips curved in a grin as he drove us away from the scene. "Nasty car accident by the look of things. These out-of-towners don't know how to drive on icy roads."

Frost's dark chuckle on the speaker made me squirm. *Why had he kissed me like that?*

"Is Stormy safe?"

I frowned, mouthing the name to Nick in question. He just raised a brow with a bemused smile on his lips, giving a small shake of his head to say *not now*.

"She's fine," Nick replied instead. "The sheriff has a hard

on for killing her, though, so I'm taking her to Doc Kane's cabin on Lake Swan."

"Good idea," Frost agreed, sounding grim. "I'll meet you there."

He ended the call without saying anything further, and I gave Nick a probing stare. "Stormy?"

He tossed me a quick smirk. "Nothing to do with me, Rainbow. I need to grab the keys from Candice and let Alf know where we're heading. Do you need anything? Alf can bring supplies after he closes up the clinic tonight."

I already had my bags packed and in the back of Nick's truck, so I shook my head. "No, I've got everything."

Five minutes later he slowed us to stop right in front of the medical clinic, all decked out in its colorful lights and tinsel. "Come on, let's be quick before any of the sheriff's lackeys see you."

I swallowed hard, shaking my head. "I should just wait here then. Less chance of being seen, right? And um, my knees are shaking pretty hard right now so I don't really want to slip and—"

"It's fine, Rayne, I get it," he assured me, reaching out to thread his fingers into the back of my hair again. Fuck I liked how that felt. "Keep the doors locked. Do you know how to use a gun?"

I shook my head, never feeling more pathetic in my *life*. Okay, that wasn't true. But it'd been a hot second since I'd been a damsel in distress. But fucking hell, I was a journalist and a homebody, why would I have ever needed to learn to shoot?

Nick grimaced then gave a thoughtful nod. "Okay, then *don't* use the one in the glove compartment. If you get scared, or need me fast, lean on the horn. Got it?"

I nodded quickly. "Loud and clear, Saint Nick."

His eyes darkened with desire, and his fingers flexed

against my skull. "Don't start something you can't finish, Rainbow. I've waited my whole life to have you, and now that we've gone there it's taking all my self control not to—"

I cut off whatever he was saying by crushing my lips to his. I needed to feel his kiss. I needed to lose myself in the sweet security of his caresses and chase away the haunting fear of yet another attempt on my life.

Nick groaned, kissing me back without even the slightest hesitation and giving me exactly what I'd been craving. When his kisses became slower and his hand slipped beneath my shirt, I arched into his touch. Was I really trying to tempt him into more than just a kiss while parked in front of the medical clinic? Yes. Yes, I was.

"Rayne..." he moaned my name in the sexiest way imaginable.

"Who says I can't finish what I'm starting, Saint Nick?" I challenged, responding to his earlier warning. "You already proved you don't mind a little exhibitionism."

To reinforce how serious I was, I ran a hand over the hard ridge in his pants, giving him a firm stroke through the fabric. His breath hitched and he kissed me harder, biting my lip with a delicious nip of pain.

"Hmmm I'll have to remember this," he commented between kisses. "Adrenaline and fear make my Rainbow horny. I'll park somewhere more secluded next time and pack condoms."

To my disappointment, he planted one last kiss on my lips then broke away with his hand on the door. "I'll be quick," he assured me. "Remember, keep the doors locked, and if you need me—"

"Lean on the horn. Got it." I licked my lips, his taste still lingering. His eyes tracked the movement, too, and he seemed to sway back closer before he remembered what he was doing. I *liked* having that kind of power over Nick, after all this time.

"Fuck," he cursed under his breath, climbing out of the truck with a groan. He slammed the door shut, then waited while I leaned across to press the central locking button. Once he tested the door handle to ensure it was, in fact, locked, he blew me a kiss and winked. Then he strode into the clinic with his erection not even slightly disguised in his suit pants. The man had confidence in spades, I'd give him that.

He was right, too. Apparently the adrenaline got me all hot and bothered, because I was left squirming and silently praying he'd return quickly to finish what we just started. I wasn't going to invest too much brain power or guilt into the fact that I was sleeping with both him and Alfie at the same time and had just locked lips with Frost this morning.

I wasn't here permanently. This was a bit of fun, a trip down memory lane—the good parts of it, anyway—and nothing more. No need to do mental gymnastics about how it could work out long term, not when I had every intention of being gone before Christmas morning.

For now, I wanted to take whatever they wanted to give. If that meant both Alfie and Nick in my bed... great. If it meant them at the same time? Even better. And if Frost ever managed to thaw his utterly baseless grudge, maybe we could make it a real team sport?

A sharp knock on the window jerked me out of my sexy four-way sex fantasy, and I nearly choked on my tongue with fright. Someone was standing at my window, but the heat from my tryst with Nick had steamed up the windows something awful, so I tried to wipe a patch clear with my sleeve.

It was ineffective at best thanks to the ice and snow stuck to the outside, so I nervously wound the window down just a crack. "Yes?" I asked, squinting to make out the person's face through the tiny gap.

It wasn't Sheriff Vynachts, that much I could be sure. The person was far too small.

"Rayne Dear," a woman responded. "It *is* you."

My mouth went dry, and disbelief made my brain turn to static. Surely not? Unable to help myself, I wound the window down further. Not enough to put myself in danger, but enough that the fog started to clear and I could confirm...

"Matron," I whispered with horror.

CHAPTER

EIGHTEEN

The old woman looked exactly as I remembered. Her soft white hair pulled back into a perfectly neat chignon, and her plump cheeks rosy. The dainty spectacles perched on her nose were identical to the ones I remembered, because of course they were. It was all part of her *image*.

"Oh, silly girl, you know to call me Grandmother," she chastised with a smile like a hungry croc. "When Sheriff Vynachts told me you were back in Northland, I thought surely he'd been mistaken. But here you are. Alive and well, and all grown up."

Grandmother.

I touched my tongue against my teeth. It was like all I could taste was copper. There'd been blood in my mouth that night. It was the first time.

It wasn't the last.

My stomach rolled as *Grandmother* stared at me, the corners of her lips turned up into the gentlest of smiles. It was the kind of smile you used on the disturbed because, well, they were disturbed.

I guess I was the disturbed one here.

"I still can't believe it's you," she continued. "Of all my pretty little partridges coming home—I didn't see you doing that."

Words formed and failed as her pale, milky blue eyes bore into me. There was something soulless about her; you just had to look beyond the filter she showed the world. Long before TikTok and Snapchat, Grandmother mastered the perfect image.

"You really should open the window or step out, my darling little Rayne Dear." She practically tutted at me with a click of her tongue. "Funnily enough, your timing couldn't be better. Mr. Schneemann is back as well, and he was asking about you."

The world faded around me and spots danced across my vision.

Schneemann.

Grandmother.

Vynachts.

My skin went hot, then cold, then hot again. Then she tugged on the handle, but the doors were still locked. The metal made a thud, the sound cracked through the ice freezing me into place, and I slammed my hand down on the horn.

Hit it and leaned into it.

The sound blasted through the air like a trumpet. Grandmother jerked backwards. The raucous sound shattered the illusion of the morning and yanked attention from those passing by on the sidewalks, cars driving past, and even the people inside the shops.

A familiar dark-haired figure raced around the truck. Nick came, just like he'd promised. Alfie came from the rear. They had *Grandmother* in a pincer move. But it wasn't her they were looking at.

It was me.

I let off the horn as Nick cut a look from me to the matron and then back.

"Goodness," Grandmother said, tutting again. "So upset. Maybe you should let the doctor take a look at you. It's like you've seen a ghost, sweet child."

Sweet child.

I was going to throw up.

"Mrs. Mechante," Nick said in that utterly polite tone. "Sorry to interrupt, but we've got to get going."

"Of course," she said, then gave them both a smile. "It's always good to see my young ones thriving." Then she cast me the saddest look. "Even if my most difficult one continues to struggle."

Rage burned in my belly. Heartburn that threatened to eat me up.

"Take care," Alfie told her, and with some reluctance and the iciest warmth, the matron made her way around the truck and onto the sidewalk. Her pace was glacially slow, and I didn't take my eyes off her for an instant.

Alfie knocked on the door of the truck and I almost screamed. I jerked my head to look at him. "Open up, Rayne-drop."

Where had Nick—oh. I twisted in the seat. Nick had moved back to the driver's side, but Alfie was right there at the passenger. With fingers that wouldn't stop shaking, I hit the unlock button twice.

The sound was unnaturally loud.

Like gunshots.

Sweat dotted my skin. The air washing into the truck cab

was chilly, and the burn in my stomach threatened to climb my esophagus.

"Easy, I got you." Nick's voice snapped me back to the present. I hadn't even recognized the two of them getting in the truck. I was buckled into the passenger seat in Alfie's lap.

This couldn't be legal.

"Breathe with me, Rayne-drop," Alfie ordered in a voice so calm and confident, I wanted to obey. But I forgot how to get air into my lungs. I couldn't take a deeper breath.

It was all short and shallow. I looked out the front window. There were people everywhere. They kept staring at us.

Matron had gone that way.

The Grand Marne.

Grandmother.

Mechante.

"What the hell is going on?" Nick asked in a harsh whisper.

"I don't know," Alfie said, worry filling his voice. "She's shaking and her pulse is racing. Get us the fuck out of here. Tell me you didn't let her see those guys..."

"I'm not a fucking idiot," Nick retorted, the insult in his voice clear. "I told her to stay down and she was a good girl. She did it."

The soothing nature washed over me, and yes, I was violently aware that they were talking about me. Aware, but incapable of responding.

The world kept flashing in and out. It was like I couldn't break out of a nightmare that used to haunt me. A nightmare I'd thought I'd abandoned, but it was here. I was right in the middle of the damn thing.

I could have been on a beach drinking frothy, fruity concoctions with little umbrellas. Was I? Nope, I was—the fuzzy static receded, and we weren't in Northland anymore.

Gone were the charming little storefronts hiding all their

dark and bloody secrets under the gloss of snowy decorations and fanciful lights. We were on a snowy backroad, following a path through the thick trees.

Heavy spruce and pines were everywhere. The evergreens that survived in the frigid winters. Places where the snow ran so deep and the water was so cold, the bodies would never come to the surface.

The tremors struck all over again as I shuddered. Arms banded around me, embracing me rather than shackling me in place. I turned my face to hide it in Alfie's throat. The rich, masculine scents of leather and pine with hints of snow and peppermint kissed my nostrils.

Alfie. Sweet. Loving.

Hot.

"Hey," he murmured, his voice low and husky like it had been in bed when he'd been wrapped all around me. "You back with us?"

Had I gone away? "I don't know," I admitted, and it was hard to push those words out. Harder still to say it. A hand came to rest on my thigh, a squeeze that reminded me we weren't alone.

"We've got you," Nick said, and I had a feeling like he'd said that before.

Maybe a few times. The farther we drove away from North-land, the better I should feel and yet, the emptiness was still there.

The place they'd carved out and left hollow. I'd filled it with so much over the years but nothing stuck. Nothing stayed.

When we followed the curve of the last bend, a cabin came into view. It wasn't the log building that captured me, but the location.

The last time I'd been here—I'd nearly died.

"Doc Kane…" I murmured, memories trickling back. "How is he doing?"

"You remember him from when we were kids?" Alfie asked, his fingers tracing soothing patterns over my back.

"I remember more than I want to," I murmured, shuddering as my mind dredged up the horror of the first night Doc Kane needed to treat me. And the last. "Is he here?"

There was a silence between the guys, and I moved to glance at them both with suspicion. "What?"

"Sweetheart, no one has seen or heard from Doc Kane in almost a year," Nick informed me with a gentle tone.

I frowned, confused but considerably calmer than I'd been just moments ago. My mind was latching onto the mystery of Doc Kane and allowing me to push aside the fresh wound Grandmother had torn through my sanity. "He's missing? Or dead?"

"Uncertain," Alfie murmured. "He reached out to me about eighteen months ago with some… medical concerns regarding a patient. We talked often, back and forth, then one day about six months ago I received a certified mail package containing the keys and title deed for the clinic, transferred into my name."

I wrinkled my nose in confusion, sitting up straighter while Nick turned off the truck and climbed out. He circled around to the passenger side and opened the door to lift me out. Instead of setting me on my feet, though, he just scooped me into his arms and carried me up the porch steps.

"I'm capable of walking, Saint Nick," I muttered, glowering up at him.

His lips curled up. "And I'm capable of carrying, Rainbow. See?" Just to show off, he lifted me higher in his arms, then lowered me. Fucking hell, he was biceps curling me.

"Come on, let's get inside," Alfie said, unlocking the front door for us to enter, "I'm freezing my balls off out here. Nick, put my girl down and get a fire started, would you?"

"*My* girl," Nick retorted, holding me tighter.

I shoved against his chest, forcing him to release me. "I'm no one's *girl*, so dial down the testosterone."

Nick's smile turned heated, and he slipped that pesky hand into the back of my hair once more, using his gentle grip on my roots to tilt my head back. "That's not the impression I got in the truck earlier, Rainbow. When you were all hot and tingly from the adrenaline rushing through your veins, damn near begging me to—"

"Yes, well, that was then," I quickly spoke over him, my voice high and tight with anxiety. "And it doesn't change the fact I'm not a *girl* at all. In case it escaped your notice, Saint Nick, I'm all grown up."

Because it sure as fuck didn't escape Grandmother's notice, or Sheriff Vynachts' for that matter. Neither of them had been too pleased about it either, and that made me quietly relieved. After all, their business didn't deal in fully grown adults. I was of absolutely no use any more. Except, maybe, to one man.

A shudder of fear and revulsion ran through me, chattering my teeth.

Schneemann.

If he was in Northland... maybe Frost was right. I should leave now and never look back.

"I'll get some firewood," Nick said, cutting through my paralyzing thoughts. "Sit with Alf, Rayne. You might be in a little bit of shock."

Alfie took the hint, gently placing a hand on my waist to direct me over to the deep leather sofa in front of the fireplace. "Do you want to talk about what's put that haunted look on your face, Rayne-drop?"

I shook my head firmly. "No. I really, really don't."

Alfie nodded his understanding and ran a hand over his neat beard as I snuggled into his side. "Okay, well... change the subject, then?"

"Please," I agreed, closing my eyes to breathe him in. His strong arm draped over me, and I leaned my head against his navy blue work shirt.

He hummed a thoughtful sound, his strong fingers stroking my waist. "You and Nick..."

I grimaced. "Not really the subject change I was hoping for, Alfie."

A low chuckle rolled out of him. "Yeah, well... curiosity and jealousy are getting the better of me, and I want to know where *I* stand. If it helps, he didn't actually tell me that you'd had sex."

"Then how do you—*oh*." The STD test. Alfie was probably the only doctor in town, so it stood to reason he was who Nick got to do the test. "Well... at least the result was negative," I murmured, my cheeks flaming hot.

Alfie gripped my waist, lifting me from my position at his side and seating me across his lap, my knees on either side of his waist and our noses touching. "You blush so prettily, Rayne-drop, but there's nothing to be embarrassed about. Did you forget what Nick told you about me?"

I blinked, confused, but also comfortable as all hell sitting in Alfie's lap like I was. It made me wonder what might have been, if things turned out differently all those years ago. If the three of them hadn't enlisted in the navy the *second* they could, and if Grandmother hadn't grown so greedy that first Christmas I spent without them.

"What did he say?" I murmured, trying to keep my head in the present and way out of the past. Alfie's deep brown eyes and comforting gaze helped immensely with that. As did the stroke of his fingers on my spine, beneath my shirt.

Alfie's lips kicked up in the corner. "That I greatly enjoy team sports, Rayne. Do you?"

My eyes widened. Was he asking what I thought he was asking?

"I don't know," I replied honestly. "But I'd like to find out."

His lips brushed mine, light and teasing. "Good answer."

This time, I kissed him. My Alfie wanted a threeway and I couldn't think of anything I'd rather be doing. Except, maybe Frost.

CHAPTER
NINETEEN

Anchoring myself through kisses probably displayed some kind of unhealthy coping mechanisms. Sure, fine, whatever. I was pretty sure there'd been articles I'd written in the past about using people's weaknesses against them or whatever.

I bound and gagged the armchair psychologist hmming in the back of my brain and shoved them into the closet with the creepy elf that people liked to stick on their shelves and those angels that reminded me of the even creepier *Doctor Who* episodes.

A rumble escaped Alfie as he sucked on my tongue. Compartmentalizing my life had saved my sanity. But with all the boxes ripping open and spilling on the broken landscape, I needed to get out of my head desperately.

The night before it had been too dark to appreciate the muscle rippling under my hands or the casual strength in his hands where he gripped my ass. Somewhere a door opened, and there was a huff of laughter.

I wanted to stretch like a cat and purr like one too. There

was a thump of wood. Then a chilled hand slid under my shirt and rested against my too-hot skin. I was being drawn too tight, a guitar string pulled to vibrating tautness.

Fresh wood, snow, and something indefinable teased my nostrils as Alfie held my mouth captive. Then there was a second hand in my hair and the tug pulled me away from Alfie's mouth. His low growl went straight to my cunt then bounced up to my diamond hard nipples.

We were all wearing entirely too many clothes. But I half-twisted in Alfie's lap, grinding down against the very present cock that pressed up like a steel bar. Too many clothes.

Nick's gaze on mine held me in absolute demand as Alfie kissed along my bruised throat. The belated reminder that I was bruised and a little beaten didn't turn me off in the slightest.

The gleam of Nick's damp lips shimmered in the corner of my eye. "Weren't you getting firewood?" I murmured, somehow excavating that thought from under the sensual onslaught of Alfie's hand cupping one breast while Nick cupped the other.

Seriously, too many clothes.

"I think Alf got the fire going without the wood." Nick teased his tongue along the seam of my lips and I was torn between laughing and groaning.

"I think you both bought wood for me." Then Nick grinned before he kissed me. Someone undid my jeans and then there was a hand sliding down my abdomen and into Alf's boxer briefs.

Nick's growl actually pulled laughter out of me. A moment of incalculable, unfettered joy that I hadn't felt in too long. I choked on that laughter when he slid his fingers right between my soaking labia. Or maybe it was the fact that Alfie had worked his hand down the back of my jeans and the contrasting motion, pulled the fabric tight when Alfie teasing his finger around the rim of my ass.

They were going to kill me with edging, and I was here for it. Third murder attempt was the charm right...

"Are you two out of your fucking minds?" Frost's distinctly unhappy snarl ripped through the haze of pleasure blanketing me even as Nick thrust a finger into me and Alfie twisted one of my nipples almost painfully.

I literally didn't know which direction to move in. I wanted to push down on Nick's finger, but there was intrigue in Alfie teasing the tightness of my puckered asshole while Nick suffocated me, not allowing me much in the way of breath as he devoured my mouth.

The slam of the front door reverberated and Alfie nipped my throat before he said, "Sit down and shut up if you're not playing. Some of us have waited a long fucking time."

"Some of us need to use their brains and not their balls, or have you fucking forgotten why we're here? Or for that matter *what* she did?"

I wasn't sure if it was the content of Frost's accusation or the absolute disgust in his voice that had me surfacing from the pleasure the boys were drowning me in, but I managed to peel my lips off Nick's to glare at Frost.

What *I* did? Anger caught fire in me all over again, ripping through the chill of shock that came from someone trying to *kill* me again in quick succession with running into one of the worst parts of my past.

"What the fuck is your problem?" I snapped, meeting Frost glare for glare. "If your dick is in a knot, that's 'cause you took off like a little bitch."

Alfie let out a long sigh and Nick groaned. "Thanks for killing the mood, you absolute asshole." Whether Nick meant me or Frost, I really didn't care. Suddenly, it didn't matter just how soaked my cunt was or how achingly empty.

I unbent myself to get free of the most sensual game of Twister ever with *some* assistance from the guys. Nick dragged his fingers out of me and I shuddered as he gave my clit a solid pinch. The combo of pain and pleasure sent electric shocks vibrating through me.

The absolute shit knew exactly what he'd done too as he licked his fingers clean. It took some effort, but I was off Alfie's lap and had my pants buttoned back up, then smoothed down my shirt over my aching nipples.

The entire time, Frost watched with his arms folded, his expression a raw, wintry tundra that managed to freeze the passion boiling over in here five minutes earlier.

What. A. Dick.

Rising and making no effort to conceal the absolute beast of a bulge in his slacks, Nick rolled his head from side to side. "Did you handle the clean-up?"

A scratch at the door interrupted Frost, and he finally transferred that vicious stare from me to Nick. Honestly, he looked more angry with him than me. Looked like a personal problem.

"Of course I took care of it. I wasn't sniffing after Bad Weather there like she was a bitch in heat."

"Dude," Alfie said. "Grow up." He pushed out of the chair we'd been sharing, adjusting himself with a shake of his head. Frost just flashed his teeth as he pulled open the door like he was the lumbering beast that came in with a hard shake.

Jolly. In the bright light of day, he was even bigger than I imagined. The dog rubbed up against Frost as he trotted into the cabin. His head easily reached Frost's hip. My guys were not small men, that dog was just an absolute monster.

As if summoned by the thought, Jolly weaved his way

through the room, brushing Nick and then Alfie as he made a beeline for me.

"Start the fire, Nick," Alfie said with a sigh. "I'm making coffee. Did we restock the liquor when we were out here?"

I wasn't really registering the words as Jolly dropped to sit on his haunches and *stared* at me. There was a thing about dogs looking like their owners, and Jolly didn't really look all that friendly currently. In fact, if he was taking after Frost at all, he might be considering ripping the flesh from my bones like he had that guy in the woods.

All at once, I could smell the copper and the snow. Hear the screams. Then the abruptness of the gunshot ending the asshole's suffering.

The asshole who'd had his hands around my throat. He'd lifted me off the ground, throttling me. It wasn't the first time someone tried to beat me to death. The world went gray and spots danced across my vision.

"Breathe," Alfie ordered, a hand on my back as I had my head between my knees. It was like sucking air through a straw, but I managed to fill my lungs. Once. Twice.

The darkness receded and I opened my eyes to see Jolly laying on his back staring up at me. Mouth open, tongue lolling, and his icy blue eyes so Frost, my heart twisted and laughter escaped on an explosive huff.

"There she is," Alfie said, still soothing as he rubbed my back. I dragged my head upward. There was a crackle of fire and hints of woodsmoke to enhance the homey feeling. The heavenly perfume of coffee in the air made for a far more compelling siren.

As I drank in the room, I glanced from where Frost sat with an ice pack pressed against his chin to Nick who stood somewhere between where Frost sat and Alfie and I were on the hearth.

Oh that explained the heat, I glanced back at the fire licking over the wood. A head bumped my leg and I looked down at Jolly. The crazy expression on his face tugged at me.

Bit by bit, the last few minutes put themselves back together. It was kind of like assembling a three dimensional puzzle while drunk and no idea what shape it was supposed to have.

"Just breathe," Alfie repeated, a reminder he was right there. The solidness of him, which had been such a turn-on twenty minutes ago, was a comfort now. "We're right here."

"You want coffee, Rainbow?" Nick asked, but he hadn't taken his gaze off Frost. As I got my shit back together, the rising tension in the room was impossible to miss. Jolly nudged me again and I dropped my hand down toward that massive jaw. I swore the dog stretched out like a cat when I began to rub his belly.

"Please tell me it comes with alcohol," I said, the plaintive note escaping before I even realized how torn my voice was. It was like having a thirty-year smoker's voice.

Had someone throttled me again?

"I got it," Alfie said, before he pressed his lips to my temple. He lingered there a moment, one arm around my shoulders. I wanted to sink into that comfort and stay there. "Then we need to talk, Rayne-drop."

I so didn't want to talk.

"I know," I admitted.

"Two attempts in two days, and that's not the first panic attack you've had." Where Nick's tone was smooth like melted chocolate, Alfie's was richer, and warmer. It filled me to the brim with the sense of *caring*.

I'd kind of forgotten what that felt like. Being buffeted on all sides. It was so much easier to keep my walls up and the world out. How they kept tearing mine down, I didn't know.

Was I going to survive this? The past was visible through this sooty little pinhole. I'd kept those windows bolted and blocked. I didn't want to clean them off and look back.

I just...

"Yeah," I said, and it wasn't agreement so much as acknowledgement. I hadn't had a panic attack in eight years.

Eight years since I'd found a way to pack it all up, bolt the chest, barricade it behind a door, and wallpaper over the cracks so I could pretend it wasn't there.

A chill touched my side as Alfie moved away. A shiver raced through me, and it wasn't remotely pleasant. The rasp of a tongue against my fingers helped to ground me. Petting Jolly was kind of nice, so I made myself do it while forcing deeper breaths.

In front of me, there was a huge, furious argument playing out in silent, death stares between Nick and Frost. They were *pissed* and it eddied in the air like hot steam disrupting the frozen landscape. Once upon a time, I might have been able to interpret the non-verbal communication.

Once.

Alfie came back with the biggest mug of coffee I'd ever seen. It had to be about thirty ounces in size. I had to wrap both of my hands around it.

It was scalding hot on my fingers, helping to burn through the ice, and when I took a sip of it. I savored the heat that was both a suggestion of a scald on my tongue and then the deeper, lazier heat that detonated in my stomach.

"Butterscotch."

The reverence for that flavor unfurled as I took another deeper drink. It was perfect. The bitterness of strong, dark coffee, freshly brewed and laced with butterscotch schnapps.

"Your favorite," Alfie said, and while he'd taken the seat

next to me on the stone hearth again, he'd also put a little distance between us. Probably a good plan.

Good call.

Since clearly, my hormones were out of control where he and Nick were concerned. Not that it had been my call to break off the kiss with Frost earlier, so maybe they were all my kryptonite.

Another deep drink helped to chip away at the ice inside me, and I freed up a hand to pet Jolly. *Right, let's go Rayne.* "Where do you want to start?" Because I might need a minute.

"Let's talk about why you're here," Alfie said.

"She's doing a story on missing kids," Frost supplied. "For her magazine."

Helpful.

"You are?" Alfie looked surprised. "Why?"

"Why wouldn't I? It's Pulitzer prize winning material, you know? Nothing says Christmas like missing orphans—wait, nothing says Christmas like missing wealthy kids, you know? You need a family to be remembered."

Nick shifted his stance, pivoting to take that glare off Frost to focus on me. "Rainbow, I get it, you're upset. I'm calling bullshit on you chasing some prize. There are people actively trying to kill you—read us in."

"I'm pretty sure I'm still beaten up from the last couple of go-rounds, Nick. I'm not an idiot."

"Then stop acting like one," Frost swore as he shoved to his feet. All at once, Alfie was on his, and Nick swung around and the three of them were back in that furious non-verbal fight again.

Jolly rolled over at my feet, but he didn't leave me as we both watched the three of them.

"I'm not going to sit here and coddle her. This isn't like when we were kids," Frost said, finally including me in this battle. "You two can't get over getting your dicks wet, fine. But this isn't just us making some fucking toys so Grandmother can turn a profit. There's a lot worse going on here, Bad Weather."

"No shit," I said when no one else responded. "Unlike you three, I was here when it started."

That yanked them all around to me.

"I know exactly how bad it was—so much worse than what *you* remember." I was practically spitting the words. Then I took another longer, deeper drink, draining the coffee for the alcohol and letting the liquid courage bolster me.

"Rainbow?" Worry crept into Nick's voice. "What happened?"

"After you three left? After Alfie aged out and joined the navy and you followed him, what? A month later, Nick? You begged me to wait for you and then you couldn't even wait for the sun to set on your birthday before you were out the door." Their expressions were taut, but I drifted past all of them to focus on Frost. "Or maybe after you went—it was just you and me, that's what you said, right? You and me. We were going to kick it all in the head."

Bitterness from the coffee seeped into my blood.

"You'd get a job in town, and wait... I was always the youngest. I didn't age out until the end of next spring and it was almost Halloween..."

"Stormy," Frost said, for the first time the ice in his voice was gone. "I'd signed the contract...I didn't realize it wouldn't give me a lot of options."

"Yep, not a lot of options, so there was no dust growing on you. You left. And then it was just me...and Grandmother, and a house full of kids working their asses off. Weird how a recession even hits a sweatshop."

I hadn't realized it at the time. No—that came later.

"Right as the town was trying to really put itself on the map." Suddenly, I wasn't in this room with them anymore. I was staring across the desk at Mr. Schneemann as he made his proposal.

"What do you say, Mrs. Mechante? I know you could use the extra around here, and Rayne here," he said, sliding me a warm smile. But it wasn't his smile that I was trying to avoid, but the heat in his eyes when he looked me over. "Be something different for you. We're making big plans. Three or four days a week, you come clean my house, maybe do some work around the office. Then we'll look at the new lodge once it's opened."

"That's a lot of time to be taking her away," Grandmother said.

"I can afford it," Schneemann said with a grin, and then he rested a hand on my shoulder. A devil with an offer that I didn't see the small print on until it was too late. "What do you think, Rayne? Want to have some fun and get out of here?"

Rising, I left the fire and Jolly, I crossed the room to look out at the snow. Doc Kane was missing. Grandmother knew I was back. Vynachts murdered people blatantly and wanted me dead.

"What happened?" Nick asked, cracking the silence. "What happened after we left?"

"Everything." The last thing I wanted to do was tell them. I didn't want to tell anyone. Not again. No one believed me before. Why would they be any different? I blew out a breath and forced myself to face the three of them. "Do you really want to know? Can you handle knowing?"

Could I?

"Tell us," Frost said. His eyes didn't hold the dark comfort of Alfie's, or the somber faith in Nick's. There were no promises in Frost's eyes at all, just violence.

Violence I trusted.

CHAPTER
TWENTY

THIRTEEN YEARS EARLIER...

"Are your bags packed?" Grandmother asked as she stood in the doorway to my room. The two-hundred-foot square room boasted two beds, but I actually had it to myself. I'd won the stupid competition over the summer, more because of a dare than anything else. It was nice, though, having my own room.

First time ever.

It had helped in the last few weeks.

"I just packed one bag," I told her. "You said they were providing uniforms." It sounded better than I didn't have enough clothes for two bags. Grandmother really didn't like it when we complained. She also tended to take the cost of any extra clothes out of what little allowance we were given.

"Good call," she said as she nodded. "Remember, it's for the next four weeks." She checked her watch before she signed the paper and then she held it out to me. But she didn't release it when I touched it. "What are the rules?"

"I am to behave as though I am still here. I am not to take advantage of the generosity of Mr. Schneeman. I will still attend school and complete my exams in addition to my job. I am to do whatever is asked of me and behave in a courteous manner. I will be given one day a week off and I am not restricted when it comes to watching whatever I want on television."

The last was huge, particularly because I would have one in my room for the next few weeks while working for Mr. Schneemann and staying on his property.

"Well done," Grandmother said. "You will make me proud. As tight as funds have been, this is another way to benefit the others."

Our state funding took a hit every time one of us aged out. This year it had also been slashed due to other concerns that I didn't really understand. The guys being gone also cut into productivity. I'd tried to double mine, but there never seemed to be enough hours in the day.

Working for Mr. Schneemann would not only offer a potential windfall to Grandmother and the kids here, but it would give me something else to focus on.

Six weeks since Frost left. Six weeks since I'd heard even one of their voices. I thought I'd get a letter or a postcard. Alfie had promised postcards from every single place he went.

Each day when I asked, Grandmother had given me a look of such quiet sorrow when she had to tell me no, I'd resolved to stop asking.

Still... "If a card comes..." I hated myself for even bringing it up.

Grandmother wrapped a bony arm around me. The woman was so slight, yet she seemed so much larger than life. "Don't worry, I will make sure you get it. I promise."

That helped. I mean, Christmas was coming, and despite

all the toys we made all year long here, it had been Alfie's favorite time of year. Nick's too. Frost and I didn't care so much, but we always got three days off at Christmas, and the past four years, we'd always spent it together.

Grandmother walked me downstairs. The old gothic manor had been home for so long, I was almost sad to see the wear and tear age had wrought on the fixtures. Grandmother had a wishlist of upgrades and repairs. I used to wish we could win the lottery or something, then make the place magical.

A car waited for me, and that gave me a bit of a start. I thought I'd have to hike it, but the driver got out to take my bag, and Grandmother waved me off after I climbed into the back.

It was really nice back here. The driver didn't chat on the drive over. The drive from the orphanage was a lot longer than I expected. Mr. Schneemann had purchased a huge tract of land and had a house built. It was a giant place.

But the driver went right past the mansion and followed the road down to a smaller house tucked in the back. Mr. Schneemann was waiting for me.

"Rayne, you made it. Are you excited?" he asked as he took my bag from the driver and dismissed him.

"Yes, sir," I told him. I'd met him only once before, and he hadn't changed much. Tall, white hair, open smile, and a bit of a belly. But he was a lot older, and his eyes were practically dancing.

"It's really nice to see you again, Rayne," he said as he took my hand in his. The man had huge hands; they practically swallowed mine. "Come in, come in. Let me show you around."

While nowhere near as large as the mansion we'd passed, the house was definitely large. He gave me a quick tour, leading me upstairs to where my bedroom was located. I almost forgot to breathe; it was twice the size of my room at the orphanage, and it had the biggest bed.

As promised there was a television on the wall and an ensuite bathroom. It was like all those fancy movies we used to watch.

"As I told Mrs. Mechante, the house isn't finished, but you'll have plenty of work up there. We're hosting a big event for the New Year there that will be the debut of the main house. For now though, we'll live out here."

"That's great," I said. "I really appreciate the work."

"I've heard you're a good girl," he said, his smile growing. "Go ahead and unpack. I'll go downstairs and make us some hot chocolate, and then we can discuss your work. Sound good?"

It kind of did. In my head, I pictured Mr. Schneemann as this stuffy businessman type. He'd been in a suit the last two times I'd seen him, but here he was in this plaid fleece shirt, a happy grin on his face and his cheeks ruddy.

He was so *nice*.

"That sounds great. I won't be long at all."

"Take your time," he said from the door. "Think of this as your home too. I want you to be very comfortable here."

"Thanks."

As soon as he slipped out, I pinched myself. The house was nice. Schneemann seemed really kind, and I had this huge room to myself. I unpacked my bag and set my stuff neatly into the dresser drawers. He'd told me there were uniforms in the closet and sure enough, I found them all hung neatly. The sizes looked right.

Should I change now?

He didn't say anything about changing, so I took the risk of just going down as I was. Pulling my hair out of the pony tail, I ran my fingers through it to ease some of the pressure and then followed my nose to where Mr. Schneemann was.

The next week passed like a virtual paradise, even with the cleaning at the mansion. He hadn't been kidding about the work that needed to be done. The house had a lot of tradesmen in it, but as they finished, it was time for me to take over.

Floors cleaned, bathrooms scrubbed, and everything dusted. Every day, Mr. Schneemann's driver took me to school and picked me up. Even with the back breaking work of cleaning and decorating, it was still worth it. Some of the other girls were jealous. I didn't blame them, I would have been too.

Each evening, when Mr. Schneemann returned, he'd come inspect whatever I'd worked on to clean, and then we'd go back to his house for dinner and a movie. A Christmas tree had been delivered and decorated one day while I was gone.

I liked the lights, and every night I enjoyed a hot cocoa before bed. On the last day of school, Mr. Schneemann surprised me by being home, and he'd gotten me a present. To be fair, it wasn't really a present for me; it was the new jacuzzi tub fully installed at the big house, and he invited me to test it out.

Despite the bit of unease, he'd teased me and said he was going out to dinner. So I could enjoy the amenities at the big house—including the movie room. It was all so wild. Yes I'd been doing the work, but it was positively hedonistic to enjoy it.

Week two, the workload increased as we got closer to Christmas. Mr. Schneemann was almost always around. When I'd been on the ladder in the library, organizing the books, he'd worked at his desk. When I was making beds, he followed me from room to room.

While I thought the little black maid's dress with the pinafore apron was hard to keep clean, it was even harder to keep my ass from being in his face when he kept showing up behind me.

More than once, he'd come to tuck me into bed, which was weird. But Mr. Schneemann was nice, I reminded myself. He was very nice. Grandfatherly, I supposed... not that I knew what that was really like.

Three days before Christmas, all the work at the big house was done. I half-expected that I would be sent back to the orphanage, at least for the holiday. But Mr. Schneemann had other plans.

"Come in here," he called from the living room when I would have gone upstairs to change. I was still in the maid's dress, and I was tired. He'd insisted on an inspection of every single room.

"Sir?"

He smiled as he flipped a switch. The lights were off except for the Christmas ones on the tree. It really was lovely. There was a fire burning. The scent of pine mingled with the woodsmoke.

"Come here, sweet girl," Mr. Schneemann said, and when I glanced at him again, he'd dropped a cushion on the floor in front of him. "Come. Now." He held out his hand to me, and apprehension slithered through me.

"I need to get changed—"

"No," he said, a snap in his voice. "You don't. You're perfect. Get over here."

The command was wildly at odds with his normally genial expression. Maybe he'd just had a bad day or something. I looked for any excuse about why he seemed distant.

Had I done something wrong?

When I finally got to him, he grasped my hand and pulled me forward. I almost fell on him and he gripped my ass in a heavy hand.

"That's my girl. You've been so good for me." Then his hot breath was against my cheek. What the hell was he doing? I flattened my hands against his chest, but I couldn't get the leverage to push him away.

Then his hot mouth was on mine, and I screamed. I was sure I screamed. But the sound didn't come out. Instead, his tongue was just there. It wasn't like kissing Frost or Nick or Alfie. Their kisses—even the distant memory of them—seemed to pop and evaporate at the hard thrust of his tongue as he fisted my hair.

"You've been such a good girl, Rayne," he told me, licking the side of my face. "Now you're going to keep being a good girl."

"Mr. Schneemann…"

He yanked my hair, so hard it burned my scalp. "Sir," he ordered me in a dark voice. "Call me, Sir." I couldn't see his face in the shadows.

"Sir…" I wanted to swallow and spit at the same time. I didn't dare move; he had my hair in a death grip.

His smile softened. "Better. You're a good girl. You take orders so well, and you know how to be a good girl for me, don't you?"

Terror crawled through me. Did he want me to answer? "How, Sir?"

"Have you ever sucked a man's cock before?"

My stomach bottomed out, and he chuckled. He was undoing his belt and then unzipped his pants with his free hand. The whole time, he kept my head still with his hand in my hair.

"See how hard I am for you?"

I didn't want to look at his cock. I didn't even want to acknowledge he had one. When I didn't answer, he jerked my hair again. Pain lit my scalp and tears dotted my eyes.

"Oh, that's even prettier...will you cry for me, sweet Rayne, while you choke on my cock?"

He didn't really let me answer. 'Cause suddenly, I was face to face with it and he forced my mouth open. I dug my fingers into his thighs, but he wrapped my hair even tighter and I was torn between having my hair ripped out and trying to breathe.

Pain made me cry out and he slammed his cock into my throat. The next fifteen minutes passed in a blur of tears and grunts. I almost passed out twice, because I couldn't breathe around his fat dick.

He smelled of cinnamon, apples, and cloves. When I wasn't gagging on his dick, he was dragging my hair so hard I couldn't stop crying.

The more my tears fell, the happier he was. Positively jolly.

Then he came in a grunting rush. Spit and cum splashed my face, and he let out a happy sigh before he ground my face to him, stroking my hair.

"That was good, but not great," he said, exhaling hard. "You just need some practice, my girl. And we have the next two weeks..."

I was pretty sure I blacked out then. He locked the door to my room that night. The next morning, he was there next to my bed, and his dick was out.

On my knees, on the bed and he yanked and pulled my hair as he fucked my throat.

For three days, he repeated the maneuver. On my bed. On the floor. In his office. He wrapped his belt around my throat and kept me with him.

My clothes disappeared on the third day.

I only had the maid outfits. One by one, he would rip them apart. When he got tired of my mouth, he pushed me down on the ottoman, the belt tightening on my throat and cutting off my air.

I wanted to pass out but then he crammed his cock into my pussy and grunted as he tore through what innocence I had left.

"We need to get you some lube," he told me as he grunted away. "Dry pussy is awful and you won't bleed every time."

Christmas eve, he tied me down in front of his tree and used my ass. Pain and humiliation were my constant companions. The last day, my clothes returned, my bag was packed, and I was limping—and bleeding.

He didn't seem to mind when he woke me up to suck him off and then fucked my ass one more time before he dropped three thousand dollars on the bedside table.

"I'll see you in a few weeks," he told me. "When I get back to town."

Then he was gone, and when I got back to the orphanage, I confessed it all to Grandmother, sobbing my heart out and pleading with her to help me.

She took the money I'd "stolen" and slapped me for complaining. Hard enough to split my lip.

Just a week later, she hired me out to someone new. He paid me a bonus too...apparently, I cried pretty.

The third time, I didn't give the money to Grandmother. That man had said it was a *bonus* so I made sure to keep it for myself.

I also never had to make another toy in the basement sweatshop. She'd found a good business in selling me.

It didn't matter how much it hurt.

Or who I told... My worst mistake came when I told Deputy Vynachts what had happened.

That was the first time old Doc Kane had to stitch me up.

It wasn't the last.

TWENTY-ONE

PRESENT.

Unable to keep going, I tightened my lips, breathing quickly through my nose as I attempted to fight back the rising nausea. It was like this every time I tried to talk about my assaults—plural—and I'd long since come to terms with my physical reactions to my own lingering trauma.

"Rayne..." one of the guys said in a broken voice. I didn't know which of them spoke, because I couldn't look at them. Keeping my eyes on the floor had been the only way I could disassociate enough to tell them *that* much. Making myself mentally aware that it was the three of them who were hearing what'd been done to me? It wouldn't have worked. I never could have got it out.

"I don't want or need your pity," I said in a firm voice, regaining a little steel. "This happened thirteen years ago, and trust me when I say I've spent thousands of hours in therapy to deal with it all."

"Rayne," Frost said. I knew it was him, because of the way Jolly perked his ears up and swiveled his head. "I am so—"

"I said I don't want your pity, Frost!" I exploded, surging to my feet. "What part of that did you fail to understand? It happened. I got myself out. The end."

"Except it's not *the end*, Stormy, is it? Because you're here in Northland and Vynachts wants you dead because of what *you* know. Because of what he did to you." Frost was on his feet, too, like he was ready for anything I was likely to throw his way. "Why? Why now? I don't get it. Why won't you *leave*?"

"Because it didn't end when I escaped!" I shouted back at him, poking a finger into his chest. "I got out but left *how many* kids to take my place? How many little girls went through what I did, or worse, because I never had the guts to come back here? How many are dead now? Because Grandmother did her damn best to try and kill me the night before I aged out. If it wasn't for Doc Kane, she'd have succeeded."

Alfie stood up also, positioning himself to separate Frost and me, like he really thought we were about to throw down. "Okay, everyone is really heated right now, maybe we need to—"

"So, what?" Frost snapped back at me, totally ignoring Alfie's peace attempt. "You're suddenly back in Northland after thirteen years to save the kids Mrs. Mechante has been whoring out under the guise of housekeeping?"

I threw my hands up, hearing how stupid it sounded but too far down the rabbit hole to see reason. "Maybe!" I yelled. "Someone has to! And if Doc Kane isn't here any more, then those kids have got no one looking out for them!"

"What the fuck do we look like?" Frost roared back, "Fucking lawn ornaments?"

Anger and stubborn combativeness damn near choked me. "You look like a big dumb f—"

"Okay, that's enough, you two," Nick interjected before I could get my snappy insult out of my mouth. "Maybe let's all take a breath and refocus."

Frost's lip curled in a sneer, his glare positively deadly. "Yeah, Bad Weather. Calm down, your hormones are making you irrational."

"Oh, fucking hell," Alfie muttered with a groan. "Do you have a death wish?"

"Rainbow, baby," Nick attempted to soothe, "he's just trying to—"

It was too late. I was already seeing nothing but red and dove at Frost with pure anger and not an ounce of skill. All I wanted to do was smack his obstinate face until he shut the hell up, but Nick had other ideas, intercepting me mid-pounce and physically holding me back.

"Case in point," Frost smirked, then whistled to Jolly. "Come, Jolly. Walkies." He stalked out of the cabin with his shoulders hunched and steps crisp.

Nick's grip on my waist loosened, but I was *far* from calm. "Rainbow, just let him take a minute to realize what a fucking moron he is."

He was right. Frost's temper hit like a cold front but often dissipated as quickly as it came, so I reluctantly sat my ass back down on the couch with a huff of frustration.

"Rayne..." Alfie said gently, but the look in his warm eyes was enough to send me running.

"You know what?" I announced, springing back to my feet. "I have a few more things I wanted to say to Frost after all." Before Nick could grab me again, I darted out the front door and took off after Frost's dark coat disappearing into the snow-coated forest.

Jolly's paw prints were clear enough to follow, but I caught up quickly and pegged Frost with a snowball to announce my arrival.

"I swear to fuck, Rayne, if you don't give me five minutes to calm down I'll—"

"You'll what, Frost? Hmm? You'll *what?* Say mean words? Ooh I'm so scared." I gave him an exaggerated pout and batted my lashes, scooping up another handful of snow to throw. "Did you sleep through that story I just told? The worst has already happened to me. Nothing you *say* can hurt me."

"I don't want to hurt you!" he bellowed, grabbing my wrist before I could throw the snow at close range. "Don't you get it, Stormy? I've never wanted to hurt you!"

His furious, tortured gaze darted to my mouth, his desire etched over every inch of his face for a moment only to be wiped clean in the next breath. He wanted to kiss me. I was *sure* of it.

I stepped closer, tipping my head back to hold his gaze. "So what *do* you want, Frost?"

His lips parted, and I thought *finally* he's going to tell the truth. *Finally* he's going to admit that the suffocating love I had for him wasn't one-sided after all. But then he gave a slow head shake, and his expression softened to something uncomfortably close to pity.

"Rayne, I'm not—" he broke off, running a hand over his white hair. "You're in a vulnerable state, I won't—"

"Don't you dare," I whispered with hot fury filling my chest. "Don't you fucking dare treat me like I'm breakable, Frost Jackson. I deserve more respect than that."

He straightened up a little at that and his eyes narrowed. "Like how Nick and Alfie are *respecting* you, Bad Weather? Is that what you want from me?"

My brows shot up. "Slut shaming, Frost? I didn't expect

that from you. Is it such a crazy concept to accept the fact that I was more than just an enthusiastic participant with both of them? In fact, I was the one who initiated that scene you interrupted earlier. Does that shock you?"

The confusion was obvious in his frown. "Rayne, the things that happened to you—"

"Happened thirteen years ago, Frost. Thirteen years. Nearly half our lives. Trust me when I say I've done my time in therapy, I've made my peace with who I am now. Don't take that away from me just because it's news to you."

Shock parted his lips, and I finally saw my words getting through to him.

"What do you want me to do, Stormy?" he asked softly, damn near pleading. "Tell me what you need, because my mind is pure chaos right now."

I wet my lips, anticipation building in my gut and excitement making my breathing quicken. "I want you to pretend I never told you all that shit. Act like... like how we were on that last night. Remember? When we went on the hayride at Old Man Crow's pumpkin patch?"

A nostalgic smile touched his lips as his gaze unfocused. "Of course I remember. How could I forget?"

"So... pretend with me, Frost." I reached up and cupped his cheek with my frozen fingers, tilting his face down to meet my eyes. "You kissed me that night, for the first time."

He leaned into me, his forehead resting on mine, and his eyes drifted closed. He was remembering that sweet night. "I did," he murmured. "But I warned you I would."

I smiled, butterflies setting flight within my stomach. "You did. We were in the corn field and you told me to *run*... and if you caught me, you'd kiss me."

His breathing hitched. "Jolly, *home*." The sharp command in his voice made me jump, then his ice blue eyes locked on me with determination as his enormous dog bounded back toward the cabin. "Rayne... be careful what you're asking of me. We aren't children anymore."

I smiled. "Good. You're so much sexier as an adult, Frost."

A rumbling sort of growl escaped his chest. "If I catch you..."

"Do you promise?" I whispered, my heart in my throat.

Surprise flashed across his face, quickly followed by raw hunger. "I'll give you a twenty second head start," he generously offered. "Starting *now*."

I was off running before he even finished that word, sprinting into the trees away from the cabin but also well away from the road. I knew this area decently well, so I knew we were as safe and secluded as we could hope for, and if I stuck roughly to the lake edge...

Seventeen...

I'd started counting down in my head from the moment I started running. I wanted him to catch me, but I was too competitive to make it easy.

Sixteen... fifteen... my feet crunched the snow with each step and I shivered. I wasn't in a coat, but at least I had shoes on. And surely Frost could warm me up soon enough.

Fourteen... thirteen... twelve...

"Gotcha!" Frost popped out of goddamn nowhere, snagging an arm around my waist and lifting me clean off my feet.

"What happened to my head start?" I protested, laughter bubbling out of me nonetheless.

"Changed my mind," he replied, and then his mouth was on mine, devouring me in a way that I never thought I'd experience again, searing heat to contrast the ice of his demeanor. "Are you scared, Stormy?"

Of what? I nodded, though. "Yes." I was scared of so many things...

"Do you want me to stop?" His fingers popped the button on my jeans, dipping down to stroke my mound.

I shook my head. "No. Never."

"Thank fuck," he said on a harsh exhale then crushed his lips back to mine once more.

Pure rapture ripped through me at his kiss. My lips still tingled from Alfie's earlier kisses and Nick's. It was like they were all determined to brand themselves on my soul.

The rough, callused tips of his fingers stroked across my cunt. Despite the damn story, I was slick as ever. I'd had some issues over the years—but apparently not with these guys.

He thrust two fingers into me with such force, I arched my whole body upward. His mouth devoured mine, swallowing every single sound.

Frost curled his fingers as he shoved them deeper, and I had to spread my legs more even as I kept my arms around his shoulders. Not like I was going anywhere; he was a solid wall, keeping me trapped.

"I'm going to fuck you," he whispered against my mouth. "I'm going to fuck you harder than you've ever been fucked."

The spots dancing in front of my vision this time were laced with anticipation and pleasure. "Is that all you're going to do to me?" I panted in between his stolen kisses.

The crunch of snow as he moved reminded me of where we were...in the woods, near the lake, and the only two people close by were his best friends.

Men I would more than welcome right now. Need had me strung so tight, I wanted to come and I wanted to come now, but the angle of his fingers was just torment layered upon torment.

"You want me to tell you what I'm going to do to you, Stormy?" The rasp in his voice was a sensual scrape over my senses. "I can do that."

He tugged his fingers from my cunt abruptly and set me on my feet. A little whimper escaped me, but he slid his damp fingers between my lips and I sucked the taste of me off him.

Snow. Salt. Me. Frost. His pale blue eyes were perfect in their icy heat, threatening to consume me.

"I'm going to turn you around, pull these jeans down and you're going to hold that tree while I fuck your cunt the way I've wanted to forever." He leaned in close and I swore I got dizzy. "I'm going to fill that pussy of yours to the brim, and you're going to feel me for days. After we take the edge off, we're going back to the cabin and you're going to suck me off while you let one of those other assholes fuck you through my cum."

Oh. Shit.

"Frost..." Wonder filled me.

"Oh, I'm not done," he told me, spinning me until I faced the tree. We were in a copse of them, surrounded by evergreens and pine. Woodsmoke drifted by on a breeze that tasted of snow and—

My heart stuttered, but Frost pulled my pants down and the cold air was flush against my bare skin. His hand landed with a rough smack against one cheek and I shuddered at the fire.

"You don't go anywhere," Frost said, his lips at my ear and his breath hot. "You're here, with me. The only cock you're going to feel is mine..."

He didn't give me a chance to even think about it as he pulled my hips back and then the blunt, hard tip of him was at my entrance.

"My cock, Stormy," he said and then thrust into me so hard, the tree bark scraped my shirt. The roughness added to the stroke as he sank balls deep. "My cock is in you—you feel that?"

I opened my mouth to respond, but he pulled back and then landed another slap. This one stung so bad tears filled my eyes, and then he filled me to the brim. The stretch was painful, but fuck I wanted this pain.

It was Frost.

"That's it, your cunt is so goddamn hot," he whispered as he began to saw in and out of me. "I am never getting enough of you..."

Was that a promise or a threat?"

He was kissing a path along my damaged throat.

"I'm going to wreck this cunt," he said. "Fuckers in there already know how good this feels, but I'm going to ruin you. All of us are..."

They already had, and then he began working his fingers over my clit as he delivered on his promise. The stretch of his cock burned me every single time he slammed into me. He pursued my orgasm with a kind of single-minded relentlessness that turned me inside out.

"That's it," he growled, every syllable a grunt because he was grinding against my soul with every thrust. "Fucking come for me, Stormy. I want to feel you come on my cock..."

"You're—fuck—" Words failed me as that orgasm struck and he bit me. He sank his teeth into my bruised flesh and all of it faded except for his cock and his teeth as he fucked me right through that orgasm before he came in a rush so hot, I wanted to scream.

We leaned there, shuddering, and I tilted my head back to find him staring down at me with heavy-lidded eyes. "You still feeling me?"

"Frost..." I licked my lips. If I thought my voice was hoarse before, it was utterly wrecked now. "Did you mean it when you said I could suck you off?"

Because that sounded good.

"Team sports," he rumbled, and I spasmed around his half-stiff cock. His grin turned almost feral. "You're not going to be walking for a while, Stormy."

"Got no place else to be."

I wanted this.

I deserved this.

We all did.

I'd survived and they were here and, goddammit, I wanted to feel them for days.

There was still a story to chase and killers to deal with, but I wanted my guys right now. I wanted them and they wanted me.

I could feel him soaking Alf's boxer briefs as he dragged them back up. A minute later, I was over his shoulder as Frost stalked back to the cabin like a caveman.

"You crazy asshole," Nick yelled, but there was something darker in his voice. Lust. We might be crazy, but he fucking wanted me too. "She could have gotten frost bite."

"I did," I told him, almost cheerfully. "Frost totally bit me."

Laughter and groans answered my pun, then Frost landed another slap on my ass. Worth it.

TWENTY-TWO

awn arrived and two of the three men in my life left grumbling, but Alfie stayed in bed with me. Even Jolly had gone. I debated getting up. There was so much work to do, but between my very sore, very well-used pussy and the ache blanketing me elsewhere, I burrowed back into Alfie's arms to go back to sleep.

The next time I woke up, I was alone in the bed and there was not much in the way of light creeping in around the blinds. My bladder demanded I get up. We'd all crashed in the master suite, so I just used the bathroom in here.

There were tiny bruises all over my breasts. Hickeys. A stupid little thrill went through me at the sight of them. Frost, like Nick before him, hadn't used a condom.

That sparked the best lecture ever from Alfie. One that ended with him locked out of the bedroom for a while and Nick's face buried between my legs.

The man ate pussy like a champ. By the time Frost reminded me of his promised blowjob, I had almost zero compunction about doing it in front of the other guys—only he locked them out too.

Between them, I didn't leave that bed once we were back at the cabin, but it was never all of us at once. Hell, it was barely two of them at once.

Not that I was complaining.

"Sounds like a complaint," I snarked at myself. After I showered, I got dressed—oh look at that, Alfie had more boxer briefs here. I shrugged them on and then got dressed.

Saint Nick the panty thief.

I followed the scent of coffee and breakfast foods. While there was a soft, bluesy kind of jazz horn playing Christmas music, it was far more pensive than upbeat and sugary sweet. At the foot of the stairs, I glanced around the living room.

It hadn't changed much in the years since I was last here. Even the rug on the floor was the same. Doc Kane had disappeared.

Not dead, disappeared.

That couldn't be a good sign though. A scuff of a step pulled me out of my reverie, and I found Alfie standing in the doorway to the kitchen. He wore a dark blue button-down shirt, with the sleeves rolled up to the elbows. His jeans were old and worn. They looked comfy as hell.

The past few times I'd seen him, he'd been in scrubs. This was...

"You look—"

Before I could finish the sentence, my phone rang and I dug it out of my pocket. The cracked screen was a mess. But Connie's name was not hard to read.

"Shit," I muttered before I hit answer and put the phone to my ear. "I haven't checked in cause I'm still nailing the story down."

"Good morning to you too," Connie said. "It is a good morning, right?"

Oh someone got up on the wrong side of the bed. Were his in-laws still staying with him? "Yes and I haven't had coffee yet. Fair warning."

His laugh carried not an ounce of real humor. "But you're alive and in one piece?"

Alfie had drawn back into the kitchen at my approach, but he made no pretense of not listening to my conversation as he poured me a huge mug of coffee.

"I'm alive," I told Connie. "Alive and kicking." Still this was a weird call. "What's wrong?"

He carried it over to the table where he'd been working on —something. Not that I got a look at it as he snapped his folders closed. Alfie dropped into a chair and looped an arm around my waist.

Dragging me back, he settled me in his lap, and I sighed as silently as I could. Then he pressed his chin against my shoulder.

"I think I should be asking you that," Connie said in a stern tone that said no more games.

Since I wasn't really awake enough, or in the mood for that matter, to play games, I just said, "I'm fine."

"So was your rental car stolen and then wrecked?" I had the coffee halfway to my mouth when Connie asked. "I know you didn't file a police report, at least not that we were able to find, and I avoided calling them directly."

I took a long drink of the coffee. It was hot and perfect. Setting the mug down, I said, "Yes, there was an accident, and no, I didn't report it. I have my reasons. I'm fine. Barely even a scratch."

That earned me a sour look from Alfie. But Connie couldn't

see me, and if he could, he might be tempted to pull me off this story.

"You gave me this story for a reason, Connie. Trust me. Let me do my job."

"I do trust you, but two of our sources are no longer answering calls, and the third one turned up dead." Connie's blunt statement got another jerk out of Alfie. "You will check in with me, even if it's just a text. I want a message every twenty-four hours. Are we clear?"

"I'll do my best. Before you start yelling at me, remember, you hired me because I wasn't afraid to get dirty."

"I hired you because you're a damn good writer. I also happen to value you more than a story. Don't be a damn hero."

I snorted. "I'll message you tomorrow."

Connie didn't want to let it go, but he did and then we were off the phone. Alfie wrapped his arms more tightly around me.

"Friend?"

"He's—my boss. Worked for him for almost eight years. He gave me my first break when I was a freelancer and put me on the payroll a couple of years ago even when I said I didn't want a permanent spot."

"Why not?" The curiosity in his voice unfurled and I debated how much I wanted to share. Did it really matter?

"It's easier to move on if you're not tied down. For a long time, I worried that my IDs wouldn't hold up. So I always did everything in cash. When you work full time, they like shit like direct deposit." Another shrug. "We worked it out."

"You don't even have a digital footprint, do you?" The question was a weird one, but since he'd made me coffee, I was a little more willing to play along.

"I have social media accounts under some anonymous names that use stock photos for my pictures." It had taken me years to think I'd shaken this town off, and to make sure no one could find me.

Then I came right back like a Christmas goose ready to be cooked. Not the best move, but I wanted to nail these bastards even more now.

Alfie just held me while I sipped my coffee. It was nice. Ridiculously so. Eventually, when my stomach grumbled, he settled me in his chair and refilled my coffee before he made me pancakes.

There was bacon in the warmer that he added to my plate along with warmed maple syrup and butter. I devoured the food. We hadn't really eaten the night before, a fact I'd pretty much ignored because I was more interested in them than food.

Alfie didn't say much while I ate, but I was very aware of his watchful gaze drifting over me. A hand on my knee, my shoulder, or his leg against mine. He kept touching me, and it was nice.

When food was done, he led me back out to the living room with two fresh mugs of coffee. Yeah, there wasn't a lot I wouldn't do for coffee. Once we were on the sofa, he turned partially to face me.

"I want to talk to you about something."

"Okay," I said, reaching forward to put my mug back down. "If it's about me leaving, you can save your breath. I'm finishing my story."

"As much as I want you safe," Alfie told me, "I don't want you gone."

Well, that was something. Folding my arms, I met his gaze. "Okay, then what did you want to talk about?"

"Yesterday..."

I braced myself. I didn't want their pity. I didn't want it from Frost or Nick or Alfie. It had happened. I told them because they needed to know I was more aware of the shit going on here than they were.

"You said...you said we never sent cards."

I lifted my shoulders. "It's done, Alfie. We were stupid kids making stupid promises..."

"Don't," he said, cutting me off and then blowing out a breath. "Don't belittle us that way. We've—we've spent years thinking you left us and now..."

"Oh, is this the grudge thing?" I was trying very hard *not* to scoff. "Nick said all three of you were holding one, especially Frost."

I stood by my earlier assessment of that: they could all get fucked.

"Yes," Alfie admitted, but it was the genuine sorrow in his voice that stilled my next smart-ass response. "We thought you ran away from us."

"Wait—what?" I gaped at him as he brushed his fingers over my hand and then tugged my arms so I'd unfold them. Then he was holding my hand between his. "Why the fuck would I be hiding from you guys?"

"You didn't look us up—you had our names," Alfie said with a sigh. "You knew we'd signed up for the Navy. You had ways of finding us."

I stared at him. "But why would I look? One after another, you left and didn't send a single word. Not even a postcard. It took me a long time to stop hoping to see them, Alfie. Months. I waited months and then that Christmas happened and I stopped waiting."

The confession earned me another sigh. "I wish to fuck we'd known, Rayne-drop. I'd have gutted them. Autopsy on the living would be brutal..."

A faint smile pulled at my lips. "You guys always looked

after me, but then it was just me and I had to take care of me. I thought—you'd moved on."

"We didn't," Alfie said. "None of us did. Soon as I finished boot, I got kicked right to my next assignment. Scores were great. I had classes and more. I was also already studying medicine. Nick too—not Frost though, he went back as soon as he could."

He what...

"He came back here looking for you."

"When?"

"February."

"I was still here." That was bullshit. I never saw him.

"He came back here and Grandmother told him you ran away over Christmas. She even showed him the missing persons report she filed."

I was going to kill her...February would have been when Mr. Schneemann had come back. She'd sent me to him for a week.

"She didn't give me the postcards either, did she?"

Alfie dipped his chin. "I sent them, Rayne-drop. I sent you tickets too, open-ended so you could come to us. Frost...Frost said you were gone then he went to apply to Navy SEALs and it was a while before we heard from him again. By the time it occurred to me to ask someone else—you probably already were gone."

Pain fisted in my chest.

"You kept your word?"

"I swear to you," Alfie said, bringing his hand up to cup my cheek. "I did—I should have known better than to trust her, but she even arranged for us to meet with the recruiters. No one ever stuck around after aging out."

We would know, we'd grown up there.

"But she found other ways to make money with me." Fuck I

hated her. I hated her and hated... "You really thought I ran away from you?"

"I didn't want to," he said with a long sigh. "But like I said, we couldn't find you and we looked. When Nick won the damn lottery..."

"When he *what*?"

Alfie laughed but it wasn't remotely humorous. "You know how he loved to play it. He was always stealing scratch-offs."

"He actually won the lottery?"

"A hundred thousand. Doesn't seem like much now, but the Navy put us through school, me through med school and him through law school. He invested the money and kept putting it away—except the part he paid to private investigators to see if they could find you."

My heart sank. "I didn't know..."

"I know you didn't," he said. "I wish like fuck we'd known what she was doing to you."

But they hadn't known either.

"What do we do now?"

Alfie pulled me to him and wrapped me up. The hug was everything. I closed my eyes and sank into him. The crackle of the fire, the warmth of his arms and—

An engine roared from outside. The sudden loudness sent adrenaline spiking through me. Alfie was on his feet and a gun appeared in his hand. He pointed me back toward the kitchen, even as he went to the door.

"Shit," he swore and holstered the gun before he pulled the locks and opened the door. Nick was there, carrying a kid—a badly injured kid.

"You weren't answering your phone," he snarled at him and I forgot how to breathe. Frost and Jolly weren't far behind and Frost had another kid with them.

Teenagers.

"Take her through to the backroom," Alfie said, all business. "Frost, I'm going to need backup."

The three men moved like they knew what they were doing, and I half-followed, aware of the teenager who was also moving in their wake.

"Is she going to be okay?" she was asking, tears coating her voice. "We were trying to get to the meeting point...I didn't know they'd followed us."

"It's going to be fine," Nick told her. "Stay with Rayne. She'll look after you."

The girl turned toward me, her eyes wide and the pain in them all too familiar.

Puzzle pieces began to slot into place.

Why the guys were here.

Why they didn't want me to investigate the missing kids.

I was looking at two of them right now.

TWENTY-THREE

Alfie went straight into doctor mode, barking orders to Nick and Frost as he went to work trying to save the little girl's life. I wanted to help, but it became quickly apparent that the boys knew how to work together more efficiently and I was better off staying out of the way. So I took the other girl through to the kitchen and made her cocoa.

She sobbed uncontrollably for a good twenty minutes, and I let her. When she started shivering, I wrapped a blanket over her shoulders and found some warm socks in the bedroom for her feet.

Eventually, warmed with the hot cocoa, she calmed enough to tell me what'd happened.

"How long have you been at Yule House?" I asked her, using the official name of the *Home for Misfit Children*.

She huddled in on herself, her eyes low. "About two years. My parents died in a crash when I was eight and I've been bounced from one group home to another until being transferred here. I didn't even know places like that still existed."

I nodded my understanding. "Orphanages crammed to the

rafters with a hundred odd kids? Yeah. Unfortunately there are a few that somehow seem to escape the notice of CPS."

"A hundred?" she repeated, wrinkling her nose. "At *least*. There were twelve girls living in my room, and there's *dozens* of rooms."

My jaw dropped. Even at its most crowded when I was growing up, there were no more than four girls in my room. Grandmother must be seriously lubricating the pockets of someone in a position of power.

"Fucking hell," I whispered. "What's your name? I'm Rach — um. Rayne. I'm Rayne." It was pointless to keep running from my past, especially now. Here.

"I'm Holly," she murmured. "I don't even know that girl's name. She's new."

I wet my lips, mentally reminding myself that falling to pieces wouldn't help anyone. These girls had been through some *shit* and it was a hell of a lot fresher than what I'd suffered. They needed our help.

Ours. The guys... that's why they'd come back to Northland?

"What happened to her?" I asked, not wanting to know as much as I *needed* to know.

Holly shrugged. "I don't— it's all a bit of a blur. We saw an opportunity to run, and we knew where we needed to go to get out... They've been getting kids out for months now, one by one, just making them disappear like they never existed..." She trailed off, chewing her lip.

They. My guys. They'd taken over more than just Doc Kane's clinic apparently.

"So when we thought no one was watching, we ran. But they followed us and... and... they hit her with their car. Just stepped on the gas and drove straight at her. I jumped out of the way and screamed for her to do the same but she was too slow and..."

"And they mowed her down," I whispered, horrified.

Then again, that checked out. Grandmother had nearly killed me when I threatened to expose her just before I turned eighteen. By all accounts, she'd only escalated since then.

"Holly, I am so sorry," I told the fragile girl, choking back my own tears. The guilt was damn near suffocating me, thinking how I should have done more after getting out. I should have tried harder to make someone *listen* to what was going on.

In fairness to myself, I had tried once. It'd gone nowhere, though, since Grandmother held the Northland sheriff department tight within her gnarled fist. The blowback had compromised my hard won anonymity and I'd walked away.

Holly just gave a sad nod and buried her face in her mug once more.

I didn't push her to talk further, instead going to check if Alfie and the guys needed anything.

For the next hour, Alfie worked on the little girl and eventually Nick came out to make coffee for everyone. I got Holly set up in one of the bedrooms, and left Jolly lying in front of her door when she climbed into bed to rest.

"How is she?" Nick asked when I returned to the kitchen.

"Holly? She's okay… I guess. Shaken up, for sure, but doesn't seem hurt from what I could see." I raked my fingers through my hair. "Might not be a bad idea for Alfie to check her over when he's done with the other girl, though."

Nick nodded. "We don't know her name?"

"No, Holly didn't know. Apparently she's new, but when they saw the opportunity to run, they did." I took one of the fresh mugs of coffee—black and unsweetened—and sat on a barstool beside Nick. "Do you want to tell me more about that?"

He sighed heavily, visibly exhausted. "I do. I really do. I thought—" he broke off with a whispered curse. "Rayne... I'm so fucking sorry. If we'd known..."

"But you didn't know," I said softly, turning on my stool so I faced him directly. "None of you knew. The worst that ever happened while you were there, was the sweatshop conditions of the toy factory in the basement. Yeah, it sucked to essentially work for free our entire lives, but that wasn't... this." I gestured to the room where Alfie was working on the injured girl.

"Definitely not," he agreed in a soft voice. "This... what happened to you? None of us could have predicted that's what would happen. Mrs Mechante was always an opportunistic fuck, but human trafficking and underage sex work is a a huge departure from child labor."

I sipped my coffee, humming my agreement.

Alfie and Frost emerged from the guest room Doc had converted back in the day where they'd been treating the girl, looking exhausted. Alfie had streaks of blood all over his shirt, and Frost's expression was grim, making me fear the worst.

"She's stable," Alfie announced as my heart caught in my throat. "But she really needs proper medical attention. More than I can provide here. I'm going to place a call to East and arrange a transfer to Mercy."

Nick blew out a long breath, echoing how I was feeling. "Good. Yeah, good plan. Once you get it all set up we can take her to the meeting point."

"Yep, let's leave her to rest as long as we can," Alfie agreed. "Is one of those for me?" He nodded to the coffee, and Nick pushed one of the mugs across the counter to him.

Alfie took a huge gulp then put it back down with a sigh. "I need to wash up. Then, I guess we need to talk." He arched a brow my way and I nodded firmly.

Damn fucking right we needed to talk.

Frost remained silent as he scrubbed his hands clean in the kitchen sink, his brow set in a deep frown. I watched him, questions sitting on the tip of my tongue, but the moment his cold eyes met mine I swallowed them all back. Frost wasn't tired or pensive, he was *pissed*.

"Frost—" I squeaked, taking in the icy fury in his gaze.

"Shut up," he snapped, grabbing a tea towel to dry his hands.

"Whoa, don't talk to Rainbow like that!" Nick barked back, ready to go to bat for me. That in itself made me all warm and fuzzy inside, but I *really* didn't need them getting into an argument over me. Not now. Not with two scared little girls in the house, one of whom was fighting for her life.

"Okay, that's enough. Nick, I'm a big girl and I can handle snappy Frost just fine."

Frost scoffed a bitter laugh, circling the counter to where I sat on a bar stool. "I said, *shut up*." He gripped my face in one hand, his fingers tight on my jaw.

I narrowed my eyes. "Make me."

Heat cut through the cold of his gaze, and his lips tilted in a smirk just a split second before his lips met mine in a soul shattering kind of kiss. A kiss that stole the breath straight out of my lungs then filled me back up with warmth and desire, curling through me with absolute adoration.

"Oh," Nick murmured. "That was Frost flirting? Fucking weird but alright, who am I to judge?"

The laugh that rumbled through Frost poured into my kiss, and I grinned against his lips. It felt *good* to have him kiss me without reservation. Even if he did have to still be a dick about it.

Before things could get *too* heated, Frost reluctantly released my jaw and took a seat on one of the vacant bar stools. "Coffee me, Saint."

Nick obliged, passing over the remaining mug of black heaven. Frost took his coffee the same as mine, while both Nick and Alfie loaded theirs with syrups and creams.

"God that's good," Frost sighed after a long sip, his hand finding my knee in a gesture that was both totally new and entirely familiar at the same time. Fuck, I'd missed him.

"The other girl is called Holly," Nick informed Frost, catching him up on what little information I'd gleaned over cocoa. "We don't know the injured girl's name."

"Ginger said it's Karol," Frost replied, scrubbing a hand over his dark stubble. "She's fourteen, recently transferred from a foster home in Montreal and was slated to be *fostered* with one of Mrs. Mechante's friends next week. That was why Holly decided to bolt with her now."

Nick grunted. "Fucking hell. Business must be booming if she's gone across the border."

My stomach twisted into knots, but I refused to back away from this conversation. I needed to know. I needed *proof* if I still intended to write my exposé, and now more than ever I was determined to rip the mask away from Northland.

"How does she have so many customers?" I asked in a hoarse voice, hating that this was a reality. "How are there *so many* evil people willing to use and abuse children in this way, and say *nothing* about it?"

Neither of the guys had an answer for that. Because the sad reality was that the world contained *a lot* of evil, walking around wearing a pleasant face.

"Wait, you said Ginger?" I tipped my head in Frost's direction. "She's involved in this?"

He nodded. "Yes. There's a network set up, which Doc Kane

started but lacked the connections to do much more than one kid every few months. He was terrified of tipping his hand to Mrs. Mechante and Sheriff Vynachts, so he waited until he was absolutely sure he could get them out before acting."

That rang true. "I know. He was the one who got me out… eventually."

Alfie returned to join us then, his hair and short beard wet from the shower and a towel in his hands. His feet were bare, and it was a curiously unfamiliar look for him. "Tell us," he urged.

I wet my lips, thinking it over. I'd already told them the worst of it—Schneemann—so I started from the end. "Over those months between Christmas and my birthday she booked me out every opportunity she possibly could. It was just me, no one else, so I was her most profitable source of income."

"Why do you think it was only you?" Nick asked, pensive.

It was something I'd asked myself plenty of times when I was trapped in the worst of it. "I was the only seventeen-year-old girl. Remember? We were the only ones in our age range… the other girls were all several years younger, and at the time I'm guessing none of her clients wanted boys? I'm assuming that's changed since then, having seen the profiles of the missing kids."

None of them answered that, so I sighed and drained the last of my coffee.

"Well. Anyway. I got taken to see Doc Kane plenty of times in those months. Grandmother only had one rule for her clients, and that was to return me alive. Everything else… acceptable. She looked the other way. I learned pretty quickly that the bonus payments were in addition to her fees, though, so I started keeping them for myself. If a client didn't offer one, I ballsed up and demanded it. Making it seem like a requirement, then stowing the cash with Doc Kane before returning to Yule House."

"Smart," Frost murmured, squeezing my knee. "Building the finance to disappear."

I nodded. "Yep. It worked well, until Grandmother figured out what I was doing. She lost her shit, demanding I give her all the cash I'd been hiding. When I refused, she had one of her staff beat me within an inch of my life. She would have kept going, if Doc hadn't come by for a house call and found me broken and bleeding in the foyer."

"Fucking hell," Alfie whispered, leaning his elbows on the counter opposite us. "He took you back to the clinic?"

"Yeah. I was there for a while, but we both agreed I couldn't go back to Yule House. He helped me get out, driving me out of town himself and setting me up with my fake IDs and admitting me at Mercy under my new name. They cared for me as his niece—under his insurance—then one of his friends helped me get set up as far from here as my cash could take me. I quite literally owe him my life."

"A lot of kids over the years owe *you* their lives, Rayne," Alfie informed me with his steady gaze locked on me without even a hint of pity. "If not for you, Doc Kane maybe never would have started his mission. You inspired him, and when things escalated here—when he found himself treating a seven-year-old *child* with injuries like yours—he reached out to us for help. I don't think that was a coincidence."

Frost's hand on my knee helped to keep me grounded, and I leaned into his warmth. "You think he remembered we were friends?"

Nick scoffed. "We were never just friends, Rayne. You were —*are*—the sun of our solar system."

"Yes," Alfie answered. "I think that was why he thought of us. But we'd been in contact over the years, always searching for you, and he had a vague idea that we might have the right connections to do what needed to be done."

Curiosity sparked within me at that. "Because of the Navy?"

Alfie's answering smile was full of secrets. "In broad terms, yes." His phone beeped in his pocket, and he pulled it out to check the message. Then he groaned a curse before dialing someone and putting it on speakerphone. "Ginger, how urgent are we talking?"

"Eight out of ten. Either you three show up here for questioning, or they go looking... and we don't want them finding Doc's cabin while the girls are there." The fluffy, sweet as pie woman was all business on the other end of the phone. "Are they safe there without you for an hour?"

My brows rose, and the guys exchanged silent glances.

"I can leave Jolly," Frost suggested. "And a gun."

"Rayne can't shoot," Nick disagreed. "But Jolly is a good idea."

"All of us?" Alfie asked Ginger, "Or can I send Nick and Frost so I can stay?"

"All of you," she replied, grim. "You especially, Alfred. They've already looked for Karol in the clinic. Candice just called to let me know."

"Fuck!" Alfie exclaimed, raking a hand over his hair. "Okay. Let me make some calls and get East to collect the girls directly from here. We'll be back shortly, Ginger. Just keep that leech occupied."

"Drive safe, hon. It's about to come down thick out there." She ended the call, and I glanced out the window. Sure enough, fluffy white flakes had started falling.

"We aren't leaving Rayne alone," Nick growled, his jaw set with determination.

Shit. This was surely the rock and proverbial hard place. I

also didn't want them to leave, but if it stopped them finding Karol and Holly... "You have to," I said firmly. "Keep Vynachts away from this cabin, so it can stay our safe space."

"I can shoot," a small voice interrupted, and we all swiveled to find Holly standing awkwardly in the doorway with Jolly flopping down between us and the door. "I learned how to handle a Glock when I was fostered in Detroit."

Frost was the one who moved first, sliding off his chair and pulling a gun from his own holster. He handed it to Holly butt first, and locked eyes with her. "You shoot to kill, am I clear?"

The girl nodded quickly. "Crystal."

Within minutes, the guys were gone, and I was alone in Doc Kane's cabin by the lake. Alone, with one girl barely clinging to life and a scared teen holding a gun like a lifeline. Oh, and a snoring polar bear. What could go wrong?

CHAPTER
TWENTY-FOUR

Arms folded, I stared out the front windows. The angle of the blinds and the sheer curtains offered me some anonymity from being spotted. Our isolation also helped. We'd see anyone approaching. The cabin's location, nestled near the lake, was great for fishing in the summer. That was what Doc used to say. It'd be great for fishing in the winter too, when he was in the mood for ice fishing.

Doc was missing.

A sigh rippled through me. A part of me thought he'd died when I'd seen Candice working at the clinic and no sign of Doc. Retired was a fanciful thought, one I'd never really allowed myself 'cause I worked so damn hard to forget about this place. The reality, however, was he was most likely dead. Especially after what I'd seen with Tinker.

"Do you think she's going to be okay?" Like me, Holly had gone quiet after the guys left. Jolly had only shifted his position so he could lie on the rug near the front door. It was like he knew his job was to guard us.

He could do it too. He was easily a hundred and fifty

pounds of white fur, teeth, and claws. Though, the more I was around him, the dopier the grin on his face seemed to be. Maybe he was channeling Frost's inner sweet side. I almost snorted at myself before shaking it off to focus on Holly.

She was a kid. She was alone. She'd been through hell. These were all things I recognized. "I hope so. Alfie's a good doctor." I didn't have to know much about his career to know that, but Alfie had always been the one who cared about all of us. "When we were kids," I told her, "he saved a baby bird. Nursed it back to health. I thought it was crazy. Nick told him it was crazy, but I think the only one who was pretty certain of him was Frost."

One more glance out the window and I headed to the kitchen. Holly needed food, and I needed more coffee. The guys had checked on Karol before they left, and the door was cracked so we could hear her. Doc had turned that room into a pseudo-treatment suite. It let him handle emergencies without leaving the cabin.

Now, I supposed, it was letting Alfie treat kids who couldn't be seen in town.

"You grew up with them?" Holly asked as she perched on a stool. She'd brought the gun with her, and she set it down carefully with the muzzle pointed away from me. I was trusting a fourteen-year-old with a gun. Frost had given it to her. But I wasn't wrong and neither was he. The sobriety in her eyes was definitely beyond her years.

"I did," I said, and ripped the Band-Aid off. "At Yule House."

Surprise filled Holly's expression as I told her about my first year there—and the first year I met the guys. I sanitized some of it, but not all. She clearly had a taste of what the place had become. A transition I'd experienced and my guys had been spared.

It wasn't until I set the grilled ham and cheese sandwich in front of her that I realized that for once, I was grateful they'd missed that instead of resenting them for being gone. We hadn't had any control then.

None of us.

"What happened to the bird?"

"Well," I said. "Spoiler alert, *she* made it. Soon as her wing was healed, he let her go and she flew away."

"Did you ever see her again?" That was a loaded question.

"No," I told her. "But the fact she healed and she could fly meant she could have the life she deserved. We didn't need to see her again to know."

Holly looked at her sandwich. "But it would have been nice."

Yeah. It would have been. "I'm going to give you an address. It's a PO Box. When you're ready, send me a postcard so I know you're okay too."

She blinked. "I don't even know that I have any wings left to heal..."

"I know," I told her and she frowned at me. "They'll regrow, believe me. You're tough. You're a survivor. You're going to heal, and you're going to be stronger. You already saved Karol."

The surprise in her eyes gave way tears, and she blinked furiously down at her food. I left her to get her composure back. Crying in front of other people wasn't my thing either. I checked on Karol; the tiny thing was still sleeping. Her breathing seemed steady, and Alfie seemed okay with leaving her—well not okay with it, but sure she would be fine until their ride got here.

When I returned to the kitchen and my coffee, Holly said, "Could you tell me more stories about when you were kids?"

I'd have to edit some of them. The boys were terrible as

teens. Absolute wretches. Frost stole his first car when he was fourteen. The same age Holly was now. He stole it just to see if he could and because I said I'd never seen a drive-in movie. We made it three towns over and watched the movie in the car, then ditched it closer to Northland before sneaking back into the manor.

We'd almost been caught, but Nick took the heat. Pretended it was just him sneaking back in while Alfie and Frost got me back to my room. Nick got punished. Three days in the sack room in the basement by himself. But he'd said it was worth it. Took me a minute to come up with some stories where we weren't total hellraisers. Some were even fun.

The memories weren't all bad. Maybe I could just cherry pick the ones I wanted. The next hour dragged past. I checked my cracked cellphone screen a few times to see if the guys messaged me. I'd actually texted Nick my number so he'd have it when they were leaving.

No word.

They still had to drive to Ginger's and deal with whomever was there searching. Probably Sheriff Vynachts—the bastard. Jolly's calmness kept my pacing to a minimum. That and the desire to keep things easy for Holly. Jolly heard the arrival of a vehicle before I did. He was up from his snooze on the rug to face the door, his whole body one long line of tension.

He didn't bark like some dogs did when visitors approached. He didn't wag his tail or move closer. His whole being seemed fixed on the front of the cabin like he could see right through the wood to the person approaching. Fuck, maybe he could.

Holly had the gun in her hand and she'd moved to stand in front of the little hall leading to the bedrooms. Brave girl. I moved to the windows, staying to the edge where I could see out.

The monster truck parked outside already sported snow on the top, but the flakes weren't sticking to the hood. Too warm. The guy moved like a lumbering giant. I thought my guys were big and I curled my hand around my phone. I stared right at him as the guy climbed up the steps and stomped his feet clear of snow before he reached the door. I still jumped when he pounded on the door.

"Rayne-drop?"

That name coming from someone *not* Alfie made me glare and a rumbling growl escaped Jolly. His teeth were bared and his whole body vibrated, ready to be loosed with one command.

"Name's East, Doc Bud said to tell you he sent me."

Relief cut the strings of tension holding me hostage. That was why he said *Rayne-drop*. Alfie didn't shout that name from the rooftops. They hadn't even done that when we were kids.

I cut a look to Holly. "It's okay." Then to Jolly—I put a pin in the fact that rhymed—"Stay boy. He's a friendly, I think."

With that, I went to the door. "Can you tell me why Doc Bud sent you?" I didn't open the door, I just listened. Doc Bud was kind of an adorable name for Alfie.

"Said I had two little angels to transport, one to Mercy and the other to Hope."

Hope.

Hope was a sweet thought. I looked over at Holly again, the tension in her echoed the same in me.

"Safe?" she mouthed and I nodded but motioned her back. Jolly and I would take the first risk. So I unlocked the door.

"Jolly, stay," I repeated, and while he didn't take a single step forward, he continued to growl as the door swung wide letting in what could arguably be an Abominable Snowman— or a lumberjack. Damn, he was tall.

"Does he have ID?" Holly asked and since the same question was on the tip of my tongue, I focused on him.

"I do." The man pulled off the knit cap, not that it revealed much. He had a bushy beard to go with his bushy head of hair. "I'm East," he said, then glanced at Jolly. "Friendly, remember?"

For his part, the polar bear of a dog just sat, but he didn't look any happier to see the huge man. That said, he didn't automatically attack either. Good.

"I'm going to reach into my pocket for my wallet." He telegraphed every move, opening his jacket to snag the wallet out of his pocket. He wasn't wearing a gun anywhere I could see one. Didn't mean he didn't have it. When he handed it to me, I studied the driver's license. It had his full name—Has East—age, details, and an address that was in Oschter, which was a good twenty plus miles away. Satisfied the details matched, I snapped a picture of it with my phone and fired it off to Nick.

"Smart," East said, not taking a single step inside. He also kept his hands loose and open.

Holly moved over next to me, and she took the wallet, glanced at the identification. "You look a lot younger in the picture." She eyed him again, and kept the gun trained on him as steady as Jolly's stare was, but East seemed patient even if we were letting the cold air in.

"It's the beard," East said with a grin. "Makes me distinguished."

I snorted, but my phone buzzed and Nick's message was succinct. *That's him.* Relief spilled through me, and when I showed Holly, her shoulders dipped a fraction and then she pointed the gun away from East.

"Right. I'd like to stay and chat, but Doc Bud said the littlest one was in a bad way."

"She is," I said, handing him his wallet back as I let him in and closed the door behind him. He got the snow stomped off his boots before I led him to where Karol was. Holly watched him the whole time, eyes wary and knuckles white on the handle of the gun.

"I'm a nurse," East said. "Gimme a minute to grab the plastic stretcher. Then we can get her secure."

He didn't wait for my response. Nor did it take him long to return with the orange stretcher, we kept her wrapped in blankets so she wouldn't get cold and then secured the straps to hold her in place. He checked her IV before he secured it.

"Can you carry this bag?" That he directed at me, but Holly stepped forward.

"I can." With that, she handed me the gun. She'd also pulled on her coat and a pair of boots. Despite a certain amount of wariness, East's no-nonsense actions and directness made both of us feel better.

Jolly not just killing him helped too.

He even stopped growling. I stuffed my feet in boots and debated giving the gun back to Holly before I detoured to the kitchen. I dug a knife out of the drawer. It was a sharp one. Then I wrapped it in a tea towel, before I moved to help them get Karol in the back of the truck.

Poor darling never once even woke up. A good thing, I hoped. Then East told Holly to get in and I pressed the towel-wrapped knife into her hand. She stared at it for a moment, then gave me a hug. I returned it, careful of her cause I had no idea if she had any injuries or not.

"Remember," I told her. "You can heal. You will fly again... one day."

"Thank you." Another squeeze and then she was in the truck, and I retreated to the porch. Snow clung to my hair and my lashes, but I didn't duck back inside as the truck backed out. Jolly walked out to where I was on the porch and came to stand next to me. I stood there as they drove away and the snow kept coming down.

Then the sound of the engine disappeared into the hush. The snow blanketed everything. It wouldn't be long until even the truck's tire tracks would vanish under it all. We'd saved two kids.

The guys had.

I got to help.

That was definitely something.

A sound of running water pierced the silence and I turned to see Jolly at the foot of the steps, leg cocked as he pissed a river. He looked very pleased with himself and a laugh huffed out of me.

Right. The kids were safe. I was stuck out here until the guys got back.

Time to get some work done.

Fuck, I hope the cabin had wifi.

CHAPTER

TWENTY-FIVE

The guys didn't return that night, but Nick checked in on me every fifteen minutes without fail until I fell asleep with my phone in my hand just before midnight. When I woke up the next morning, I found myself sharing a bed with a bear-sized dog and an inbox overflowing with messages.

Smiling, I answered the most recent and let the guys know I was still safe. Then I snapped a picture of Jolly lying on his back, tongue lolling out the side of his huge snout as he snored. That one I sent to Frost, who'd also texted me overnight asking for pics.

His response was an immediate eye roll emoji followed by *not the pics I meant, Bad Weather.*

As I made my coffee, Alfie called me.

"Good morning, Doc Bud," I greeted him, grinning to myself.

"Good morning, Rayne-drop," he murmured back quietly, like he was worried about being overheard. "How'd you sleep?"

I yawned, dragging my fingers through my tangled hair.

"Not great. I was worried... I think maybe Jolly got sick of me jumping at every noise and that was why he climbed into bed with me."

Alfie chuckled. "Nah, he just thinks he's a cat. Or a person. Have you scratched his belly for him yet? It's almost embarrassing to watch."

"Well, whatever he is, he's good company. It helps that I have first-hand knowledge of how capable he is of killing. How are things in town?" I bit my lip, nervous to hear the answer.

Alfie blew out a long breath, causing my stomach to flip over. "It's going to be okay, I think. They were focusing pretty hard on me last night because they know I'm the only person in town trained for surgery and emergency medicine so if anyone had helped Karol it would be me... but without evidence they can't do much. Not without admitting they'd run a child over."

"Fucking hell, Alfie, this is insane."

"Agreed. But we're doing everything we can to end it, Rayne-drop. Now more than ever." The reassurance warmed me, and I rubbed my breastbone where my chest hurt.

"So... what now? Are you coming back?"

"Soon. I hope. Nick's working on things right now, and Frost is worried about us leading Vynachts straight back to you." Alfie yawned in my ear, and I silently questioned whether he'd slept at all. "I'm at the clinic today anyway, seeing patients. Hopefully by end of day it'll be smoothed out."

"I hope so, too." I poured my coffee, letting the rich aroma fill my nose. "Nick being a fancy lawyer must come in handy. Why hasn't he tried shutting Grandmother down the legal way, though?"

"He did. Try, I mean. He spent months trying to get Yule House shut down permanently, but Mrs. Mechante has friends in high places. Even the *random* checks from CPS had enough forewarning that she cleaned the place up and nothing was ever found amiss. Worse yet, the kids seemed to suffer after each attempt through legal channels."

"So you took matters into your own hands," I concluded, taking a sip of my coffee. It made sense. Even back in my time, the men she sent me to were wealthy, influential, and powerful. I could only imagine the client list she held after thirteen years.

Some voices murmured in the background of the phone, and Alfie answered in a muffled tone.

"You gotta go?" I guessed, a bit sad that we couldn't chat all day.

"Yeah, my first patient for the day is here. I'll call you when I get a break, okay? Stay safe, Rayne-drop. I can't lose you again."

He ended the call before I could reply, and it was a good thing too, because my heart was right in my throat and I couldn't have gotten words out if I'd tried. Nick and Frost had both sent me messages so I read those before taking my coffee to the dining table where I'd left my laptop set up.

For the rest of the morning, I worked on cobbling together a bare bones outline of the story I wanted to write. It wasn't the investigatory meat that Connie wanted, but it did expose Grandmother's operation... in a different way.

I needed proof. I needed credible sources and documented evidence to back my accusations and protect the magazine from a defamation lawsuit. The only problem was *getting* that proof without being killed in the process.

Around midday, Jolly was whining and pawing at the door *again,* so I pulled on a coat and boots to take the overgrown pup outside for another firehose piss.

"Come on, Jolly," I moaned when he took his sweet fucking time choosing which tree he wanted to water, wandering farther into the woods surrounding the cabin. The big dog looked back at me and woofed softly, as if to say *shut the fuck up and let me do my thing.*

I stomped my feet in the snow, grumbling under my breath about pet maintenance. Jolly finally decided on the *perfect* tree and did his thing, melting a huge patch of snow in the process, then grabbed a stick in his teeth as he trotted back to me.

"What's that for?" I asked when he dropped the stick at my feet. Jolly looked at me, then down at the stick, then back at me. "Seriously?" I moaned. "You want to play fetch in the snow? Jolly, come on!"

Damn dog just poked the stick with a huge paw and twitched his ears.

Mentally cursing Frost, I picked up the stick and threw it without a whole lot of effort. The dog took off like a bullet out of a gun, snatching the stick from the air before it could even land and my jaw dropped.

"Holy shit, Jolly," I muttered. "That was actually impressive."

He delivered the stick back to me, tongue lolling out and tail wagging madly as he waited for me to throw it again.

A little more enthusiastically, I hurled the stick into the trees and once again the damn dog seemed to teleport himself to catch it before it could hit the snow. Crazy fast, and incredibly accurate. Frost hadn't been joking when he said Jolly was well-trained.

Pretty soon, it became a challenge for me to try and get the stick to actually *land* before Jolly caught it and we ended up deeper and deeper into the uninhabited woods, laughing and barking with joy all the while. It was the most clean fun I'd had in years.

Eventually cold set in through my coat, and I suffered Jolly's exaggerated puppy eyes as I told him the game was over, we needed to get back to the cabin. As we approached the cabin, though, I slowed my steps and hesitated near a thick tree trunk.

An unfamiliar blue pickup sat parked in front of the cabin, and the front door stood open.

Jolly trotted out of the woods, totally unconcerned, even though I hissed his name in panic. I hadn't taken the gun with me, because it just wasn't a natural thing for me to do when I didn't know how to safely handle it. All I had was the stick Jolly had been playing with, and if that was Sheriff Vynachts inside the cabin right now, it wouldn't be much use.

I should run. Or hide. Or... something. Call the guys? Crap, my phone was inside. I hadn't anticipated the dog pee break to take so long, dammit.

When Jolly disappeared inside, I braced to listen for blood curdling screams. The memory of what he'd done to steroid-elf was still fresh in my mind, but the silence stretched...

"Fucking dog," I whispered, making up my mind and darting across the clearing in front of the cabin to get a better look inside. I couldn't take off and run without Jolly, and if it was an enemy they'd be screaming in agony by now. Right?

A familiar deep rumble met my ears as I cautiously approached the front door, and the relief washing over me was so intense I nearly sobbed.

"There she is!" Nick announced as I stepped inside. "Good boy, Jolly, you took good care of my Rainbow. Yes, you did. Who's a good guard dog, hmm? You are. Yes, you are."

The stupid animal was on his back, paws in the air as Nick shamelessly scratched Jolly's white belly fur, making his back paw kick.

"What happened to *your* truck? You scared me," I admitted with a sheepish smile, coming closer. Then I paused and eyed the new addition to the already cozy living room. "Um. What the hell?"

Nick grinned so bright he rivaled any Christmas lights. "You hate it, don't you?"

I wrinkled my nose, smelling the fresh pine of the enormous tree parked in a bucket beside the fireplace. "Um... *hate* is a strong word... but... I don't *not* hate it."

Nick hummed a thoughtful sound, nodding as he climbed to his feet and stepped over Jolly to reach for me. "Rayne... after everything you told us yesterday, and everything you went through, it's understandable that you hate everything Christmas. Now we *get* why Ginger insisted on making flowering plant cookies instead of Christmas trees."

I jerked a nod, not wanting to delve back into that whole sour tale all over again. "Yeah. So... why bring back a tree?"

His hands on my waist, he pulled me into his embrace and held me tight. Safe. "Because I want to help you regain the parts that old bitch stole from you. You deserve all the best things in life, Rayne, and Christmas used to be one of the times when you really sparkled."

I sighed, melting into his hug. His heart was in the right place. "That had nothing to do with Christmas, Nick, and everything to do with you guys. You all loved the holidays so much, it was an infectious energy."

He said nothing for a moment, then slid a hand to the nape of my neck, tilting my head back so he could kiss me. "I'll get rid of it if you want," he whispered between kisses. "Or..."

"Or what?" I asked, already breathless. That was what he constantly did to me, left me totally breathless.

"Or you could help me decorate it, and build some new core memories around Christmas?" One hand slipped inside my jeans, and showed me exactly what sort of core memories he meant.

I groaned, rocking against his hand as he found my clit, the denim biting into my hips with how far he was stretching the waistband. "I mean… I'm not against that idea."

"Excellent," he murmured, kissing me deeply. "Take that coat off and get comfy. I'll grab the box of decorations from the car." He started for the door, then paused and gave me a sly smile. "Take the jeans off, too. Alfie won't be back until later and Frost is keeping Vynachts busy, so we have all afternoon. Just us."

Jolly huffed, and Nick rolled his eyes. "Just us *and* Jolly."

I laughed, a weight shifting off my mind with the sound, and started stripping out of my clothes. Forget just the coat and jeans, I was playing Nick's game now. When he returned inside with a huge box of decorations in hand, I was totally naked in front of the tree.

"Holy shit," he croaked, dropping the box.

I grinned. "Are we off to a good start, Saint Nick?"

"Twelve out of ten," he replied, kicking the front door shut and shedding his own coat. "Merry fucking Christmas to me."

I cupped my own breasts, playing with them as I watched him strip naked, my mouth watering as each inch of his tanned, tattoo-decorated skin was exposed. "How do you want me, Saint Nick? Are you going to use me like a good little ho, ho, ho?"

Neither one of us could keep a straight face at that, but it sure as fuck didn't dampen the mood. Nick got on his knees before me, kissing my belly all over while whispering sweet promises… then he lay down and pulled me onto his face, demanding I suffocate him with my pussy.

I did as I was told, riding his mouth like a rodeo bull and relishing the bite of his fingertips in my thighs as he held me firm, drinking in my first climax like it was the finest champagne.

CHAPTER
TWENTY-SIX

J olly got bored with us when I kissed my way down Nick's body, this time. The plan called for me to suck him off right in front of the fire. The warmth washed over me as Nick gripped my hair. For a moment, he paused as he fisted my hair while I was on my knees. I looked up at him and met his gaze.

"How tight?"

His hard cock rested on my tongue and I teased the vein throbbing along the underside of it. How tight had he yanked my hair?

"Or not at all?"

Closing my eyes, I savored the heavy weight of him in my mouth. I had my hands on his thighs. The dark springy hair there tickled my palms. Blowjobs were an exercise in trust. I'd had a couple of lovers over the last few years I'd been willing to do this for, but yanking my hair had always been a hard limit.

A no.

Pulling off his cock with a slow pop, I took a deep breath. The storm outside continued, leaving us with the light of the fire playing over us and the dark evergreen next to it. It was still naked, just like us. There was something poetic about it. While woodsmoke and pine were in the air, the heavy musk that was all Nick was the predominant scent and it made my cunt slick with just that thought.

"He damn near yanked it out at the roots," I said slowly, not really wanting that bastard in this moment. My saint was trying to paint over those memories, with more than just paper on the cracks. "I don't usually do blow jobs...but I don't hate it. So—tug and if I don't like it, I'll tap your right thigh."

That would take some thought on my part. His eyes held mine captive. The flames seemed to dance in them, and his smile grew. "Good girl. If you want more, you pat my left thigh."

"Right," I said as I tapped his thigh. "Ease up. Left," I repeated the tap to his left thigh. "Go harder."

He licked his lips and I swore his cock gave a little jerk. "Got it."

"What if I dig my nails into both?" No idea what inspired the question, but there was something intoxicating about the open desire on Nick's face. He knew me...all the dark and broken bits alongside the ridiculous and the silly. First loves were difficult to get over, and if I were honest, I'd never gotten over any of them.

Thank fuck they didn't seem to have gotten over me.

"Then I'll take it as a cue to just fuck your mouth, but—" The sting of command surrounded that last word. "If your throat starts to bother you, Rainbow, right thigh scratch and I'll pull back."

"So many game cheat codes," I teased. "You're going to spoil me."

"Good." The firmness in that one word fisted around my

heart and dug in for the long haul. "I'm going to do everything with you Rainbow. *Everything.*"

A shiver went up my spine, and I focused on his cock again. The pre-cum beading on the tip made me want to lick it, so I did. Nick let out a little groan.

"You're going to kill me with that tongue." Not that he sounded remotely opposed. "What a way to go…"

He didn't rush me along as I sucked his cock against my lips or when I began to move my mouth along his length. I'd felt this beast in my cunt. It was thick and heavy. His balls hung low, and there was darker, springier hair at the base that tickled my nose when I took him all the way to my throat.

The whole time I explored, his eyes remained on mine as he wrapped my hair around the fist of his hand. When I patted his left thigh, nostrils full of the scent of him, he let out a low groan. "Thank fuck."

I softened my mouth as he gave a gentle tug and then thrust at the same time. The bitter, salty taste of pre-cum flooded my mouth, and I was pretty sure I drooled a little. Tears sparked when he gave another thrust, and when he stilled I patted his left thigh.

I was okay.

I was *more* than okay. Because I drank in the ecstasy in his eyes and let the bliss roll through me. I was probably still hopped up on endorphins and the fact his beard glistened with the evidence of my own release. That said, Nick was *beautiful.* Rugged and thick in all the right places. The cut of his muscles was like someone had sculpted him.

There were also scars, and I wanted to explore all of them. I wanted to know where they came from and the life he had without me. I wanted to know *everything.* Later. For now, I concentrated on bringing him to the edge and when his fingers flexed against my hair and my scalp lit up, I shuddered.

Not in fear, or pain, but delight.

I took him right to the edge and then eased off a little.

"Fuck," he swore. "You're killing me, Rainbow." He huffed out a laugh. "Don't ever stop."

Something inside of me flipped over at the declaration, and I had zero intentions of stopping. Between us, we found the rhythm that drove him mad, and I increased the suction as I pursued his orgasm. I wanted to see him fall apart. A memory to savor. And when he thrust deeper into my throat, I swallowed around him.

"I'm going to come..." The warning was appreciated, but I didn't need it. I dug my nails into his thigh and held on as he threw his head back and came. Choking on his release, I fought to swallow every damn drop, but he was a big boy and some escaped with my drool.

What a sight I had to be, but he went to his knees in front of me. The cradle of his huge hands on my face made me feel small and cherished. He rained kisses down on me, and as I gripped his wrists, it hit me that he was shaking. When I wrapped my arms around him it was like we collapsed inwards. The tears on my cheeks hit me then.

That was why he'd been kissing me, and fuck me, I was crying. But I had to tell him. I just couldn't get the words out. When he picked me up and settled me in his lap, I held on as he kept up a litany of comforting sounds. Some of them were words. Maybe. It was his voice and his body and his arms, and I held onto my saint.

Eventually, the sobs stopped and I could catch my breath, and his words penetrated the haze. "You should have stopped me, Rainbow," he whispered, adding, "I'm sorry."

"No," I said, and it came out hoarse. Yes my throat was still sore from being throttled, and I still had a bruise across my chest. Neither bothered me right now, and I pulled back so I could see his face and he could see mine. "I loved that..."

Surprise flickered across his tortured expression. "You were crying..."

"You have a huge dick," I countered, and his surprise turned to a wicked grin. Laughter swelled up inside of me. "Tears are normal when you're rubbing the back of my throat... and I was trying to swallow all of you."

"You were amazing," he whispered. "I just don't ever want to hurt you. Not like that. Not ever."

"You didn't," I promised. "I just think we might need to practice that a few times, and find all the ways we like it."

The heat in his eyes promised he was onboard, then he fisted the hair at my nape and tilted my head back for another soul-stealing kiss. "Every day," he swore. "Twice on Sundays."

I cracked up at his grin. "Might need to spread that out a little or my jaw is gonna break. Frost and Alfie will not want to be left out."

"Pfft," Nick said, then nuzzled a kiss to the corner of my mouth. "What do we think about the tree now?"

I shifted against his lap and stared up at the tree. "It's naked."

He rubbed his cheek against my hair. "We don't have to decorate it." We didn't. He was right. But once upon a time, I was thrilled to see how much of Christmas these assholes enjoyed even when none of us gave a damn about toys.

If you made enough of them, those weren't the presents you wanted. This—this was a present I could give them and make with my own hands. I glanced down at my nails. Despite the last few days, they weren't in terrible condition, but the polish was a standard pale red with no suggestion of Christmas. Then I looked up at the tree.

"Let's do it... Hot cocoa to go with?"

His smile was almost its own reward. "Good thing I got the ornaments in. I think naked Christmas decorating is a tradition I can get behind." He rose, lifting me with him, and then set me on my feet. He moved on unsteady legs, and another thrill went through me.

Traditions.

Traditions were for people who had futures and pasts to mingle. We definitely had shared pasts. Shared experiences. Did we have a future? All four of us?

"Music?" Nick asked as he held up his phone.

"Can we do wintry but not quite Christmas music?" I wasn't sure I was up for the sensory overload, and Nick was absolutely going overboard to do everything to make this work for me.

"I know just the thing..." He did a search on his phone as I headed for the kitchen.

Music began to drift from the phone and it was—pretty. I frowned as I pulled milk from the fridge. "That's..."

"Enya," he said. "I got some Loreena McKennitt on here too." The mirth in his smile was contagious. They'd been favorites of mine, and I hadn't listened to them in years. "If you're a very good girl, I'll throw on some Trans-Siberian Orchestra."

"Hmm—tempting." I winked, and I swore his dick thickened at the suggestion. The next two hours passed almost magically. We decorated the tree with care. Some ornaments were right out. I didn't want anything Santa up there.

I just wasn't ready for that.

But the red, green, and blue balls were perfect. Crystal ornaments that reflected the light. Multi-colored garland that added to the glistening effect. Multicolor lights too. I also discovered just how meticulous Nick was. If he decided something was off, he just took it all back off and redid it.

I was giggling more and more, particularly when he got that fierce expression. The tree was just a hint lopsided. The more he tried to fix it, the worse it looked. When we ran out of ornaments, he grunted.

"It's only like half of it."

"But we can't see the back, so I think it's fine…"

Nick made a face. He stood behind me, arms wrapped around me, and his very erect dick stiff against my ass. A shiver went through me as I studied the tree. We'd turned off all the lights and he'd stoked up the fire. I could still catch whiffs of chocolate and vanilla from when I'd made the cocoa and added the whipped cream. The woodsmoke. The pine. Nick. Even a hint of wet dog.

The last made me grin as Jolly rolled over on his back. He was in front of the fire and snoring away like the polar bear he was. The music wrapped around us and gradually it hit me that Nick was swaying us.

Dancing.

"Nick…"

"Hmm?"

"Will you help me make a new memory?"

"Anything."

"Anything?" That was a lot of latitude.

"Well, short of tattooing your name on my ass, and that's only because we don't have the tools here."

Laughter burst through me. "That's an image."

He cupped my breasts, massaging them and I sighed. "I want to put mine on yours. Maybe I'll do it with an ink pen later so we can see how it looks."

That was definitely a delicious thought. "Weirdly, I'd like that. But I was thinking of something a little more intimate…"

"Name it, Rainbow. If it's mine to give you, I will."

253

The solemnity in that oath sparked fresh tears in my eyes. "I want you to fuck my ass while I look at the tree."

Stillness held him as he processed what I asked, and then he shuddered, wrapping me up closer. With soft lips, he tickled my ear. "Two caveats...you have to promise to tell me to stop if you need me to stop."

"I can do that." I could. "But I need you to push me if I don't tell you."

It was my time to shiver. Nick squeezed me closer. "I will." Another promise.

"Second caveat?"

"You ride my face first, I want to have my Rainbow come at least three more times before we do that."

"Done."

He bit my ear. "Not yet. But soon." He spread a huge furry blanket out on the floor right next to the tree and when Jolly would have joined us, Nick sent him back to the rug. My first orgasm took no time. And I kept my gaze on the tree as I sat on my man's face.

I was damn near boneless by orgasm three, and every muscle trembled. Nick had to do most of the work of curving me over the ottoman. I'd worried about lube, but no, the boys had that here.

Always prepared. He warmed it before he began to work my ass with his fingers. The whole time, he rained kisses down along my back and my spine. Kisses and praise. I floated on a haze of bliss that even the first press of his fingers couldn't disturb. The second finger added to the burn, and he stretched me.

I began to shake and then Nick was at my ear, whispering to me. "I'm here, Rainbow. This is me. Can you feel me?"

Licking my lips, I clenched around him and then began to relax again. He never let me forget it was him. He refused to rush me, and when I would break out sweating, he slowed us down and went back to petting me.

"When you're ready," he would murmur.

"I'm ready," I told him, but it wasn't until I was damn near weeping in need that he added a third finger and I rocked back onto his hand.

"That's my girl," Nick said before pressing a kiss to my shoulder blades. Replacing his fingers with his dick was a whole new experience.

"Fuck," I exhaled as he eased in not even an inch before my whole body seemed to catch fire. The burn and the pressure was exquisite. More because it was Nick. He added more lube and chuckled.

"Soon, Rainbow... very soon."

It took time, but he worked his way into me with such tender slowness that it was the most exquisite form of torture for both of us. When he finally sank balls deep the only things I was aware of were my Saint and the tree we'd decorated together.

"This," he said in between panting breaths that exposed how challenging this was for him, "is a tradition I can get behind."

The comment popped the expanding tension and I laughed. The laughter became a gasp as he pulled back and then thrust in and it was my turn to gasp. "Again," I demanded and Nick groaned.

The tree lights blurred as he found a rhythm and I pushed back to meet him. The cabin smelled like Christmas and sex.

It was glorious—the sex part at least. I still wasn't sure about Christmas.

CHAPTER
TWENTY-SEVEN

Frost was being all kind of mysterious as he bundled me into his car a few days later, having woken me up well before sunrise. Nick was still fast asleep and Alfie was at the clinic for an overnight shift, but Frost assured me it'd be fine. No one would panic. He'd left a note.

I yawned heavily, snuggling into the huge coat he'd dressed me in after waking me up.

"It's really early, Frost," I mumbled, giving him a narrow-eyed glare. "Really, really early." Early even for Jolly apparently because the big bear hadn't even looked up from where he'd taken our place in the bed.

Frost quirked a brow as he drove away from the cabin. "Suck it up, Stormy. You'll live."

I snorted a sleepy laugh. "Why do you keep calling me that? It's always been Rayne or Bad Weather with you. Where'd the new nickname come from?"

He glanced over, his blue gaze piercing in the dim light of the dash. "You've always been Stormy to me. My own personal storm cloud, permanently pissing me off whenever you flirted with Nick and Alfie in front of me."

I didn't really know what to say to that. "I thought you were okay with... you know... sharing?"

Frost breathed out a long sigh, drumming his fingers on the steering wheel. "I am. Now. I wasn't, back then. But every time I held back and put you at arm's length, it gutted me inside. Back then, I thought we had our whole lives ahead of us and that eventually you'd be forced to make a choice... and I was scared as hell you wouldn't choose me."

That made sense. I nodded my understanding, hugging my coat tighter around myself. "You know better now, right?"

He flashed me a quick grin. "I definitely do."

"Good," I muttered. "Because I like you, Frost."

He frowned, shooting a glance at me. Then he steered the car onto the shoulder and put his foot on the brake, stopping us completely. "Say it again, Stormy."

Confused, I shifted to face him. "Um, I like you?"

He grabbed my throat, not hard enough to hurt but more than enough to show his control issues in full swing. The way my thighs clenched instantly said I was just as damaged. Using his grip on me, he pulled me close and kissed me so soundly I forgot where we were, and what we'd been talking about.

"Say it again," he demanded in a husky voice, barely releasing my lips from his kiss.

"I *like* you, Frost Jackson," I repeated.

He rumbled a sexy sound. "Well, I *love* you, Rayne Dear. Always have and never stopped." He kissed me again, stealing all the air from my lungs and coherent thought from my head, then released me abruptly. "Reach under your seat, beautiful, I packed a thermos of coffee for the drive."

My brain was still back on that kiss, then I swore it stumbled and forgot how to run the brain cells together at all. He *loved* me. *He* loved me. It was like I played the declaration on repeat.

"Coffee, Stormy," Frost said with the darkest chuckle that was more decadent than chocolate before he resumed driving. Like he didn't know what that announcement did to me. I snagged the thermos from under the seat, still licking the taste of him off my lips.

When I glanced over, I caught him watching me more than the road. So I crossed my eyes and stuck out my tongue. His laughter was a magical invitation, warm and inviting. Unscrewing the lid on the thermos, I had a little mini-gasm as the scent of the coffee drifted out like a lover to wrap me in its hot embrace.

"Should I leave you two alone?" Frost asked, humor still decorating his dry tone.

"No," I said after doing a little mental weighing of the scales. It was close though. "Although, if I needed evidence that I really like you this is it."

"The fact I made you coffee?" He didn't scoff but he did sound flat out amused. Hmm, snarky Frost or soft-serve Frost? I liked them both. He definitely still had a bite.

"The fact I'm willing to share it with you," I told him before I took a deep drink. Dark, bitter, and strong. "Oh my god, that's good."

"Fuck, that's hot."

"Good coffee should be." Still I took another drink and groaned my appreciation before I passed him the thermos. The weight of his fingers had left an impression on my throat. Frankly, I liked his hand as a necklace. If anyone was going to lock their hand there, I wanted it to be Frost.

It was also the first time in days his eyes didn't turn into a frozen tundra of solid ice when he looked at my throat. The bruises were better. Much better. It barely hurt at all now, and I could almost forget it happened. I was ready to ditch the turtlenecks I'd started wearing to keep his surly temper in check.

"Frost," I said after he took a drink then passed the coffee back to me.

"Stormy?"

I could get used to that. "Alfie told me you came back...the February after you left."

"Fucker. You didn't need to hear that."

"Actually, I kind of did," I said, then took another sip of the coffee. It was so dark out there, and the snow was piled thick on the fields, but the roads were pretty open.

"You didn't need to know that I came back and didn't get you out of all that." The gruffness in his voice raked across my heart with what he didn't say. That he didn't *save* me.

"I needed to know I wasn't forgotten," I said. "I needed to know you cared enough to come back."

"If I'd—"

"You would have," I told him and I knew it like I knew my own name. "I know."

"I wish I had."

"Me too," I said, then cleared my throat. "But maybe we wouldn't be who we are now..." Maybe I would have had to have chosen, and I didn't want to do that either. "I have regrets, Frost. You're not one of them."

Not any longer.

"Cause Alf told you I came back?" The skepticism rifling the words didn't fool me.

"Nope," I said. "'Cause you made me coffee."

That earned me another huff of laughter and a flash of heat in his eyes. The interior of the SUV warmed. The seat warmer on my ass helped, and the warm air flowing from the vents did too. Or maybe it was the hot coffee and Frost. He didn't say anything about our destination, and I found myself studying the snowy landscape trying to identify where we were.

We'd skipped the turn that would have taken us back toward Northland. But we were angling east, bypassing going through town apparently. "Where are we going?"

"I win," Frost said almost smugly, and I shot him a look as he reached for the coffee.

"What did you win?" I surrendered the thermos.

"You." He winked and I rolled my eyes. "But I made a bet with myself that you wouldn't just trust me about where we were going. You'd ask questions."

"I can trust you and still ask questions."

"Sure," he said. "But the journalist in you wanted to know."

"It's in the job description."

"I read some of your articles by the way—Rachel Dean." The way he said my assumed name made me shiver. Despite my attempts at getting them to use Rachel in the beginning, I didn't want to be Rachel for them.

"And?"

"You're good," he said. "Really good. You write—biting pieces and really acerbic exposés."

"Thank you. That doesn't tell me where we're going."

The curve of his lips into a smirk made it clear he wasn't planning on answering. "I did have a couple of thoughts on some of those jobs... the one you did on illegal immigrants entering the country."

"Yeah?"

"Did you really use a coyote to bring you over from Mexico to see what happened and how brutal some of those paths are?"

I shrugged. "Sometimes, first-hand experience is a better story, and it's harder to call me a liar if I can say I was in those trucks, I dealt with the extortion, I saw the crimes..."

He shook his head. "You don't know how to fire a gun?"

"I don't like guns." That earned me a look. "The point is, I don't like them, I never learned how to use one, and I think it'd be more dangerous to me than someone else if I had it. I can use a knife."

"That's hot."

I snorted. "The point, Frost, is that I know my strengths. Yes, I went on that investigation. I got up close and personal. I got names. I got routes. I helped people. That's why I write those stories."

"You take risks to save people," Frost said softly.

"Love me, love my damage." Because I was damaged. "It's why I'm here too."

He set a hand on my thigh, strength conveyed in a gentle squeeze. "You're good at what you do, Stormy."

"But?" 'Cause I heard it there, hanging off that sentence, unspoken but waving a red flag.

"But," he said, picking up the handed-off line before he pulled off the road and we bounced a little as he followed a barely discernible track into the woods. "I don't want you tackling stuff like that without backup. One of us can go with you. Probably me. I have more free time than they do. Just—we'll be clear, some guy tries to rape you to get his cost for transport, you won't have to stab him. I'll rip his dick off and shove it down his throat."

He really had read my work. I stared at him, mouth agape for a moment and damn near missed when he stopped the car and put it in park. We were definitely out of sight of the road and tucked into the trees.

"Okay," I said, finally gathering my thoughts back together.

"Good girl," he said. "Stay there. I'm coming round." Then he was out of the SUV and circling it. "Time for your surprise."

I had a surprise? What surprise? It hit me that he was all in black, just like he'd been the night I "hit" him with the car. He tugged a knit cap over my ears and zipped up my jacket. I was in unrelieved black too. He shouldered a bag from the back. Then gloved hand in hand, he led the way back up the track we'd followed to some huge boulders that were in sight of the road. Tucked up against them, we were out of the wind.

"What are we doing?" I asked and he winked.

"You are staying right here for a minute." With that, he took off across the snow. It was still dark, but the sun would be up in... I checked my watch... another hour. He pulled something out of his bag and rolled it across the road before he jogged back to me.

I didn't get a chance to ask anything as a truck appeared on the road. It was a large box truck, not diesel, but definitely huge.

"Wait for it," Frost warned, then small explosions of sound hit as the truck's tires went over the—

"You put a spike strip out." Shock held me in place, but Frost just grinned. The truck swerved, but they had no choice but to pull over. All four tires were flat. From behind the truck came another vehicle, it slowed, but not fast enough to avoid the spike strip. It skidded, sliding before it nearly hit the truck.

The driver of the truck was out, then the driver of the other vehicle. They were yelling at each other. Another man appeared and Frost murmured, "Come on, just need number four..."

Then as if on command a man appeared from the far side of the truck. Despite the cold, a wild exhilaration went through me. Frost focused on them, his stare locked and steady but violence seemed to shimmer around him. Violence he was about to unleash. I had no idea who these men were, and I wasn't sure I should care.

Frost pulled something out of his pocket, twisted the end,

then flicked a switch. The engine of the truck in the front exploded. The men were knocked back and then more shouts went up.

"Three," Frost murmured. "Two..." Then he flicked a second switch and the second car gave a bounce as it blew upward. The concussive force of it knocked the men on their ass and then they were scrambling. One after another, dragging each to their feet and running. The second vehicle had slammed back into the pavement, and it was burning.

The truck's engine was on fire.

Frost grinned at me. Proud.

"I'll be happy to give you all the head pats after you tell me what we just did."

"Holding you to that." He grabbed my hand and then we were off, heading to the road. The four men were gone; they'd vanished around the curve, but what if they came back? It wasn't until we were close to the trucks that the heat hit and the sign on the big box truck was visible.

All Yule Toys.

All. Yule. Toys.

"This is from..."

"Yep," Frost said, his cold satisfaction and happiness shone in his eyes as he pulled out something from the bag and used it to cut off the lock on the back. When he shoved the back door upward, it revealed all the boxes inside.

Toys.

Handmade toys.

She made a fortune off these.

"It's not the trafficking," Frost said. "Grandmother may make a lot of money off of it, but she still sells these for even more now than she did then. They are custom, handmade, and people think they are coming from craftsmen and not kids."

"This'll hurt if she loses the shipment." I saw where he was going.

"Not enough," Frost said. "But it's a start. You want the honors?"

At the question, I glanced at him and then the grenade he was holding in his hand. It was an *actual* grenade. Just like—

"You know what," I said. "Yes, I do."

"That's my girl."

CHAPTER
TWENTY-EIGHT

We didn't linger for too long as the truck and its contents burned. Long enough to make sure they wouldn't be recovering anything, particularly as the engine fires approached their fuel tanks. It wasn't quite like the movies, but at the same time there was something deeply satisfying about watching those toys go up in flames.

Grandmother wasn't going to like that. Once we were back in the SUV, Frost drove us along the path deeper into the woods. Eventually we reached a different track and the bouncing ride was impressive as we climbed up a little hill and then onto another road.

I didn't recognize it, but Frost seemed to know where he was going. He dropped a hand onto my thigh once we were on the road. The sun was rising, flashing red and pink against the clouds. We wouldn't get all of it because there was another snow-filled storm heading our way.

"You okay?" The question pierced the bubble around me

and I flicked a look over to find Frost glancing at me, his concern evident.

"I was just thinking about the kids...the ones who made all those toys and what Grandmother's gonna do when she realizes how much we just torched." On the one hand, I had zero regrets. I almost wished the old bitch had been there to see what we'd done. On the other...

"Well, if she's true to form, she will want to fill the orders she just lost out on and maybe—just maybe that will keep the kids closer to the big house and not on the market." The last came out a bit of a growl as if he had to grind the words up and tear them off.

"You think?" I chewed the inside of my cheek and Frost gave my thigh a gentle squeeze.

"Yeah, I do. But don't worry, we've been working on getting the kids out of there, we're just going to escalate the plan."

Escalate the plan. "I want to help." Granted that wasn't the story Connie sent me here for, but this was important. "If I'd done more when I was younger maybe these kids wouldn't be in this position."

"You were a kid too," Frost said. "And you help by being here, by letting us make it up to you that we left..."

He sighed and I put my hand over his. That was about the time I realized we were heading back into Northland proper and I was torn between sitting up higher and slinking down in my seat. "Frost..."

"We're fine," he said in a half-chuckle that was also half-soothing, and the fact he was squeezing my thigh in a petting motion chased away some of the apprehension.

"What if the sheriff..."

"If Vynachts so much as blinks in your direction, Nick will have his badge on a silver platter. That's if I leave him anything to roast. Trust me, Nick took care of their so-called search. It's all good. We just wanted you to heal up before we headed back into town."

Oh. That helped, but at the same time, my nerves twisted my guts into knots.

"Thought we'd stop at Rudolph's Attic for breakfast and then into the Wonderland Emporium for pies."

Pies? "Pies as in multiple?"

"Yep," Frost said. "We all like pie—and Alf's been pulling a lot of long nights at the clinic. I figured we could drop him off some food and some pie for the staff there."

A smile worked its way free of my nerves, and I was having a hard time not laughing. "You're a big ol' softy, Frost."

"Oh, I'll show you how very not soft I am when we get back." That sent a thrill through me. Rudolph's Attic was as hosed down as the rest of the town with the Christmas spirit, including the red-nosed reindeer sign that looked like it had crashed through the roof.

Inside, the diner was familiar. This was one of the older ones from when we were kids. I'd thought about getting a waitressing job here at one point, but Grandmother wouldn't hear of it. If I worked, it was going to be in her basement sweatshop, and then later it…

I shoved all of that aside. I was on a date with Frost. We'd blown up the toy trucks, and now we were going to have food, which turned out to be strawberry crepes, hash browns so crispy they crunched, the perfect eggs and English muffins. Frost got extras of the bacon and sausage, when he offered to share, and I fed him some of my strawberry crepes.

The best part, the coffee here was perfectly strong and super dark. I could almost tune out the Christmas music, because Frost kept knocking his booted foot against mine each time it would start to sink in.

"Having fun?" he asked when we were almost done, and yeah. I was.

"Might be hard to top this." I mean how did you beat blowing up some trucks?

His grin was pure wicked adventure. "I'm sure I'll figure something out." That sent another shiver of anticipation through me. When the waitress came over with the breakfast burritos he'd ordered for Alfie, he peeled off several bills and left them on the table before taking my hand. The Wonderland Emporium was next door. The bakery smelled sinful with chocolate, sugar, and more.

If I hadn't just had breakfast, I might have died. "Look for something you want," Frost suggested, nudging me toward the cupcake case. Oh, I hadn't been hungry, but now that he mentioned it.

His smirk said he didn't miss my interest. He went to talk to the lady at the register about picking up five different types of pie. I half-listened as I studied the various kinds of cupcakes.

Yes, they had the assortment of Christmas monstrosities, but there were other fluffier, more normal looking ones, and I swore when I caught sight of the yin-yang dark and white chocolate one, my eyes half-bulged.

"And two of these kitten cakes," Frost said as he snaked an arm around my middle. Oh, they were *kitten* cakes. They were little black and white kittens curled up together. It was violently adorable. "Jolly is gonna be jealous," Frost warned before he nipped my ear and I laughed.

"We should get him something."

"Solid plan. Want to pick something out of the dog treat case?" They had a dog treat case? Apparently they did. Sadly, they were as Christmas as it got, so I picked out three elf cookies just for Jolly.

He'd done so well with the giant-elf. Amusement curved

through me as Frost collected our baked goods and carried them. I offered to help, but the look he sent me was one that said absolutely not, so I just raised my hands and followed him back out to the SUV. Stuffing my hands in my pockets while Frost put the goodies in the back, I studied the streets and fixed on a dark sedan that pulled in down the block.

The man who stepped out of the back was—

My stomach did a flip.

No.

The man in question still had a round gut. It had expanded some. His suit tried to slim it, but he couldn't quite disguise the way it hung over his belt. His snowy white hair might be a little thinner, but it was still fluffy. His cheeks were ruddy red as he clapped his hands together and then he turned and locked gazes with me.

Fear was a bear-trap shaped set of shackles that ripped into me as recognition flickered. Surprise wavered over his face and then a smile.

"Hey, Stormy..." Frost suddenly stepped in front of me, cutting off Schneemann's gaze, and I dragged my eyes upward. "What the fuck just happened?"

He cut a look from me then over his shoulder then back. When he shifted, I saw Schneemann still standing there. Still staring in our direction. And I wanted to be anywhere but here.

"That's him," Frost said in a lethally soft voice. "That's the mother fucker who..." He already had a hand inside his jacket, going for his gun, and I lurched forward, gripping his wrist.

"You can't."

"I sure as shit can. That fucker needs to die..."

"You can't. His brother is a senator. He's a popular candidate, and there's a chance he'll be his party's nominee for president. You can't just shoot him." The words seemed to matter very little to Frost. The ice in his eyes, the raw fury in them, it was for me. For my pain. And I adored him for it. "Frost, please... if you do this and they take you away... I don't want you to spend the rest of your life in prison."

His jaw clenched, and that muscle in his cheek ticked away. He spared a look back, but Schneemann was gone. He'd gone inside or whatever. Frankly, I didn't care. I didn't want to see him. I didn't want to talk to him.

"It's okay," Frost said abruptly, letting go of his gun and catching my hand in his before he pulled me to him in a rough hug. "It's okay. No one is taking me away from you."

This was far from done. He wasn't remotely offering me a promise to leave Schneemann alone, and fuck it if I wasn't more than a little thrilled that he wanted that vengeance for me.

I just didn't want it to cost me Frost.

Ten minutes later, we were at Alfie's clinic, and despite the rapid approach of Christmas, or maybe because of it, they had a lot of patients in the waiting room. Candice looked up from the reception desk and hit the buzzer to let us in the back with a laugh. "You darling boy..."

Frost dropped off a pair of the pies to her, and she flashed me a smile. Doc Kane's wife had always been a good lady, and for the first time since I came back to this town, I had no problem smiling at her.

"Is Alfie free?" I asked.

"He will be in a couple of minutes. Go on back to his office. I'll let him know you're here."

Frost led the way, totally at ease in the clinic, and held the door to Aflie's office open. The nameplate on the door professionally displayed *Dr. Alfred Buddie, MD* and I traced it with my finger, smiling as I did. I was *so* proud of him for chasing his dreams, no matter how unattainable the idea of medical school had been while working our fingers to the bone in Yule House sweatshop.

"Was there ever a doubt?" Frost asked, seeming to read my mind.

"No... He was destined for this. I'm glad the Navy gave him —all of you—the opportunities we never could have accessed otherwise." I headed inside the office and glanced around. It was a much smaller space than the treatment room where he'd fixed Frost's shoulder

Curious, I circled around the desk and picked up the framed picture that'd been positioned for Alfie to see while sitting at his computer. I'd expected to find a photo of the three of them, or maybe an ex-girlfriend... but it wasn't a photo at all. It was a black and white pencil sketch of a woman who seemed strikingly similar to *me*.

"Who is this?" I asked Frost, turning the picture to show him.

A bemused smile tilted his lips and he closed the door, coming around the desk to stand behind me. His arms looped around my waist and his chin rested on my shoulder. "You know that's you, Stormy."

I hummed a thoughtful sound. "There's a resemblance... but she's a lot prettier."

Frost plucked the frame out of my grip and returned it to Alfie's desk before spinning me around to face him. "Rayne Dear, you shut your mouth with that slander." His expression fierce, one hand drifted up to cup my face, holding me firm.

I wet my lips, my breath quickening. "Or what?"

A wicked smile touched his lips. "Or I'll give your mouth something else to do."

My heart raced and my nipples peaked hard. "Don't threaten me with a good time, Mr. Jackson." I gave him a firm push, making him sit heavily in Alfie's office chair, then sank to my knees in front of him. "I can think of one better use for my mouth..."

Frost's brows rose as I unbuckled his belt, holding eye contact when I slowly tugged his zipper down and freed his already straining erection. Of course he was a commando kind of guy. Easy access.

"Stormy—" he started to protest, but I cut him off by closing my lips around his tip, sucking on it like my favorite lollipop. "Oh, *fuck*. Alf is going to murder me but it'll be worth it."

I hummed a laugh as I took him deeper in my mouth, my tongue exploring every inch of his hot, tight flesh. He tentatively gripped my hair, and I scraped my teeth over him with warning.

Frost laughed on a moan. "Okay, okay, message received. Don't treat you like a breakable thing." His fingers flexed, tightening in my hair and pushing my face down harder, forcing his length into my throat. He moaned again, and it was such a delicious sound I pushed myself further, taking him even deeper still.

I took my time sucking Frost's cock, teasing him to the brink of climax then backing off and shifting my mouth to his balls. Ever so gently I sucked his sack, rolling the hard stones in my mouth and loving the panicked, excited gasps he made. It was an exercise in trust, and Frost showed he trusted me implicitly.

"I'm so fucking close to blowing," he groaned after a while. "But I want to make you come first. Will you be quiet while you ride my cock, beautiful?"

I released him with a wet pop and mimed zipping my lips. He barked a laugh, but helped me wiggle out of my jeans and straddle him in Alfie's office chair. I was already so wet he just slid straight in despite his size, and I gasped with pleasure.

"Fuck," Frost whispered as I shifted my weight, getting him deeper inside. "I didn't lock the door."

I didn't care, already lost in the euphoria of fucking Frost Jackson. Breathing hard, I braced my hands on his shoulders and started to move, rising and falling on his rigid cock as I took what I needed.

"Why am I not even a little bit surprised," Alfie said from somewhere near the door, and I looked over my shoulder without even an ounce of guilt. "You probably should have locked the door, though. What if Mrs. Kane walked in on this, hmmm?" He turned the lock latch and gave me a scolding look which only made me smile wider.

Of course, Frost's thick cock buried in my cunt had something to do with the smile on my lips.

"She'd have very politely reminded me to use protection and left us to it," Frost replied, kissing my throat.

Alfie prowled closer, shucking off his white coat. "And are you?"

My face flamed and Frost rocked beneath me. "Hell no, barebacking in Rayne's sweet pussy is too fucking good."

Alfie clicked his tongue, rolling his sleeves up like some kind of thirst trap. "So, you're both being bad. What do I do about that, hmm?"

"I have an idea," Frost murmured, still sucking and biting at my throat. Leaving his own marks where the bruises were fading. "How long do you have?"

Alfie checked his watch, leaning his ass against the desk right behind me, facing Frost. "Fifteen minutes."

"Good enough," Frost decided.

Wait, what?

CHAPTER
TWENTY-NINE

One minute I was straddling Frost, riding his dick while trying really hard to follow the cryptic conversation between them, then the next he was spinning me around to face Alfie where he leaned against the desk.

Gripping my ass cheeks, Frost spread me wide and thrust back into my pussy from his seated position. He groaned as I gasped, and his strong grip pulled me down to sit across his thighs. "Oh yeah, that's it," he murmured. "Now, Rayne, be a good girl and suck Alfie's dick while I fuck your cunt."

A deep shiver ran through me at the use of *be a good girl,* but here, with these men, it hit different. So very different.

Alfie watched and waited for my reaction, gripping the edge the desk with white knuckles as I cycled from shock to confusion and finally settling on excitement, all in the matter of a moment. He seemed to sense my decision and held my gaze while tugging his navy pants and briefs down. His cock sprang free, already hard as a rock and beaded with pre-cum on the tip, making my mouth water.

Ever since that day with Nick, where he'd tested the limits of how rough he could be, I was becoming quite the blow-job enthusiast. Something the guys had been all too happy to work on with me in the last few days.

"Cannot believe we're doing this *here*," Alfie murmured while gathering my hair up into his fist, holding it out of the way as I wrapped my lips around him. He gave a sweet moan as I sucked, his hips jerking forward, and I braced my hands on his thighs. "Not complaining, though. Fuck you're good at that, Rayne-drop."

Frost hummed his appreciation of our new position, holding my hips and thrusting into me from below. "I like this angle," he admitted, his thickness stretching me and his tip hitting deep.

Trapped as I was between the two of them, I could do little more than let them have their dirty way with my body. Frost from below, Alfie in my mouth. Wetness splattered my crack, and I dimly realized Frost had just spat a mouthful of saliva on my asshole. When he shifted his hand from my hip and pushed his thumb into my ass, I exploded. My orgasm hit me so fucking hard there was little warning, and slick moisture coated my thighs and Frost's lap.

"Oh *fuck*," he gasped. "That's so fucking hot." Instead of easing off, it spurred him on, and he swapped his thumb for a finger, then two, using my own juices for lube while his cock pumped into me from below with ferocity.

Alfie wasn't backing off, either, gripping my head with both hands and holding me still as he fucked my throat.

I was utterly helpless, and came again so hard it seemed like a dam had burst. Liquid gushed and Frost lost it. He barked a curse as his cock jerked, cum painting my inner walls as he climaxed.

Alfie followed just a moment later, holding my face against

his crotch with his dick as far down my throat as I could take it as he grunted and jerked. I swallowed eagerly around his length, and he moaned long and low.

"Holy shit," Frost panted as Alfie released my hair, and I sat up with my head spinning.

"That... was a pretty great way to start the day," Alfie murmured, cupping my face as he leaned in to kiss me soundly. He gave zero fucks about the taste of his own semen on my tongue, and I loved that. "You two should stop by to visit more often."

I hummed happily, squirming on Frost's lap. He was still buried inside my cunt, and honestly I wasn't against going again already...

"Uh, I don't suppose you have spare pants here, Alf? My little Puddle made a mess of mine." Frost chuckled, kissing my throat as I gasped.

Glancing down in horror, I realized I hadn't been imagining anything... I'd actually drenched him. "Fuck, that's a first," I admitted, equally embarrassed as I was impressed. "I didn't know I could do that."

"Neither did I," Alfie agreed, his heated gaze locked on my pussy. I was still sitting on Frost, my legs spread across his thighs and his semi-soft cock still nestled inside, and with the way Alfie was staring I had no intention of moving off. Instead, I just leaned back against Frost's chest and spread my legs wider.

"See something you like, Alfie baby?" I was practically purring with post-orgasm bliss.

Frost whispered a curse, but banded an arm around my ribs, holding me there.

Alfie arched a brow at me, then checked his watch. With infuriating timing, a knock sounded at the door, and Mrs. Kane called out that his nine o'clock appointment was here. I pouted, and Alfie stroked a hand over his short beard.

"I'll just be a minute, Candice!" he called back, then sank to his knees in front of me. "Now, Rayne-drop, not a sound from you. Am I clear?"

I nodded enthusiastically, then he went to work diving head first into my drenched pussy.

"Shit," Frost groaned, hardening inside my cunt. "I've always bounced back quick, but this would be a record..."

Alfie didn't even seem to mind being in such close proximity with Frost's dick, licking and sucking at my clit like it was rock candy. He moaned against my flesh, inhaling deeply as he explored every fold, then gently scraped his teeth over my clit and made me buck.

Frost growled, his arm tightening around me, but he remained still. This was Alfie's turn and Frost was just a bystander... sort of.

I was well aware we were on the clock, but given how sensitive and swollen everything already was—and the rapidly hardening cock still buried within me—it wasn't a hard task for Alfie to make me come again. Another short gush of fluid exploded out of me, soaking Alfie's face, and I gasped.

"Oh. This changes things," he purred, licking his lips. "Take her home to rest, Frost. I want to explore that phenomenon in detail when I get home."

He reluctantly got back to his feet and righted his clothes, wiped his wet face off with some tissues then sighed dramatically as he headed back out of the office.

"So... how about that, hmm?" Frost murmured, lifting me up off his lap and setting me on my feet. "My little Puddle..." He took my hands in his, then placed them flat on the desk.

I shivered with overstimulation and delight as he left me standing there bent over, and tugged open one of Alfie's desk drawers. Sure enough, there was a bottle of lube hanging out in there like it wasn't uncommon for Alfie to jerk off on his breaks.

"What are we doing, Frost?" I asked, breathless and excited. Today was really turning out to be the best date I'd ever been on.

He squirted a pump of lube on his hand, then stroked his cock, watching me watch him do it.

"I'm going to fuck your ass over Alfie's desk, little Puddle, and see if you squirt again. Then we're going to do what the good doctor said, and go home to rest. And maybe, *maybe*, if you're good... Nick will join us when Alfie gets home."

The cold squirt of lube on my asshole made me gasp and squirm, but within moments I was moaning so loudly Frost had to clap a hand over my mouth while he fucked me hard and fast from behind.

This time when I came only a tiny amount of liquid gushed free, to which Frost hummed and simply told me we should hydrate.

Luckily, Alfie *did* have spare pants in his closet, so Frost wasn't walking out of the clinic with saturated jeans, but the mess we left on Alfie's office chair was shocking.

"Leave it," Frost said when I tried to mop it up. "Trust me, he won't be mad."

We left the clinic giggling like teenagers in love, and drove home in a haze of happiness and post-coital bliss.

And then we saw Nick standing on the cabin porch with a face like a thundercloud and my stomach dropped out my ass.

"Um, I thought you said you left a note?" I hissed to Frost, seeing his own smile evaporate as fast as mine had.

He flashed me a slightly panicked look. "I did! I don't know why he's all scowly like that."

Nick stalked toward the car, not even waiting for me to

unbuckle my seatbelt before he yanked open the door. "Where the *hell* have you two been?" he snarled, stabbing my belt clicker to free it, then lifting me out with strong arms.

I yelped as he tossed me over his shoulder, and smacked his tight rear end as hard as I could. "Dammit, Nick, put me down!"

"I have been worried *sick* about the two of you, all damn morning. Jolly has been beside himself, too, pacing up and down the living room and I—"

"We brought you pie," Frost cut him off.

Nick stopped in his tracks, turning to—I presume—glare at Frost. Since I was still hanging upside down with my face near Nick's ass, it was hard to know for sure.

"What kind of pie?" he growled.

I could fucking *hear* the grin in Frost's voice as he replied. "Apple and cherry."

Silence for a moment while I dangled there, blood rushing to my head. "That's my favorite pie," Nick grudgingly admitted. "You know that."

"We got cream and custard, too," I added, trying to play whatever game Frost was playing.

Nick grumbled something under his breath and continued inside, but then set me down on the edge of the kitchen counter.

"I cannot be bribed," he informed us both with narrowed eyes. "But I will allow you the opportunity to mount your defense while I sample this pie you speak of."

"I thought Frost left you a note?" I implored, trying out Jolly's trick of puppy eyes.

Nick glowered. "*Gone out with Bad Weather, back soon. Frost.*"

Ah.

Frost placed the remaining pie box on the counter beside where I sat and grinned widely at Nick. "Stormy's a squirter."

Nick's mouth fell open and I tossed my hands in the air. "Way to change the subject, Frost! Real smooth."

Frost just shrugged, totally unrepentant. "Facts are facts, Puddle, my love. And this is relevant information to temper Saint's... uh... temper. As it may be. Right, Nick?"

The big doofus just nodded enthusiastically. "Very relevant discovery."

Rolling my eyes, I pushed off the counter and grabbed a glass to fill with water. I gulped it down, because I was at a loss for what to say.

"That's it, hydrate well, my little Puddle," Frost murmured seductively, and I choked on the water. Bastard.

"Where did you go?" Nick asked as he popped open one of the pie boxes. I finished my water and stripped out of my jacket just as Jolly joined us in the kitchen. He nosed at my leg and I dropped a hand to scritch him between the ears.

"Oh, here and there," Frost said as he snagged my jacket and headed to the coat rack by the door, where he hung mine before stripping off his to hang it next.

"Care to expand on that answer?" Nick's chilly tone pulled a smile from me as I fished out the treats we got for Jolly and made nice with him.

Boots off, Frost prowled over to the sofa and flopped down, kicking his legs up. "Went to town, picked up pies, had breakfast, had Stormy—a few times—"

Heat scorched my face at the description, all too aware of Nick's speculative gaze.

"Dropped off breakfast for Alf, shared Stormy with him—" Frost stretched out the last word with a yawn then hooked an arm under his head.

"And you had to leave well before *dawn* to do that?" Nick wasn't looking at Frost, but at me, and I couldn't stop my grin.

"Oh, yeah, took Stormy out on a date," Frost said, then dropped a hand to stroke Jolly's head as the polar bear stretched out on the rug in front of the sofa. "We blew some shit up."

Nick blinked and whipped his head around to glare at the sofa, but a gentle snore was already rising from Frost. I poured myself another glass of water and then met Nick's penetrating stare with a grin.

"Blew shit up?"

At his question, I shrugged. "Allegedly."

Laughter filled his eyes, and the corners creased as he grinned. "Going to make me work to get it out of you?"

My pussy gave a clench. "I could be persuaded...maybe."

Unsurprisingly, as soon as I finished the water, I was upside down over Nick's shoulder, again, and we left Frost and Jolly snoring in the living room with the crackle of the fire and the twinkling lights on the tree.

Once in the bedroom, Nick tossed me down. "Permission to treat you like a hostile witness?"

I swore I came and soaked my panties at the dark promise in those eyes.

"Yes, please."

Thirty minutes later, I was panting and I needed more water.

The guys were right—hydration was definitely the key.

CHAPTER
THIRTY

"Be good," Alfie ordered before he gave me a kiss that had my toes curling.

"Or bad," Nick suggested, a smirk on his lips. "I'll be back to grab you at lunch." Then he left me with his own kiss before he headed out the door with Alfie. Frost was still in bed, but he hadn't even come to bed until nearly dawn. Now that I knew what they were doing, his after dark activities made more sense.

They had a series of safe houses for the kids. Frost and Jolly often moved them after dark if necessary, they also retrieved kids they could from the "helper" locations from all over Northland.

The last surprised me more than anything. The town was helping.

"Not everyone," Nick explained. "There are teachers in some of the schools, newcomers, nurses like Candice, and some of the newer shop owners. Northland's growth may have been built on the backs of these kids, but it has also brought in people who want to help and are. It's not perfect... but the more we can get out now while we go through channels to shut it all down..."

Yeah, I got that. "Is it realistic?" I asked, and the minute the question escaped me, I regretted it. "Is shutting them down, legally, something we can really do?" Grandmother had always been on a crooked path. She started down the darker one with me, but I couldn't fool myself. If there wasn't a market for it, she wouldn't have been able to keep her secrets and profits. She had people to bury the stories, bury the reports, and since she'd tried to bury me—I didn't doubt that there were bodies out there.

Powerful people made up her customer base, and that made them powerful allies—for her. Mutually assured destruction tended to motivate even the most selfish.

"Yes," Nick said without an ounce of hesitation. The same determination filled Alfie's expression. "Trust us, Rainbow. We have your back."

"We'll have theirs too." Theirs. The kids who came after us. After me. The kids who'd lived in that hell for longer than I had. I wanted to believe them. As much as I didn't believe in happily ever afters or the so-called miracle of Christmas—gag me—I did believe in these three men.

My best friends.

My lovers.

So I chose to believe in their ferocity now. We would figure it out.

Or—as Frost would say—we could just blow it all up.

That was a thought.

Frost continued to snooze on the sofa after the guys left, and I went to my laptop to work. My brewing coffee and moving around didn't seem to faze him in the slightest. Still, the longer I wrote, deleted, then rewrote my notes for the article I'd come to Northland to research, the more unease settled in my stomach.

Every story was personal. I'd always thrown myself into them, invested myself not only in the situation but the outcome. Maybe I'd always been looking for the elusive happily ever after or a resolution that truly did make a life better. The problem with this story was I didn't have to project myself into it to make the experience real.

I was a part of the story.

Grabbing my laptop and phone, I left Frost snoring and ducked into the bedroom, where I closed the door. Someone had made the bed—they'd also changed the bedding. A little laugh escaped me. The guys all seemed to delight in making me squirt, which did not make for comfortable sleeping conditions after.

Shaking that off, I curled up into the chair in the corner and put my feet up on the ottoman while balancing my laptop, and then I called Connie. He deserved a heads up, because my investment here went way beyond the story.

"Rachel," Connie greeted me, his tone gruff when he answered the phone. "Glad to know you still remember how to use a phone."

I winced. "Fair. I know I haven't checked in much."

"Much?" He snorted. "You haven't talked to me since your rental car turned up in a ditch about fifty miles away from Northland."

True. "I've been working." While I'd also been doing a lot of other things too, I hadn't forgotten the story. "That's why I'm calling."

"Gimme a sec." In the background there were sounds of kids playing and yelling along with music, what was definitely a dog barking, and beyond that, a woman's laughter as she scolded. Connie was working at home. There was the sound of a door closing, cutting off that ambient noise. "There, got us some privacy. Talk to me. What do we have?"

"A lot," I told him, not bothering to look for more poetic phrasing. "This is about more than missing kids. It's human trafficking, child slave labor, and murder all against the romantic, Christmassy backdrop of Northland."

Connie let out a low whistle. "You have secondary sources?"

"I have first hand accounts," I said carefully. "And supporting evidence."

"Are you in any danger?" There was something careful about that question, but I'd known Connie for too long. He wasn't trying to coddle me; he was reading between the lines.

"Not my first time," I said, deflecting. "That's not why I'm calling you... I wanted to give you a heads up that this story isn't going to be what you pitched when you sent me here."

"I don't care about that," Connie said, as though hand waving me off. "I never have. You go where the story takes you. If I just wanted to manufacture bullshit for column inches, you'd be on a beach right now."

A snort escaped me. That was where I wanted to be—that beach, having drinks with their little umbrellas, and slathering on the sun block so I could bake safely. "It's entirely possible that I'm going to do more than just blow the doors open on this operation. I could destroy this town and everything about it."

On the one hand, it was hard to really feel regret. Blowing the snow off the roofs and destroying Christmas for all the Northers in Northland might seem a Grinch move. Yet, their "magical joy" was built on the blood, sweat, and tears of some of its most vulnerable population.

"The thing is, I don't even mind doing it to those who

deserve it. If I thought it would help, I'd blow up the big tree in the center of the town square."

Connie didn't laugh, but then again, I wasn't joking.

"The thing is, it's not just about the assholes. There are some good people here." People like Ginger and Candice. People like East. The teachers who reported the changes in behavior. The families and shop owners who were helping to form the chain to funnel those kids out. "The ones who help. This could destroy their lives too—by proximity."

The town's major industry was Christmas. The majority of its tourists came this time of year. What would happen once all the doors were thrown open and the victims were given their time in the light. Fuck, what would happen to those kids?

"Rachel—" Connie said with a sigh. "Do you mind if I call you Rayne for a moment?"

The words penetrated the cloud of emotional turbulence around me, and I snapped my head up. "What?"

"I know you changed your name. I know who you are, Firecracker. I've known from the first month you showed up here looking for freelance work."

The panic clawing up inside of me kept my jaw locked.

"Thing is, people like us, we don't change everything about ourselves unless we're running. We don't run unless it's bad. Real bad."

I swallowed around the sudden lump in my throat.

"You've been running for a long time, and when I saw the link to where you grew up, I knew you had to be the one who did this story. Even if you told me to get fucked and quit, you needed the chance to do it."

"Connie…"

"Yeah, I'm an asshole." He chuckled. "But this is the thing, Firecracker, you can't close the book on the past until you write the end of that story. The only one who can write the ending is you."

"How...how did you find out?"

He sighed. "Well, I know I look like all I do is hang out in the office, harangue my best writers, and occasionally get in eighteen holes, but once upon a time, I did my own investigative writing. Not my first time around the block."

A wet laugh escaped me.

"Some things stick, you know. I put together the pieces. One of your references was a university professor, and he remembered an uncle—"

I put a hand over my face.

"You never mentioned an uncle. You barely mentioned the parents you made up, but I love how creative you were about them. Then I met the man and he didn't let your name slip, not once. But I could see the worry there, feel it in my bones. I knew there was a story there, a darker one. I could have kept digging, and I thought about it, but you seemed happy, so I left it be."

"Until the missing kids..."

"And the missing uncle."

A second shock hit me. "Doc Kane was one of your sources?"

"Yeah, he reached out to me last year—tried to feel me out all careful like. Said he might have a story I'd be interested in. I hesitated, more 'cause it had been years and you seemed better. I kept notes, but then we heard from those teachers near Crenneck, the ones who'd been substituting in Northland... More and more, the story took on its own dark shape. When I tried to check on the doc, I found out he'd gone missing."

"Then you got the runaround from law enforcement." That explained some of the holes in the file.

"Yeah, you hadn't said anything or acted worried, so I didn't think you knew. Your reaction to me handing you the story—that told me the rest." He blew out a long breath. "I didn't know everything I was sending you into, but—I knew enough to know it wouldn't be easy. That you'd have to deal with some shit you might not want to."

That was an understatement.

"No," I said slowly. "I don't think I could have pictured this either." In my mind, it was a dark and evil place. I'd blown it up to be huge because it was to me. But piece by piece, I was tearing that down. I was finishing what the therapist and I started all those years back. "Throwing me at Northland was a real dick move."

"Accepted."

"Thank you."

Silence greeted that, and he cleared his throat. "I'm sorry, we must have a bad connection. What did you say?"

I chuckled. "I'm not repeating it, 'cause you're not hard of hearing and you don't miss a step. I'm going to write the story, and when I'm done, you can decide whether you want to run it or not."

"Sounds like a plan to me—and the byline?"

"We'll discuss that later. Talk to you soon, Connie."

"You do that." Then the call was over, and I was left staring at the cracked screen on my phone. He'd known who I was. He'd always known, and he hadn't let on—ever. I wasn't sure whether to be impressed with his skill or annoyed with my own failures. Maybe a little of both.

Snuffling at the door followed by a gentle thud as the polar bear settled just outside the closed room made me smile. Closing the book on the past had started a whole new series for me. Better, it had dropped me right into the spicy scenes, and instead of slowing down, it just seemed to be getting hotter.

Phone down, I opened the laptop once more and clicked open to a new document. My fingers hovered over the keys as I stared at the blinking cursor.

Christmas memories are meant to be cherished, passed down in families, and pulled out each new season to decorate our present with relics of the past in hope for the future. But for some, Christmas brings up haunting memories that are tattooed onto our very identities...

CHAPTER THIRTY-ONE

I had four thousand words roughed out when Jolly whuffed from the far side of the door. While I hadn't meant to leave him out there, once I got on a tear, I didn't want to stop. I saved the story for now and shut down the laptop before I headed out to the hall. Jolly bounded to his feet at my arrival and charged into the living room. A minute later there was a thud as Jolly literally dragged Frost off the sofa.

"Damn dog," Frost grumbled as he sat up. His hair was adorably askew, his face decorated with a day's worth of stubble. In a word, he looked delicious. "I really hate Jolly right now."

Surprise filtered through me at that declaration. "Why?"

"Because when you look at me like that, I want to strip you naked and bury my face in that cunt until you give me a bath." The raw description sent heat pulsing through me.

"Well, that wasn't exactly on the agenda—but it's definitely going on the list." Cause goddamn. I fanned myself. "And you don't hate Jolly."

The big-ass dog open-mouth grinned at me, tongue lolling, but he glanced from me to the door then back.

Standing, Frost cracked his back and then glanced at his watch. "Fuck, I'm tired. Right. Let's walk the dog, then we'll come back and I'll feast on you."

I almost hated to do this to him... almost. "Can't, I'm afraid. I can absolutely go on the walk with you two." I went for my boots as he did.

"Why not the fun stuff?" I swore he and Jolly stared at me with the same put out expression. It was laughably adorable.

Sitting, I stuffed my feet into my boots. "Cause I'm going to town with Nick, and he's due here in..." My phone buzzed and I didn't quite pull it out with triumph, but there was a message from Nick on it. "Twenty minutes tops."

Frost grunted. Granted, he hadn't had any coffee, so he was definitely doing much better than me in a similar situation. When I stood, he held up my coat and then helped me slide it on before he nuzzled a kiss to my ear.

"I'll go have lunch with you. Maybe we can take food to Alf and play doctor in his office again, Puddle."

He barely dodged my elbow, but I couldn't help laughing at his unrepentant grin. After the last few hours detailing out some of the uglier details of the past, I needed the laughter. As soon as we opened the door, Jolly raced out. Frost caught my hand, and we followed at a more sedate pace while Jolly investigated the morning news on the various trees.

The breeze off the lake was definitely colder today, and there was a bitterness in the air. It wasn't quite snow, but we were going to get more. The whole area looked like something off a Christmas card. The peace masked something so much darker at the base.

"Hey," Frost said, giving me a tug. "What's wrong?"

The automatic "nothing," I was about to offer died unspoken. "Actually, do you mind if I wait for Nick to get here? I'd rather Alfie was too—but I kind of only want to have to say it all once."

He studied me for a beat then nodded. Nick was just pulling up to the cabin as we got back, and Jolly bounded over to greet him. Turned out, Jolly was coming with us along with Frost. We piled into the SUV—Nick's truck wouldn't fit all four of us. I kind of missed the bigger one he'd had, but it was getting repaired after ramming the pursuing car, and the smaller truck was cover.

They thought of everything.

"Okay, Bad Weather," Frost said, cutting me a look via the rearview mirror, and Nick half-twisted in his seat to look at me. "Read us in."

"I talked to Connie today." Probably better to lay it all out, including the fact that Connie had at least known Doc Kane enough to talk to him. Nick's expression flattened when I mentioned Connie was aware of my ties to the town. His eyes narrowed. I could almost see the way he cataloged each thing I was saying.

He searched for the trap.

Still, I trusted Connie. He'd known me for years and he'd *known* for years. The man was good people. As I pushed on, some of Nick's wariness eased. Then I moved onto the compiling I'd begun with the story.

"Over the past several days, you've arranged for me to talk to Ginger—" The woman was even more amazing than I'd realized. She'd actually worked at Yule House a long time ago; she got fired by Grandmother when she questioned some of her methods. "She's a fount of knowledge, but so much of it is background. Candice has also been helpful. But she admitted that Doc kept a lot of it from her."

"To protect her," Frost said, drumming his fingers against

the steering wheel. "We've given you as much as we can, Stormy. I suppose we could reach out to the kids..."

"I thought about that. Particularly Holly, because I met her, and maybe before this is all done I should talk to her. But what I need is hard evidence. My story. Candice's. The teachers. Even you guys—we're all hearsay..."

"You had first-hand experience," Nick drawled. "That's not hearsay, Rainbow."

"It's biased then; what you need in a court of law is different from what I need for a court of opinion. I have to be able to back up the assertions with evidence. If Doc had taken a rape kit on me—I don't know about it. I know he wanted to help me report it, but after my one run-in with the then deputy..." I shook my head. "I didn't want people to know. When I left, I tried to erase it like it didn't happen. So while I know in here...I don't have the evidence to back it up for the story."

"Fuck," Nick muttered. "I hate that you have to think about it like that at all. Your word is enough for me."

"And me," Frost agreed. Jolly bumped my hand with his nose, and I lifted it to begin stroking his head. My fingers were trembling, but only a little.

"I adore you both for that, but I'm a big girl. I can handle this. I even know where I want to start."

That whipped Nick's head around to look at me. "That's a terrible idea."

"You haven't even heard what it is."

He snorted and shook his head. "It involves something dangerous."

"Why do you think that?" I mean, it did, but why would he go there automatically?

"'Cause you're walking us into the idea the long way," Frost said drily. "Whenever you thought we were going to tell you no, you always worked us around to why it was the only way you saw for it to work."

Okay, that was an uncomfortable level of insight to have into me. Still... "You think that's what I'm doing now?"

"I know it is," Nick said, tapping his head against the seat. "I don't want you anywhere near Yule House."

"I'm not in a rush to get back there unless it's with gasoline and a match." Burning it to the ground sounded like the best idea for a Yule Log.

"We could do that," Frost said easily.

"We could," Nick groaned even as he seemed to agree. "But we're not quite ready for it *yet.*"

Which was enough for me. "What I want to do is corroborate everything I can with police reports, files kept by the sheriff..."

That jerked both of their gazes to me.

"Vynachts is up to his neck in this. He's already tried to have me killed, and I saw him shoot someone. Again, I don't have evidence other than what I saw. You told me that Tinker died, Nick, but you also said it was marked as an accident..."

None of us believed it, but we also didn't have proof.

"You're not going to the sheriff's office," Frost said. "You want something from in there, I'll fucking go in and get it."

"I don't think it will be there. It would be available to far too many people."

Nick turned in his seat. "You want to go to that asshole's house?"

"It's gotta be there. He has to have dirt on the people involved. Sure, he could have destroyed the evidence to protect the people or..."

"He kept it for blackmail purposes." Nick latched right onto that. "He might literally know where all the bodies are buried." Like me, he would need more than his word. "He'd need the evidence to apply the leverage."

"And to stay alive," Frost mused. "Powerful people don't like anyone holding shit over them. If he was an obstacle, they can remove him and hire someone else."

"We know he was here *before* she changed business tactics, which means, there's a solid chance he's been tied up in her choices from the beginning." I swallowed. No amount of distance could ease the disgust I felt. When I was seventeen and begging him for help, he'd made me feel like a piece of shit to be scraped off his shoe.

How dare I talk about the fine people in the town that way. Obviously, the one with the problem was me. For a little while —I actually believed him.

"He took a report when I spoke to him," I said, holding onto my impartiality with every ounce of my strength. "Whether it was him playing tic-tac-toe with himself or not, I don't know. But he did listen to me, so if he wrote it down, he would have had the names. That report would be *evidence* that I tried to speak to law enforcement when it happened."

"That makes it a supporting claim." Nick gritted his teeth. "Fine, I see your point. Breaking into his house to get them could compromise the evidence for a court of law..."

"I get that, but are we in any position to get a search warrant? To legally obtain it based on an investigation they aren't even doing because we don't know how far the cover-up goes?"

Their silence was the answer. The only answer.

"Sometimes, the press can go places that law can't because I'm a private citizen. Paint the picture, drum up the outrage, and you can put law enforcement agencies into a corner where they have no choice but to kick over every single rock. Even the ones on their payroll will be lining up to take them down."

"To cover their own ass," Nick murmured, stroking his beard. He kept it neat and trimmed, but I loved how soft it was. "I don't like it, but I see where you're going and why you want to go there."

"If we go, it's all of us," Frost said. "We need a full op, I want one of us with Stormy at all times, and we need someone on lookout. Jolly won't work in the house, but he can be backup for the lookout."

Just like that, they were onboard and mapped out a plan before we got to Wise Man's Pub. That was a new place. It was a new place, but an older establishment, and the guy behind the bar didn't even bat an eye at Jolly coming in with us.

Alfie was waiting inside, a surprise for me. The guys were proud of themselves. Of course, it also meant that we had to bring him up to speed on the plan. The guys briefed in short order, giving him the details as a done deal rather than the discussion I'd made it.

Fair, they were already signed on. Alfie didn't like it any more than they had, but he focused on me for a long moment. "You sure you're up for this?" From Nick or Frost, that question probably would have pissed me the hell off. "I think you can handle it, but you've been charging right at the past for the past few weeks."

I nodded. "I'll be fine," I promised. "You guys are going to be with me."

"Damn straight," Nick said as our beers arrived. "So… let's go over the plan…"

Just like that, we were a team, and something that had been clenched tight and holding on for dear life since they first left, let go and relaxed.

It was us against the world.

Frost nudged a glass of water over toward me as I took a long drink of the beer. At my amused look, he winked. Yeah, us against the world, and apparently dehydration.

THIRTY-TWO

The way my insides flip flopped between euphoric excitement and soul-shaking terror would have been all kinds of amusing if it wasn't, in fact, *my* insides. As it was, I was left with a jittery feeling of nausea and really regretting the gingerbread loaf Alfie had talked me into trying earlier. Not to mention all the copious amounts of cream he'd served with it... *and* the dairy type too.

"What if he's home?" I whispered, despite already having gone over the plan sixty thousand times. "What if he catches us?"

Nick gave me a patient smile, then reached over to roll my black ski mask down over my face. All that showed was my eyes, and the fabric instantly became damp with my elevated breathing.

"That's why we wear these, Rainbow. So no one knows it's us." He winked, then rolled down his own mask. Alfie and Frost did the same, and we all climbed out of the truck.

Licking my lips, I shifted from foot to foot and eyed the three of them. Then I bit my cheek to remind myself we were about to break into the sheriff's house, so it really wasn't the time to confess my darkest fantasies about three masked men chasing me down in the woods and having their way with me.

"I know that look, Rayne-drop," Alfie murmured, linking an arm around my waist. "Later." He gave me a squeeze, and I desperately tried to calm myself.

"I'll hold you to that," I whispered. "Since you don't know what you're agreeing to."

He laughed a dark chuckle. "Nothing is off limits, beautiful girl. Nothing."

Well shit. That was dangerous.

"Let's do this," Frost barked, all business. He drew his gun, and Alfie peeled off with Jolly to stand guard in front of the property.

Our intel—basic as it was—said that Vynachts would be at his buddy's house for poker night, so we shouldn't have any interruptions. Never could be too careful, though.

Despite all three of the guys' best efforts, I was heading inside with Nick and Frost. I needed to face my demons head on, and that meant seeing the plan through *myself*. Was it stupid to think I was capable when I couldn't even handle a gun? Maybe. Probably. Yes, almost certainly. But if Vynachts wasn't home and I didn't leave fingerprints anywhere... What was the risk, really?

Besides, Frost had armed me with two knives from his personal stash, and I felt a whole lot safer knowing I wasn't defenseless.

Nick and Frost communicated with one another in a series of hand gestures, and I didn't even try to work out the code. I just stuck close to Nick and watched as Frost forcefully broke the lock on Vynachts' patio door and pushed it open.

He disappeared inside, and Nick placed a reassuring hand

on my stomach like he knew my anxiety had just spiked dramatically. He wasn't wrong; it definitely had.

An owl hooted somewhere nearby, and Nick gave me a nudge, telling me to follow him. Was that our cue? I couldn't remember. Thankfully, I didn't have to, because Nick wanted me with him at all times.

That part of the plan had been drilled into me. It was weird to think of some of the shit I'd managed over the years without them, but breaking into this one house had me ready to vomit. As soon as we stepped inside, I held my breath. I didn't want to smell his house.

Unfortunately, even trying to breathe only through my mouth, there was no escaping the hints of old tobacco and cigar smoke, a splash of cologne, liberal pine-scented air freshener that had just a bit too much antiseptic in it, and garlic. Good god, did the man have some fear of vampires? The eau de garlic was fucking heavy.

"Apparently, he eats nothing but Italian," Nick said after Frost reappeared, giving us a thumbs up.

"He didn't set the system," Frost said, "but there are cameras and motion sensors. I just overloaded the board so they don't kick on while we're here and it'll look like a power surge."

I understood most of that, and I kind of stared at Frost. He noticed because his eyes were dancing.

"Yes, Bad Weather?"

"You're a damn superhero."

Nick snorted. "Great, now he's going to have a super-inflated ego." Still, he pressed something on his phone. A single thumbs-up emoji that would go to Alfie and let him know we were in.

"Five bedrooms," Nick said and motioned toward the stairs. We would work our way down. Frost was starting downstairs in the basement. I was going with Nick. On our way toward the stairs, I studied the layout of the room. There was a Christmas tree in the corner, decorated, and it even had presents under it. There were nutcrackers on the shelves around it.

Instead of a fireplace, there was a fat, pot-bellied stove that would more than warm the whole place up when it was loaded. The furniture was older, but it wasn't shabby. There were throws and colorful pillows. It had a feminine touch, and that made my skin crawl more if possible.

That and the collection of family photos on the mantle. Vynachts was married or had been. Or maybe those were siblings and nieces and nephews in the pictures. Monsters didn't always look like monsters. I knew that, intellectually, but it was still a sucker punch to be reminded.

Nick gripped my hand at the staircase, and I went up with him. The needy little part of me that was still that seventeen-year-old kid clasped on tightly to him. I didn't want to be that person. And most of the time, I wasn't. She'd been alone and abandoned, real or imagined, and while I'd survived it—the girl I'd been then had no idea how we would.

Shaking off the past was like passing through sticky cobwebs. It continued to trail against my skin even as I tried to rip it away. There were kids' rooms up here. One smelled kind of musty, and looked more like a teen's room. Instead of ignoring it, we were thorough. Maybe his eldest kid's room and they'd moved out?

There was a guest room, and it seemed fresher; there was also a suitcase stored in the corner. Nothing jumped out as a clue, and Nick checked the closets. He knocked on every wall. I even swept under the bed with my flashlight. Beyond the guest room, the other bedrooms also seemed "empty" despite being kids' rooms. Were he and his wife separated?

There weren't a lot of feminine items in the bedroom, and it definitely smelled like more tobacco, sweat, and something vaguely unpleasant like body odor. Where the rest of the house was at least clean, it wasn't in here. Disheveled bedclothes. Dirty laundry. And under the bed? I found sex toys. It was enough to make my gorge rise up, but I kept the search as clinical as possible.

It was a long shot that anything would be up here, still, we had to check. In the bathroom, I found a number of prescriptions—including Viagra.

Gross.

Downstairs, we found Frost coming up from the basement. He just shook his head, and the three of us scanned the living room. The idea of him keeping anything out in the open *here* didn't make any sense. He had a home office. That was the right spot, yeah? By the time the three of us converged in there, it seemed the most logical.

The filing cabinets were locked, but Nick had them open with very little trouble. He had some work files here. Taxes. Bank statements. I took pictures of a bunch in case it proved useful later, but the office was almost too clean.

Frost stared at the bookcases and at first I thought he was just scanning the titles but then he tapped the third one. "Nick, help me here."

Help him—the two of them went over it starting at the top then working their way down until there was a sudden click and the bookcase swung open.

It was a secret door. Fuck, I almost wished I could be excited, but you didn't go to that much trouble to hide a room for something good. At least, not in my experience. Frost went through first and then Nick, and I had to force myself to breathe through my mouth again.

The smell of him was worse in this "second" office. There were new file cabinets and boxes lined the wall.

Case boxes.

Labeled. Numbered.

Dated.

The last part registered just as Frost went to the far end and yanked out what was probably one of the first ones stored here. He set it on the desk and then flipped it open. The photo on top was me.

A badly beaten me. I had a black eye, a split lip. There was a pure circle of bruises around my throat and the very distinct shape of a belt buckle that had seemed engraved there for the longest time.

"You guys don't need to see those," I said, finding my voice, but Nick dragged me to him, then pressed a kiss to my lips that robbed me of breath.

"Evidence," he reminded me. "We're taking everything. But we have to know what's in here, Rainbow."

Behind him, Frost met my gaze before he reached in for the thick bundled file with its dark brown folder that had to be rubber banded closed because there was too much. It was all there.

Medical reports.

Photos.

The rape kit.

I picked up the sealed medical box. They kept the damn rape kit. It was probably not remotely viable after all this time. There were so many photos, including ones from the hospital.

The heart wrenching ones were the ones that came after that Christmas. The ones dated in January.

Then February.

Frost went rigid as he paged through them.

"It's all here," Nick said, as he flipped through a secondary file. "Including your statements. You gave him names."

The last was almost disbelief but also reverence.

"I tried," I told him. "Never seemed to do any good."

"There are no more after February," Frost said, his voice raw. "What happened after this last report?"

I shook my head.

"Stormy," Frost said and the snap made me look at him. "What happened?"

"The next beating I took from him, since I wasn't getting the message...I never reported another one. I managed to patch myself together and Doc Kane did—but after that last time, I never went back."

It didn't do any good. So why bother?

The guys repacked the boxes, and I turned to the others. There were so many. Girls. Some the same age I'd been then. Some far younger. Those made me just want to vomit. Frost pulled apart his desk, while Nick went through the files. We were taking everything but they were looking for—

"Bingo," Nick said as he pulled out a book. "Ledger."

A ledger.

Payments.

Names.

The first one in the book went back to when all four of us were kids. I was right, Vynachts had been on Mechante's payroll for a long time. Too long.

"Let's pack this up." By pack it up, they meant we were taking everything out to the SUV. Alfie met us as we were coming out. He helped. Soon we had everything from the private office emptied. Then Frost made a call, but the guys weren't leaving the house.

"What are we doing?" I asked, all too aware of the stillness

313

that had gone through all of them. I hadn't missed the consultation that had gone on between Nick and Alfie either.

"You know what we're doing, Stormy," Frost said. "The only thing you need to tell us is if you want one of us to take you back to the cabin."

They were staying here and waiting for Vynachts.

The images had been the final nail in his coffin. After everything, the attacks, telling them what happened, and the realization of what so many of these kids had been going through was even worse than they'd imagined...

It was time.

"I'll take you," Alfie offered, but it wasn't hard to read the desire to stay in his eyes. An angry storm had been writhing in the air around Frost and Nick since we found the box.

"I'm staying." This was our fight. They wanted to avenge me, and I couldn't begin to describe what that meant to me, but I needed to be here.

I needed to see him pay.

I *wanted* to see him pay.

I lifted my chin. "How are we doing this?"

"That's my girl," Nick said and there was a distinctly unfriendly smile on his face, one that echoed on Frost's.

"*Our* girl, greedy fuck," he corrected, and Alfie wrapped an arm around my waist and pulled me in tight. I leaned on him. Leaned on all of them.

'Cause they were mine, dammit.

THIRTY-THREE

We didn't have to wait long. When Vynachts' car pulled up in the driveway Nick yanked me swiftly into our chosen hiding place, bracketing me with his body so I saw nothing—and couldn't be seen—when the sorry piece of shit sheriff entered his home.

Frost and Alfie had the task of surprising him and they were so efficient Vynachts barely gave a grunt before he hit the floor in a thud. It was another tense moment before Alfie gave us the okay.

Nick released me and bit my lip to try and keep my harsh breathing in check. Alfie and Frost had Vynachts knocked out, bound and gagged already, and Frost was in the process of dragging him through to the hidden office where we'd left his single chair in the middle of the room.

Between the three of them, they manhandled the heavy man into the seat and trussed him up even tighter. I stood back, my arms wrapped around myself and guts churning with anxiety.

"Are you sure you want to stay?" Alfie asked for the

dozenth time. "You don't have to see this, Rayne-drop. I can take you back to the cabin."

I shook my head. "No. No, I need to see this with my own eyes. I'm fine."

"It's going to be messy," Frost commented, emotionless as he tugged his ski mask off. There was no need to hide his face if Vynachts wouldn't be leaving the room alive... and that was the plan.

"It's premeditated murder," Nick added, having already removed his own mask. He folded his thick arms and leaned against the empty desk, eyeing me with concern. "It's a heavy weight on your conscience."

I nodded quickly. "I'm aware." I paused, my eyes shifting to the unconscious man tied efficiently to the chair. "Have you guys done this before?"

"Murder?" Alfie asked, tilting his head in question.

"Yeah."

"More than we'd ever care to admit," he replied with a haunted look in his eyes. "But they all deserved it. Every last one of them."

It was on the tip of my tongue to ask how murder aligned with his Hippocratic oath, but it really wasn't the time or place for those sort of discussions. Not when I wanted this plan to go ahead... and I did. I really fucking did. Seeing how many other girls had suffered when Vynachts was in a position to stop it all? He couldn't be left to do it again. Men like him didn't deserve to live, let alone hold such a position of power in the community. Evil. Pure evil.

Before the guys could take another run at convincing me to go home, Vynachts started to stir, and their attention shifted back to him.

"What—" he mumbled, blinking groggily. "What the fuck?"

The bright overhead light was on, filling the small office with light so there was no mistaking where he was... or who had put him there. My mask was still on, though, and he zeroed in on me with a sneer.

"You little bitch." He spat the words with venom, and I shivered. Apparently my mask did little to hide my identity when in the company of my three guys, so I tugged it off. Better that than have Vynachts think I was afraid.

Nick gave a grunt of irritation at my decision—they'd been adamant I keep my mask on—but it was too late.

"Hello again, Deputy Vynachts," I said in a cool voice, channeling Frost's energy.

The red-faced man snarled. "It's *sheriff* now, bitch."

"Not for long," Nick commented with a shrug. "Karma has officially caught up with you, Scut."

Confusion rippled through me, and I tipped my head in question. Alfie was the one who answered, quietly murmuring in my ear that Scut was Vynachts' first name. Scut Vynachts. It was the kind of name that screamed sleazy asshole, but maybe that's because I knew the man personally.

"What do you want?" he snapped, narrowing his glare on Nick. "There's no way you're getting away with this. Breaking into the sheriff's house? Assault? Torture? You're a lawyer, aren't you? You know what happens to criminals who lay their hands on the law. They get—"

Vynachts bullshit cut off abruptly as Nick laid a powerful right hook across the sheriff's face, making his chair rock dangerously.

"Like that? Is that what you mean by laying hands on the law?" Nick smirked, shaking out his gloved hand. My guys weren't risking leaving fingerprints anywhere and I was glad for that caution.

Vynachts groaned and started to say something, but Nick hit him again before he could get any words out.

"You good?" Alfie asked quietly, and I nodded firmly. He nodded back, accepting my answer, then turned to Vynachts. "Notice anything missing from this office, Scut?"

The sheriff glared daggers, blood running down his chin from a split in his lip. "You have no idea who you're messing with here, Doc."

"Oh, we know exactly who we're *messing* with, and wanted to personally thank you for providing the copious amounts of evidence that can seal their fates. That was very diligent of you, but not very smart." Alfie smiled like a damn shark and nodded to Frost. "Shall we get this started?"

Frost silently started taking little circular discs from a bag he'd retrieved out of the truck while we'd been waiting for Vynachts to come home. Each one had a sticky backing and he took his time peeling the top layer off before sticking the discs to each of Vynacht's limbs. His feet and hands all bound to the chair got one, then his knees and elbows, and finally one either side of his neck.

All the while, the sheriff babbled and bullshitted, spouting threats and pleas in equal measures while I just tried to work out what those sticky things even *were*. When the guys had made the decision to kill Vynachts, they hadn't elaborated on the *how* of it all, and I hadn't asked.

If I thought about it, I'd just expected one of them to shoot him execution style like how Vynachts killed Tinker, then set up the scene to look like suicide. Poetic justice for old Tinker. But this... seemed like they had another idea.

"Now, Scut, you might not be familiar with these devices that my good friend has just attached to your body, so let me inform you," Nick said in a scarily calm voice, his thick arms folded over his chest. "These are little explosives. Isn't that fun?"

"So fun," Frost agreed, grinning with pure violence all over his handsome features. "Technically they're used for exploding passage locks and shit like that... so they're not *too* powerful."

"True," Nick agreed. "But an explosion is an explosion, right? And we thought it'd be festively appropriate to turn you into a Christmas Cracker."

"Whatever you want from me, I'll tell you!" Vynachts howled. "You can't kill me, I have a family!"

"Had." Nick corrected. "You *had* a family. According to my sources, they left you several years ago and went so far as changing their names to keep you away. Not to mention the dozens of domestic abuse reports and child endangerment... CPS had quite the file on you, Scut. I don't think your so-called family will shed a tear when they hear of your tragic passing."

My mouth went dry, and a shudder of disgust ran through me. Of course he was the kind of sick fuck who hurt his own kids. He'd never flinched away from hurting me after I'd been abused for weeks and sought out *help* from the sheriff's office.

"Make him sing," I croaked out, not even fully processing the thought before it exited my mouth. "Make him sing 'Jingle Bells.'" It'd been playing through the speakers in his office that first time he'd beaten the shit out of me, after subjecting me to hours of photographs and interviews.

The guys all cast me a curious look, but no one questioned me.

Nick shrugged and turned his attention back to Vynachts. "You heard her. Sing."

"Wh-what? I'm not—" his protest cut off quickly when Nick drew a huge knife from the sheath at his belt.

"I won't say it again, *Scut*. Sing 'Jingle Bells.'"

Frost shifted closer to where I stood as Vynachts shakingly started to sing, then offered me the little device in his hand. I didn't pretend to know how all his little explosive devices worked, but it didn't take a rocket scientist to work out that he'd just handed me the detonator. For all of them? Or one at a time?

One way to find out, I guessed.

"*...in a one horse open sleigh...*" Vynachts sang hesitantly, his panicked gaze skipping between the four of us with utter confusion."

"Keep going," Nick instructed, making a rolling gesture with his knife.

Vynachts swallowed hard, then did as he was told. "*Dashing through the snow, in a one-horse open sleigh, o'er the fields we go...*" He paused, fear all over his face. He knew. He *remembered* now. His gaze locked on mine, he spoke the next line of the song. "*Laughing all the way.*"

"*Ha,*" I said, pressing the detonator. Vynachts' left hand exploded in a spray of blood and chunks, but I didn't flinch. I didn't even blink. "*Ha.*" Another press of the detonator and his right foot exploded. "*Ha.*" This time his left foot.

Vynachts howled his agony, but my mind was locked in the past, hearing that fucking song as the deputy sheriff had beaten the shit out of me, delivering kicks to my ribs with each *laugh* of the song while he'd hummed it under his breath.

I don't know how long I stood there staring at the sheriff bleeding out all over the carpet, but eventually Frost pried the detonator from my grip and kissed my cheek.

Then he started singing the remainder of the song himself as he blew off the remainder of Vynachts' limbs, one by one, painting all of us in blood until finally all that was left were the two devices on the sheriff's neck.

"*Now the ground is* red, *go it while you're young, take care of* our girl *tonight, and sing this sleighing song,*" Frost sang with a bemused smile on his lips. He had a lovely voice. *"Just get a bob tailed bay, two forty as his speed, hitch him to an open sleigh... and crack,* we're going to have some fun!"

Bang.

Then his head exploded and my guts lurched.

"Oh fuck, I think I might throw up," I admitted, clutching my stomach.

"Deep breath through your mouth, Rayne-drop," Alfie coached, moving to stand in front of me, effectively blocking the sight of Vynachts' remains. The bloody stumps that were once his arms and legs... and head. Fuck.

I tried to follow Alfie's instructions but foolishly inhaled through my nose and smelled the thick hot scent of blood. Bile rose up and I choked it back.

"Okay, let's head outside and let Nick and Frost clean up," Alfie suggested, his hand soothing on my back as he spun me around and steered me out of the hidden office, then out of the house entirely. He didn't stop until we were in the garden where he stripped off the plastic outfit they'd had me wear over my clothes. We'd all worn them. I hadn't really thought about the why until now. Once I was stripped of the bloody mess, he nudged me to sit on a little seat beside a fish pond.

"Thank you," I whispered, taking deep inhales of the clean, crisp night air. "I needed this."

I meant more than the fresh air, and Alfie understood me perfectly. At some point, he'd stripped off his own. He plucked a handkerchief from his pocket and wiped something wet from my cheek. Was I crying?

Nope. That was blood. Ew.

"I've said it before, Rayne-drop, and I'll say it again. Nothing is off limits when it comes to making you happy."

"Including violent murder," I added with a weak laugh, losing myself in the warmth of his gentle gaze.

"That and so much more, sweetheart." He paused, his gaze shifting to the house for a moment where we knew Frost and Nick would be *cleaning the scene*, whatever that entailed.

He seemed pensive all of a sudden, and I nudged him in the ribs. "Hey, what's up?"

Alfie's gaze returned to me, and a smile touched his lips. "I've been holding this in because it's only been a little over a week since you walked back into our lives but... there's something I need to say. Something I wanted to say the moment I saw you standing there in my clinic after running Frost over."

Worry chilled my skin. "What is it?"

He wet his lips and drew a breath. "I love you, Rayne Dear. I'm *in* love with you, and I think I have been since we were twelve. It never went away, it never got weaker, and I only realized how intense it was when I saw you again that day. I love you so fucking much."

Shock held me speechless once again, but before I could muster up the words to tell Alfie that I felt the same, Nick and Frost came bursting out of the house on a run.

"Let's go!" Nick called out, and Alfie grabbed my hand.

We ran to where our vehicle was parked with Jolly napping inside, sliding in just as the first flames licked at the windows of Vynachts' house.

By morning the news had broken. Such a tragedy, that the sheriff had been burned alive in a house fire sparked by a faulty electrical plug.

The only regret was that no one knew what he'd done in his position of power and influence.

Not yet, anyway.

CHAPTER
THIRTY-FOUR

The first nightmare woke me up an hour after I fell asleep. It didn't seem to matter that I'd collapsed, boneless, replete, and pretty much drunk on multiple orgasms. The shadowy fingers of the past came for me like Krampus on crack.

"I'm right here," Alfie murmured, arms curling around me tighter.

"I'm here too, Rainbow," Nick soothed, rubbing his foot along my leg.

"Go the fuck back to sleep, Stormy," Frost ordered, cupping my chin and kissing me breathless. They surrounded me, and it eased the chills wracking through me. The stubble on Frost's cheeks scraped against mine. Alfie pressed kisses behind my ear, and Nick literally reached over Frost to catch my hand in his, threading our fingers together.

We were playing sensual Twister, and the thought wriggled loose from under the suffocation of the past in the form of a soft laugh.

"Sleep," Frost ordered, adding a pinch to my nipple to go with his kiss. Alfie cupped my cunt and began to work my clit, and between them, they pursued my orgasm so relentlessly, it left me gasping and exhausted. The abrasive and the soothing chased it all away, and I burrowed into them.

The next time I jerked awake, it was Nick holding me, and he just rolled me over, pinned me to the bed and kissed me until I forgot I'd been having nightmares. The first thrust of his cock had me gasping, and then I forgot how to think at all. When I went back to sleep this time, he was still buried inside of me.

Dawn was gray outside the window when my eyes jerked open the next time, and Frost gave me a long look from where he perched in the chair, lacing up his boots. The shower was on and I was bundled up in the bed, alone.

I'd complain, but my pussy was on the bruised side along with my ass. I didn't think it was possible to come as many times as I had. A snore rose up from behind me and I twisted to find Jolly flopped on his back, head on Alfie's pillow. It was —adorable.

"Hey," Frost said as I rolled back over to find him kneeling next to the bed. "Jolly's been out and he's been fed. There's breakfast cooked for you in the kitchen already."

I frowned. "How long have you guys been up?" I'd never been a huge fan of mornings, but it wasn't like they'd slept any more than I had. Probably less.

He chuckled, stroking his hand through my hair. "Not all that long. Alf got called an hour ago, kids got stupid with some snowmobiles."

I winced.

"Hopefully, they'll be fine. But he's the closest doctor, and he couldn't stay here. East messaged me about fifteen minutes ago."

East. The nurse. That had me struggling to sit up. "The girls?"

"They should be fine, Karol's recovering well and Holly is still with her. They were admitted under different IDs."

That sounded so familiar. Despite the steadiness of Frost's words and his tone, there was a darkness moving in his eyes.

"But something's wrong?"

"There's been 'people' asking around the hospital. Karol's well enough to move, so I'm going to take them to the next stop. Get them secure. It means I'll be gone for a few hours. Nick's here though… just waiting for him to get out of the shower."

As if summoned by the words, the shower cut off and Frost wrapped his hand around my nape and dragged me forward so we were forehead to forehead.

"How are you doing this morning, Stormy?"

This close there was no hiding my reactions, and I didn't try to bury them. "I'm okay. The nightmares sucked." I wouldn't lie about that. "I haven't had those in a long time…"

"But the pictures," Frost said, his expression grim.

"I still wish you hadn't seen them."

"I don't," he said. "I'm glad we saw them."

That gave me a start. "Why?" I couldn't quite keep the skepticism and faint disgust from twining together.

"Because everything that happened to you—good or bad—is important to me. I want to know. I wanted to know how much of a pound of flesh we needed to take…"

That shouldn't be funny. It wasn't funny. At the same time, my lips twitched, "So you just went for all of it?"

"He's lucky I didn't cut his dick off with a rusty knife and let him die from the infection, slowly." There wasn't an ounce of laughter in Frost's voice. "What that fucker did to you? That signed his death warrant. What he has been doing since? Just meant he was the trash that needed taking out. My *only* regret is I wasn't here that December or January or February..."

"You can't think like that." It was something I'd learned in therapy. What ifs existed, there was no escaping it. "What happened to me wasn't your fault."

"It wasn't your fault either. Stormy, understand this, I chose you from day one. I'm always going to choose you. The people who hurt you? They are choosing to die. The only thing that's left is how we take them out."

A delicious shiver unfolded within me at that fierce declaration.

He pressed a long, hard kiss to my lips. "Be a good girl today. Hydrate. Rest. I'll be back as soon as I can."

"Take care of those girls," I murmured against his jaw, wrapping my arms around him to indulge in one long hug.

"I will." Then he was gone and the room was colder in his absence. Jolly's snort from behind me made me laugh. Then the door to the bathroom opened and let out a billow of hot steam and spicy hot male.

"Hi," I said.

"Hey... shower is free."

"Pity," I said, and that had him raising his eyebrows. "I was just thinking about joining you." Well, not before the water shut off, but to be fair, I was definitely thinking about it now. Who cared about a bruised cunt? The hunger they woke up in me was damn near starvation.

"You know, I'm a two-showers-a-day kind of guy." Then he strode across the room and lifted me right out of the covers. While the room was chilly, Nick was definitely not. The water came out hot when he turned it back on, and then my back was against the tile and Nick thrust into me.

Fucking in the shower was now my new favorite thing.

An hour later and maybe a little bow-legged, I wandered out to the kitchen. Nick had brewed up fresh coffee and reheated the food the guys had left us. Frankly, totally worth it. Jolly followed along and I split my bacon with him. Technically, there was enough bacon here for all four of us, but since two of us were out being superheroes, Jolly got to have their share.

Nick chuckled at me and I grinned.

"Do me a favor," he murmured.

"Stop wearing panties?" I suggested. "Pretty sure you made it impossible for me to wear them."

It hadn't escaped my notice that even Alfie's boxer briefs were now absent from the house. Or maybe they were hidden.

"Good," he murmured with a smug smile.

Dick.

I chuckled before taking a sip of my coffee. "What favor would you like?"

"Tell me how you're doing. For real?"

Like Frost before him, and I suppose Alfie would be too even if he wasn't here to express it, Nick worried about me. He worried because he cared.

Alfie loved me.

Frost loved me.

I wanted to burrow into all that hot mushiness and stay there forever. Still... "I'm okay. Really. I told Frost this morning... I haven't had nightmares like that in a while. A long while."

"But it was about what happened... it was why you whimpered for him to stop."

I'd said something? Surprise flickered through me. Nick's grim, even expression held me steady. "I didn't know I'd said anything at all."

331

"The first time it was just a sob. The second, you said 'please don't'." His eyes narrowed.

"What did I say the third time?"

'Cause I remembered three different times I'd woken up. Had I woken up more? Shit...

"I don't know, Rainbow, you were begging again...but I didn't want you trapped there so I kissed you until you woke up."

Then he fucked me. Pulled me back to the here and the now.

"Thank you."

"For fucking you?" That earned me a real smirk and I rolled my eyes. "You're always welcome to that. But enough deflection, tell me how you are. Please."

"I'm really okay. The pictures threw me. It reminded me of a lot. Blowing up the sheriff? That helped. Being with you guys, that helps. Being in the now... I'm okay, Nick."

"You're so goddamn strong," he whispered, reaching across the island to cup my cheek. "You take my breath away."

"Mine now," I whispered and he grinned.

"Damn straight." Then his phone went off and he made a face. "No rest for the wicked." He winked as he pulled it out then grimaced as he read his screen. "Sorry, Rainbow. Five minutes. Let me deal with this."

I saluted him with my coffee as he went down the hall to take his call. It took him a little longer than five minutes, because I was out curled up on the sofa with Jolly and a fresh cup of coffee after doing the dishes by the time he returned.

His expression was pure thunder, and I straightened. "What happened?"

"Fucking bureaucracy," he muttered as he shrugged his coat on. He'd also changed into a suit, and damn, it was a really good look on him. "Judge Bailey wants me in his chambers about papers we filed, and if I don't get my ass down there, he'll rule against me because he wants his docket clear before Christmas."

"Is it about me?"

"No, sweetheart," he promised, leaning down to drop a kiss on my lips. "It's actually about Ginger's boarding house and the zoning changes. One of her neighbors decided she didn't want Ginger converting the place and filed a complaint. It's a nuisance and it's aggravating, but I promised Ginger I would take care of this, and that's what I'm going to do."

"You are a good man, Nick Klores."

"No, I'm not," he told me with a wink. "But I am damn good at what I do." He frowned abruptly. "I want to take you with me, but there's no way you can come into the judge's chambers with me, and I talked to Candice at the clinic, Alf is swamped. He actually had to do a minor surgery there."

I hoped those kids were going to be okay. "Go, I'll be fine. I have Jolly here, and you guys said the cabin is still safe, right?"

"It is," he said, but he clearly didn't like it. "Next up on our to-do list, getting you firearm certified. I'd be happier if you were more comfortable with a gun."

"That's how you know it's real love."

"Because I want you to be able to shoot a gun?" That earned me a hard, skeptical look, but I just grinned.

"That you want to teach me when you know I have a temper and that we used to fight *all* the time."

That gave him a moment's pause. "I have a few objections to that argument, but I'll make them later." Then he winked and gave me another kiss. "Be a good girl."

"Give them hell."

"Oh, I intend to." Then he was gone too, leaving me to the quiet of the cabin, the crackle of the fire. Jolly moved his beast of a head over to lie against my lap, and I gave him gentle scritches.

I studied the tree and gave a little sigh.

"You know, Jolly," I murmured. "I almost don't mind it." Then I spotted the—were those presents *under* the tree? When the fuck had they put presents under there? Curiosity spiked through me, and I made a face. "Should I check them?"

Jolly yawned.

"You're no help."

Then he bumped my hand and I chuckled. Fine, I wouldn't check them. Not now. But I was going to have some words with my boys later. No one agreed to presents.

And by no one, I meant me.

Then it was my turn to yawn and I leaned back. The warmth, the dog, and the fire were all lulling and my eyes drifted shut.

The next time they snapped open, I stared around the—what the fuck? *Stable?* I was in a stable. It was cold on my bare arms and legs. The fire was gone and the hay I was lying in made my skin itch.

I pushed my hands down to sit up and a jingling noise crawled out of the depths of my memories. The sound was made by the chain rattling along the wooden wall. With one hand, I reached up to touch my throat and the silver bells on the collar jingled when I disturbed it.

Horror chased away even the remnants of warmth. "Wake up," I told myself. "Wake up." I was in a nightmare again.

I'd fallen asleep on the sofa and I was back in one of those nightmares.

The cold on my skin made me shiver. The little black-and-white maid's uniform left nothing to the imagination, but it evoked *everything* from some of my worst memories.

"Oh good," a bright, cheerful voice said and I squeezed my

eyes shut. *Wake up, Rayne.* I ordered. *Wake. The. Fuck. Up.* "I'm so glad you're back..."

But when I opened my eyes, Olaf Schneemann grinned at me.

"My very favorite Rayne Dear."

THIRTY-FIVE

T his couldn't be happening. This could *not* be fucking happening! It was a dream, it had to be. A really nasty fucked up dream my mind had conjured in the wake of seeing those photos in Vynachts' office. After reading snippets of my own statements surrounding the violent assaults from Schneemann. This was... trauma. Nothing more.

"Oh, sweet girl, you're not dreaming," the man of my nightmares said with a merry chuckle, his ruddy cheeks glowing as he crouched down to my level. "I know that look. You think if you pinch yourself hard enough, you'll wake up and be safe and cozy back in Doc Kane's fishing cabin."

I did think that. *Please let this all be a fucked-up figment of my imagination.*

"Here, let me help speed up the process." Schneemann reached out and grabbed my freezing cold nipple through the tissue-paper-thin dress, pinching it savagely and giving a twist for good measure.

I screamed, pain and horror wracking through me at his

touch, and I frantically scrambled backwards out of his reach. My surroundings remained, and I didn't wake up.

"See?" he smiled, eyes glassy with a familiar desire. "It's not a dream. I finally have you back, my sweet, sweet girl."

A panicked sob rattled my chest, and my breathing quickened with terror. *How did I get here?* The last thing I remembered was falling asleep beside the fire with Jolly. How the hell had Schneemann got me *here* without me knowing?

"I can't wait to get reacquainted with you, Rayne," my captor murmured, licking his lips as he straightened back to his feet. The tent in his pants was unmistakable, and my stomach lurched. "I just need to pay my associates for the damages caused by your stupid dog, and then we have no more interruptions. You'll be all mine... for as long as you last."

Dog? Jolly. He'd hurt whoever grabbed me, but the fact I was *here* said he hadn't succeeded. Was he okay? I needed to know.

"Wait," I choked out between panicked sobs. "How—?"

Schneemann smirked. "Nitrous oxide pumped into the cabin when you were already asleep, then a shot in your arm to keep you out for transport. Should have been a simple job, if your dog hadn't tried to shake off the gas too soon."

My mouth went dry. Had he hurt Jolly? I couldn't ask, because on the chance Jolly was still okay, I couldn't risk giving Schneemann leverage. So I kept my mouth shut and watched my original abuser stroll out of the stables, whistling "Deck The Halls" merrily as he went.

Deep shudders of fear trembled my body as I shrank against the wall. I was wearing the black maid's uniform again, the very same one he'd forced me to wear in his house all those years ago, and nothing else. No shoes, no underwear, just the flimsy black fabric, which tore far too easily in his pockmarked hands.

He wouldn't be gone for long. If I wanted to get myself free, I needed to be quick about it. That thought sobered me somewhat from my borderline hysteria, and I choked back my tears as I explored the collar with my ice-cold fingertips.

Every movement I made, the bells jingled and my mind assaulted me with the darkest of memories.

When Schneemann returned, I'd made no progress. Quite the opposite, in fact: I'd worked myself up into such a panicked state that I was dry heaving and shaking uncontrollably, which only made him grin wider when he saw the state of me.

"Look at you, Rayne Dear," he purred, crouching down once more and stroking a weathered finger across my tear-soaked cheek. "Prettier than I could have ever imagined. How'd you hide from me for so long, sweet girl? How'd you get away? Was it Kane who stole you back then, like he's been stealing all my pretty dolls now, hmm?"

Disgust made me retch. Of course Olaf Schneemann was still visiting town for Grandmother's services. A monster didn't simply grow tired of being a monster and give up. "You're disgusting," I spat with venom. "Perverted, deranged, sick in the head. You don't deserve to live in this world."

He shrugged. "And yet, I don't just live in it, sweet girl. I *thrive*. Now then, we have so very many years to catch up on, you and me, and I don't intend to waste another minute."

Grabbing a rough handful of my hair, he dragged me to my knees, and I cried out in pain. My scalp had barely started to heal after the muscle elf's attack, so it was extra sensitive to yanking and tears streamed down my face once more.

"That's it, Rayne Dear," Schneemann purred, loosening his belt as he stood over me. "You remember how I love when you cry. Let's see if you remember what else I like, and maybe I'll bring you in from the cold. I have a lovely tree decorated in there, and the fire is crackling."

I gagged as he flopped out his engorged cock, smacking my cheek with the seeping tip.

"Suck my cock like the good girl I know you can be," he ordered, his grip on my hair agonizing as he rammed his spongey tip against my tightly clenched lips. "Suck it, or I'll drag you down to the sheriff's office and let Vynachts have his filthy way with you in one of the holding cells. You have no idea the sick shit that man is into."

I laughed without meaning to, thinking how he clearly didn't know about Vynachts' untimely demise yet, but it was enough that my mouth loosened. Schneemann jabbed his thick fingers into the side of my jaw, prying my teeth apart and jamming his cock into my throat.

"Good girl," he grunted, withdrawing his fingers. "You bite down and I'll make you wish for death, over, and over, and over..." he thrust hard, grunting, and with each assault on my tonsils I nearly vomited. Fear, shock, and my own lingering trauma held me immobile that long... but then I remembered who the fuck I was.

More than that, I remembered who the fuck I *wasn't*.

I'd left that scared, broken, defeated little girl long in my past and vowed never to become her again. That girl was easily coerced and controlled. That girl had been terrified of the *something worse* since it'd been proven time and time again that it could, and would, get worse.

But she was not me. Not anymore.

Fuck the threats, I'd rather die fighting than let him win.

I bit down.

Blood burst into my mouth, and Schneemann howled a blood-curdling scream of agony, jerking out of my mouth and stumbling backwards with his pants around his knees.

I heaved, vomiting on the straw-covered stable floor and spitting his blood out in the process. Trusting my luck I'd just caught some kind of blood-borne disease from him, but seeing him shrieking and clutching his flaccid, bleeding dick, I found it hard to care.

Trouble was... I was still collared with fucking jingle bells and chained to the wall of the stable, so utterly helpless when Schneemann charged at me, red-faced and fists swinging.

A solid blow to my left cheek knocked me to the ground, and several more rained down on me before a feral, animalistic snarl ripped through the stables and something huge slammed into my attacker.

Ears ringing and face thumping with agony, I lifted my head to find Jolly standing over Schneemann with his huge jaws locked around the old man's throat... growling.

He wasn't savaging him, yet. He was just holding him there and waiting for the *kill* command from his owner.

"Frost," I called weakly, seeing a dark figure approaching through the stables.

Another rushed toward me, and gentle hands touched my shoulders. Instant calm washed through me as the warmth of Alfie's touch sank in.

They were here.

They found me.

"I've got you, Rayne-drop," he murmured in a reassuring voice. "Stay still, I need to get this collar off you, okay?"

I whimpered, nodding and then flinching at the jingle of bells from my own throat. Alfie cursed under his breath, his fingers tracing the collar as he searched for the buckle. I'd done the same thing, and found it padlocked in the back where the chain attached.

"It's locked," he growled. "I can't—"

"Cut it off," I told him. The collar itself was leather, so even though it was padlocked it *could* be cut off between the bells. Surely. "Please, Alfie, cut it off. Get it off me. Please."

His panicked gaze met mine, but whatever he saw there made his brow dip and he nodded firmly. "Okay. Just stay really still, I don't want to cut you as well."

He drew a knife from somewhere and carefully threaded it between the collar and my skin, then in quick, precise tugs he sliced through the leather. Finally he got through, and the cursed bells dropped to the floor, flooding me with such staggering relief I sagged in Alfie's arms.

"Rayne, baby, stay with me," he exclaimed, panicked as he stroked my hair. "I need to check you for concussion and—"

"I'm fine," I lied, locking eyes with Schneemann on the ground just outside the stall he'd kept me locked up in. Jolly's teeth remained locked on his throat, saliva pooling all over his face, but he clearly recognized the danger and remained statue still.

Frost stood over him with pure murder etched across his handsome face and a string of colorful Christmas lights in his hands. Nick came running into the stables just a moment later, panting heavily and pale as a ghost.

"Rayne!" he exclaimed, seeing me on the floor in Alfie's arms. His horrified gaze took in the scene, from my outfit, to the cut jingle bell collar and chain, to the white haired old man on the ground with his pants still down and Jolly's teeth in his throat.

"What do you want us to do, Stormy?" Frost asked, ignoring everyone but me. "How would you like us to handle this? Like Vynachts? Or..."

"More," I croaked. "More pain, more agony, more fear. Make him pay for what he did to me, and to so many other girls since me. Make him *wish* for death. Make him fucking earn it."

"R-rayne," Schneemann murmured, very careful not to

move in Jolly's grip. "Rayne, think about this. You know who I am. You can't possibly think you'll get away with this."

I gave a cold laugh, pushing out of Alfie's embrace to face my abuser head on. "Oh, I don't think, I *know*. Your time is up, Olaf. You are on the goddamn naughty list and the only thing you deserve is flaming coal shoved up your ass."

"Nick, help me get this sack of shit trussed up, would you?" Frost tossed an end of the Christmas lights to Nick, who eagerly participated in binding Schneemann with the wire.

Jolly held his position, growling menacingly and drooling like crazy, until Frost ordered him to release. Then the big dog sat back on his haunches and licked his chops, pouting. Poor baby needed a steak.

"Can I take you home?" Alfie asked in a low, warm voice as I scrambled to my feet. At some stage he'd draped his coat around me, and I was a lot warmer for it.

I nodded, numb, my gaze following as Frost and Nick dragged Schneemann—screaming and thrashing—through the stable like a netted tree. My feet moved without conscious thought, stumbling after the guys, and Alfie cursed.

"Your feet are bare," he informed me, like I wasn't aware. I couldn't even feel them.

Not waiting for my response, he swept me up in his arms and carried me out of the stables to where Frost and Nick were attaching the trussed up pervert to the back of a sleigh. A sleigh hooked up to a team of reindeer.

A slightly unhinged laugh escaped me at the image of it all. I couldn't have come up with a better idea if I'd tried.

"Do you want to come along for the ride?" Frost offered, crossing the snow covered ground to where Alfie stood holding me. "If you need to see this with your own eyes?"

I bit my lip, then shook my head. "I trust you, Frost."

A strange look crossed his face, his eyes going glassy for a moment like he was about to cry. Then he jerked a nod. "I won't let you down, Stormcloud. I'll take my time and make him regret ever laying a hand on you."

He kissed me hard, then turned and jogged back to the sleigh to hop in on the driver's seat.

Nick kissed me next, then gave me a feral smirk. "Before he dies," he told me in a dark promise, "I'll cut off his dick and make him choke on it."

My heart thumped hard in my chest, making my ribs hurt. "Perfect."

Nick joined Frost in the sleigh, and they cracked a whip to set the reindeer in motion. Bells jingled as the animals started moving, and Schneemann's screams played a harmony as Frost loudly began singing "We Wish You A Merry Christmas" while disappearing across the snow, into the night.

CHAPTER

THIRTY-SIX

THE FALL OF THE HOUSE OF YULE

BY R. DEAR

Christmas memories are meant to be cherished, passed down in families, and pulled out each new season to decorate our present with relics of the past in hope for the future. But for some, Christmas brings up haunting memories that are tattooed onto our very identities. For some, like those of us who grew up in Yule House, an orphanage on the outskirts of Northland, one the country's prettiest Christmas towns, the holidays aren't about pageantry at all.

For us, Christmas is about childhood slavery, sex trafficking, and abuse from those who were meant to look after the most vulnerable. Mère Mechante, also known as Grandmother, a moniker she demanded the children of

Yule House give her, has been the sole executive matron of Yule House for more than thirty years.

With a staff of more than a dozen who reported to her, she turned to the idea of productivity keeping the orphans in her charge out of trouble. While one can only speculate why she thought a sweatshop was a good idea, she turned a tidy profit using child slave labor to create handmade toys that would later be sold in and out of Northland under the brand All Yule Toys.

Ostensibly, she only reported a minor increase in income, using "some" of the profits in the form of an allowance to provide the growing children with new clothes or shoes, while actually pocketing the majority along with the government stipends provided by the state for the children in her care.

Eventually, her profits took a hit as demand for hand-crafted toys declined. So she turned to the only other resource she had available to sell—the children in her care. Children she betrayed in every way possible. Children, like me, who found ourselves being traded as a commodity. Nothing was sacred or safe.

The first time, Grandmother described it as a job I should be grateful to have received. A special time, where I would clean a house and do manual labor for a stipend. The profits, of course, were hers. Still, she wanted me to appreciate the fact I'd get to stay in a nice house, with my own room, and a television, for several weeks. This was a real luxury for a kid who'd grown up sharing a room with three other girls.

What I didn't know, and couldn't have imagined at the time, was the client she "rented" me out to for the holidays had plans of his own. Plans that would include grooming, sexual assault, and torture. When my time was up, he tossed me a few bills as a bonus. A bonus I thought I was supposed to deliver to Grandmother.

She'd been pleased by the profit, but not by my protests or complaints. When I tried to report the assault, I was gaslit by local law enforcement. Deputy (Now Sheriff) Scut Vynachts took my interview personally. He also documented all the evidence, and then he boxed it away and told me I needed to stop making trouble.

I asked for help and I got a beating for my trouble.

Grandmother rented me out again the following month. Then the next. The only rule she had for the clients—they couldn't kill me. Eventually, I gave up reporting it and looking for help and just tried to survive. Fortunately, a local doctor took an interest in my case, and when he realized the extent of the abuse, he helped me to escape.

My story is sadly not unique. Instead, it was the first in a long list of children who suffered over the next decade at the hands of Grandmother, her conspirators, and her very twisted clients. Northland's snowy facade bedecked in lights, garland, toys, and music served as the camouflage for a far deeper, uglier underbelly. Rotten to the core, this conspiracy has been using Northland's legacy to line their pockets even as they destroyed so many other children.

Grandmother's clients, however, had grown more demanding. Her conspirators, including a state senator, members of law enforcement, executives in multi-million-dollar corporations, and more than a few celebrities, helped pave the way to increasing her productivity with a pay-to-play mentality that sent kids with no families to be "lost" in the system here.

After all, if no one reports you missing or hurt, no one

investigates. Even teachers, nurses, and local business owners who begin to see the injuries and the signs are hamstrung when the law enforcement they report it to just bury the evidence. If necessary, they bury the victims. And if that's not enough, they bury the samaritans.

Samaritans like Doctor Christopher Kane. Doc Kane was born and raised in Northland. He was here before Yule House came under Mère Mechante's care, and he was the doctor who helped me to escape. Like me, he tried to report what was going on, but he had little success when people like Deputy Vynachts, Mayor Wilkens, and a couple of county judges were in charge of what was going on. When they, those in authority, enjoyed their profits over people.

Thankfully, Doc Kane didn't give up. He kept trying to save kids. He created a network to help funnel them away. Still, Yule House kept growing, more kids were sent there, more were sold, and more suffered. It seemed for each child Doctor Kane saved, two more arrived to take their place.

He was one man with a huge heart. When he reached out for help the last time, he reached out to kids who'd grown up in Yule House. Kids who'd grown up, survived, and become men who could protect themselves. They came to town to advocate and to help Doc.

Like all of us who have been ensnared in this wicked trap, they had no idea how truly terrible it had become for those in Yule House. Doc Kane disappeared and is believed to have been killed. While no body has been found, his widow and the kids he saved have no intentions of giving up looking for him.

His wife, Candice Kane, continues to work at the Northland clinic, continuing to help her community as well as the kids her husband had been trying to protect. She proved instrumental in helping to gather the information for this article. Ginger Bridges, the owner of the Ginger Bridge Boarding House, also played a part, helping to ferry children away to safety.

Doctors. Nurses. Teachers. Business owners. The people in Northland are not all like Yule House or Sheriff Vynachts or even businessman Olaf Schneemann, who is allegedly responsible for the deaths of five teenage girls over the last ten years in addition to the multiple girls he assaulted, including myself.

While not everyone will face charges, some have passed away due to accidents and others to natural causes, still more—like Olaf Schneemann—have fled the jurisdiction and are currently being sought by law enforcement for questioning related to these matters. Senator Hans Schneemann, once believed to be his party's candidate for the presidency, has announced an abrupt retirement from politics in order to look after his family during these difficult times.

Elaine Vynachts, the widow of Sheriff Vynachts, has come forward to offer some insights into her deceased husband's violent and abusive behavior at home toward her and their children. Mayor Wilkens' wife has also filed for a restraining order in light of her husband's arrest.

Currently, the FBI has taken control of the investigation into all the allegations both at Yule House and in Northland proper as multiple local, county, and state agencies vied for control. Christmas may not be as merry in Northland as visitors might expect this year, but for those who have suffered the most, it might just be the brightest.

The article went live seven days before Christmas. The first look had gone up on the website three days earlier, but today, the print copies were hitting the stands. We'd come into town for breakfast. Alfie met us at Egbert's Nog for breakfast, and Jolly was snoring under the table.

After the incident with Schneemann, I'd been a wreck. The nightmares had returned in full force, but I had gotten a lot better about shaking them loose. The guys hovered a lot more, but they'd also fired off the evidence to a friend of Nick's at Justice in Washington.

The FBI had shown up three days later. The rumor mill in Northland had gone wild. It was Ginger who let us know that the mayor's wife filed for a restraining order. More than one of the new resort owners had tried to hurry out of town as people started making deals for snitching.

The biggest change though, the one I was waiting to see, went down this morning. The sneak peeks at the article that Connie had been getting out there had been whipping the online audience up into a frenzy. Between that and the Feds getting involved, there was no hole deep enough for her.

We had a front row seat when the line of black SUVs pulled up in front of the sheriff's office. Deputy Brick seemed to be one of the only deputies working for Vynachts to have survived the purge. He also seemed to be walking around with a permanently dazed look, like he had on now, as the Feds in their dark suits exited the vehicles and started removing the arrested from the back seats.

First in line? Mère Mechante. Grandmother was under arrest for a long, long list of crimes. I was also planning to testify if they needed me to. While the statute of limitations might still be a factor, I could testify to prior bad acts, and I'd still been a minor, which meant there was a possibility to "halt" the clock.

Nick had explained it, but I didn't care about the details. I cared that Grandmother was losing everything. There were people lining up on the streets, pointing and talking about her. It didn't matter how fucking cold it was out there. How icy the conditions. The unfriendly looks and the gossip would be going full tilt. My article would fill in the blanks.

A hand wrapped around my nape, warm fingers massaging the tension along my neck, and I leaned into the contact. A second hand settled on my thigh. My guys were right here, watching it all go down with me. If I'd tried to tell myself when I fled from this town that someday, I would be sitting here in a window, clearly visible to the woman across the street as she was marched inside and arrested, I would have laughed in my face.

As if she felt my eyes on her, Grandmother looked around and then slowly she focused on me. The corners of my lips twitched into the first real smile I'd felt in days. I might have to survive the nightmares again. It might be a while before the panic attacks faded again.

She glared at me and my smile grew.

Suck it up, bitch. I raised my coffee and smirked at her before I took a sip. Nick's soft chuckle tickled my ears, and I turned my head away, ignoring her now, to look at my guys. They were all studying me, their expressions a range of indulgence to worry to exasperation.

I made them crazy. Fair enough.

"Hey guys, did I mention that I love you?"

It seemed about time they knew.

THIRTY-SEVEN

Christmas morning dawned beautifully. The sun was just coming up in the distance, the snow storm from the night before had left another five inches of fresh white powder to blanket the postcard perfect landscape. From the crackling fireplace to the decorated tree, to the men giving each other a ration of shit in the kitchen of Doc Kane's cabin on the lake, it was perfect.

The most perfect Christmas I'd spent in forever. I almost didn't mind that I wasn't on a beach. Maybe next year I could lure the boys out to Aruba or St. Barts. Connie had sent a present the night before, it arrived at Alfie's clinic, and he brought it home with him. New York cheesecake with strawberries. The guys had practically salivated. It was my favorite, and I was happy to share.

"Hey," Alfie said as if summoned by my thought. "Ready for breakfast?"

"Hmm," I said, leaning back against him as he looped his arms around my middle. "I could eat."

"Then bring that gorgeous ass over here," Nick said. "We've got omelets, fried potatoes, and grilled ham."

"We also have cheesecake," Frost said around a mouthful. I laughed as Alfie walked me back into the kitchen. At my look, Frost held up his spoon with the next bite of cheesecake on it.

"Hmm, having the good stuff first."

I opened my mouth and let him feed me. The creamy smoothness was perfect, and then Frost kissed me, chasing the cheesecake with his tongue. Laughter bubbled up through me as I waged war to hang onto my bite, but he looked damn pleased with himself because he managed to swipe back about half.

Nick shook his head then stole the spoon and offered me a bite with a wicked grin. "Game for a second round?"

"I'd kiss you without the cheesecake," I teased him, but I still let him feed me the bite. Alfie laughed at both of us as Nick deepened the kiss. He wasn't remotely trying to steal my cheesecake, but I swore he was going to leave an impression on my tongue. Lazy heat stole through me as he dipped me, and it remained after he straightened.

"How are you feeling about me saying 'Merry Christmas'? Or any of us, really." Nick studied me as I slid onto the chair in front of the bar. How did I feel about that?

Really good question. "I don't hate it," I said after a long moment.

"But not sure you like it yet," Frost suggested, looking thoughtful.

"Which means we still have room to grow and work on this. This is our first Christmas in a long time, so—I like goals." Alfie grinned, and that warm bubbly feeling that I was still getting used to surged through me.

The guys looked at each other, and the silent communication passing through their glances wasn't lost on me. "I like goals too," I told them, and Nick's shoulders betrayed just a hint of relief.

Alfie nodded slowly, but Frost grinned.

"Personally, I like challenges," he told me. "But I love you."

"You know, I think you mentioned that." The stupid dopey grin came back to me, and Frost gave me a narrow-eyed look. He was waiting. I huffed a dramatic sigh. "I love you too."

"Better. Food. Then presents."

Presents. The presents that had been under the tree. I stole a look over at them. I'd wrestled with the idea of being excited or not when I first saw them. Now? I was just happy to be with my guys. To be fair, the last thing I expected when it was time to open presents was to find a key in one of the boxes, a helmet in another and a heavy winter suit in the third.

"Those aren't technically the presents," Alfie said.

"Nope," Nick agreed.

"Go get changed," Frost ordered.

"Boys, just because I love you doesn't mean I can't kick your asses."

"Absolutely not," Nick said.

"We agree, Rayne-drop," Alfie told me with an angelic smile, but Frost just snorted.

"Move it, Stormcloud, we've got the rest of our present to give you."

The rest of...

Oh fuck it; curiosity consuming me, I got changed. I'd give them one thing, they were not predictable, and I was having my best Christmas in ever.

"Okay, is someone going to tell me why we're all dressed to leave the house when we're so thoroughly snowed in?" I parked my hands on my hips, watching as Nick finished lacing his boots. The snow had fallen *heavy* overnight, and everything was blanketed in several feet of fresh powder. "Are we going plowing?"

Alfie chuckled, shaking his head. "Aw it's cute you think we would spend our Christmas day plowing the road instead of plowing you. Come on, hot stuff, we have places to be."

He smacked me on the ass, then led the way out of the cabin and stomped his way through the snow across to the barn. I followed eagerly—how could I not when he suggested I might get plowed on this adventure?

Jolly had practically pouted when Frost made him stay home, and I was curious, but then Alfie threw the barn doors open to reveal a line of shiny black snowmobiles.

Excitement zapped through me like a live wire.

"We're going snowmobiling?" It came out as a squeaky borderline shriek.

Alfie grinned. "Yes..." There seemed to be more to that response, but I was overflowing with too much excitement to push it further.

"Hop on," Frost ordered, pointing to the second one in line. The one with a "bad weather warning" bumper sticker on it. Funny man.

I just laughed as I did as I was told, climbing into the seat and accepting the helmet and gloves the guys handed to me to wear. Within a few minutes, we were all suited up and ready to go, our snowmobiles out of the shed and on the pristine snow.

"Have you ever done this before, Rainbow?" Nick asked, his helmet visor still raised.

I smirked back at him, feeling the rumble of the engine between my thighs. "No, but I've also never had three dicks all at once, but I reckon I'd be good at that, too."

Frost barked a loud laugh, gunning his engine, and I flipped my visor down, doing the same. When he lurched into motion, I was right on his tail.

Utterly exhilarating.

Frost led the way from the cabin, following a path I couldn't see between the trees and over copious little rises and valleys, showing me the best backcountry adventure Northland could possibly offer. Until finally, he slowed to a stop in front of what seemed to be an on-going construction project all smothered in plastic sheeting and scaffolding.

"Where are we?" I asked, turning off my vehicle and removing my helmet when he did.

Nick and Alfie arrived just a moment later and also parked. This must be where they wanted to bring me today?

Frost climbed off and held out a hand to me, helping my shaking legs.

"Remember we told you about the house we're renovating?" Nick said, taking the lead as we approached the construction site on foot. "This is it."

Surprise held my tongue. I'd forgotten all about that, to be fair.

"This?" I finally squeezed out. "Here? In Northland?"

Alfie cast me a bemused look. "Where else? This is our home."

"Besides," Frost took over. "This house being under construction provided us a safe and easy way to transport kids out of town without being seen. Maybe you didn't notice in the dark, but East's vehicle is decal-ed to look like a carpentry van. Everyone knew this house was being repaired, so his coming and going raised no suspicions. Especially when we rarely visited."

They'd already filled me in on a lot of how their network had colluded in transporting kids out of Northland and making them disappear off the map, but it was different to *see* the house.

"It looks weirdly familiar," I commented as Nick held back

a sheet of plastic for me and Alfie opened the carved wooden front door.

"Because it is," Nick replied. "This house was built by the same architect who designed Yule House. It's been vacant for decades but we all just... resonated with the property. We wanted to restore it to what it once was."

I had no words for that, instead just staring around at the foyer with awe. It looked a lot like Yule House, but with none of the nasty memories. It was the beauty of our childhood home, and the warmth of my three guys.

"I'll get the fire going," Alfie announced, tugging off his gloves and striding through to what must be the living area. It was set up with couches and rugs, plenty of floor cushions, and even a decorated Christmas tree. But it was definitely cold.

"This is incredible," I whispered, trying to take it all in as Nick helped me out of my heavy coat. He guided me over to the couch directly in front of where Alfie was preparing the fire, and nudged me to sit so he could unlace my boots.

Frost sat down beside me and poured a cup of something hot from a thermos. Rich scents of apple and cinnamon filled my nose, but for once I didn't gag with disgust.

"Hot apple cider," he informed me, handing the cup over. "To warm you up while Alfie takes his sweet fucking time on that fire." The last was delivered in a dry voice, and Alfie extended a middle finger in response.

I took a sip, moaning as the warmth traveled through me. "This is delicious. But I can think of another way to get warm..."

What could I say? Apparently I had a high sex drive at Christmas.

"So can I," Nick agreed, tossing his own coat and boots aside. "What was that you said earlier about taking three dicks at once? It just so happens... we have three available."

I grinned, then gulped another huge mouthful of cider before handing the cup back to Frost. Wouldn't want to get scalded when things heated up, after all.

"Oh, you do? How convenient. I don't suppose you brought lube?" Because as eager as I was to get the trifecta, I wasn't stupid.

Alfie reached into his coat pocket and tossed a bottle of lube across to Nick. "Always prepared, Rayne-drop," he called over his shoulder, then struck a match to light the little tepee of kindling he'd built.

I laughed out loud, my pussy already pulsing with arousal. "In that case, why the fuck are we all still clothed?"

It was all the coaxing they needed. In less than a minute, all four of us were naked and shivering, but my guys were quick to warm me up with a little skin-on-skin action. And more. The whole "make Rayne squirt" game was getting out of hand and by the time Nick sat me on Frost's dick, pushed me forward and started to work his way into my ass... lube was unnecessary.

But still, better too lubed than not lubed enough, in my opinion.

"Oh my *god*," I moaned as his thick cock pushed into my ass, my pussy already stretched around Frost's hard length as it was. We'd done all kinds of combinations in bed the past few weeks, but *this* was new. New, and so fucking good.

"Not god, Rainbow," Nick replied with a husky laugh. "You know."

I moaned again, forcing my body to relax and take him deeper. "Saint..." I gasped, waves upon waves of euphoria rolling through me. "Fuck me, Saint Nick. Fuck my ass and come down my chimney."

Frost snickered a laugh beneath me, grabbing my face. "I

love when you talk Christmas-dirty, Stormy." Then he kissed me hard as he started to move in my cunt.

I gasped as Nick found a harmonious rhythm with Frost's thrusts, then Alfie was grabbing my hair in a ponytail to tilt my face up.

"You're so beautiful, Rayne-drop," he murmured, tracing my lower lip with his thumb. His erect cock bobbed, still slick from my last orgasm when I'd gushed so hard the couch was soaked. "Merry Christmas, gorgeous."

My response was to open my mouth wide, humming as he threaded his cock down my throat.

Who the fuck needed three wise men when you could have three well-hung ones instead? Merry Christmas to me, indeed.

EPILOGUE

CHRISTMAS DAY... ONE YEAR LATER.

I'd never really been one for holiday traditions. For most of my life, Christmas was not a time of joy and harmony, but just the end of an exhaustive toy-making season and then later the source of my worst traumas.

On my second Christmas Day as a woman in love three times over—and my first Christmas as a married woman—I was nostalgic enough to want traditions of my own.

Evergreen House was still under construction thanks to a particularly harsh winter, and our stringent requirements to restore the house with attention to original materials, so we'd lived in Doc Kane's cabin all year. Candice had told us it was ours as long as we needed it, since it was too painful for her to visit for upkeep.

Doc Kane's body had been found stuffed in a freezer at one of Schneemann's properties during the investigation. It was the same property where he'd first raped me.

I had no idea what Frost and Nick had done with Olaf Schneemann's body that night, but he was still a missing person. And would remain that way.

"Good morning, beautiful wife," Alfie murmured in a sleepy voice, cuddling me from behind as I poured my coffee. It'd been less than two months since our less than conventional wedding in Nepal—one of the few countries where polyandry was legal and recognized—but the label of *wife* sat as comfortably on me as Alfie's boxers, which I'd stolen again.

I finished pouring my coffee and leaned back into his chest. "Good morning, husband."

The enormous triple diamond ring on my hand sparkled with the dozens of fairy lights strung around the cabin, and I gave a happy sigh.

"How late did you stay up working last night?" he asked with a yawn, nuzzling into my neck.

"Um, I think I came to bed around two? I wanted to get that story on that insane diamond heist turned into Connie before it was due, so we could enjoy a break." I sipped my coffee and hummed my delight. There weren't many better ways to spend Christmas morning, in my opinion. Only two things could make it better.

"Merry fucking Christmas, you two!" Nick sang out, striding into the kitchen totally naked and half-erect from whatever he'd been dreaming about. He grabbed me out of Alfie's embrace—being careful not to spill my coffee—and kissed me so soundly I was convinced he'd been dreaming of me.

The front door opened, letting in a flurry of wind and snow-flakes, along with Frost Jackson decked out head to toe in black.

Now it was the perfect morning.

Two steps behind Frost, Jolly came bounding into the cabin, shaking snow all over the floor before trotting over for a head scratch.

I made a mental note to correct that this *now* was perfect... how could I have left the dumb dog out of my equation?

"Merry Christmas, Jolly dog," I cooed, crouching down to smother him in love. He'd taken a hard blow to the head a year ago when Schneemann captured me, still, he'd joined the guys when they came to rescue me and he'd been a part of it. After, we took him to see the vet, and he needed an extensive stay at the animal hospital before they let him come home. He was okay, and still had plenty of years left in him, but he walked lopsided now and drooled more than ever. Poor baby.

"Did you get that story turned in?" Frost asked with a smug smile.

I glared up at him. "No thanks to you and your distractions, yes. I did. Connie already had his out of office turned on, but that's not my problem. I'm officially on vacation."

"Until your next assignment," he replied, pouting. "You turn these in early, and Connie just slaps you with a new one the next day. The fucking man doesn't understand healthy sex-work balance."

I arched a brow. "And you do?"

"Okay, not today you two," Alfie interjected before Frost and I could slide into a heated argument... again. It certainly wasn't the first time we'd had this same debate, and it wouldn't be the last, but it always, always ended up in the most explosive angry sex that neither of us could get enough of.

"What do you want to do today, Rainbow?" Nick asked, drinking my coffee then wincing at the bitterness.

I licked my lips, remembering where my mind had been going while making coffee. "I want to take a snowmobile ride," I announced, "and visit Evergreen House. Maybe take some hot apple cider with us?"

My smile spread wider as Nick's cock stood to attention. He knew. They all did.

"I'll pack the lube," Alfie offered, already on his way back to our shared bedroom.

Nick groaned, palming his dick as he followed, grumbling about having to ride the snowmobile with a hardon.

Frost hadn't said anything, though, and I tilted my head his way. "You aren't into this as our Christmas tradition, Iceman?"

He wet his lips, a soft smile sitting there. "I am. I really am. But I promised the kids I'd stop by this morning with those cookies we baked yesterday. Would you mind if we swing past Yule House on the way to Evergreen?"

Fuck he was a big softie under all that gruff exterior. "Of course I don't mind. I'll pack them up into boxes now. Did Dash end up getting his Santa suit in time? I was so lost in writing my story yesterday I forgot to ask."

Dasher Berri was one of our best staff at the *new* Yule House—the one owned by Nick, Alfie, Frost, and me together. The one which served as a sanctuary, rehab, and most importantly, as a *home* for the dozens of children who'd been victimized by Mrs. Mechante's schemes and others like hers that'd been blown wide open in the months after her arrest.

Dr. Dasher Berri was technically a psychologist with special interest in children of abuse, but to our kids he was just Dash. Loveable, friendly, easy to talk to Dash. The kind of man who would rather cut his own throat than harm a spider, let alone a child.

Most recently, he'd started dating Nick's "ex", Donna. She was actually pretty fun, and funny. Despite everyone thinking we'd have a hard time with each other, I pointed out that I had a sex life before the three of them too.

"Yeah, that's where I've been this morning," Frost

confirmed with a yawn. "It got stuck over in Westgarden, so I drove over to pick it up and drop it to Dash before the kids woke up."

A fuzzy warmth filled me with thoughts of how magical this Christmas morning would be for our kids.

"Go change," I told Frost. "I'll get the cookies packed up and we can go straight there on the snowmobiles. It'll be quicker than driving in these conditions anyway."

He grabbed my throat, pulling me toward him with a demanding grip and kissed me until I stopped breathing. I just about short-circuited every time he did that, and he damn well knew it.

Ten minutes later we were all zipped up in snowsuits and speeding through the forest track on our snowmobiles. Jolly was with us, secured in his little sled attachment. None of us wanted to leave him behind. Where we would usually turn off to head through the north forest to Evergreen House, we veered south toward Yule House.

It was still just as impressive now as it had been when we were kids. Huge, ornate, looming high on the top of a hill overlooking Northland. Now, though, with nearly a mile of fairy lights twinkling all around the exterior and the glittery sparkle of dozens of window wreaths, it was an entirely different house. It wasn't the house of nightmares anymore; it was that of dreams. It was warmth and safety in a physical building. I couldn't be prouder of what my guys had achieved.

Frost carried the tubs of homemade cookies inside to share with the kids, and we all got to watch the littlest children lose their shit over the fact that *Santa* had joined them for breakfast. Jolly was the second-favorite, but the big doofus soaked up all the attention. It was fucking adorable, and I was glad Frost suggested stopping by.

When I overheard a little girl sitting on Dash's lap and

sweetly asking if Santa would help Miss Rayne have a baby, I had to leave the room. Fucking Nick must have been talking around the kids again. For the record, it wasn't even remotely on our agendas with how busy we all were in our careers.

If Nick had any say in the matter we'd get started tomorrow, but we all kept telling him we had plenty of children at Yule House. And besides, we were having more than enough fun *practicing*. Maybe one day, though.

"You good?" Alfie asked, joining me outside in the softly falling snow.

I nodded, smiling. "Yeah. This has been perfect. Maybe I don't hate Christmas so much after all."

He smiled back, but it didn't touch his eyes. There was a reserved, almost haunted look hanging over his expression. "Rayne-drop... I just had some news and I really don't want to tell you today. I don't want to ruin this incredible morning. But..."

"But?" I prompted, officially worried. Alfie didn't keep secrets from me. He just didn't.

He grimaced. "But I have a feeling I need to, so you aren't blindsided."

Oh god. What could possibly have happened on Christmas day?

"Mrs. Mechante was released from prison a couple of days ago," he told me with a heavy sigh. "Her lawyer has been pushing hard on the courts for compassion due to her advanced age, and last week she got diagnosed with stage four liver cancer. The court released her so she could die peacefully at home."

My jaw dropped. "They—*what?*"

"Our sources indicate she might have returned to Northland. Rayne, we think she has come to see you..." Alfie looked positively sick as he said it.

Dread and disappointment curled through me. I should have known she would slither out from behind bars sooner or later. In those weeks after her arrest, I kept having nightmares that she'd get out and come after us for revenge.

"We should have dealt with her like we did Vynachts and Schneemann," I muttered, bitterness coating my tongue.

Spirits tanked, I sighed and headed back over to my snowmobile. Nick and Frost were still inside, but I needed to go. I couldn't stay here at Yule House with the threat of Grandmother returning looming over my head. If I had any hope of salvaging Christmas, I had to push on to Evergreen House and rekindle the magic once more.

"Rayne-drop, please don't—" Alfie started to protest, then cut off as a black Lincoln Town Car crawled through the front gate. He frowned at the car, and my stomach churned with anxiety.

Surely not.

The door opened, and I held my breath. Out stepped the white haired little old lady who'd haunted my nightmares and nearly drove me to suicide before my eighteenth birthday.

She walked with a cane, decorated with red and white ribbons to look like peppermint, the sick bitch, and she tapped the driver's window to tell him to leave. Why? Was she planning on staying in her old suite?

"Did that cancer diagnosis fry your brain, Mère Mechante? Have you forgotten the restraining order against you, filed by almost every resident within Yule House?" Alfie spoke up where my mouth had gone dry. He was reading my mind beautifully, though.

The old woman chuckled a jolly laugh, her cheeks pink and healthy. I called bullshit on her cancer. That cruel twist of fate never seemed to claim the people who deserved to die, always seeming to target the good souls.

"Oh, Alfred, you always were such a delight," the sick and twisted bitch commented with a warm smile as her car rolled out of the driveway once more. "It's such a shame you chose to return to *her*."

Her smile froze to ice as she swung her milky blue eyes my way. Then drew a gun from her knitted cardigan and pointed it at me.

"You had to know, Rayne Dear, that I'd be taking you with me." She flicked off the safety with her thumb, then as my breath caught in my throat... the psychotic old hag turned the gun on Alfie.

"Oh, hell no!" I bellowed, kicking my snowmobile into gear and doing the one and only thing I could think to do. I had to stop her... so I ran the bitch over.

It was surprisingly quick, and shockingly easy. She wasn't a large woman, nor was she very strong apparently. She went down like a sack of bricks and my vehicle mowed straight over her without much trouble at all.

I didn't even fully realize what I'd done until I stopped a few feet past her, and turned my stunned gaze to Alfie's. "Oh fuck," I whispered, scrambling off the snowmobile and jogging back to the flattened old murderess. She'd taken a track right across her face, ripping her thin, aged skin right off and leaving a red stain all across the fresh snow.

"She's dead?" I asked in disbelief as Alfie crouched to check her pulse. "So quickly? No suffering or... anything? Just... dead?"

He sighed, standing back up to take my hands in his. "As old as she was, her heart probably gave out before you even hit her. But we probably don't want the kids to see, so... wait here for a moment? I'll tell the guys to ensure no one comes out."

He smacked a kiss on my mouth, then disappeared, leaving

me standing there looking down at the blood stain which once formed a monster. A cruel, greedy, power-drunk monster, who'd ruined so many more lives than just mine. But not any more... now she was just roadkill.

Another car drove through the gates and the motion startled me out of my daze. Panic shook my hands for a moment, wondering how in the fuck I'd explain what was happening... but then I recognized the decal on the side of the van.

"Rayne!" the little blonde teenager screamed, jumping out before the van even stopped. "We need to warn you, Mrs. Mech— oh."

Holly stopped dead a few yards away, staring at the bloody mess on the snow at my feet. Her wide eyes shifted from the body, to the discarded walking stick, to me. Then she nodded slowly. "Well, shit. I guess she beat us here."

East, the lumberjack nurse, jogged over and had a similar reaction before patting me on the back. "You did the world a favor, Dear. We can clean this up, no worries."

Men's voices rumbled behind me, and I dimly recognised that Nick and Frost had come out to help... clean. But all I could focus on was Holly's face. Her stricken expression.

"Holly, I'm so sorry," I said softly. "I didn't—"

She cut me off by stepping right over the body and wrapping me in a huge hug.

"Thank you, Rayne," she whispered into my puffy coat. "Thank you. This is the best Christmas present anyone could have gotten me. Merry Christmas, Rayne Dear."

Relief and understanding washed through me in heavy waves. She was me... and I was so glad she got to live her life without fear of Mère Mechante ever finding her again.

"Merry Christmas, Holly," I murmured back with tears in my eyes.

A very merry Christmas, indeed.

THE END

Afterword

Well, I mean... it could have been worse.

Probably not what you wanted to hear, but—I mean it could have been.

Still not buying that?

Fine. I've got to dive into working on Deceptive Truce anyway!!

You guys are the best!

xoxo

Heather

P.S. Yes, I am heading right back to my corner!

Reader groups:
facebook.com/groups/heatherspack
facebook.com/groups/TateJames.TheFoxHole

WHAT SHOULD YOU READ NEXT FOR HEATHER?

Check out the **Bay Ridge Royals** by Heather Long

Deceptive Truce

Book 3 of 6

Life has been a series of exquisite disasters...

Do you ever lie to yourself? I do. Making friends has been the cruelest choice I ever inflicted upon myself. I like to say I don't regret it, and for the most part that's true.

I resent it.

I despise him because he left me behind, following another battle in this war we've been waging. I thought we were partners, best friends, allies, and that he would always have my back as I've fought to have his.

I hate her because she's perfection and everything he's ever wanted, untouchable, brilliant, and capable. Yet, I want her too. Need her. Still, she gave herself to someone else.

Telling myself one taste would have to be enough even when I knew it never could be is just another deception I sold myself on this trail of disaster.

No matter what I do, I'm not enough for them, for my

family, for this world we inhabit. Now—alliances are shifting, and our enemies are closing in.

I know the difference and I know I need to leave them to face it all on their own. That's the choice I should make. That's the choice I have to make.

Or at least, that's the newest lie I tell myself.

Book 1 - Shamelessly Loyal
Book 2 - Battle Lines
Book 3 - Deceptive Truce
Book 4 - Wicked Surrender
Books 5 & 6 to be announced

WHAT'S SHOULD YOU READ NEXT FOR TATE?

Check out the **Valenshek Legacy** by Tate James

Heist

Book 1 of 3

Every four years, the criminal underworld engages in a game. *The* Game. The challenges range from the impossible to the deadly to the truly insane. Things that only a crazy person would tackle.

I've won the game 5 times. This time will be no different.

I'm at the top of my field now, the best of the world's thieves. There's nothing I can't steal, and this time, the game is all about theft, subterfuge, and sleight of hand. Starting with a legendary painting of poppy flowers.

It's a painting that disappeared into the blackmarket decades ago, but I know where to find it. The only person standing in my way is *her*.

Nothing will stop me winning the game, not even the sultry, quick witted brunette who lures me into her painting studio with the most irresistible bait.

I have no option to fail at The Game. It's my legacy.

The Valenshek Legacy.

Book 1 - Heist
Book 2 - Forgery
Book 3 - Restoration
Series Complete

About Heather Long

I *love* books. Not just a little bit, but a lot. Books were my best friends when I was growing up. Books didn't care if I was new to a town or to a class. They were always there, my trustiest of companions. Until they turned on me and said I had to write them.

I can tell you that my own personal happily ever after included writing books. I've always said that an HEA is a work in progress. It's true in my marriage, my friendships, and in my career. I am constantly nurturing my muse as we dive into new tales, new tropes, new characters and more.

After seventeen years in Texas, we relocated to the Pacific Northwest in search of seasons, new experiences, and new geography. I can't wait to discover what life (and my muse) have in store for me.

Maybe writing was always my destiny and romance my fate. After all, my grandmother wasn't a fan of picture books and used to read me her Harlequin Romance novels.

Follow Heather & Sign up for her newsletter:
www.heatherlong.net
TikTok

ABOUT TATE JAMES

Tate James is a USA Today Bestselling Author of Contemporary Romance, Romantic Suspense, and sometimes dabbles in Paranormal Romance, and Urban Fantasy. She was born and raised in the Land of the Long White Cloud (New Zealand) but now lives in Australia with her husband, babies and furbaby.

She is a lover of books, red wine, cats and coffee and is most definitely not a morning person. She is a bit too sarcastic and swears too much for polite society and definitely tells too many dirty jokes.

She also thought she didn't have an about the author, but we fixed it.

Follow Tate & Sign up for her newsletter:

tatejamesauthor.com

Also by Heather Long

Bravo Team Wolf

When Danger Bites

Bitten Under Fire

Cardinal Sins

Kill Song

First Chorus

High Note

Last Word

Chance Monroe

Earth Witches Aren't Easy

Plan Witch from Out of Town

Bad Witch Rising

Fevered Hearts

Marshal of Hel Dorado

Brave are the Lonely

Micah & Mrs. Miller

A Fistful of Dreams

Raising Kane

Wanted: Fevered or Alive

Wild and Fevered

The Quick & The Fevered

A Man Called Wyatt

Heart of the Nebula

Queenmaker

Wolf Bite

Caged Wolf

Wolf Claim

Wolf Next Door

Rogue Wolf

Bayou Wolf

Untamed Wolf

Wolf with Benefits

River Wolf

Single Wicked Wolf

Desert Wolf

Snow Wolf

Wolf on Board

Holly Jolly Wolf

Shadow Wolf

His Moonstruck Wolf

Thunder Wolf

Ghost Wolf

Outlaw Wolves

Wolf Unleashed

Also by Tate James

Madison Kate

#1 HATE

#2 LIAR

#3 FAKE

#4 KATE

#4.5 VAULT (to be read after Hades series)

Hades

#1 7th Circle

#2 Anarchy

#3 Club 22

#4 Timber

The Guild

#1 Honey Trap

#2 Dead Drop

#3 Kill Order

Valenshek Legacy

#1 Heist

#2 Forgery

#3 Restoration

Printed in Great Britain
by Amazon

35921352R00227